SOLOMON'S
ARROW

SOLOMON'S ARROW

A Novel

J. Dalton Jennings

TALOS PRESS

Talos Press books may be purchased in bulk at special discounts for sales promotion, corporate gifts, fund-raising, or educational purposes. Special editions can also be created to specifications. For details, contact the Special Sales Department, Talos Press, 307 West 36th Street, 11th Floor, New York, NY 10018 or info@talospress.com.

Talos Press is an imprint of Skyhorse Publishing, Inc.*, a Delaware corporation.

Visit our website at www.talospress.com.

10 9 8 7 6 5 4 3 2 1

Library of Congress Control Number: 2015933719

Cover design by Owen Corrigan
Cover photo credit: Thinkstock

ISBN: 978-1-940456-22-5
Ebook ISBN: 978-1-940456-32-4
Printed in the United States of America

TABLE OF CONTENTS

"The illimitable, silent, never-resting thing called Time, rolling, rushing on, swift . . . like an all-embracing ocean tide, on which we and all the universe swim like exhalations, like apparitions which are, and then are not . . ."
—Thomas Carlyle

"You are the bows from which your children, as living arrows, are sent forth."
—Khalil Gibran

PROLOGUE

The conference room was packed with reporters of all stripes, each there to hear from and hopefully pose a question to Dr. Solomon Chavez—President and CEO of Chavez International Medical Research & Development, Inc., otherwise known as CIMRAD. Over the previous months, speculation about the reclusive son of the corporation's late founder, Dr. Juan Chavez, had been running rampant. Only one clear photo existed of him, and it was a publicity shot distributed to the press shortly after his father's funeral. He was a cipher: no one knew he existed until the day of his father's funeral.

The elder Chavez was one of the most famous people in the world: scientist, philanthropist, inventor, and the world's first trillionaire. A certifiable genius, he'd made his name in genome sequencing and industrial cloning. The scientific community had dubbed him a wunderkind, and his knack for innovation soon allowed him to open his own research lab. In the year 2023, he burst upon the public consciousness by inventing the first workable, artificial womb, supplying replacement organs cloned from a patient's own stem cells. This groundbreaking achievement heralded a new era in transplant surgery, eliminating the need for anti-rejection drugs and saving millions of lives. Fame and fortune followed in its wake, and within ten years, Dr. Juan Chavez was the richest man in the world.

Then disaster struck . . .

On the morning of April 10, 2051, the world learned of the great man's death. Nearly every Holovision channel interrupted its programming to report that he had perished in a single-person airplane crash while en route to his home in Pacifica, the floating city that he, along with a thousand of the richest people on Earth, had built in the Pacific Ocean, off the coast of Peru. Very little wreckage was recovered, and the authorities found no trace of his body.

During the days leading up to the funeral, conspiracy theorists argued that he'd been murdered by one of the terrorist organizations located in the United States of America, possibly even the Christian Republican Army itself. The CRA's leader, Reverend William Mannheim, had branded Chavez a heretic, so there was ample reason to suspect foul play. But no amount of investigation—by police or journalists—could tie the good doctor's death to terrorism.

The funeral had been private, followed by a public memorial at the Pacifica Concert Hall. Many dignitaries from the scientific, political, and entertainment world had attended. The incomparable mezzo-soprano, Claudette Mulroney, sang a powerful rendition of "Ave Maria" that brought many to tears. Her performance, combined with a long list of testimonials, made for a magnificent send-off. The memorial was talked about for days, yet it was the lone figure seated in the late doctor's private box that sparked the most speculation.

The stranger appeared to be in his thirties and wore dark sunglasses. His body was cloaked in shadows, yet it was plain to see he bore a striking resemblance to the day's honoree. The service had no sooner ended than a tremendous buzz flooded the social media and news networks: Who was this man? Why was he allowed in the doctor's private box? Was he related to Chavez, and if so, in what way? The deceased had never been married, nor had children—to the world's knowledge.

The following day, a press release identified the young man as Dr. Solomon Chavez, son and sole heir to Dr. Juan Chavez. The release was accompanied by a somber publicity photo that looked remarkably like the good doctor in his youth. This revelation was followed by another round of intense speculation: Why was the public hearing about him now? Where was he raised? What schools had he attended? And the most pernicious of questions: Was he really Dr. Juan Chavez's son, or a clone?

For the next three weeks, little was learned except that Solomon was adjusting nicely to his new role as head of CIMRAD. As with every news cycle, the buzz faded and other news took its place: the civil unrest in Africa; floods in Tennessee; water shortages; food shortages; terrorist attacks in the American heartland; the fifteenth anniversary of the Hebrew/Islamic Peace Accord; and the premieres, scandals, and deaths in the entertainment world. The public focus was elsewhere on the day CIMRAD issued a press release stating that in one week, Solomon would be holding a news conference at their headquarters and that all the major news organizations should attend.

On the scheduled date, a huge crowd of reporters gathered in the company auditorium, waiting impatiently for the mystery man to arrive. The air was electric. Most of the reporters were speaking via interlink, with network anchors located in studios half a world away, when Solomon entered the room. They immediately switched off their link-implants, took their seats, and turned their attention to the lectern.

Stepping up to the microphone was CIMRAD press secretary Lawrence Murchison. Most of the reporters in the room had dealt with Murchison over the years and knew him to be a smooth operator. The blond, blue-eyed, thirty-eight-year-old ladies' man was famous in his own right, having been the company's face for the past six years, and from all appearances, it looked as though he'd been asked to continue in that position.

"Ladies and gentlemen, Dr. Chavez will be making an important announcement. Please note that he will *not* be taking questions at the end of this press conference. However, each of you will receive a press packet with supplementary info regarding today's announcement."

A low murmur filled the auditorium. With disappointment registering on the reporters' faces, they glanced from Murchison to Chavez, who stood beside the press secretary, his hands clasped behind his back, looking not the least bit nervous about addressing the public for the first time. He wore an expensive silk black suit and a red power-tie; his face was angular; his jet-black hair perfectly coifed in a style similar to his father's, making him look remarkably like Dr. Juan Chavez, with only subtle differences telling them apart.

"I'm sure you have many questions about Dr. Chavez's background," Murchison continued, "but this press conference is not about him, specifically. He is as security conscious as his father was before him, and he will decide whether to disclose further details about his upbringing. I assure you, what he plans to say is much more important. So, without further ado, I'm pleased to present Dr. Solomon Chavez."

There was no applause—as was protocol with the press—when Murchison relinquished the stage to the man who'd garnered so much speculation over the previous months.

"Good afternoon, ladies and gentlemen," Dr. Solomon Chavez said, sounding confident. "As you know, twenty years ago my father built this magnificent city. He envisioned an ocean community that would be self-sufficient—a model for the future. Overpopulation was the impetus for that ambitious vision. With 75 percent of the Earth covered in water, he felt that Pacifica could serve as an example for future generations, proving that humans—being so adaptive—could live on water. By taking some of the load off the landmasses, he instilled hope that the human race wasn't teetering on its last legs.

"Twelve years ago, his vision was fulfilled, and thus began an influx of businesses and families that continues to this very day. Pacifica is a success . . . despite some controversy." A few of the reporters chuckled knowingly. The project had been a favorite target of environmental extremists from the day it was first announced. "However, not a person alive can say my father's heart was out of place. He was always looking to the future, always concerned about the welfare of the human race. But after observing the continuing hardships around the globe—the food riots, water shortages, the inability to stem the tide of over-population, the religious strife in America, and numerous other issues—he became worried for humanity's future. Being an optimist, he knew that an even more ambitious program than Pacifica was called for . . . a program to prevent the human race from vanishing, due to its own shortsightedness."

Solomon paused momentarily to let those dramatic words sink in.

"Unfortunately, his tragic death left this announcement up to me. I'm here to let the people of the world know that CIMRAD, in league with the scientific community and the world's most prosperous corporations and nations, will develop the most ambitious construction project ever attempted, which is tentatively titled, the *Ark Project.*"

A low rumble of excitement rippled through the auditorium.

"We hope to complete this venture within the next ten to twelve years, and—"

"Could you be more specific, Doctor," shouted a reporter standing near the back of the room, known for his combative style. "You're being a bit vague. I'm sure we'd all appreciate it if you—"

"*Mr. Brantley* . . . if you possessed a modicum of patience, you'd know I was getting to the point," Solomon snapped back, his face clouding with obvious contempt. "Unlike you, I am patient. However, if you interrupt me one more time, you will be escorted from the room. This is not *The Darren Brantley Show.* Have I made myself clear?"

The reporter appeared as though he would launch into one of his famous diatribes about the freedom of the press when his producer ordered him to quiet down and listen. Chastened, he nodded and glumly took his seat.

"Very well," Solomon said, taking a deep breath to collect his thoughts. "As I was saying, within the next ten to twelve years, the Ark Project will be ready to proceed. But what exactly, you might ask, is the Ark Project?" Solomon cut a quick glance at Brantley, his eyes narrowing to slits. "Utilizing the Lake Victoria Space Elevator, we will soon begin transporting equipment, hardware, and prefabricated components into orbit, whereupon we will assemble a massive spacecraft that will leave on a one-way voyage to the Epsilon Eridani star system, where an Earth-like planet has recently been discovered. After reaching the planet, we will set up a colony designed to perpetuate the species."

A collective gasp swept through the room.

"We can no longer afford to keep all our eggs in one basket," Solomon stated, looking straight into the camera. "If not dealt with, the human race's shortsightedness *will* be our undoing. My friends, it is my fervent hope that we will solve our problems before the tipping point is reached. We are capable of great things, as proved by what science and the arts have accomplished thus far. But we must not be blinded by optimism. We can no longer rely on nature to heal the wounds we've inflicted upon Mother Earth—we must be realistic and hedge our bets. It's imperative we develop a contingency plan that will ensure the survival of the species. By coming together in a common cause, we can accomplish miracles.

"Thank you for your time, ladies and gentlemen. Good day." And with that, Dr. Solomon Chavez exited the auditorium amid a frantic swarm of unanswered questions.

PART ONE:
STRINGING THE BOW

"Time passes!" Men in fond delusion say.
"No!" Time demurs; "'tis men that pass away."
—From the poem "Man and Time" by Arthur Guiterman

I

●● **H**urry and finish your breakfast, young man. We need to be downstairs in ten minutes."

The curly-haired six-year-old tore his eyes from the frenetic cartoon playing on the seventy-two-inch HV set mounted on the hotel suite's wall, responding with a loud whine, "Mom . . . *The Benzie Badger Show*'s not over yet."

"Listen to your mother, David. You don't want us to be late, do you? After all, you've been looking forward to this as much as we have."

"Yes, papa," the boy grumbled. "Computer—end program."

The crystal-clear, holographic image of Benzie Badger—who was set to whack Needles the Porcupine over the head with a club—faded to black. Hopping to his feet, David took his cereal bowl into the kitchen.

Adjusting his tie, Richard Allison smiled at Erin, his wife of eight years, thinking how lucky he was to have such a beautiful, devoted partner in his life. She stood five-foot-seven in her stocking feet, had long blonde hair, a button nose, and the bluest eyes he'd ever seen. Her creamy-white, Nordic complexion was in sharp contrast to his own mocha coloration.

Naval Commander Richard Allison stood six-foot-two inches tall and was thirty-five years old. He was in excellent physical condition, was exceedingly handsome—in an Old Hollywood sort of way—and was one of the world's premiere astronauts. He'd just been hired by CIMRAD to oversee the final stages of pilot training for *Solomon's Arrow*, the interstellar spacecraft at the hub of the Ark Program. With his exemplary service record, he would've been the perfect candidate to pilot the craft; unfortunately, one of the set requirements was that each crew member *must* be single, with no family members to grieve over during the interstellar journey. This requirement made it more difficult to fill certain technical positions. But with ten months until launch, the crew complement was nearly complete.

Nine years ago he would've scraped and clawed his way into the pilot's seat, but having a family changed his priorities. Still, it was hard not to envy the chosen pilot, Russell Takahashi. They were high school classmates, attended the U.S. Naval Academy together, and were often referred to as "Russ 'n Rich."

Then along came Erin . . .

The two men had met the blonde beauty at the Navy's annual ball. Russell had asked her to dance and afterward introduced her to Richard. The two were drawn together like magnets. Over the next few months, Richard and Erin spent every free moment together, which obviously upset Russell. However, their devotion to each other was apparent, and Russell's bruised ego soon gave way to happiness. He even accepted Richard's offer to be best man at their wedding.

Soon after, his and Richard's paths diverged, though their reputations took a parallel course: Both were considered the best in their field, with Russell edging out Richard in his devotion to flying and keeping his piloting skills fresh, but only barely. When Russell was hired as chief pilot for the Ark Project, Richard wasn't surprised. His friend deserved the honor.

Richard hadn't seen Russell in four months, but after his hiring by CIMRAD, the two would be working together on a daily basis and be reunited as "Russ 'n Rich." It was hard to believe that he would soon be sitting with Russell and a number of other dignitaries on the tarmac of Sky Harbor International Airport, ensconced in the luxury of Dr. Solomon Chavez's private Space-plane, taxiing toward a new, better future in the floating city of Pacifica.

Picking up his Personal Interlink Device and slipping the flexible, rectangular gadget—about the size of a playing card and twice as thick—into the breast pocket of his shirt, Richard turned to his wife and son, and said with an excited smile, "Our lives are about to change forever. We've made sacrifices—bidding goodbye to family and friends—but it won't be forever. Erin, you're a freelance writer— your job isn't affected by where you live. And David, you'll have a brand new set of friends before you know it."

Erin smiled and began to scoot her son toward the door. The boy was understandably nervous to start this new phase of life, but also excited. Shortly after learning where they were moving, he began to study everything he could download about ocean-ography. David's young, inquisitive mind reminded Richard of himself at that age—only his field of interest had centered on the history of aircraft, then later, the anatomy of girls.

These days, the only female anatomy he was interested in was Erin's. After eight years of marriage, their passion had yet to wane. He was sure he couldn't be more in love with another person . . . unless that other person was David. When his son was born, a completely different part of Richard's heart opened up as he learned to love in a powerful new way.

As he exited the suite with his family, Richard could barely contain his joy. "This is it," he gushed. "Let's go touch the wild blue yonder."

●

When Richard and his family exited the sumptuous lobby of the Arizona Biltmore Hotel and boarded their waiting limousine, the car's automated voice began: "Welcome to Sky Harbor Limousine Service. Our goal is to make your ride a pleasant one. If you prefer to use your PID in place of this vehicle's interlink device, please insert it in the appropriate slot."

Removing the PID from his shirt pocket, Richard slid it into the armrest console slot. The limo's mechanical voice was replaced by a pleasantly sultry, female one, which the three knew by heart.

"Good morning, Richard; good morning, Erin; good morning, David."

"Good morning, Miri," they all said in unison.

"This vehicle's program has informed me that your destination is Sky Harbor International Airport, in Phoenix, Arizona. Are you ready to proceed?"

Erin, having just finished buckling David's seat belt, leaned back into her faux suede seat and quickly buckled herself in. "That we are, Miri, that we are."

The teardrop-shaped electric limousine pulled away from the curb, hummed by the carefully manicured shrubbery that spelled *Biltmore*, and was soon merging with traffic on the Piestewa Freeway headed south toward the airport.

"Miri, please provide us with a synopsis of the morning news," Erin said.

The device took on a more serious tone. "President Cranston has announced that she will be speaking at the memorial for the slain officers who died protecting her in last week's foiled assassination attempt. . . . Congress is still fighting over the budget impasse. . . . Climatologists have released their yearly study, which states that the world's oceans have risen another nine inches. . . ." David's ears perked up. "The Department of Transportation has determined that last month's automobile accident in Maine, which resulted in two deaths, was the result of mechanical failure and not a breakdown of the vehicle's GPS system. Including those two deaths, that brings the total this year in the United States to seven fatalities. At this rate, the present year will exceed last year's total of fifteen by a significant margin—"

"Thank you, Miri," Richard cut in. "I think that will be enough news for now."

"As you wish, Richard. Please let me know if you need anything else."

Before he could respond, David spoke up. "Papa, I learned that people once drove cars with their hands, not GPS. Ms. Fletcher said that thousands of people died each year. That must have been *really* scary."

"I'm sure it was, son." Leaning forward, he gave the boy's knee a comforting pat. "You don't need to worry about us . . . automobile accidents are rare these days. Miri, open my play list. Start with 'Moonlight Sonata' and then shuffle."

"Yes, Richard."

The soothing strains of Beethoven's classic piano number began to waft through the vehicle's interior. David rolled his eyes, groaned, and reached for his portable game controller. Erin took hold of Richard's hand and squeezed; she knew the significance of the song. It had been playing when they first met, and from that day forward he made a point to play it whenever a special occasion arose. This was just such an occasion.

Lighthearted, Richard gazed out the side window at the gorgeous mountains looming in the distance and felt the music wash through his soul.

●

THIRTY-FIVE MINUTES LATER

The terrified, middle-aged woman sat tied to a wooden chair, staring into a pair of cruel, blue eyes framed by a heavy brow. She wanted to scream, but the rag stuffed in her mouth made that impossible. She wanted to struggle against her bindings but knew that would result in a severe beating, as evidenced by her black, puffy eyes and bruised ribs. Her kidnapper loomed over her, daring her to make a sound as he spoke into his PID.

"Are you positive he's on board?" the kidnapper asked, pausing for the answer. "Good, you know what to do . . . yes, she's fine. . . . You're in no position to make demands, Reverend," he snarled. "Very well . . . I'll put her on speaker."

The whip-thin kidnapper looked over toward the woman and pressed the mute button on his PID. "I'm gonna remove your gag so you can speak to your husband. If you let on that you've been mistreated, I'll kill you . . . and then, I'll hunt down and do the same thing to your children. Do you understand?"

The woman nodded vigorously.

After removing the soiled gag from the woman's mouth, the kidnapper pressed the talk button on his PID and held the device up to the side of her head. Her eyes were filled with tears.

"You may speak with your wife."

"Winifred . . . Winifred . . . are you all right?"

"Y–yes, dearest."

"Thank God! How are you? Have they been treating you well?"

She wanted to scream the truth. She wanted to shout through the phone. *They've hurt me! Don't give in to their demands!* She wanted the courage to defy this man, but the faces of her children floated in her mind, overriding all other concerns.

The kidnapper made a circular motion with his hand, telling her to hurry up and speak.

"What? Oh, yes . . . I'm, I'm fine, dear. They've been treating me well. I've had plenty to eat and a soft bed to sleep on. They've assured me that I'll be taken home when this is over. The funny thing is—I believe them. You know how good I am at judging people."

"Hmm . . . yes . . . " Reverend Thurgood Creswell's voice quavered momentarily. *"When you see the kids next, send them my love."*

"You can plan on it. God loves you, Goodie."

"I love you, Winnie."

The kidnapper held the PID up to his ear. "Just remember, don't deviate from the plan. When this is over, you'll be the man who destroyed the biggest threat to God's plan the world has ever known. May the Lord bless your sacrifice and welcome you into his loving embrace."

Ending the call, he placed the PID on the nearby nightstand, reached behind his back, and removed a 9mm handgun from his waistband. Leveling the firearm, he pulled the trigger and scattered Winifred Creswell's brains across her bedroom wall.

●

"In the next couple of days, we need to go out and show those clowns in Pacifica how real men party," chuckled Russell Takahashi. Standing in the aisle of their employer's private space-plane, he smiled down at Richard Allison, knowing full well his friend's answer: Married men seldom partied with single men. Their wives simply wouldn't allow it.

With a twinkle in his eye, Richard glanced at Erin hoping she would give him the go-ahead. Her expression was neutral, which was not a good sign. She liked Russell well enough, but his reputation as a Lothario had been a bone of contention between them while they were dating and after the wedding. It wasn't that she didn't trust her husband; it was Russell with whom she had the problem. A whiff of infidelity, however false, would place a cloud over Richard's career that could result in lasting consequences. Infidelity was punishable by court-martial and could result in the accused landing in the brig. No . . . Erin would have none of the infamous Russ 'n Rich party action during their time in Pacifica.

"I'm not sure I'll have much free time, Russ . . . but we'll see," Richard said.

A look of mock disappointment crossed Russell's face. "I guess the only time we'll have to catch up on old times will be during lunch, *at the cafeteria*, over a grilled cheese sandwich and a cup of coffee . . . *not* pretzels and beer at a strip club."

Richard's eyebrows shot up. Pursing his lips in anger, he cut his eyes toward David, who was seated between him and Erin. The youngster was studying Russell closely, a look of confusion on his angelic face. Beside him, Erin looked anything but angelic. She was so infuriated that her face had turned beet red, causing Richard to think the devil himself might make an appearance.

"I'm only kidding, Erin," Russell said, trying to backtrack. "You don't have to worry—"

"Excuse me, sir." A sultry voice, attached to a young, female flight attendant, interrupted Russell's train of thought. With a smile, he turned sideways to let her pass, but she instead leaned forward to address Richard. "Forgive my intrusion, but according to our records, you're Naval Commander Richard Allison, correct?"

"Yes . . . how may I help you, miss?"

"The pilot was wondering if you would like to join her in the cockpit. She said to tell you, 'If he's not too busy twiddling his thumbs, he can sit in the jump seat during takeoff.'"

A befuddled expression momentarily crossed Richard's face, quickly followed by a dawning realization. "Is Captain Janice Ball the pilot?"

"Yes, sir."

Richard's face fairly glowed with joy. He turned toward Erin, but before he could voice the question, she was telling him, "Go ahead, we'll be fine. Just remember to give Janice my love while you're there."

As he rose to his feet, a small voice asked, "Can I go too, Papa?"

Richard gazed down into his son's expectant face and felt a pang of guilt. "Not this time, buddy. It'll be cramped during takeoff, and the pilot needs to pay attention to the controls, not to curious little boys. Besides, you don't want your mother to be alone back here, do you?"

"No, Papa."

Richard gave David's curly mop of hair a quick tussle as he turned to leave.

"Hey, Rich. Who's Janice Ball?"

By the keen look on Russell's face, Richard knew his friend was jealous over not being invited to the cockpit. After all, he was the world-famous pilot who'd been interviewed by nearly every talk show host on HV. "She was my wingman from '56 to '58, after you were reassigned."

"Hmm . . ." one eyebrow rose. "Is she pretty?"

"I suppose so. But more importantly, she's very married."

Normally that answer would've dissuaded most men, but Richard couldn't tell if Russell's shrug meant he understood Janice to be off-limits or that her being married didn't matter to him.

Richard stepped into the aisle, and the flight attendant motioned him forward, while at the same time telling Russell, "Sir, you need to return to your seat. Takeoff is in two minutes."

"Is it okay if I sit here, instead?"

The attendant looked to Richard, "I don't mind, as long as my wife doesn't."

Erin's only sign of disappointment (if one looked close enough) was the tight smile on her face. "He's more than welcome. In fact, he can educate David in the ways of men . . . while you're hanging out with Janice."

His wife's needling reply was offset by the twinkle in her eye. Richard chuckled and shook his head. "I'll see the three of you in thirty minutes . . . when we land in Pacifica."

Erin studied Russell as he watched Richard depart. A trace of envy clouded his expression. "Well, are you just going to stand there admiring the view, or are you going to take a seat?"

Her comment elicited a sound from Russell that landed somewhere between a cough and a laugh. "Your tongue is as sharp as ever, Erin," he said, taking the now empty seat. "So, when are you going to come to your senses and see that I'm the better man for you?"

"Not anytime soon. I suppose I still enjoy being crazy . . . in love."

Russell chuckled. "From the look of things, crazy suits you." He was about to say something else when he glanced down at David, who was seated between them. The boy's eyes were knit in a fierce glare. "What's up with you, little man?"

With a pout, David crossed his arms, looked away, and sank in his seat.

Reaching over, Erin gave David's leg a comforting pat. "It's all right, sweetheart. Your Uncle Russell and I are only teasing each other. That's what grownups do."

"He's not my uncle."

The boy's surly tone prompted Russell to burst out laughing. His amusement only served to make David's mood grow darker by the second.

"Richard has quite the champion here, Erin." A loud, dramatic sigh escaped Russell's lips. "I suppose I should return to my actual seat before your son decides to blacken my eye."

"I wouldn't worry so much about David as I would your girl-friend."

Russell's head whipped back toward the front of the plane. Standing five rows away in the middle of the aisle, hands on hips, was a beautiful, statuesque blonde who could've easily passed for one of Erin's cousins. She did not look pleased.

A female voice came over the intercom. "Ladies and gentle-men, this is your captain speaking. Please fasten your seat belts. The plane will be taking off in one minute. I've been instructed to inform you that the noon briefing with Dr. Solomon Chavez has been postponed. He was called away unexpectedly and will be taking a later shuttle. The meeting is rescheduled for 10:30 tomorrow morning. I hope your stay in the great city of Phoenix, Arizona, was a pleasant one. Please adhere to the safety protocol provided by the flight attendant."

"I guess that's my cue," Russell said, quickly rising to his feet. "Have a nice flight, Erin."

As he strode rapidly up the aisle toward his seat, an irritated flight attendant shouted, "Sir, you *cannot* be moving around! Take your seat, *now*!"

"Yeah, yeah," Russell grumbled. Waving dismissively, he plopped down beside his girlfriend and hastily fumbled with his seat belt.

Excited chatter could be heard throughout the aircraft. Eighty-nine passengers were onboard: ten reporters, thirty-two new CIMRAD employees, Richard and his family, Russell Takahashi, the elderly gentleman seated across the aisle from Erin and David (who'd arrived the day before), and other invited guests who would be given a personal tour by Dr. Solomon Chavez upon their arrival in Pacifica.

After checking to make sure David's seat belt was secure, Erin leaned forward to study the elderly gentleman seated across the aisle. He looked very familiar . . . and extremely nervous.

"Is this your first time flying, sir?" she asked.

"What . . . um, no, I, ah, I've flown many times." Looking back down, he stared at the PID he'd been speaking into less than two minutes earlier. His bottom lip was quivering.

"You look very familiar," Erin continued. She felt the space-plane begin to move. An uneasy feeling began to grow in the pit of her stomach. "Have we met before?"

Tearing his gaze from the now silent PID, the man tucked the device into the breast pocket of his expensive Italian suit and faced Erin. His eyes dropped immediately to David, whose face glowed with childlike anticipation. The plane was now moving faster. The elderly man's expression was sad, almost pained, as he spoke, his gaze fixed on David. "No, I don't believe we've ever met before, Madame. You probably recognize me from the news or from my many appearances on HV. My name is Reverend Thurgood Creswell."

●

Richard was speaking as he strapped himself into the jump seat. "So, how've you been, Jan? I hear that CIMRAD pays its pilots a fortune to fly Chavez to Bangkok or Washington or wherever else he wants to go."

Captain Janice Ball kept one eye on the controls as she spoke. The plane was moving down the runway at a fast clip. "I'll just say this, Rich. It's been a while since potted meat sandwiches were on my plate."

Richard's shoulders shook with amusement at the memory of barely having enough time to eat a proper meal, what with flight training and missions and saving their money for a rainy day. Potted meat sandwiches had been the go-to food when a quick meal was called for—plus, it was cheap. The trick to scarfing them down day after day was ignoring the ingredients.

"How long will you be in Pacifica?" he asked, watching how deftly she handled the controls.

"A few days, maybe more . . . by the way, we're livin' there now. I'll talk to Patrick . . . the four of us oughta get together while I'm on standby."

"Sounds great," replied Richard. As the plane left the runway, he was pressed into his seat, his blood pounding with the familiar thrill of flight. If he hadn't known better, he'd have sworn it was climbing vertically; the angle of ascent was so steep. Despite his mounting excitement, he felt a calm satisfaction wash over him, as his former wingman's skills were top-notch.

"How're Erin and David?" Janice asked, her West Texas twang becoming more pronounced.

"Couldn't be better."

He experienced a momentary pang of guilt wondering if David had been frightened during take-off. Ha! The youngster was probably thrilled to death. Erin would be the one gripping her seat so tightly her manicured nails would threaten to snap off.

The plane was accelerating rapidly through the upper stratosphere.

"Yeehaw!"

"Ride'm cowgirl!"

As the two burst out laughing, the co-pilot shook his head and refocused his attention on the control panel.

•

With the news that Chavez was not onboard the flight, Reverend Thurgood Creswell's heart sank. As panic set in, he nearly stood up and shouted, "Let me off this plane!" but fear held him fast. His wife's captors would not take kindly to him revealing their plan. This had been their best opportunity to take out "God's enemy," and now it was ruined. All that remained was for him to face the consequences in stoic silence.

It won't be long now, he thought, scratching absently at the barely healed five-inch scar running beneath his rib cage across the left side of his abdomen. The implanted explosive device would be triggered when the suborbital space-plane reached 110 miles above the Earth and would then detonate after the plane began its descent and reached 90 miles.

The G-forces were strong, but they would soon reach the upper atmosphere and it would ease off for a bit. His life—and those aboard the plane—would be over in a matter of minutes. He ached at the thought. The lovely young boy seated across the aisle didn't deserve this fate. Few onboard did. Unfortunately, the only individual who did deserve to die had skipped out.

Damn that Solomon Chavez! He is *the enemy of God's plan, just as the terrorists claimed!*

Though Creswell was not an active member of the Christian Republican Army, he was sympathetic to their cause. He understood and approved of their agenda, though he disagreed with their methods (for the most part). The CRA was a brutal organization that bombed government buildings, beheaded abortion doctors, was implicated in assassination attempts on federal judges and the president herself, among other, more generalized acts of terrorism.

One month earlier, when the news broke that Reverend Creswell had been invited to attend a prayer breakfast in Pacifica, and that he would be personally escorted there by Chavez himself, the CRA had sprung into action. They kidnapped the reverend and his wife and forced them to send a message via social media, saying they were going on a much-needed vacation and would be out of touch for a few weeks. The CRA had implanted the explosive device in Thurgood that same day. After three weeks of postoperative recovery, coupled with a generous helping of indoctrination, the two had been whisked back to their home in Palm Springs, California. They had been monitored around the clock, with assurances that if either of them breathed a word of the group's intentions, they and their entire family would be killed.

Not that it mattered. During the previous week, the reverend was afforded little opportunity to talk with friends or employees, and when he did, he'd been too overwhelmed by the situation to say a word. Naturally, no one had suspected a thing, which he chalked up to the acting classes he'd taken in seminary school.

Upon his arrival in Phoenix, he'd been met at the hotel by the mystery man himself, Dr. Solomon Chavez. The reverend hadn't known what to expect, given that there were so many conspiracy theories about the secretive bastard. He'd half expected to see horns sprouting from the man's forehead and smell brimstone on his breath. After all, the CRA had convinced him that Chavez was the Antichrist. But there were no horns, no hint of brimstone; instead, he was a handsome, reasonably pleasant individual. But what did he expect? The devil wouldn't appear as a demon from a horror movie. He'd appear in beauteous guise, bearing the gift of health and long life, exactly as Dr. Solomon Chavez had done.

He was a tricky one . . . the devil himself . . . which meant failure for the CRA's plan. Chavez's destruction was preordained. The Antichrist would be personally killed by Jesus, not by a group of deluded terrorists.

The plane began to level off. They'd reached the desired altitude. The Reverend Thurgood Creswell felt the slightest twitch in his gut, telling him that the explosive device had been triggered. He began to pray with all his might, fervently hoping his wife would be safe and his children could one day forgive him.

●

"Ladies and gentlemen, this is your captain speaking. Those of you with window seats on the left-hand side of the plane will see most of Central America. Those of you on the right-hand side will see Hawaii . . . if you adjust the window magnification to 3.85. We will begin to make our descent in approximately seven minutes. Thank you."

Richard watched his former wingman switch off the intercom and swivel around in her seat. "I hear Russell Takahashi's onboard," she said, studying him closely. With her long, brown hair pulled back in a bun, her countenance appeared somewhat severe. She was an attractive woman with black eyes (thanks to a Latino grandfather), was smart as a whip, and would've made a valuable member of the space corps had she chosen that path. However, she aspired to use her exceptional skills in private industry.

In a way, Richard almost envied Janice: She had a cushy job, made a good salary, and was still able to travel. Then he remembered: working for CIMRAD meant he *also* had a cushy job, made a good salary, and . . . well, he wouldn't be flying space-planes, and his astronaut days were over for the time being, but two out of three wasn't so bad. Of course, he could always reenlist once the Ark Project was under way and his services were no longer needed. By then, however, his lifestyle would've changed and reenlisting would be a difficult adjustment. He'd probably end up like every other topnotch pilot who'd been lured into the private sector . . . he'd stay there.

"Hey, hot-dog," Janice huffed. "Are you woolgatherin' over there?"

"What? Sorry . . . I was just thinking about . . ." he shrugged his shoulders, ". . . never mind. You heard right, Russell's onboard."

"Hmm . . ." Janice turned to her copilot. "You know, Lars, Richard here would've been *the* pilot for *Solomon's Arrow* . . . had he been single. Russell Takahashi's an excellent pilot, mind you, but he would've come in a distant second . . . I'm sure of it."

Richard groaned. "Don't remind me, Janice. Besides, Russ is more than qualified. He can still out-fly anyone placed against him . . . except me." Jutting out his chin, Richard simulated a yawn, prompting Janice and her copilot to laughter.

"Ha! That's the Richard Allison I know and love," she teased. "It's not too late to divorce your old, ugly, dried up, shrew of a wife and steal Takahashi's job out from under 'im."

"Hey! That's *my* old, ugly, dried up, shrew of a wife you're talking about," Richard snapped back. "And don't forget it. Besides, there's David to consider. Even if we did divorce—which is highly unlikely—he'd still be my tie to Earth. My application would be tossed in the trash bin."

"True enough." A green light began blinking on the control panel, signaling the crew that the plane's automated descent was about to begin.

●

Peering out the thick, round window at the coast of Central America, Erin saw the horizon tip slightly and knew the plane was preparing to drop out of low Earth orbit. They would soon be in Pacifica, settling into a new life. It was all so very exciting she could barely stand it.

"Mama, why is that man smoking?"

What an odd question for David to ask, Erin thought. *People don't smoke on planes.* Turning to tell the imaginative youngster he shouldn't tease about such things, she noticed the Reverend Thurgood Creswell having a seizure. David had been the first to notice, what with the passenger seated to the reverend's right apparently asleep. Creswell was making soft mewling sounds, his eyes had rolled back in his head, and he was beginning to twitch . . . and yes, strangely enough, wisps of smoke were emanating from his foam flecked mouth.

"Someone, help!" she screamed. "We need help back h—"

The sudden, violent explosion cut off Erin's next words, along with her life.

●

"I know this great sushi place we can go to after you've settled in."

"Huh, imagine that, a sushi place out in the middle of the ocean," Richard joked. "What, no farm-raised cattle? A good steak would be—"

In the next instant, Richard's entire world was shattered.

2

MEMPHIS, TENNESSEE: 2:15 P.M.

The final drop of smooth Arabica fell from the single-cup coffee maker into a souvenir cup containing the image of a sweat-drenched B. B. King playing his beloved guitar, Lucille. The cup then rose into the air and floated toward the hundred-year-old oak desk belonging to world-famous author and psychic detective, Bram Waters.

The steaming cup of coffee was easing itself down beside his right hand when every social media device in the office began playing "The Thrill is Gone." With his mind distracted by the racket, the cup fell the last few centimeters, with a few drops of the scalding liquid landing on the back of Bram Waters' hand.

"Shit!"

Bram ordered his devices to turn off and, while reaching for his PID, sucked on the offending burn. Having heard his outburst, his longtime secretary, Charlene Tolliver, a not unattractive, middle-aged, red-headed former exotic dancer with four kids, came bounding into the room with a concerned look on her face.

"What's goin' on, boss?" She glanced down at his hand. "You hurt?"

"It's nothing. I spilled some coffee on myself. That's all."

"Ha! Didn't see that comin', didja?"

Whenever Bram so much as stubbed his toe, Charlene was there to give him a good-natured ribbing about his psychic gifts. Most days her humor made him laugh. Today was different. He'd felt uneasy all afternoon and was having trouble concentrating on his current case, which was a typical assignment, nothing that would require more than a day or two to solve. He didn't need the money, but cases such as this kept him busy and paid her salary. Charlene was a little rough around the edges, but she was enjoyable company—and, truth be told, was still easy on the eyes. But after two solid days of rain, together with apprehension *and* his burned hand, Bram was in anything but a jovial mood.

"Could you please bring me some ointment, Ms. Tolliver?"

"Sure, *Mr. Waters*," she huffed. Spinning around, she stalked out of the room.

With an exasperated sigh, Bram looked to the heavens, then spoke to his PID. "Jake, please turn on the HV. Make it channel 57." If something important had taken place, his preferred news network would be covering it.

He was right. The familiar image of a sandy-haired, female reporter appeared on the forty-inch HV screen embedded in the office wall opposite his desk. She was broadcasting from a rapidly moving helicopter, valiantly trying to keep her composure.

"Switching to camera three, the viewer can see remnants of the downed space-plane." A wide expanse of water came into view, littered with smoking debris. "For those viewers just tuning in, a space-plane carrying ninety-four passengers and crew, and owned by Dr. Solomon Chavez, the renowned philanthropist, has crashed off the coast of South America. As you can see, Brent, there's a huge debris field. We have yet to learn of any survivors. We have also not been told whether Dr. Chavez was . . . *hold on* . . . I'm receiving word that he was *not* a passenger. However, I can confirm that Captain Russell Takahashi, command pilot for *Solomon's Arrow*—also called *Mona's Ark* by the public—was on the downed plane. I have also received confirmation that the controversial minister, Reverend Thurgood Creswell, was a passenger as well."

Bram leaned forward in his chair, not even noticing that Charlene had entered the office with the ointment. She stopped in her tracks and stared unblinking at the screen.

After a brief pause, the reporter resumed speaking, her voice tremulous. "I'm not sure if what I'm seeing is correct, but . . . if the control room would please pan in on the debris field just south of the southernmost column of smoke, I'd like to . . . yes, yes! Stop, right there! Right there!"

Bram saw a figure strapped to a mangled jump-seat floating face up in the relatively calm ocean. The camera zoomed in for a tighter shot.

"Ladies and gentlemen, there appears to be a survivor!" The reporter's excited tone added to the urgency of the moment. "We don't know if he's alive, but if . . . he's lifting his head, he lifted his head!"

With smoking wreckage floating all around him, a barely conscious Richard Allison managed to raise his wobbly head before passing out once again. A crimson stain was slowly spreading from his ruined body around the jump-seat he'd been strapped to, his life fluid returning to its primal origins, the sea. He was the plane's only survivor, but unless he was rescued—and rescued soon—that status would soon change.

"What a dramatic turn of events, ladies and gentlemen," the reporter continued. "I've just been informed that a rescue chopper will be here in a matter of minutes. If that poor soul can hold on for just a little while longer, he'll . . . oh, God. A school of hammerhead sharks have just surfaced, and are exploring the wreckage."

Six dark shapes, their hammer-shaped heads easily recognizable to the average viewer, were swimming through the water in

Richard's direction. He lay bleeding, oblivious to the danger he faced, but thankfully the sharks had not yet noticed him.

"Dear God," Charlene moaned, dropping the ointment and covering her mouth. She sank against the wall and stared at the screen, not wanting to watch, yet unable to tear her eyes away.

Bram stared at the HV set, his jaw muscles clenching; aching with the strain of impotence, of wanting desperately to do something, anything, to help that poor man in the water, yet knowing he could do nothing . . . unless, perhaps . . .

Turning his mind's eye southwest toward the wreckage, Bram tried to contact the advancing predators and force his way into their primitive brains, in an attempt to divert their trajectory. He was unsuccessful. Their blood lust was starting to take hold. The sharks would be on the injured man in a matter of moments.

Then he felt it. A nearby intelligence. Exploring the wreckage.

Making telepathic contact, he sent a call for help, using vivid imagery and a not-so-subtle psychic nudge . . .

The reporter was still carrying on a running commentary, her voice sounding desperate. "I'm sorry, ladies and gentlemen . . . but we need to cut away. It looks as if an even larger school of sharks has appeared on the scene. Through the use of facial recognition software, we've identified the injured man, but we will not be releasing his name at this time. What we can tell you is that he's a former astronaut and valued member of Dr. Chavez's team. We will rejoin the video feed later, after the, the . . . hold up, don't cut away! One of the sharks, or what we thought were sharks, has broken the water's surface. They're not sharks at all! The second group is a pod of dolphins! Ladies and gentlemen, it looks as though a pod of dolphins has arrived. This is incredible! They've formed a protective circle around the injured man. We're witnessing a truly dramatic event. Pray, ladies and gentlemen! Pray they hold the sharks off until the rescue chopper arrives. I've heard anecdotal stories about wild dolphins protecting fishermen whose boats have overturned, but to my knowledge it's never been televised. And now, here it is, *live*, on GBS International HV!"

●

THE INDEPENDENT NATION OF PACIFICA: SIX WEEKS LATER

Richard's eyes fluttered open momentarily. He was, with difficulty, swimming to the surface of consciousness.

"I believe he's finally coming around, Solomon," a female voice said, her tone hushed.

There was no response. Richard wondered at that. Who was the woman speaking to? Was she speaking to *the* Solomon Chavez? What was happening? Where was he?

Erin! David!

With the sudden, terrifying memory of his wife and child, Richard's eyes flew open. Lifting himself up, his vision swam and a surge of dizziness overtook him, forcing him to collapse into the soft mattress. He felt a set of hands on his shoulders.

"Easy now, Commander . . . easy now, take your time. Don't rush yourself," said a different voice, definitely male, though it didn't sound like Chavez.

Has something happened to Erin and David? Damn it all to Hell. Room . . . stop spinning!

Richard's stomach felt queasy. "I think I'm going to puke," he moaned.

A strong set of hands belonging to a muscular young man of Peruvian descent helped him up and positioned a plastic bedpan under his chin. His stomach lurched, yet little fluid appeared. He felt better, nonetheless. As Richard's head was lowered back onto the pillow, he caught a glimpse of a middle-aged gentleman in a white coat, a stocky, middle-aged woman with short, jet-black hair, and Solomon Chavez. All three were standing at the foot of his bed.

"Nurse, give the commander four milligrams of Zofran to ease his nausea. After that, elevate his bed fifteen degrees, enough that he isn't forced to lift his head during our conversation."

"Yes, Doctor."

Moments later, the anti-nausea medication kicked in, followed by a soft whirring noise. Soon his head was elevated enough for him to see the three visitors clearly.

"Welcome back to the land of the living, Commander. My name is Dr. Gurdev Singh. I'm sure you have many questions." Reaching up, Dr. Singh brushed a lock of wavy, salt-and-pepper hair off his forehead. "Before you start, I'd like to apprise you of your condition. Thanks to Dr. Chavez, you'll make a full recovery. Your spleen and one of your kidneys needed replacing. You suffered third-degree burns over 10 percent of your body, but we regrew that skin and grafted it a few weeks ago. It is responding well. In a few months, you'll never know you'd ever been bur—"

"Where're my wife and child?" Richard croaked. "Why aren't they here?"

The doctor glanced nervously at Chavez, who caught his eye and offered a barely perceptible shake of the head. "How much do you remember about the day you were injured, Commander?" he asked, trying to avoid the question.

"Not much, Doc." Richard's eyebrows furrowed in deep thought. "I vaguely recall leaving the Biltmore and asking my PID to play . . . let's see . . . oh, yes . . . "Moonlight Sonata." But after that, I don't . . .'" Richard paused to study the doctor's face. The man's lips were pursed, and the other two stood like statues. "Like I asked before, where are my wife and child?"

"There was an accident, Commander. As a result, you've been kept in a chemically induced coma during your recovery. You're lucky to be—"

"Enough already! Where are they?!" Richard barked. "Where's my family?! Tell me where . . . they . . . where are . . . why . . . won't . . . you . . ."

Dr. Singh's thumb held the button on the remote a moment longer, allowing the powerful sedative to flood Richard's system. "Go back to sleep, Commander. This discussion can wait."

Grunting softly, Richard fought to stay awake, but the sedative worked its magic. All his cares floated away, and he sank into a comforting, dreamless sleep.

●

TWO DAYS LATER

The images on the hospital HV flickered at the edges of Richard's awareness, yet he paid them little attention. His sadness was overwhelming. All he could manage was to stare blankly at the light-green hospital wall, his mind numb to the world. His pain and anguish sat like a vulture, waiting patiently to consume him.

He felt completely alone. Without Erin and David in his life, nothing really mattered.

During the past two days of knowing that his family was dead, he'd gone through the motions, not caring what he ate or if he ate, letting nurses do the work of helping him to the bathroom, of giving him sponge baths. His massive depression was giving them plenty of cause to worry. But he didn't really care. His heart was empty.

Earlier that morning, Richard had been informed that Solomon Chavez would be stopping by to pay him a visit, yet even that news had gone in one ear and out the other without a twitch of anticipation. As he absently watched a stray piece of lint floating in a shaft of sunlight beaming through the room's window, he realized someone had just spoken his name. How could that be?

He was alone. That's when he noticed his smiling face plastered on the HV embedded in the wall at the foot of his bed. He recognized the man who was speaking: Darren Brantley, of *The Darren Brantley Show*.

". . . and later in this hour I'll be speaking with Dr. Alice Shively about Commander Allison's long-term prognosis. The public is still clamoring to learn about his condition. Since his dramatic rescue at sea, which was viewed by over 1.2 billion people on various network and interlink outlets, Commander Richard Allison has become one of the most talked-about people on the planet."

The news of his celebrity status was an unpleasant jolt back to reality. Richard was aghast as images from six weeks earlier appeared on the screen. He'd avoided watching the HV up until this morning, but his nurse had insisted, thinking some light entertainment would help alleviate his doldrums. Richard had shrugged, not caring whether the HV was on or off. But this, this was different. This was the first he'd seen of his body floating in the dark-blue waters of the Pacific, surrounded by smoking debris, surrounded by sharks and dolphins.

"Who can forget the horrific carnage or the heart-stopping minutes surrounding Commander Allison's rescue?" Darren Brantley intoned, his famous baritone voice evoking the perfect amount of empathy from his audience. "I know I never will."

As the camera zoomed in, the holographic picture looked so vivid, so real, that it was easy to imagine he was watching the scene take place through a window in his room. He saw himself floating unconscious, oblivious to the battle raging around him. Richard watched as the dolphins surrounded him seconds before the hammerhead sharks' arrival, their dorsal fins cutting through the water on an intercept course. At the last second the sharks veered off, forced aside by the fast-moving dolphins. Not dissuaded, they kept circling, making dashes toward his damaged body, trying to keep the madly protective dolphins off guard.

As for the dolphins, they were ready and waiting, coordinated, sensing when the sharks were about to strike. The mammals were darting about, ramming sharks with their hard snouts. During the actual event, each time a shark attacked, the viewer at home would gasp in horror, thinking Richard's luck had run out, followed by a cheer, praising the valiant dolphin's courage when the shark was driven away.

Despite knowing he was watching a prerecorded broadcast, Richard's heart nearly leapt from his throat when he saw the first shark attack. While watching the nerve-racking battle between deadly predators and peaceful protectors, Richard began to appreciate why the real-time audience had become so invested in the outcome. It felt like he was having an out-of-body experience, like he was watching a stranger in jeopardy, not himself. When the rescue chopper finally arrived, he caught himself breathing a sigh of relief. The appearance of the chopper was the last straw for the sharks. Whether it was the noise or the downdraft from the whirring blades, the sharks suddenly fled the scene. Not so for the dolphins: half gave chase, leaving the other half to circle protectively around Richard.

While his body was being lifted to the safety of the rescue chopper, the pursuing dolphins rejoined their brethren. With their permanent grins pointing skyward, the dolphins rose halfway out of the water, watching attentively until Richard was safely within the chopper. In unison, they began to chatter and leap backward through the air. After slashing down, they spread out, returning to the business of inspecting the plane's smoldering wreckage.

"By God, I could watch that footage all day," Darren Brantley gushed. "Why, if I had a nickel for every goose bump that scene's given me over the past six weeks, I'd be rich."

The camera switched back to the smiling HV host. His snow-white teeth, perfectly coifed, light-brown hair, and wide amiable face had been gracing the airwaves for well over two decades.

Lacing his fingers together and leaning forward at his desk, he affected a more serious demeanor.

"After the break, I'll be speaking with a panel of experts about the mystery of Reverend Creswell's involvement in the plane's downing. Was he a willing pawn of the CRA? Could he have been the mastermind behind the failed plot to assassinate Solomon Chavez? Or, as some people believe, was the CRA using his wife as a tool to—"

"Computer, turn off the HV," Richard grunted, feeling drained and deeply disturbed. With a frown, he turned his head to gaze out the window.

"It seems you've become quite the celebrity, Commander Allison."

Startled, Richard whipped his head toward the voice and saw Solomon Chavez standing in the doorway, his arms crossed as he leaned against the doorframe.

"May I come in?"

"Of course . . . have a seat." Richard watched as his employer, who was wearing a faded pair of jeans, a gray V-neck sweater with white t-shirt underneath, positioned a chair beside his bed. The man's casual attire was a bit jarring. "To what do I owe this unexpected honor, Dr. Chavez?"

Crossing one leg over the other, Solomon studied Richard's face. "In a matter of weeks, you won't be able to tell that most of the skin from your left temple down to your jaw was replaced. And the new skin on your neck looks great." Most of Richard's injuries were barely noticeable due to the advances in treatment brought about by CIMRAD technology. "You should be able to leave the hospital by the end of the week."

Richard's heart sank at the thought of living in an empty apartment.

Solomon continued: "I apologize for not coming sooner. I've been very busy with . . ." he paused to shake his head. "I am so sorry for the loss of your wife and child. Their deaths were a senseless, terrible tragedy. I understand how you must . . ." Solomon stopped to clear his throat. "I can only imagine how you must feel right now, Commander Allison. This Sunday there will be a special memorial service for all those lost in the crash. We've delayed it, waiting for you to be well enough to attend."

Richard looked away, unsure if he could deal with the thought of sitting in a pew, staring at wreaths of flowers, listening to mournful tunes. "I . . . I don't know if—"

"The public expects you to be there, Commander," Chavez cut in. "Since the crash, you've become the face of the Ark Project . . . together with your son, David—a beautiful boy if I've ever since one."

"David? I don't understand."

"As I said earlier, you've become quite the celebrity, Commander. Of course, the public was outraged by what happened to the other passengers, but it was the picture of your son that set a billion tears flowing. For weeks the public was beside itself, calling for vengeance, retribution for David's death. As a result, the CRA was forced even further underground. Even some of their right-wing supporters have been calling for their heads. So, you see, you simply must attend the memorial, Commander. It's as much for the public, who's invested a piece of their hearts in your boy, as it is for you and the families of the other victims."

Richard offered a slow, hesitant nod.

"Good, I have one more thing—"

"Can't this wait, Dr. Chavez? I'm exhausted."

"Just one more thing and I'll be out of your hair, Commander," he said, glancing toward the HV screen. "I have someone who'd like to speak with you. Computer, connect with M-103."

The screen came to life. There, staring back at Richard was the face of a woman he hoped to never see again: Admiral Katherine "Battleaxe" Axelrod, former supreme commander of NATO and

Captain of *Solomon's Arrow*. Her prematurely gray hair was pulled back in a severe bun, her stern, angular features seemingly carved from granite, her navy-blue officer's uniform adorned with the many ribbons awarded during her twenty-three-year career in the British navy.

"Hello, Richard. I'm pleased to see you're recovering so nicely. Sorry about your family."

The admiral's characteristically indifferent manner grated on his nerves. Richard forced his irritation aside. "Hello, sir. You're also looking well." He always addressed her as *sir*, remembering vividly how, as a young lieutenant under her command, he'd made the mistake of calling her *ma'am*. He'd received a tongue-lashing he could still quote word for word. She'd said, "I'm not your mother," and for him to call her sir, which was a sign of respect, and to never again insult her with that other appellation. One thing Richard would never call her was a friend; though he did respect her, which meant he was all ears when she appeared on screen.

"As you well know, Richard, we lost many good people in the bombing, including Russell Takahashi. He will be sorely missed. But he's not irreplaceable. There are other qualified pilots who could do the job nearly as well, but there is only one person who could do the job better, and that's you. We'd like you to honor Russell's memory by stepping into his shoes. What say you?"

"But I'm not qualified for the . . ." that's when Richard remembered: *now* he was qualified for the job. The main precondition for joining The *Arrow*'s crew was that their life be devoid of family. Six weeks ago he'd become eligible, and he hated it with a passion.

Both Solomon Chavez and Admiral Axelrod waited patiently while he wrestled with the idea of their offer. *It was too soon*, Richard thought. They needed to find someone else. "I . . . I'm sorry, but

I can't accept your generous offer. I'm leaving the program. I need time to grieve, time to come to terms with what's happened."

"Nonsense, Richard," the admiral barked. "What you need more than anything is to work. You need to immerse yourself in your job, distract yourself with work. Lying around in bed all day does you no good. You've had too much time to dwell on your misfortune."

"Misfortune?!" Richard snapped. "What happened was not a *misfortune*, sir! Who the hell do you think you are? My life is destroyed! If you think I'll—"

"That's enough, Commander Allison!" she warned. "You're acting like a daft prick teetering on the edge of insubordination." Her eyes flared with anger. "For the sake of what you've been through, I'm willing to overlook your behavior this time, but not again. Do you understand my meaning?" Richard's glare should have made her explode with fury. Instead, her voice lowered, becoming cold, monotone. "Answer me, Commander."

Swallowing his resentment, Richard grumbled, "Yes, *sir*. Your meaning is perfectly clear, *sir*. However, that doesn't change the fact that I have reservations about remaining in Pacifica, much less joining the mission."

That's when Chavez chimed in. "Well then, let me clear those reservations up for you, Commander. I have your name on a contract. You are legally required to work for CIMRAD for the next eighteen months. And I'll be holding you to that contract."

Stunned, Richard stared open-mouthed at Solomon Chavez, unable to believe his ears.

"I wish it wasn't so, Commander. Nevertheless, I *will* put the hammer down if required. All I ask is for you to not make any rash decisions. Start the job you were originally hired for. And if, in a month or two, you want to decline the Admiral's offer, I'm confident we can find someone else to take your place. However, you owe it to your son's memory to pick yourself up, dust yourself off, and set a good example for all those who've come to care for you."

Letting his head fall dejectedly to his pillow, Richard lay staring at the light-green ceiling, feeling his future slip from his control like water through a sieve. With a barely perceptible nod, he murmured, "Fine . . . I'll *consider* the offer."

•

Having earlier that day returned to the Lake Victoria complex from Pacifica, Dr. Mona Levin, the fifty-one-year-old designer and engineer of *Solomon's Arrow*, stared out her penthouse window at the massive, circular structure lying at the heart of Elevator City. Owned and operated by a multinational conglomerate and constructed sixteen years earlier, the space-elevator was hailed as one of the world's greatest technological marvels.

At the turn of the century, the prevailing theory was to anchor the space-elevator with a carbon-nanotube cable, which would rise tens of thousands of miles into space to counteract the effects of gravity. This theory proved unrealistic and was mothballed until the year 2032, when a young quantum engineer, Dr. Mona Levin, designed the first independent, magnetic-levitation engine. After that breakthrough, it didn't take long for the notion of a space-elevator to resurface. The maglev-engine could use a laser guidance system, allowing the orbital platform to be built closer to Earth, thus shaving what would've taken days to reach space down to hours and turning an impractical dream into a practical reality.

The platform, orbiting three-hundred miles above Kenya, housed a rotating crew composed of seventy-eight scientists, administrators, and technicians, all of whom were working feverishly to build *Solomon's Arrow*, aka *Mona's Ark*. She hated the nickname, but also secretly relished it, knowing the reference applied to her Jewish heritage—a play on the ancient story of Noah's Ark, of which the project was a modern day equivalent.

The huge ground-side complex employed vast numbers of people, all of whom required housing and entertainment. Elevator City was built to accommodate their needs, and before long a booming economy was established.

Mona studied a small dot rising through the atmosphere. The dot was the elevator's transport container, and it was filled with supplies destined for the Arrow of Time (a nickname she coined, though it never stuck). As the transport passed the elevator's midway point, Mona's thoughts turned to Pacifica, causing her temper to flare once again.

Damn that Solomon Chavez and his fucking rules!

The junior Chavez was just like his father, a stickler for protocol and procedures. Everyone knew that she was the foremost quantum engineer on the planet and obvious choice to be the *Arrow's* chief engineer. But no, her mother was still alive. Hell, her mother was pushing eighty and in poor health. As for Mona's age, she was barely one year past the cutoff. There should be some leeway when it came to people such as her . . . important people, valuable people, people who put their heart and soul—their blood, sweat, and tears—into this momentous project.

It wasn't fair, and she stressed that fact in the only way she knew how, without much tact, while accompanying Solomon to Commander Allison's room. She'd been present when the poor fellow awoke from his chemically induced coma.

"You're a son-of-a-bitch for not bending the rules, Solomon," she'd snapped before entering the commander's room. "You need me on this mission and you know it!"

Solomon had come to an abrupt halt and faced her, a cold anger burning in his eyes. The timbre of his voice remained steady and he seemed his usual unflappable self, but she could tell he was furious over her continued attempts to change his mind. But he was a cool one . . . just like his father.

"Mona, you need to stop harassing me about this. You know the rules better than anyone. If I break them for you, everyone from aging movie stars to pop tarts and their idiot brothers will be calling me up." Solomon appeared sympathetic. "You and I both know you're the best person for the job. But you don't meet the qualifications, and that's final. You belong here. After all, who's better qualified than you to run the show once I'm fast asleep in a cryo-chamber?"

Right, he just *had* to remind her that he was a member of the invited elite.

Over six thousand people from various fields and professions had already been invited or would soon be invited to embark on the grandest, riskiest adventure mankind had ever attempted. They would arrive the week before liftoff to begin the process of cryogenic freezing, each person being kept alive in suspended animation using a recently discovered chemical treatment (from CIMRAD, *naturally*) that replaces their bodily fluids with a synthetic glucose designed to prevent the destruction of the body's cellular integrity during the freezing process.

Solomon, along with the other colonists, would fall asleep one day and, through the miracle of modern technology, awaken ten years later feeling as though they'd merely taken a cat nap. There would be minimal side effects, the most pronounced being a headache which, if treated promptly, would fade within twenty-four hours. During their ten-year *nap*, the *Arrow* would accelerate to just below the speed of light, using a zero-point electric engine (designed by her) together with a warp bubble to protect the ship from expanding to infinity, which, according to Einstein's Theory of Relativity, would occur as the vehicle approached light-speed. The theory also maintained that during those ten years—two of which would be spent accelerating and then decelerating—the Earth would age nearly three thousand years.

This prospect was what infuriated Mona the most. Her bones would be long turned to dust by the time Solomon climbed from his cryogenic chamber and set foot on humanity's new home.

Stepping away from her apartment window, Mona crossed the bedroom, slipped on her work jacket, and gazed at the full-length mirror hanging on her bedroom door. She wore no makeup, which accentuated every minute of her fifty-one years. Examining her dark-brown hair, which she'd always kept in a pageboy style, she noticed a couple of gray strands here and there. Perhaps it was time to visit a stylist and wash that gray right out of her hair, like the advertisement said.

Although her features were plain, she was far from ugly. Her body was slightly overweight, not stick-thin like the models she saw in fashion magazines. Fortunately, her curves fell in all the right places. And she was certainly not a shrinking violet. She'd gone to bed with her fair share of men—and a few women—over the years. She was a well-respected, highly-intelligent scientist who was good at solving engineering problems . . . and getting her way.

After a decade of working her fingers to the bone for Solomon Chavez, combined with the previous five years working for his father, she would not be relegated to the sidelines. She ached to be named chief engineer of the *Arrow*. If that dream was thwarted, Mona would be forced to take matters into her own hands . . . and institute plan B.

3

TEN MILES EAST OF MEMPHIS, TENNESSEE: 3:57 P.M., MAY, 15, 2060

B ram guided his antique, electric-powered, candy-apple red trike down the dusty back roads of his adopted home state, enjoying the spring breeze in his hair. He'd bought the three-wheeler months ago, but this was its first road trip. Shortly after noon he'd loaded the trike in the bed of his pickup and programmed the GPS to take him to an isolated stretch of dirt.

Gunning the accelerator, Bram pushed the humming motorbike's speed up to 45 mph. He'd never driven a manually operated trike before, and the thrill of doing so was contagious. It was also illegal. Manually operated vehicles were outlawed twenty-eight years earlier, but by then most vehicles used GPS. The law had been passed to discourage miscreants like him.

Logically, he understood the need for the ban: There shouldn't be a bunch of anarchists on the road, swerving in and out of traffic, getting into horrific accidents, putting law-abiding citizens in harm's way. But . . . the law had also sucked the life out of the open road. Despite the advantages supplied by GPS operating systems, he often longed for the good old days of family cruises and teenage boys roaring down Main Street in *actual* gasoline-powered hot rods.

He could imagine what it must have been like to drive what amounted to a fire-breathing dragon down the highway. Now the only place a gasoline-powered engine could be found was in a museum—if one didn't count a few Third World countries where they were still being used. And even they were starting to see the light. Since the petroleum industry was focused solely on petrochemical endeavors instead of gasoline, the remaining few gas-powered vehicles had been converted to use biofuels. This meant that the streets of rural Cambodia, and equivalent habitats around the globe, smelled of French fries, hamburgers, and fried chicken.

With these thoughts swirling in his head, Bram failed to notice the police monitor affixed to a post on the side of the road. Moments later, his reverie was interrupted by the ringtone version of Robert Johnson's "Hellhound on My Trail." Pulling to the side of the road, he placed the trike in neutral and reached for his Personal Interlink Device, feeling perturbed. He'd specifically asked Eric—his PID's artificial personality—to transfer all his calls to voice mail for the duration of the trip. That's when an image came to mind of a star, with the words "Tennessee State Police" wrapped around its outer edge.

"Dammit!" Bram glanced around, looking for the monitor; it was around a bend in the road. Shoulders slumping, he spoke to his PID, "Connect me with the men in blue, Eric."

"There's no need for that, Bram." Eric's voice sounded exactly like another one of Bram's idols, an English guitar-god from the twentieth century. "The state police traffic computer has instructed me to forward this information: 'Bram Waters, you will immediately cease and desist driving your manually operated vehicle. If you do not, said vehicle will be impounded. If you have the means, arrange for its pick up. If not, the state police will make arrangements for you, which will include a nominal towing fee. Expect a fine of one-thousand one-hundred fifty-three dollars for blatantly failing to comply with existing state and federal laws. Have a nice day.'"

"What a crock!" Bram seethed. He wanted to grind his PID into the dirt, but instead heaved a heavy sigh. "Eric, program my truck with these coordinates. By the way . . . do I have any other messages?"

"Yes, Bram, you have eleven messages in all."

"Jeez . . . okay, give me the bad news."

"Is that sarcasm or an actual premonition, Bram?"

Frowning at the PID, he grumbled, "Just play the messages."

What followed was a message from Charlene telling him that she was through for the day and heading home; two robo-calls, which he quickly deleted; five advertisements, which were also deleted; one lead on a current case; and one from a potential client before the final message was played. He bolted upright in the trike's seat, his mouth hanging open in shock.

"This is Lawrence Murchison, press secretary for Dr. Solomon Chavez. I am pleased to inform you that you have been chosen to participate in the greatest adventure ever envisioned by the mind of man: The Ark Project. Most of the other six thousand people chosen were informed by underlings or by computer; however, I'm calling you personally, Mr. Waters, because we want to offer you a special position as a crew member, the details of which I'll outline when you return my call. Please contact me by four o'clock. If you receive this message after that time, please call first thing in the morning. I'm looking forward to speaking with you . . . but I suppose you already knew that." Bram heard a soft chuckle. "Sorry, I couldn't resist. Good day, Mr. Waters."

Variations on that lame joke had plagued Bram long before his memoir became a bestseller. Lawrence Murchison's attempt at humor hadn't fazed him—it was the message itself that threw him for a loop. Bram stared at his PID, stunned, not having seen this coming.

"What the fuck?" was the only reaction that came to mind.

●

ORANGE COUNTY. CALIFORNIA:
9:27 P.M.. MAY. 29. 2060

Shaking his head in disgust, Jimmy Jamison glared at the HV, his eyes following President Gale Cranston as she strode from the podium and out of the White House press room. The president had just finished giving one of her all-too-frequent press conferences, once again trying to reassure the American people that the faltering economy was on the upswing.

It was bullshit! Everyone knew she was a lying, devil-loving, Hollywood liberal.

"Sarah, turn this crap off," he spat.

"You betcha, Jimmy." The computer's chipper, North Dakotan accent always made the seventy-eight-year-old former software engineer smile.

Rising from his plush leather couch, Jimmy Jamison cinched the red, silk robe tighter around his slight, five-foot seven-inch frame, opened the sliding glass window located in his mahogany-paneled study, and stepped onto the terrace overlooking his kidney-shaped swimming pool.

"Sarah dear, connect me with Dahlgren. And use the secure channel."

Seconds later, a man's husky voice sounded in his Bluetooth implant. "Dahlgren here, Mr. Jamison. How can I help you?"

"I'm curious how the Victoria Proposal is coming along."

"It's right on schedule, sir. Our inside contact has sent word of the shipment's arrival. It will be loaded the day after tomorrow."

"Excellent! We are doing the Lord's Work, my friend. A great reward will be awaiting our arrival in heaven."

"I'm sure that's true. However, the money *you're* paying me will come in handy while awaiting the heavenly version."

Philistine! Doesn't he know that money is a poor substitute for God's love? "Of course, my friend, you will be well rewarded when the plan succeeds. When the modern-day tower of Babel tumbles to the earth, a cry—no—a *roar* of joy will erupt from the mouths of the faithful, unlike anything heard since the walls of Jericho came tumbling down."

"Amen, brother."

Jimmy Jamison looked to the heavens and pursed his thin lips. "Call me the instant you learn of our success. Sarah, disconnect."

Placing his blue-veined hands on the veranda's white, marble railing, Jamison watched his grandchildren frolic in the pool, their happy voices sounding as if there wasn't a care in the world. *If they only knew the truth*, he thought. If only they knew that the Antichrist walked the Earth, weaving his evil plot to subvert the Lord's will, they would be shivering with pure terror instead of splashing and cavorting with unmitigated joy.

Perhaps it was best they didn't know. Their happy, carefree voices were like a balm to his soul. The young shouldn't suffer from the horrific truths that plague adults.

•

LAKE VICTORIA COMPLEX, KENYA: 4:12 A.M. MAY 30, 2060

Three sharp beeps woke Floyd Sullivant from a peaceful night's sleep without disturbing his boyfriend. Floyd's eyes snapped open, knowing that the sonically directed alarm clock, which could only be heard by the individual it was focused on, was programmed to activate only in case of an emergency involving his job as head of security.

Swinging his legs over the side of their queen-size bed, he arched his back and stretched his muscular, two-hundred twenty-five pound, six-foot three-inch frame. After a massive yawn, he rubbed his close-cropped brown hair and sub-vocalized, knowing that Madge, his PID artificial personality, would hear and respond.

"What's the emergency, girl?"

The directional function was still in effect. "Security has detected an anomaly at dock 9-B. It requires your immediate attention."

An anomaly. "I'll be right there. Is Fletcher on duty, or—"

He was distracted by a soft groan and the feel of his boyfriend rolling over in bed.

"What's going on, baby? Can't sleep?"

Floyd felt a smooth, callous-free hand find the small of his back and begin a gentle massage.

"It's nothing, Rudy." His deep, Welsh-accented voice sounded too loud this early in the morning. "Something's come up at work, is all. Go back to sleep."

Rudy sat up in bed. "Lights, fifteen percent," he ordered. The overhead glow-strip blushed faintly, casting his lean, Scandinavian features in a soft light. "Is it serious?"

"Don't know," Floyd said, pulling a clean, white t-shirt over his head. "I'll find out shortly."

"Let me know how it goes. I enjoy listening to you talk about work." Rudy's eyes lingered on Floyd's well-defined torso.

"If I can, babe," Floyd chuckled. Straightening his tie, he leaned over and gave Rudy a quick kiss. "I'll see you tonight. I'm cooking linguine . . . with oysters."

Rudy shook his head. "You're incorrigible."

"What can I say? I like oysters," he said, a sly grin tweaking the corners of his mouth.

Slipping his PID into his shirt pocket, Floyd left the apartment in a rush. It had been months since an anomalous security threat had been detected, and his curiosity was piqued.

Rudy was still sitting up in bed. The expression on the young man's handsome face had changed from happiness to concern. He stared at the bedroom door, wondering if Floyd's departure warranted informing the group he worked for, and he wasn't thinking about his fellow employees in the shipping division.

●

Twenty-four minutes later, Floyd was approaching a contingent of security officers gathered outside the small auxiliary office at dock 9-B. One of the security officers was Jeremy Fletcher, a gangly twenty-year-old that Floyd was quite fond of, though Jeremy's exuberance sometimes got on his nerves.

The young man noticed Floyd's arrival before anyone else. "There he is," Jeremy said, his face lighting up. Having distinguished himself as a computer whiz in the US Navy, Jeremy was quickly headhunted by CIMRAD and reassigned to administer the security upgrades at the Lake Victoria complex. Though he continued to hold the rank of ensign, the only outward sign of his military status was the navy pin he wore on the lapel of his black security uniform. "The chief will clear—"

"Mr. Fletcher!" snapped a middle-aged black man to Jeremy's right. "Wait until we're inside the hut. On second thought, stay quiet unless called upon . . . do you copy?"

The young man sheepishly nodded his head.

Floyd was intrigued by the unusual exchange. Approaching the group of five men and one woman, he motioned toward the auxiliary security office and followed them inside, concerned by the odd, furtive looks he was receiving from his most trusted lieutenants.

"Computer, display the schematics for receiving dock 9-B," said Gloria Muldoon. As usual, her tone was brusque. Her long, raven-black hair was pulled back in a regulation ponytail and, as usual, she wore no makeup. But that didn't matter, as even without makeup, she was quite stunning.

Floyd admired Gloria's commitment to her job. It had been an auspicious day when he hired her as his second-in-command. Her devotion to the Ark Project was so complete that he never saw her with a man—or woman. Perhaps it was her icy nature that got in the way. Heterosexual men tended to be intimidated by strong women—unlike him, who was fascinated with the fairer sex, icy nature notwithstanding. Being a reasonably attractive man with a muscular physique, he'd been approached by women over the years and even gone to bed with one while attending college . . . after a night of heavy drinking. It had been a pleasant enough experience (at first). However, despite her pretty face and nubile body, the sexual glow began to dim. After more than a half hour of lovemaking, he was exhausted, couldn't finish, and wanted the experience to end. Since she was lying face down at the time, he closed his eyes, thought about a former boyfriend, and picked up the pace. Welcome relief soon followed. Exhausted, he rolled off her and stared out the bedroom window. An empty, downcast feeling lurked in the pit of his stomach.

Unfortunately, he'd done his job *too* well. The girl—he couldn't even remember her name anymore—told him that she'd never been pleasured like that by any man, *ever*, and wanted more. He tried to beg off by claiming fatigue, then closed his eyes and hoped she'd get the hint. Shortly thereafter, he felt her hand close around his flaccid member. Before he could react, her lips were next. Floyd told her to stop, but she'd kept on going. He wanted to push her off but was afraid she'd grow angry, so he lay there staring at the ceiling, hoping she would arouse him, if only to avoid telling her the truth.

After ten minutes and no reaction to her efforts, she looked up into his sad eyes and with a confused expression on her face, asked if she was doing something wrong. After reassuring her that her technique was superb, he'd asked her to lie next to him. That's when he'd told her the truth. At first she didn't believe him, saying that he was too good a lay to be gay. Then, when he told her that she was the first woman he'd ever slept with, she started to yell. As she hurriedly threw on her clothes, he tried to settle her down, asking her to stay, saying he'd fix her breakfast, coffee, anything, but she'd stormed out of the apartment. Floyd never saw her again. That was his first and only heterosexual encounter. He'd never been tempted again, not even by the gorgeous ice-princess herself, Gloria Muldoon.

Standing perfectly erect, with her hands clasped behind her back, Gloria stared at the fifty-two-inch HV screen embedded in the far wall. A blue-lined, rotating, holographic schematic of dock 9-B floated within its inky blackness.

"Computer, enhance sector nineteen, bay five."

The schematic stopped rotating and zoomed in on the afore-mentioned location. A pallet stacked with non-perishable medical supplies sat apart from the rest, blinking an ominous red warning signal.

Gloria pointed at the screen. "Gentlemen, what we have here is a pallet with a net weight equaling twelve grams less than what it should be."

Floyd scowled. He was losing sleep for *this*? "Why does this warrant an emergency meeting, Gloria? Can't this discrepancy be explained? Perhaps the manufacturer used too much packing material."

Once again, he received strange looks from his staff.

"No, sir. This shipment contains medical supplies that are pack-aged in a prescribed fashion," she replied. "The supplies them-selves have a weight calculated down to the microgram. It is my considered opinion that someone is trying to smuggle contraband onto the ship. A 'sniffer' was used to test it for explosives. Though the results were inconclusive, that does not mean a bomb is not contained somewhere within its depths."

"Has it been X-rayed?"

Gloria gave him a hard look before answering. "The container is shielded to protect itself against cosmic radiation exposure; therefore, we can't determine what's inside. A bomb disposal unit has been called in and will be arriving in a matter of minutes."

"Good work," he said, "but I'm still unsure why this situation is such a high priority."

Gloria glanced toward Jeremy Fletcher and nodded.

The young man cleared his throat and nervously explained. "Well, sir. This morning I, um, found a discrepancy in the weight classification computer logs. Normally I would have reviewed the weekly statistics yesterday, but I was down with a stomach bug. I came in early to catch up and discovered that the weigh-in on the receiving dock and the official figures recorded in the permanent record were off. I did a little digging and narrowed the anomaly to dock 9-B, sector nineteen, bay five. As you know, sir, I'm a stickler for detail and—"

"Yes, yes, get to the point, Ensign," Floyd snapped.

"Yeah, um, anyway," Jeremy sputtered, glancing sidelong at Gloria. "I was m-merely . . ."

The boy seemed oddly reticent. Before he could suffer further embarrassment, Gloria held up a hand for silence—she was being notified (via Bluetooth implant) that the bomb squad had arrived. All six left the auxiliary office and hopped onboard a maglev warehouse trolley. Further discussion was put on hold as the group traveled to sector nineteen. Floyd was pleased to see the sector was cleared of workers, which would minimize casualties if something did go wrong.

The bomb squad was already set up and waiting for the order to proceed when they arrived at the dock. Floyd and the other security officers positioned themselves behind a blast shield located twenty yards away and watched as the squad, positioned behind their own blast shield, deployed a bomb-disposing robot affectionately known as Teddy. It stood three feet tall, rolled across the floor on tracks, and sported mechanical hands that could be used for finely detailed work. Atop its box-like head were two half-moon antennas that gave the impression of ears . . . hence its name.

It took nearly thirty minutes for Teddy to remove the crate's top panel and begin scanning its interior. The scan showed a ceramic object with electrical components in the middle of the crate. After a tense five minutes, the object was removed and placed in a portable detonation chamber.

Floyd turned to Gloria with an angry, determined look on his face. "Whoever's responsible for this device must be apprehended, and quickly, before word leaks out. I don't want this fucker slipping through our fingers." As his staff's hard expressions began to soften and they shot each other knowing looks, Floyd decided to confront their attitude head on. "What the hell's going on, Gloria?" he growled. "What are you not telling me?"

Once again she nodded to Jeremy Fletcher.

"Um, sir, I traced the records discrepancy to a specific security code. I immediately contacted Chief Muldoon, and she instituted a communication trace on the suspect. Ten minutes before you arrived, he attempted to place a secure call to a location in the United States. An immediate data-block was initiated, and we're narrowing down who the suspect was trying to contact. The suspect attempted to leave his apartment complex, but we disabled his vehicle's GPS system and locked him inside. A security squad arrived a few minutes later and apprehended him as he was trying to bust through the vehicle's side window."

He looked over at Gloria, who took it from there. "The suspect arrived ten minutes ago, and we're holding him in lockup. The interrogation will begin the moment we get there."

"Great! We're wasting time. I can't wait to get my hands on the bastard who thought he could pull the wool over our eyes."

Floyd saw relief on all but Gloria's face. As always, her expression remained neutral. Setting aside further questions about his team's peculiar attitude, Floyd's mind focused on the job ahead. One way or another, the suspect would give them the answers they needed.

●

Stepping out of the elevator on level G5, Floyd took the lead, striding ahead of the others down the dove-gray hallway to the installation's holding cells. As he approached the entrance, he and his team were identified using facial recognition software. The door slid open, and they entered a four-foot wide by eight-foot long chamber. Once inside, the security program requested their names, further confirming their identity through voice recognition software. The inner door slid open, allowing the group access to the holding cells.

Security for the installation was tight; like a well-run ship, with most threats contained well outside the city. As a result, there were only seven holding cells in all, with most of them empty on any particular day.

Entering the circular antechamber, Floyd nodded to the guard in charge, who sat at a small, central monitoring station. "He's in the interrogation chamber?" The guard nodded.

"Excellent . . . Gloria, you're with me. The rest of you, in the observation room; I'll want your impressions on how it goes. If you pick up on something we've missed, don't hesitate to contact us. We need to explore all avenues of questioning, understood?"

Following a chorus of "Yes, sir," the other four team members hustled inside the adjoining room. Floyd paused before the interrogation chamber door, Gloria Muldoon directly behind him.

"Do you want to be good cop or bad cop this time?" he asked, looking over his shoulder and giving Gloria a lopsided grin.

One eyebrow rose. "What do you think, sir?"

"Bad cop it is then." Chuckling, he nodded to the monitoring station guard.

The door slid open, and the two stepped inside the interrogation chamber. In the middle of the eight-foot by ten-foot room sat a small, metal table, bolted to the floor. A blond-haired man was slumped over it, his head buried in his arms. As the two entered the room, his head popped up.

Floyd staggered, nearly losing his balance. Coming to an abrupt halt, he stared at the young man, disbelief in his eyes. "What's the meaning of this?" he sputtered.

Seated at the table was his boyfriend, Rudy. *There must be some sort of mistake*, he thought. Furious, Floyd rounded on Gloria and growled, "Answer me. What's this man doing here? Don't tell me he's the suspect."

"Yes, sir," she replied. "Rudolf Luttrell *is* the suspect in question."

Directing a hard stare at his second-in-command, Floyd hissed, "Rudy . . . tell the lady she's mistaken."

"You know I can't do that, Floyd," Rudy moaned. "They've found us out."

For a split second, Floyd's mind didn't register his boyfriend's words. Tearing his gaze away from Gloria, a puzzled, frightened expression appeared on his face. "What the hell are you talking about?"

"I won't be your fall guy," Rudy said, shaking his finger. Turning to Gloria, he wailed, "It was all Floyd's idea! I didn't want to do it, but I love him! He forced me!"

Floyd's mouth fell open. He was being accused of sabotage by the man he loved, the man he planned to marry. How could this be? Gritting his teeth, eyes flashing with fury, Floyd moved toward Rudy Luttrell. Gloria immediately grabbed his arm, holding him back.

"You lying piece of shit!" Floyd yelled. "Tell them the truth or I'll break your fucking neck right here and now, before my men can save your sorry ass!"

Rudy cringed, hands up. "Don't hurt me," he whimpered. "See what I mean, he's a beast!"

"Why you little—"

Floyd tried to shake Gloria's grip.

"Dammit, sir!" she barked, pulling furiously on his arm. "Outside! Now!"

Floyd reluctantly allowed her to drag him from the interrogation chamber, not taking his livid eyes off Rudy until the door shut behind him. His rage threatened to consume him, his confusion running rampant.

Gloria seized both his arms and shook ferociously. "Get a hold of yourself! For Christ's sake, the bastard's baiting you."

Floyd was shaking with anger . . . and fear. Shutting his eyes tightly, he took a deep breath to calm his nerves, thankful that the others were still observing . . . the suspect. Floyd opened his eyes to an uncommon sight: the hint of a smile on Gloria's lips.

"I thought the plan was for me to be the bad cop, sir," she chuckled softly.

Floyd reached up and rubbed his bristly scalp. "I don't understand." Even though his voice was a whisper, it contained an ocean of sorrow and pain. "How could I have been so wrong about him? You've met Rudy. We've been together for ten months. What did I miss?"

"He's obviously very good at his job," said Gloria. "Even now, with all the evidence pointing at him, he's trying to play us by implicating you. But don't worry, despite our initial reservations, we don't believe you're involved."

"I was wondering why everyone was giving me the eye." Floyd glanced at the observation room door. "What convinced you?"

Gloria's eyes sparkled. "I've seen you play poker, sir. You can't bluff worth a shit. I doubt your acting ability's any better."

A halfhearted chuckle escaped Floyd's lips. "I'd better hold onto my day job then." Reaching up, he gave a light tap to his Bluetooth implant. "John, initiate directive 98-C." Reentering the interrogation chamber, he crossed the room and stood opposite Rudy, staring intently.

The blond-haired, blue-eyed young man leaned forward. "Perhaps we'll be consigned to the same prison. I'd like that."

Floyd and Gloria stood silently, side by side, staring down at him, their arms crossed. Rudy shifted nervously, glancing at both. He was set to say something else when the door slid open, and in walked a burly, stone-faced security officer, who marched over and, before Rudy could react, pressed the end of an inch-long cylinder against his carotid artery. A barely detectable *phifft* was heard. The security officer lowered his arm and stepped to one side.

"What the hell!" Rudy blurted out, grabbing his neck. "What did you do?" Panic set in. He shrank back from the security officer and glared at Floyd and Gloria. "Did you just imject be wit somebling?" Rudy shook his head. His words were slurring. Suddenly, his arm dropped from his neck. He sat staring into space, unable to speak or move.

Gloria purred, "What you've just been given, Mr. Luttrell, is a fast-acting paralytic that will wear off in two minutes—long enough for us to bind you to the chair and fix a pair of electronic nodes to your temples."

John, the security officer who gave Rudy the paralytic, slipped a pair of white, plastic zip ties from his belt and bound the petrified young man's wrists securely to the arms of the chair.

"The nodes are neural stabilizers," Gloria said. "They're handy little gadgets . . . and effective. They influence the brain's pre-frontal cortex, using targeted trans-cranial magnetic stimulation to prevent one from lying during an interrogation. An electronic truth serum, if you will."

Floyd watched as John threaded the second zip tie, its sound familiar to law enforcement for over seventy years. They were as low-tech a device as one could use, but effectual nonetheless. The neural stabilizers were a different matter altogether. They were non-descript, three-quarters of an inch in diameter, gray, dome-shaped objects that, when activated, sent a magnetic signal to the brain making it impossible for the interviewee to withhold the truth.

Having used this technique on numerous occasions, Floyd was looking forward to the next few minutes. They'd find out every-thing his former boyfriend knew about the terrorist plot, and then some. He felt a strange sense of satisfaction watching John attach the neural stabilizers.

"What the hell do you mean?" Gloria was talking to someone on her Bluetooth.

Tearing his eyes away from Rudy's blank-faced stare, Floyd studied his second-in-command, wondering why she was so agitated.

"Dammit!" she snapped. "Get back with me as soon as you find out *anything*!" She gave her implant two light taps. "Fletcher, get your ass in here."

She turned to face Floyd, an anxious expression on her face.

"What's the problem, Gloria?"

Her head jerked toward Rudy Luttrell, her eyes flashing anger. "The bomb was a dud, sir. It was set up to look real, but not actually be functional."

Floyd's stomach lurched. "My God!"

"Exactly."

"Are you thinking what I'm–?"

"Yes, sir!" she exclaimed. "It's all been a ruse. We have a ticking bomb out there ready to detonate, and we don't know where or when it's set to blow."

4

The wheel-shaped lift soared through the overcast Kenyan sky at one-hundred miles per hour, its central core consisting of the maglev engine and laser tracker integral to the Lake Victoria space elevator.

"Inertial dampeners are now in effect, Dr. Levin."

"Thank you, Judah," said Mona. Being the only person onboard the space elevator, she'd uploaded her personal PID into the system. It was programmed to sound like one of her favorite characters from the cinema, Judah Ben-Hur, played by Charlton Heston. The classic movie had been remade back in '49 to appeal to the modern moviegoer's taste, and was good, but didn't hold a candle to the twentieth century version. Besides, his voice was *so* manly.

Swinging her stocky legs over the side of the gel-padded, liftoff slab, Mona planted her feet and stretched. There was nothing to stop her from lying there the entire trip—she could use the three-hour nap—but she was restless, her thoughts consumed by the addition to the supply manifest she'd secreted onboard. Thankfully no one suspected a thing. Being the director of operations had its advantages: she could request additional cargo be loaded without anyone questioning her motives. So far, her scheme was working according to plan.

●

Grabbing his former boyfriend's throat, Floyd leaned in and shouted, "Where is it, damn you!? Where the hell is the other bomb?"

Gloria placed a firm hand on his arm. "He can't answer your question if you strangle him to death."

Floyd shot her a venomous look. "Fine!" Releasing his grip, he backed away and lowered his voice. "Increase the magnetic stimulation, Fletcher. Either he talks or his brain fries . . . we can't afford to coddle the bastard."

Without hesitating, a nervous Fletcher tapped a code into his Security Interlink Device. Rudy Luttrell's defiant eyes suddenly glazed over. His jaw unclenched. His facial muscles went slack. Despite his mental conditioning, the neural suppressor had finally dampened his will to resist.

"That's better," said Floyd, staring wrathfully into Rudy's blank face. "Now . . . let me repeat the question: Where is the real bomb located?"

"It's . . . it's on its way up . . . up to the sky."

Floyd was puzzled. "Be more specific."

"It's taking an elevator ride to space."

Floyd jerked upright and snapped his head around. "Gloria! Find out if a shipment's headed to the space platform."

"I'm on it, sir." She began speaking hurriedly into her Bluetooth.

Floyd leveled a frightening gaze at Jeremy Fletcher. "I need your computer skills. Discover if another package, like the one we found today, is on that transport. There's no time to lose."

He rounded again on Rudy Luttrell. "What time is the bomb set to detonate?"

The young man's glazed eyes shifted to Floyd. A confused look crossed his face. His brows furrowed as he tried to think. "Um . . . 6:30 . . . yes . . . 6:30 a.m."

"What?" Rudy's answer was like a punch to Floyd's gut. "That's . . ." he looked quickly at his watch. "That's twelve minutes from now!"

Both Jeremy and Gloria were staring at Rudy, in shock.

"Get back to work, Fletcher!" Floyd yelped.

Jeremy snapped back to his SID, his fingers flashing across the screen.

Gloria tapped her implant. "I've just been informed that a shipment is underway at this very moment. The lift is ninety miles up. If the bomb is onboard, there's not enough time to lower the lift, let alone find the bomb and defuse it. And one more thing . . . Dr. Levin's onboard."

Floyd clenched his fists involuntarily and roared, "Shit!"

●

Mona was in the middle of a third set of jumping jacks when she heard the steady hum of the lift begin to trail away. Seconds later it stopped completely. Because the inertial dampeners were engaged she didn't feel the lift come to a halt, but sensed it nonetheless. She was on the verge of ordering Judah to contact Central Command when his deep, baritone voice sounded.

"I'm receiving an emergency call for you, Dr. Levin."

"Put it through, Judah."

Floyd Sullivant, chief of security, was on the other end. "Dr. Levin, I have very little time to explain, except to say that a major security breach has been detected. A faction of the CRA has infiltrated this complex and smuggled a bomb onboard the lift."

Mona placed one hand against the wall to steady herself. Her knees felt like wet noodles. *A bomb onboard the lift? How could this be?*

"Quick action must be taken, Doctor," Floyd added. "According to our source, the bomb will detonate in less than twelve minutes."

"Dear Lord!" Mona's eyes darted around, looking in horror at the prolific amount of crates stacked side by side up to the ceiling. The lift was packed, as usual.

"If the bomb detonates," Floyd said in a rush, "the resulting explosion will disable the maglev engine. The lift will plummet to the ground causing massive destruction to the complex and surrounding city. There's no time to evacuate. Innumerable lives will be lost."

Not to mention placing the mission in jeopardy, Mona thought.

"You are our only hope, Dr. Levin."

"Me? What do you mean?"

"Hurry to the storage closet located ten feet to your left. I'll explain everything."

Sprinting to the closet, she entered her security code. Inside were four skintight, lightweight, gel-infused spacesuits with accompanying helmets and oxygen tanks. Sullivant was explaining that she must strip down as fast as possible and don the smallest of the four suits. Thankfully she was wearing the requisite jumpsuit worn by everyone traveling to the space platform. Seconds later it was lying on the floor, and she was reaching for the smallest suit.

"You need to shed your bra and panties too, Dr. Levin."

Her head jerked upward and she stared at the ceiling. She knew a tiny spy-eye was there. "Are you serious?"

"Yes, Doctor," Floyd responded, his voice sounding dispassionate. "Clothing prevents the suit from establishing a proper seal against the body. Please hurry. If it's modesty you're worried about, I'm the only one monitoring this feed."

"It's not that I'm . . . oh, whatever," she huffed.

Mona had no problem with nudity, per se; it was her own body that bothered her. She wasn't a waif-thin supermodel. Her self-consciousness, in regard to her appearance, had always informed the way she presented herself. Reaching behind her, she unhooked her bra and tossed it to one side, then hurriedly stepped out of her panties. Looking down at her thick pubic hair, she was about to ask if it would pose a problem when Sullivant answered her question before it was even asked.

"The suit has a built-in, pressurized cup to protect the genitals, Doctor. Please hurry, you're wasting precious time."

"All right, all right!"

Moving as fast as humanly possible, Mona squeezed into the suit in under a minute. It felt like a second skin. The zipper, which ran from her crotch to her neck, was covered by a Velcro gel-flap that formed an airtight seal. After securing the oxygen tank to her back, Mona fastening a cushioned brace around her neck, tucked her short hair behind her ears, attached her helmet's air hoses, slid the lightweight helmet over her head, and gave it a sharp turn, creating the final barrier against the unforgiving environment of space. As soon as the helmet clicked into place, the oxygen began to flow.

"Hurry to the emergency hatch located three meters to your left," said Floyd. "Punch in your security code, step into the pressurization chamber, and seal the hatch."

She did as she was told, trying not to think about what she was doing.

"From here on, Doctor, Ensign Jeremy Fletcher will provide instructions. He has the technical expertise to guide you the rest of the way . . . good luck."

Mona wanted to respond, but fear caught up to her. Standing in the tiny chamber, her chest and legs trembled, waiting for the pressure to equalize. The process seemed to take forever, though only thirty seconds ticked off the clock. With so little time remaining, every second was precious. She could barely hear the ensign speaking. All she could think about was how young he sounded, how she was placing her life—and the fate of the mission—in the hands of someone who sounded like a teenager.

"Look d-down at the left side of your utility belt, Dr. Levin," Fletcher said, his voice trembling almost as much as her legs. "You'll see a stainless steel clasp. When the airlock opens, pull the clasp. It's attached to a retractable safety-line. Outside, to your left, is a metal guide rail. Attach the clasp to the railing, grab hold of the ladder beside it, and climb to the top of the lift. I'll continue once you're topside."

The airlock slid open. Staring at Earth's blue curve, framed by the terrible blackness of space, Mona tried to take a step forward, but her foot refused to budge. Her breathing was rapid. She was becoming lightheaded, overwhelmed by fear and doubt.

"Calm yourself, Doctor," Floyd cut in. "Take slow, deep breaths. At this stage, you can't afford to pass out."

His deep, measured voice gave Mona the strength she needed. Closing her eyes, she took two deep breaths, opened her eyes, and stepped toward the open door.

"I'm all right," she muttered. "I can do this."

"Yes you can, Doctor," Floyd said. "You're the most capable person I've ever met. If anyone can do this, it's you. Focus on the guide rail and ladder instead of the view and you'll be fine."

Mona nodded. "Thank you, Floyd."

It was the first time she'd called the chief by his given name. For a moment, that breach of personal protocol bothered her—fleetingly. Floyd was her connection to humanity, his calming voice a lifeline to her courage.

Grabbing the handhold beside the airlock, Mona pulled on the safety line, leaned halfway out the door, and hooked the clasp to the metal guide rail. Without looking down, she reached over, clamped her fingers around a ladder rung, and swung her body into space. Her heart pounded wildly in her chest, thumping so loud that she was certain others could hear her telltale heart. After a terrifying moment of vertigo, her hands and feet connected with the ladder. Only then did she remember to breathe.

Mona spotted the top of the lift, twenty feet above her. It was framed by a swath of blackness unlike anything she'd ever witnessed. Tiny pinpricks of light, which she knew to be stars, were scattered throughout the soul-sucking void. The stars appeared smaller, less distinct. Then she remembered: There was no atmosphere to defuse the starlight and make them appear larger.

Mona gave her head a violent shake. The damned stress was causing her to lose focus.

Wrapping her fingers loosely around the outside of the ladder, she pushed off with her feet and shot upward. Being very nearly weightless, her ascent was rapid. A short five seconds later, Mona found herself climbing atop the lift.

Ensign Fletcher's voice returned. "The soles of your suit are lightly magnetized, Dr. Levin, enough that you stay attached to the lift. We have nine minutes remaining. Hurry to the end of the guide rail near the center of the lift."

Bounding forward, Mona could virtually hear the seconds ticking away.

"Once there, you'll see a maintenance hatch. Enter your command code. We're in the process of equalizing the pressure within the interior of the lift. It will take another five minutes, but—"

"That's too long!" Mona shouted, nearing the halfway point.

"We realize that, Doctor." Fletcher sounded annoyed. "Some of the pressure will be relieved, but not all. Keep your body clear of the hatch when you enter the code. The hatch will open violently and probably suffer damage. We don't want you damaged as well."

Mona arrived at the hatch, knelt down, and punched in her code. Nothing happened.

"It's not opening, Fletcher."

There was a pause. "Um . . . it probably needs an override code," he said nervously.

"Probably?!"

"Hold on, Doctor. I'm searching for it right now."

Kneeling beside the hatch, Mona waited, her left hand gripping the guide rail—the silence like a heavy blanket. The lift blocked the sun, but she could see its blazing rays growing brighter by the moment. Her helmet's faceplate darkened accordingly.

"I have the code, Doctor," Fletcher said excitedly.

Mona wanted to scream, "Quit fucking around and tell me, already." Instead, she clenched her jaw in quiet anticipation.

"Are you ready, Dr. Levin?"

"Yes, Ensign," she said in an even monotone, trying to keep the frustration out of her voice.

"Enter this sequence: One, One, Alpha, Delta, Alpha, One, Seven, One, Delta, Zero, Nine."

Pressing the final number, Mona jumped in shock as the hatch sprang open, smashing against the skin of the lift. A violent geyser of oxygenated air shot from the opening; it was filled with what must have been thousands of tiny, sparkling ice crystals. She half expected to hear a loud roar accompany the violent outpouring of air, but as it was the edge of space, there was only silence. Mona watched the geyser climb thirty feet into space and disperse, transforming into a brilliantly twinkling cloud, glowing with sunlight.

In any other situation, she would've considered the sight beautiful, but the discharge of air seemed interminable, reducing the window of opportunity needed to find the terrorist bomb. A drop of sweat trickled down her brow, making its way into her right eye.

"Shit!" She closed her burning eye.

Fletcher immediately came on line. "What's wrong, Dr. Levin?"

"Nothing . . . I got sweat in my eye. How do I cool this suit down?"

"The gel insulation regulates the suit temperature. As for the helmet, its thermostat is self-regulating. However, you can order the temperature reduced by however many degrees you think appropriate. Its controls are linked up to the lift computer."

Rapidly blinking her right eye, Mona ordered the computer to lower her suit's temperature by five degrees. A noticeably cooler stream of oxygen flooded her helmet. Seconds later, the geyser of air shooting from the maintenance hatch abruptly ceased.

Mona crawled forward. "The air's expelled. I'm entering the lift."

"Good," Fletcher rasped. "Once inside, you won't have far to go."

Mona swung her legs over the edge of the maintenance hatch. As she descended the ladder, her head drew level with the opening, and she noticed something out of the corner of her eye.

"Fletcher, when the hatch blew open, it sustained some damage. The hinges are twisted slightly. Once I've made it outside and disposed of the bomb, I don't think it'll close."

"We'll worry about that later, Dr. Levin," he hurriedly replied. "We're down to six and a half minutes to complete the mission."

"Right—what now?"

"Climb ten feet down to the first catwalk. Step off, turn to your right, go fifteen feet, and face the interior compartment wall. Once there you'll see another maintenance hatch. Your command code should work this time."

Scrambling down the ladder, Mona felt the lift's artificial gravity return in force. She hopped onto the catwalk and practically sprinted to the maintenance hatch. Fingers flying, she punched in her code . . . but once again, nothing happened.

"It didn't open."

"It's not going to open by itself, Dr. Levin," Jeremy sighed. "Remember, the pressure has equalized. Pull the handle and I'm sure it'll open."

Mona pulled the handle and peered inside. One of the crates was so near, it seemed wedged against the interior wall. Sticking her helmet through the opening, she estimated there was twenty inches between the crate and the wall. Not enough room to maneuver. With less than six minutes to go, Mona began to panic.

"There's not enough room, Fletcher! There's not enough room!"

"Calm down and tell me what you see, Doctor," Jeremy barked.

"There's less than two feet separating the cargo from the wall." She looked down. "I see a twenty-inch catwalk just below the hatch."

"That's what I expected," he said. "Take off your oxygen tank and pull it in behind you. Once you're inside, it'll be tight working conditions, but manageable."

Mona unbuckled the chest strap holding the tank to her back and quickly wriggled out of the shoulder harness. A hook on the oxygen tank corresponded to a small slot in the wall. She hung the tank and, using the handhold over the hatch, pulled herself up and swung her legs through the opening, reached in and grasped the interior handhold, and dropped to the catwalk. Seconds later, the oxygen tank was hanging by her side.

"Which way do I go now?"

"Continue clockwise another twelve feet and stop."

Moving sideways, Mona worked her way over to the next position.

"You should see—"

"Dammit, Fletcher, quit saying *should*. Be more definitive. All your *shoulds* are making me want to scream."

"S-sorry, Doctor," he replied, voice faltering. "In front of you, you'll see a stack of two-foot by four-foot plastic crates. Each crate is filled with a specific size stainless steel nut. The fourth one down shou—*will* be at waist level. That's the one we're searching for. It's marked three-quarter-inch hex nuts.

"On the right side of your utility belt, you'll find an oddly shaped pouch, kind of like a gun holster. Remove the objects inside. One is a laser cutter, and the other is the energy cartridge that powers it. Use the laser to cut a twenty-four-inch hole in the side of the shipping container. Once done, the nuts will begin to spill out. The bomb is somewhere inside. We have five minutes left."

Unsnapping the pouch, Mona yanked out the laser . . . and dropped it. The laser bounced off the catwalk, ricocheted off the wall, and landed half off the catwalk, perched precariously between two crates. It wobbled above a narrow opening, threatening to fall to the distant floor below.

Mona froze, terrified, the barest of squeaks issuing forth from her lips.

For a long, horrifying moment she was filled with dread. Gathering her courage, she eased the oxygen tank down and cautiously lowered herself to the catwalk. Slowly extending her arm, she carefully plucked the laser from the brink of disaster. Taking a deep breath, she tried to calm her hammering heart. It didn't work. Reaching into the pouch, she slid the power cartridge out and gripped it firmly, knowing that all would be lost should it slip through her fingers. Deftly inserting it into the laser's handle, Mona felt the cartridge click into place. A relieved sigh escaped her lips. Quickly rising, she faced the crate of three-quarter-inch nuts.

"How's your progress going, Dr. Levin?" Fletcher inquired.

"Swimmingly," she lied. "If you would, please let me concentrate." She knelt in front of the crate and positioned the laser. "I'll give you an update as soon as the nuts drop—so to speak."

The laser had the general shape of a small pistol, though the barrel tapered to a point. Mona pressed the button where a trigger would normally be on a handgun, and a thin blue line formed instantly between the laser's tip and the plastic container.

The material melted like a hot knife through warm butter. Twenty seconds later, the hole was cut and the nuts were clattering to the catwalk. When the flow eased off, Mona reached in and shoveled the nuts out with her hands.

"Does this suit have a flashlight?"

"Yes, Doctor. It's embedded in your helmet, just above the faceplate."

Ordering the flashlight on, she positioned her helmet partway inside the crate and swept the beam back and forth. She saw no bomb. Reaching in, Mona used her entire arm to shovel nuts through the opening. Time was running out. She *had* to locate the device. Stretching, Mona plunged her hand into the remaining nuts, feeling around, touching the bottom of the crate, desperately searching, finding nothing.

"It's not here!" she screamed. "It's the wrong crate!"

At this point, Floyd Sullivant came back online. "Are you sure?!"

"Yes, yes! It's not here!"

"It . . . has to be inside the crate above the one you just searched," he said, sounding worried.

"What if it's not, Floyd?!" Mona wailed. "What if it's in the crate below the catwalk?"

"That one's filled with different sized nuts, Dr. Levin," he said, trying to keep his voice calm. "The next crate up is filled with three-quarter-inch nuts, like the one you just searched."

"Good God," she said, rising to her feet. "I hope you're right."

"I am. Now get to work, Doc—you have less than three minutes."

Aiming the laser, she sliced into the plastic. Mona could barely think. The tension was eating at her resolve, making her want to curl into a ball and sob hysterically. Her hand shook as she made a ragged cut across the crate. For the first time in years, she began to pray, albeit silently. Despite her Jewish heritage, she seldom went to synagogue, except while visiting her mother.

She was a scientist, which meant acquiring a healthy skepticism toward all things religious. She nearly laughed when the old saying about there being no atheists in the heat of battle came to mind.

Fifteen seconds later, another torrent of nuts were falling like a stainless steel waterfall onto the catwalk. Before Mona was able to reach in and start sweeping them out of the crate, like last time, the rounded end of a cylindrical object came into view.

"I have it!" she shouted.

Without waiting for instructions, Mona pulled the bomb from the crate. It was a one-foot by two-foot metal object, shaped like a large medicine capsule—only this pill cured no disease.

"Good Lord, this thing is heavy," she said, tucking it under her arm. Using her other hand to pick up the oxygen tank, she hurried toward the maintenance hatch.

"It's probably lead lined," Fletcher said. "Helps it escape detection."

Mona gently placed the bomb on the catwalk. Working the oxygen tank through the hatch, she picked up the bomb, latched onto the access rung with her free hand, and tried to swing her feet up through the opening, but failed. Realizing she needed both hands to make it through, she decided to drop the bomb through the hatch, but balked, fearing it would land hard and explode. Positioning the bomb on the catwalk, Mona grabbed hold of the rung with both hands and pulled her legs up and through the opening. She immediately let go of the rung and dropped backward, snagging the bomb off the floor. Struggling, she worked her abdominal muscles for all they were worth, which wasn't much since she'd never been a stickler for exercise.

Red-faced from the effort, she heard Fletcher and Sullivant wondering what was taking so long. Forcing out a loud, sustained grunt, she stretched upward, snagging the rung with her free hand's fingertips. Ignoring shouts of concern, Mona pulled herself up and through to the other side, then placed the bomb on the catwalk and quickly strapped on the oxygen tank. Breathing heavily, she stumbled with the bomb to the maintenance ladder. That's when she responded to those back on Earth.

"I experienced a slight glitch getting the bomb through the hatch," she snapped, shutting them up. "Don't worry, everything's back on track."

"I hope so," Floyd responded. "You have one minute and . . . twenty-eight seconds to clear that bomb from the lift."

Mona took no time to reply, but in her mind was shouting, *fuck, fuck, fuck*.

With the bomb tucked safely under her arm, she worked her way up the ladder, well aware of being up against the clock. Scrambling through the hatch, Mona became disoriented as the weightlessness kicked in. The heavy bomb now felt light as a feather. With her adrenaline pumping, she yanked the safety line and anchored herself to the guide rail.

"I'm in position," she wheezed, her strength rapidly fading.

"Good," Floyd said, taking command. "Buck up your courage, Dr. Levin. The next step will take more nerve than all the other steps combined."

Mona did not like the sound of that. After Floyd hastily explained what she needed to do, her legs began to buckle. Bending over, she began to hyperventilate. She was exhausted, shaking inside and out, scared out of her wits.

"We only have fifty-two seconds left, Doctor," Floyd informed her. "You can do this. You're almost there. . . . Now get your shit together and start moving!"

Mona was twenty-five feet from the lift's edge. Stumbling forward, she straightened up and quickly picked up her pace. The lift was spinning. No it wasn't—she was becoming lightheaded. Clutching the bomb tightly, she kept repeating over and over in her mind: *Don't trip. Don't trip. Don't drop the bomb.*

Sprinting, sucking in great gulps of air, she watched the edge of the lift draw near. The sun was directly behind her, peeking over the opposite side, causing her pitch-black shadow to stretch out before her like a wraith. When it touched the lift's edge and merged with the void of space, she momentarily lost track of her position. Glancing from one side of the terrible blackness to the other, Mona continued her headlong rush, then came to the edge and pushed off, flinging herself as hard as possible out into space.

With the safety line reeling out behind her, she tried to keep her eyes focused straight ahead, but they shifted downward nonetheless. The whole of Africa sat below her, causing Mona to feel like she was falling from an impossible height. A terrified scream began to well up within her.

"Fifteen seconds, Mona," Floyd said, snapping her out of it.

Knowing she must be farther from the lift before releasing the bomb was causing her heart to beat like a drum. The safety line, which would extend fifty feet, was nearly maxed out. With both hands, Mona lifted the device over her head and, gathering all her remaining strength, hurled the bomb violently into the frozen abyss of space. Two seconds later the safety line played out and jerked her backward, most painfully.

"Son of a bitch!"

The force of the sudden stop acted like a bungee cord, but without the elasticity. A torturous spasm seized her lower back as she drifted toward the lift–though not fast enough. The safety line was curling and drifting, not retracting into its casing. It was jammed! Mona slapped the utility belt. Nothing happened. The line was still not retracting. She was starting to yank on the line, hoping to free the jam, when a brilliant flash blossomed in the corner of her left eye. Her scream was cut short by the bomb's blast wave.

Thankfully, Mona was far enough away to avoid being caught in the explosion itself, but the blast wave hit her hard, hurtling her toward the lift at a terrific speed. As she shot backward, she realized she'd become entangled in the line. Both her right shoulder and the back of her left thigh felt like they were on fire.

She'd been hit by shrapnel. Tiny pieces had punctured Mona's suit, leaving bits of skin exposed to the harshness of space. She was in agony. Something must be done or the frostbite would spread and she would be dead in less than a minute.

"It worked, Floyd! It worked! But I've been hit by some shrapnel."

Floyd responded at once, sounding composed over the loud background celebration. "What's your damage, Mona?"

She was too frightened to reply. The blast had thrust her beyond most of the safety line, but not all; a tangled mess was wrapped around her legs and torso. Bouncing off the edge of the lift, she tumbled a few yards then found herself floating above the lift, moaning, faint with nausea.

"Mona! Are you all right? What's your condition?" The worry in Floyd's voice was palpable. His normal reserve was wavering.

Mona didn't hear any more celebration in the background.

"I'm . . . I'm hurt, Floyd," she moaned.

"The tears in your suit," he snapped. "Are they large or small?"

"Small . . . I think."

"What you need to do is press the torn pieces together. The insulating gel will seal the tear long enough to get back inside. Can you reach them?"

"Um . . . the leg, I can. Not so sure about the shoulder."

After all she'd been through, and now this, Mona felt herself going into shock.

"Don't give up now, Doc," Floyd implored. "I have a full bottle of thirty-year-old single malt with your name on it in my office. Don't make me drink it alone."

"I'll be there, even if it's a bottle of cheap tequila."

Floyd chuckled then grew silent, not wanting to distract her while she worked to save her life. The most worrisome tear was the one on her thigh. As she floated above the lift, she strained to see the damage, located it, and pressed the small flap of suit back in place. She saw tiny globules of dark, frozen blood floating around the leg. *Damn that hurts!* Seconds later she released it and smiled; the tear had successfully sealed itself.

The shoulder, which she could barely reach, came next. As Mona arranged the pieces of her suit, her vision began to cloud. *What now?* she wondered. It was becoming difficult to catch her breath. "Judah, analyze my suit . . . is the oxygen tank damaged?"

"Yes, Doctor, the valve was damaged—either by the explosion or when you crashed against the lift. You are currently receiving five percent of the oxygen needed for survival. You must return to the airlock within fifty-two seconds or you will pass out . . . and then die."

Mona wanted to say *No shit, Sherlock*, but knew to conserve oxygen. With her shoulder tear mended, Mona snagged the mass of a safety line and began to reel herself down to the lift. The instant her feet touched, she whipped out the maintenance laser and sliced through the safety line, directing the beam carefully. She had to concentrate—the heavens were spinning like her college dorm room during a weekend of drunken revelry.

Was that Solomon's voice? If so, his voice sounded muffled. Why was he speaking when she needed to stay focused? Having freed herself from most of the safety line (which seemed to take forever), Mona wrapped the usable portion around her hand and stumbled wearily, drunkenly, toward the maintenance ladder.

She didn't think she was going to make it. *Those fifty-two seconds (or was it forty-seven?) must've expired by now*, she thought.

Swinging herself over the edge, Mona barely noticed the ladder rungs while descending.

She heard distant chatter, mingled with her own tortured gasping for breath. Her vision was filling with brilliant flashes of light.

Reaching over, she felt but couldn't see the entrance to the airlock.

The next thing she knew, she was inside, on her knees, unable to breathe. Fumbling around, feeling snow-blind, she reached outside to unhook the safety line from the guide rail but failed to locate the clasp. The line would keep the door from shutting all the way. To cycle the airlock, she needed the door completely sealed. All her efforts would be in vain if she . . . no . . . even if these were her last seconds, the mission would go on. And for that she was thankful.

But this was not enough for Mona Levin, chief engineer and architect of the Ark Project. To admit defeat was not in her nature.

Tearing the tangled safety line from her hand, Mona uttered a last, pitiful scream as another part of the suit tore, allowing the burning ice of space to bite into her skin. With her muscles twitching and her mind reeling, Mona tossed the safety line through the airlock and, in a tiny, faltering voice, wheezed, "Judah . . . close the . . . the airlock . . . now."

"Yes, Doctor."

Mona didn't hear the door close, but she did feel the pressure return. The whiteout she'd been experiencing was fading to black. Her indomitable willpower was the only thing preventing her brain from shutting down completely. Feeling as if her lungs were collapsing in on themselves, she gave her helmet a shaky twist and, pulling it free, sucked in tremendous gulps of wonderful, precious oxygen.

PART TWO:
THE ARROW OF TIME

"Time's wing half pauses in its onward sweep
across the vale of years,
as if to give hushed hearts a time to weep—
a time for prayers and tears."
—From the poem "Time's Pulse," by Mary T. Lathrap

5

THE INDEPENDENT NATION OF PACIFICA: SIX MONTHS LATER

"Tell me, Richard, what changed your mind about accepting Dr. Chavez's offer to pilot the *Arrow*?"

Richard Allison sat nervously on a comfortably upholstered armchair, staring at the telegenic host of *The Darren Brantley Show*. The man's snow-white teeth gleamed brighter in person than on HV.

"Well, Mr. Brantley—"

"Please, call me Darren."

Richard bristled inside, but kept a smile on his face. He wasn't exactly sure why the amiable newscaster tweaked his nerves. Everyone else fawned over him, like a rock star. Perhaps it was because Lawrence Murchison, press secretary to Solomon Chavez, had insisted on this interview, claiming contractual obligations. Oh well, the HV special wasn't entirely about him. A number of other passengers and crew of the *Arrow* were also being interviewed.

"Very well, *Darren*," Richard said. "Please, call me Commander."

A puzzled look flickered across Darren Brantley's wide, approachable face. He then gave his knee a slap, looked directly into the camera, and began to laugh.

"I better stay on my toes, ladies and gentlemen. It seems that Commander Allison is not only the world's most famous pilot, but he's also a comedian." Turning back to his guest, Brantley leaned forward in his chair. With fingers steepled in front of him, he gave Richard a searching look. "It must have been difficult returning to work after what you've been through. I, myself, well . . . I would've been a basket case."

"On the contrary, Darren," Richard replied. "Work was my salvation. After recovering from my injuries, I threw myself into managing the shuttle training program. Nearly two months later, I found myself laughing at one of the trainee's jokes." Richard paused momentarily, a wistful expression crossing his face. "I felt guilty for experiencing that brief flash of happiness. But after arriving home that evening, I thought about it and realized I was dishonoring the memory of my wife and son by wallowing in self-pity. They'd want me to be happy, not shut off from the world, floating in a black cloud of despair. The very next day, I met with Dr. Chavez and accepted his offer to pilot the *Arrow*."

Darren Brantley nodded understandingly. "I think I can speak for all our viewers when I say that the Ark Project is better off with you in it, Commander."

Richard wasn't sure how to respond to the newsman's praise. Thankfully, he didn't have to, for Darren Brantley went straight to the next subject.

"Have you met any of the other passengers, Commander? For instance, have you met Bram Waters, the psychic? Now he's an interesting fellow, that one."

Richard shook his head. "Not yet, though I did read his memoir in college. I'm not sure what to believe, but if half his claims are true, the mission will be gaining a valuable crew member."

Darren Brantley again turned to the camera. "If half his powers were mine, I'd be running this network." He chuckled and turned back to Richard. "What about Dr. Levin? Have you worked with her yet?"

"Yes I have, Darren. She's quite formidable."

"No doubt. I'm looking forward to interviewing her in the next few days. If the public hadn't already dubbed the starship *Mona's Ark* before the terrorist attack, they would've done so after her amazing heroics."

Richard cocked his head. "A little advice, Darren. Don't call the ship *Mona's Ark* to her face. The first time I met her I made that mistake and, let's just say . . . I'll not be doing that again."

Darren Brantley again turned to the camera. "That's good to know," he quipped, raising his eyebrows in mock fear. Richard could almost hear the audience laughing. Shifting his attention back to his guest, Brantley turned serious. "I'm curious about something, Commander: What do you think should happen to Jimmy Jamison, the fanatic billionaire who allegedly financed the attack on the space elevator? Rumor has it that he's also linked to the terrorist attack that killed your wife and child."

Richard's eyes turned to slits, his voice cold as a Siberian winter. "If the police ever find him, I hope he resists, and therefore goes straight to hell."

●

ORANGE COUNTY, CALIFORNIA: SIX DAYS LATER

What a crappy way to spend my birthday, thought Bram Waters. It was November 9, and instead of getting sloshed at B. B. King's blues bar, he was hanging around an old fart's bedroom, trying to divine the sorry bastard's location.

Behind him, a security agent assigned to the case whispered to a fellow agent. "He's stalling for time. He has no clue where Jamison's hiding."

Bram returned an obscenely expensive, ancient Chinese rhinoceros horn cup back to the suspect's mahogany nightstand. "I thought I made myself clear . . . I need complete silence to do my job."

The agent's eyebrows rose, surprised that he'd been overheard. "Sorry 'bout that."

Bram nodded curtly while scanning the room. He was looking for an object Jimmy Jamison touched while deciding where to flee. Unfortunately, the closet had been cleaned out. Shoes were ideal for the job, given that they were saturated with residual psychic energy.

The billionaire skipped town soon after his plan to destroy the space elevator went awry. The security network at the complex had promptly traced the saboteur's scrambled phone calls and, shortly after Mona Levin's heroics, notified the FBI. But by the time they arrived at Jamison's mansion, he was long gone. The bastard had dropped off the grid and remained off it for the past six months. A worldwide manhunt had been initiated but failed to uncover a single piece of evidence as to Jamison's whereabouts. That's when Bram was called in.

Bram had kept his detective work local for over ten years and was reluctant to accept the job. However, after learning how much it would pay, he reconsidered. All in all, it wasn't as if he needed the money. Royalties from his memoir continued to trickle in and, in three months' time, he'd be onboard the *Arrow*, traveling to another solar system. No, he'd accepted the offer for one purpose only: To create a trust fund for Charlene, his longtime assistant. He wanted to make sure that the old girl wouldn't be forced back into stripping (or worse) once he was gone.

"I don't think we're gonna find anything useful in here, fellas," Bram said, turning to leave the lavishly furnished bedroom. Suddenly, from the corner of his eye, he noticed something brown peeking out from under the bed. "Hello . . . what have we here?"

Kneeling beside the canopied four-poster, Bram slipped its blue, satin skirt up a few inches, exposing the heel of a house slipper. Placing both hands on the shoe, he opened his mind and the psychic impressions locked within the footwear flooded his consciousness. Most of the visions were trivial: The old man lounging by the pool or watching HV or talking on his PID. Others (of a more personal nature) Bram skipped through. A mere twenty seconds after opening his mind, he was viewing more recent events.

Agitated, Jamison was listening to his PID. He was being called a fool, and then was told he had a choice: To disappear willingly or by force. *Interesting.* Jamison was not the head honcho. *Oh well,* thought Bram. He was being paid to locate this person, not an entire ring of terrorists. He'd inform the lead agent, but he wouldn't allow himself to be roped into some long, drawn out, worldwide search for some shadowy cabal. Those days were long gone.

Delving deeper into Jamison's imprint, Bram felt the man's fear, the concern directed toward his children and grandchildren, the regret that he would probably never see them again . . . and then, Bram began to picture a place—the place where Jamison had decided to flee—to make a final stand, if needed.

Bram isolated the image, focusing on it and it alone. . . . His shoulders sagged.

"I know where the sorry bastard is. But—" he grumbled, glowering at the agent in charge, "—you're gonna need me to pinpoint his exact location! Dammit!"

●

NORTHERN CANADA: 6:23 A.M., TWO DAYS LATER

The small, picturesque log cabin was nestled in the middle of a snow-covered clearing, a steady stream of gray smoke drifting from its stone chimney.

Kneeling in a stand of evergreens located forty-six yards to the east, Bram scanned the cabin. He was accompanied by a seven-member Special Forces unit from Canada and five security officers from Elevator City, commanded by Floyd Sullivant. The sun had yet to rise, but its pink and orange rays were painting the sky a rosy glow.

"Are you sure Jamison knows we're here?" Floyd asked. Like the others, his broad, angular face was framed by the hood of a white parka designed to blend in with their snowy environs. "We've taken extreme precautions to ensure this raid succeeds."

Bram's eyes were locked on the cabin. "Yep," he whispered. "We registered on a nearby security sensor . . . one of many located around the perimeter of the clearing. In all likelihood, the sensors are there to alert him to the presence of wolves or grizzly—but also humans. I sense that he knows we're not a prowling bear."

The leader of the Special Forces unit was stationed to Bram's left, listening intently. "I want you to read Jamison's mind and find out if he'll do anything crazy, like kill himself or put up a fight when we storm the place."

"I can tell you this, Lieutenant," Bram sighed, "he's not suicidal. As for reading his mind, I don't do that. However, I sense that he's got something nasty up his sleeve."

The Special Forces leader studied Bram intently. "To be clear, are you saying that you *don't* read minds, or that you *won't* read Jamison's mind?"

"My impressions are accurate, Lieutenant," Bram replied. "As for your question, many years ago I vowed to never read minds. A person's thoughts are personal, *private*. I have no qualms about reading images and feelings, but there are places in one's mind I refuse to go. It's a form of mental rape, and I won't be party to that, no matter who that person is—even Jamison."

The Special Forces leader shook his head. "Sir, I appreciate your ethical dilemma, but you're placing us in danger. I need something better to go on than, 'He's got something nasty up his sleeve.' Do you copy?"

Bram scratched his two-day-old beard. "I don't know what to tell you, but I don't think he'll put up a fight once he's in custody."

The Special Forces leader grumbled under his breath before giving a hand signal to one of his men. The designated soldier burst from the stand of evergreens, skis hissing as his momentum increased. Tucking both ski poles under one arm, he pulled a teargas launcher from his holster, aimed at a window, and fired as he zipped by the front of the cabin. With a crash of shattering glass, the canister entered the cabin and began to emit its noxious fumes.

The soldier made it back to the group unscathed, having met no resistance. Within a matter of moments, the teargas would flood the cabin, forcing a coughing Jamison to stumble out the front door with his hands in the air. Gas could already be seen seeping from the broken pane.

Bram waited expectantly but nothing happened. No coughing. No Jamison stumbling outside.

"The bastard must be wearing a gas mask," snapped Floyd Sullivant.

"I agree," the Special Forces leader replied. "Everyone, don your masks! At my signal we'll start the assault. Mr. Waters, bring up the rear, you'll enter the cabin once it's secure."

Fine by me, Bram thought. Following the squad across the snowy clearing, Bram approached cautiously, half expecting gunfire from a window. There was none.

Kicking up sprays of white, the squad came to a halt, released their skis, and burst through the cabin door, shouting, "Special Forces!" and, "Show your hands, Jamison!"

With his back pressed against the cabin's outer wall, Bram stood wide-eyed, listening to the rapidly dwindling ruckus, his nerves too frazzled to use his powers. His eyes kept darting back and forth, searching the tree-line, half expecting Dr. Conrad Snow or one of his mindless clones to appear. Bram was still plagued with occasional nightmares from the events he experienced two decades earlier, which were documented in his bestseller *Snowbound*. He'd been held captive in a secret underground installation near the Cascade Mountains while the crazy bastard formulated his twisted plot for world domination.

Bram heard curses followed by Floyd Sullivant calling his name.

Rushing inside, Bram expected to find Jamison trussed up on the floor like a Thanksgiving turkey, but instead saw the assault team standing around with anger and puzzlement written on their faces. Jamison was nowhere in sight.

Judging by the expression on the Canadian lieutenant's face, he was not pleased. "You were wrong, Waters. We've come all this fucking way—*at great expense*—for nothing."

Bram was at a loss. Jamison had been there only moments ago. He glanced around at the interior of the cabin: kitchen in the right-hand corner; coffee cup and plate sitting beside the sink; wooden table and chair in front of an eastward-facing window by the sink; comfortable chair; end table stacked high with reading material; fireplace glowing with the flames of a freshly stoked fire; all as it should be. No, he'd not been mistaken. "Jamison's still here, I know it. Give me a moment to—" Bram abruptly stopped speaking and focused on the bedroom. One of the Canadians had opened an old trunk and was rifling through its contents. Bram had sensed the man's sudden elation. "You, in the bedroom," Bram shouted. "Don't touch that latch!" .

The man shot him a startled look. "How did you . . . ?" Exiting the bedroom, he approached the Special Forces leader. "Sir, there appears to be a trap door inside the truck I found. If Jamison is here, I think he's hiding under the cabin, waiting for us to leave."

"Take a gas canister and toss it into the hidey-hole," ordered the lieutenant. "If that doesn't flush him out, we'll use a flash grenade."

"Aye, sir," the soldier acknowledged, removing the canister from his belt.

"I don't think that's wise," Bram said.

"And why's that, Mr. Waters?" said the lieutenant.

"I . . . I'm not sure."

With an exasperated sigh the lieutenant motioned the soldier forward. Moving into position beside the weathered trunk, he removed the gas canister's arming mechanism, tossed the ring aside, and reached in the trunk.

Cacophonous alarm bells were clanging in Bram's head. Something was terribly wrong. Something horrible was set to happen. That's when he saw the auras surrounding everyone in the cabin start to flicker.

"Wait!" he screamed. "It's an ambush! The trunk's been booby trapped!"

The soldier instantly froze. With his arm halfway inside the trunk, he turned slowly toward his commanding officer. "Lieutenant?"

The Special Forces leader had his eyes locked on Bram. "You told me he's not suicidal. Is Jamison in a hidey-hole beneath the cabin, Mr. Waters?"

Bram sent a mental probe beneath the trunk. He saw a small, reinforced enclosure, along with a tunnel that surfaced in the woods west of the cabin. Jamison, who'd climbed from the tunnel, was kneeling beside something covered by a white tarp, weapon in hand. After the explosion, he would escape on what he'd hidden under the tarp: a snowmobile. With a clear view of the front door, he was ready to shoot if the team exited the cabin without triggering the booby trap.

"Well, Mr. Waters?" the lieutenant pressed. After listening to Bram's rushed explanation, the lieutenant looked worried. "What do you suggest?"

"He'll pick us off easily if we exit through the front door. We need a distraction. If we stop inside the woods and set off the explosives, he'll think we're dead and let his guard down. But we must hurry . . . he's already becoming impatient."

"But how will we detonate the bomb?" asked a steely-eyed, dark-haired woman, whom Bram knew to be Sullivant's second-in-command.

"Leave that to me," he confidently replied.

The lieutenant stared hard and piercingly at Bram. Without looking away, he said, "Sergeant Limoux, secure that gas canister. We're leaving through the window in ten seconds."

Picking the pull-ring off the floor, Limoux rejoined his unit. In a matter of seconds, they were opening the window.

Using hand signals, the group wordlessly exited the cabin and, trying to keep the crunching of snow to a minimum, trudged through the calf-deep powder back to the woods. As expected, the cabin blocked Jamison's eastern view—but the old man had ears. They were relying on the wind whistling through the trees and whatever cold-weather gear Jamison might be wearing to mask their movements.

Once they entered the woods and were lying face down on the ground, the lieutenant turned to Bram and whispered, "Does he still think we're in the cabin?"

Bram nodded. "He's getting panicky."

"Good . . . he's mistake prone. So how the fuck do you plan on detonating the bomb?"

Smiling, Bram gave the side of his head a soft tap. Without further explanation, he used his telekinetic ability to lift the trapdoor. The entrance to Jamison's escape tunnel had barely opened a quarter of an inch when a huge, deafening explosion shattered the early morning stillness.

Bram had not expected the blast to be so violent. He and the others covered their heads and curled into balls, hoping to avoid being skewered or pummeled as shrapnel rained down around them. The surrounding trees protected them . . . for the most part. One member of Floyd's unit was knocked cold when a foot-long chunk of wood ricocheted off a stump and struck his head. A more serious injury occurred when a sharp piece of ceramic embedded itself in one Canadian soldier's upper thigh. Grunting loudly, he clutched his injured leg, the white outfit swiftly turning red with blood. In obvious agony, he kept his composure, clamping down the pain. A Special Forces soldier leapt into action, tending to his bleeding comrade.

The lieutenant signaled for the remainder of the team to train their weapons on the smoking rubble. Shortly thereafter, a lean, gun-wielding figure materialized from the haze. He tentatively approached the ruined cabin, glancing around in search of human remains.

Thumbing a button on his rifle, which activated the directional speaker on his scope, the lieutenant took aim and shouted, "Toss your weapon aside, Jamison."

The old man's head whipped around to stare in their direction. His eyes were wide with terror and surprise. Glancing down at his assault-rifle, Jamison briefly considered going out in a blaze of glory.

"Toss your weapon, Jamison! Lie down with your hands behind your head!" the lieutenant commanded. "In the name of His Majesty, you are under arrest for—"

The wind changed direction, obscuring Jamison with smoke. "Shit!" exclaimed more than one soldier.

Leaping to their feet, the uninjured team members burst forth from the tree-line and raced across the clearing. Jamison was no fool. The moment the wind shifted, he turned and sprinted in the opposite direction.

The ski-less assault team was halfway across the clearing when Bram shouted, "He's starting up the snowmobile."

Being electric, the vehicle's low hum was masked by the sounds of crackling embers and whistling wind, but Bram knew; the vision flashed through his mind.

Jamison mustn't escape. They had to catch him . . . alive. He was the key to bringing down the CRA, the world's leading terrorist organization. Holding their weapons at the ready, the unit dashed through the curtain of rapidly dissipating smoke and spread out in hot pursuit. But he was nowhere to be seen. As feared, the woods were empty—Jamison had escaped.

Bram was trailing behind the others. Even if they turned back now and tried to locate their skis in all that rubble, he was fairly certain most of the skis were damaged or destroyed.

From directly behind him, Bram heard a swooshing noise. Snapping his head around, he saw a crouched figure on skis, headed like a rocket toward an opening in the trees. The figure was female, one of Sullivant's security officers.

●

Gritting her teeth and bearing down on her ski poles, Gloria Muldoon disappeared into the woods, leaving her stunned comrades behind. Floyd would probably dress her down, even if she succeeded in capturing Jamison, but it would be worth a tongue-lashing to ensure the vile, son-of-a-bitching saboteur paid for his crimes.

The snowmobile's tracks were clearly visible, making Jamison easy to follow. But tracking and catching were two separate animals. Gloria was traveling too slowly to keep pace. If something didn't change soon, she'd fall even farther behind. She knew that if Jamison was able to make it to the small mining town fifteen miles away, his escape was almost certainly guaranteed. A single-engine plane (bought under an assumed name) most likely waited for him at the town's landing field. Half the people in this godforsaken wilderness owned planes, flying them manually instead of with GPS. Gloria seriously doubted he'd file a flight plan, so tracking him would prove almost impossible.

Her Bluetooth came to life. "Muldoon, Sullivant here. What's your status?"

"I spotted—" she grunted, maneuvering around a snow-covered bush. "I spotted a serviceable pair of skis in the rubble, took the initiative, and I'm now in pursuit of Jamison." She cut sharply to her right and then left, avoiding the top of a broken tree hanging in her path. "I'll contact you once I've caught up with the suspect. Right now, I need to concentrate."

"Roger that." Floyd broke contact.

Having spent part of her teenage years in the Swiss Alps, skiing came easy to Gloria, but she was still taking chances. After jumping blindly over a knoll, she found herself flying twenty feet through the air. Refusing to panic, she assumed the classic ski-jump position, sailing forty feet before landing smoothly and tucking into a racing crouch. The angle of descent had increased, allowing her to pick up speed. She'd entered a relatively straight stretch of ground and, as a result, spotted Jamison's snowmobile in the distance as it curved to the left out of sight.

The trees in that direction were thinning—enough for her to enter, but not enough for a snowmobile. Cutting to her left, Gloria sliced into the woods. If this tactic worked, she'd gain enough ground for a clear shot. Her assault rifle was strapped to her back, but it was too unwieldy to use while skiing. Instead, she'd rely on her trusty forty-five automatic, tucked safely in a shoulder holster. Her goal was to shoot out the electric engine or one of the tracks, as a snowmobile is useless if it can't grip the snow. If that proved impossible, she'd try to wing Jamison and hope for the best. First, however, she had to make it safely through the woods. She felt like a downhill racer, zigzagging past small and large trees and dodging the low branches that threatened to take her head off. Her body sang with the intense surge of adrenaline flowing through her veins.

She caught a glimpse of the snowmobile. Her plan was working. Avoiding a snow-covered stump, Gloria burst from the woods into a long, oval clearing. Jamison was to her right, looking over his shoulder to see if he was being followed, completely unaware that he was on the verge of being intercepted.

Gloria adjusted her angle. Thirty yards and a rapidly thinning stand of leafless birch was all that separated them. She needed her gun. Pressing her ski pole tightly under her armpit, she unzipped her parka. The pole started to slip and she overcorrected, almost losing her balance as she fought to stay upright. Her sudden movement caught Jamison's eye. After a quick double-take, he gunned the orange and blue striped snowmobile.

Angrily tossing the ski poles aside, Gloria reached for her gun. They were now twenty feet apart and no longer separated by trees. She was keeping pace, but that wouldn't last for long.

Their eyes locked: Gloria's stare was icy; Jamison appeared faintly amused.

She slipped her weapon from its holster.

Jamison's arm crossed his body, in his hand a 9mm. Two shots rang out. One bullet struck her chest. Staggered by the force of impact, she lost her footing and fell, dislocating her shoulder. The remaining air in her lungs was forced out by her collision with the ground. In a spinning slide, Gloria's right ski caught a root and tore free. Her foot twisted, but didn't break. By this point, she was sliding on her stomach in a fit of fury, gasping for breath. Thankfully, her Kevlar vest had stopped the bullet and broken most of her fall. Jamison looked back, laughing at her misfortune, triumph in his eyes. She had failed.

As Gloria screamed his name, the unbelievable occurred . . .

Jamison was whooping with joy when the snowmobile collided with a snow-covered log. The momentum sent the vehicle cartwheeling and launched Jamison into the air. He tumbled end-over-end, boots flying violently from his feet. As he disappeared from view, his horrified scream was suddenly cut short.

Kicking the other ski free, Gloria pushed herself off the ground with her good arm and stood holding her dislocated shoulder, trying to catch her breath.

"Dammit!" she exploded.

Pieces of snowmobile were scattered everywhere, the largest of which lay upended against an unyielding spruce. Limping forward, Gloria approached the wreckage with a singular thought in mind: that Jamison would still be alive. If she was able to extract some useful information before he died, she didn't care if he was clinging to life by a slender thread.

As she hobbled through the debris, her hopes evaporated. Locating Jamison wasn't especially difficult, as the only requirement was to follow the trail of brain matter through the snow. The old man was laying face up, arms and legs akimbo, neck twisted at an impossible angle. Part of his skull was torn away. It must have smashed against a rock as he tumbled across the frozen ground.

Gloria activated her Bluetooth implant. The members of her team were expecting an update. She paused, biting her lip, reluctant to give them the bad news.

●

Bram's eyes were closed tightly. It was bad enough touching Jamison's cold flesh without the additional burden of gazing into his sightless eyes. When he first arrived on the scene, he tried to close the old man's eyelids, but the bitter cold had frozen them in place. Jamison had been dead for nearly an hour before he and the remainder of the team had caught up to Gloria Muldoon.

Shortly after she bolted off in pursuit of Jamison, they'd searched the debris field for their skis, which they'd left outside the cabin door. The ensuing explosion had done its damage. During their futile search, only one serviceable ski was recovered. As such, it was a slow trudge to Muldoon's position. They were barely underway when Sullivant relayed her devastating news.

"Son of a bitch!" the lieutenant erupted, flush with anger. Rounding on Bram, he'd shoved a finger in his face and roared, "It's up to you, Houdini! Get us something . . . I don't care what. Some scrap of information that helps salvage this goddamn shit storm."

"Yes, sir," Bram had replied. "By the way, Houdini was an escape artist, not a–" The ferocity of the lieutenant's stare brought his comment to a sudden halt.

The remainder of the trek was long and discomfiting. By the time they arrived, Bram was all but worn out.

While struggling to read the psychic imprint contained within Jamison's corpse, he heard a muffled pop: Sullivant had reset Muldoon's dislocated shoulder. Shaking off the image, he refocused on Jamison. The old man had grown increasingly frustrated during his long stint in isolation. He'd been ordered to hole up in the cabin—a CRA safe house—by an unknown, mechanical voice on his PID filtered through a computer program.

Bram spent thirty minutes pluming Jamison's memories. He saw boring nights by the fireplace; encounters with local wildlife; time spent reading; many naps; and colossal bouts of masturbation. From what Bram gathered, the old man was a middleman, not a top-tier member of the CRA. The only useful information derived from Bram's effort was a tidbit of information that led him to believe the main CRA headquarters was located in Europe, possibly Denmark.

When he approached the lieutenant with this information, the young man held up a finger to wait, as he was speaking on his Bluetooth. "We're located three miles southeast of your position.

We'll have the body prepped and ready when you arrive." He tapped his implant. "Sorry about that, Mr. Waters. The chopper pilot's at the cabin loading our wounded and will be heading here in five minutes. So . . . what did you find out from the old fucker's corpse?"

Bram was about to respond but stopped abruptly, sensing danger lurking in the nearby woods.

"What's going on, Waters?"

"We have company. Gather your men. A large pack of wolves are sizing us up. They're about to attack."

The lieutenant didn't waste a second. "Listen up!" he shouted, moving toward the clearing. "Wolf alert! Bring Jamison's body and form a defensive perimeter over here!"

Bram looked around, seeing gray shapes darting through the brush. The wolf pack had been drawn like flies to the scent of blood, and was slavering with hunger. There were at least eight members of the pack and, being winter-starved, they would not easily abandon their prey. After a tense, fifteen-minute standoff, the familiar *thup* of approaching helicopter blades was a welcome relief to the entire group. For the wolves, the sound of approaching helicopters meant one thing: certain death. Their survival instinct kicked in and they fled, abandoning their hunger in favor of their lives.

6

A SECLUDED ESTATE NEAR ANTWERP, BELGIUM: 10:43 P.M., DECEMBER 25, 2060

The lively strains of Mozart's "Serenade Eine Kleine Nacht-musik, K525 First Movement" could be heard wafting up from the castle's dance floor, two stories below the conference room. The 403rd annual Masked Christmas Ball was still going strong and the champagne was flowing freely, but the nine men seated around the circular conference table were neither drunk nor in the mood for holiday revelry.

All were exceedingly wealthy, their ages ranging from fifty-three to ninety-one. They wore seventeenth-century period costumes, with jewel-encrusted masks covering their faces from the nose up. All were well aware of each other's true identities but preferred to leave the masks on during the assemblage: it was a tradition that went back hundreds of years and always lent an air of mystery to the annual proceedings. On the second finger of their right hands they wore a gold ring emblazoned with the face of a roaring lion. Each ring had been passed down from generation to generation and was required before entry into the conference room. The owner of the castle was the one charged with inspecting each ring while shaking hands with its possessor.

The circular conference table around which they sat was made from the finest mahogany, its deep, reddish-brown finish polished to a high, lustrous sheen. The room itself was cozy, designed to impart a sense of camaraderie. The wood-paneled walls were lined with bookshelves, but also two paintings by Rembrandt and another by El Greco. A fireplace, which had been converted to natural gas in the previous century, occupied a sizable portion of one wall and supplied relaxing warmth during the cold Christmas night.

The castle's seventy-three-year-old owner leaned forward in his ornate mahogany chair. Each person in attendance was considered his equal, yet the back of his chair was taller than the others, signifying his seniority and unofficial leadership status.

"Gentlemen," he said in perfect English, "as you well know, all of our efforts to sabotage the Ark Project have been unsuccessful; each one stymied, either through general incompetence or a lack of opportunity."

Pausing dramatically, he reached for the demitasse coffee cup sitting before him and took a long sip of freshly ground Jamaican Blue Mountain coffee, one of the priciest in the world.

Glancing around, he noted that many of the other attendees were mimicking him, taking long sips from their own cups. His smooth, baritone voice took on an almost confessional tone. "As you also know, time is running out to quash Chavez's plan to spread humanity's corrupted seed throughout the galaxy. Our exalted organization, which has endured for nearly one thousand years, has been the bulwark against mankind's headlong rush toward technological advancement. Without us keeping a check on scientific progress, the human race would've destroyed itself ages ago. Humanity is a shortsighted, envious, adolescent race of people, filled with an abiding death wish. There are times when I look back on the pathways of history and I'm surprised we've made it this far."

He listened to the other men as they added tepid mutterings of agreement. They'd heard his harangues before, but it wasn't their unenthusiastic response that surprised him. The newest member of the group, a fifty-three-year-old French aristocrat, who'd inherited a place at the table upon his father's death, spoke up. "Monsieur Chairman, might I suggest that we have reached the point where mankind can cope with technological progress. Perhaps it is time to start guiding the human race instead of holding it back. If we were to—"

The Chairman slammed his fist on the table. "I will not listen to this heresy!"

At this, the Frenchman averted his eyes, his breathing shallow with fear.

The Chairman's steely expression softened. "Forgive me, brother. Your sentiment has been expressed many times over the centuries," he purred. "Each generation believes it will break the cycle of insanity that keeps mankind tearing at its own throat. Unfortunately, the human race has learned nothing from its mistakes, and each passing year our mission becomes more difficult. I fear we are fighting a losing battle . . . yet battle we must."

Directly across the table from the Chairman, the American representative cleared his throat. Like the others, his family was from old money; though it would appear otherwise, judging from his distinctive Texas twang. "It's a damned shame the CRA couldn't pull off their end of the deal. They're a good patsy. The thing is, now security's so tight it'd take a miracle to smuggle an unregistered fart into Elevator City. So if you don't mind me askin', what's the next step?"

"Your American colloquialisms never cease to amaze me, brother," the Chairman said. "All the same, you make a valid point. With less than a month before the *Arrow* leaves orbit, it is difficult to conceive of a way to stop its ungodly trek to the stars. I fear that any further attempt at sabotage will ultimately lead to our own destruction. We cannot allow that to happen. Therefore, I vote that we step aside and let the Ark Project proceed unimpeded by us or any other branch of this organization."

As expected, the delegates responded with disappointed grumbles.

"I realize that we are unaccustomed to failure," he continued. "However, I have reason to believe that the Ark Project will fail in the long run. Chavez will not succeed in colonizing another planet, for Earth is unique. The good Lord has placed us here for a specific reason. If a collection of foolish apostates decides to leave for greener pastures, why hinder them? They are sealing their own fate. In fact, I am confident that those pastures are anything but green. Solomon Chavez and his thrall will find, to their everlasting sorrow, that the planet they hope to turn into a new Eden will run red with the blood of their own blasphemy."

●

CENTRAL COMMAND, LAKE VICTORIA COMPLEX: 9:51 A.M., JANUARY 15, 2061

Mona sat in her office across from Dr. Solomon Chavez, pouring them both a flute of seventy-four-year-old Moet. The expensive bottle of champagne was well worth the price. She handed Solomon his glass and held up her own to propose a toast: "Here's to the fulfillment of a cherished dream . . . that one day we would leave Earth behind and reach for the stars." Leaning forward over the cherrywood coffee table, she clinked glasses with her boss and took a sip of the dry, wonderfully tasty champagne, its bubbles tickling her nose in just the right way. Chavez nodded appreciatively at his glass. "An exceptional year," he said, offering Mona a warm smile. "It's good to see you in a positive mood, my friend. When you requested this meeting . . . well . . . I have to admit I was expecting it to be another one of your attempts to worm your way onto the *Arrow*."

Frowning, Mona took another sip of champagne before sitting her glass on the table. "Don't be that way, Solomon. I haven't brought that subject up in months."

Solomon held up his hand in a conciliatory gesture. "Forgive me, Mona. I've become a bit paranoid. You wouldn't believe how many politicians, businesspeople, celebrities, and assorted other VIPs have been trying to buy their way onboard. Some have even resorted to blackmail, claiming the most outrageous things. People are also dying. A Ukrainian scientist told everyone he was on an *alternative* list of colonists. A few days ago, the authorities found his entire family poisoned. It's getting crazy out there."

Mona shook her head in dismay. "I haven't watched the news lately." Averting her gaze, a pang of guilt swept over her. There had been times over the previous few years when she wished her elderly, bedridden mother would die, so there'd be one less reason to keep her off the ship. She could be callous, even underhanded, but she'd never resort to murder to achieve her goals. "Judah, activate HV, secure channel L-1A."

The 52" set masqueraded as a framed work of art that normally displayed famous paintings from yesteryear. It switched from Picasso's *Starry Night* to the *Arrow*, three hundred fifty miles above Earth. What an impressive sight! The gray and white ship looked like an arrow . . . albeit a pregnant one; and was the most complicated construction project ever conceived by the mind of man. The exhaust and doughnut-shaped engine compartment connected to a cylindrical stage that led to a massive storage compartment containing provisions and construction equipment. A bulge housing the cryogenically frozen colonists and genetic samples taken from a wide array of plant and animal species came next, followed by the crew compartment, where they would eat, sleep, exercise, and entertain themselves during their off hours.

The workdays would be divided into two twelve-hour shifts with no days off, each crew rotation lasting a little over a year, after which a fresh crew would be decanted to take their place. The *Arrow* held a grand total of five crews in all; each crew of forty-eight personnel serving two rotations. Combined, the rotations added up to ten and a half years, the time it would take to reach the Epsilon Eridani star system. A majority of the crew members were assigned to engineering and technical maintenance, with each rotation containing seven command officers.

Dotting the ship's outer hull were the black, bead-like warp broadcasters which, when activated, would encapsulate the entire ship in a warp bubble, allowing the ship to travel near the speed of light without disintegrating. Every section of the ship had been tested and retested, every nut and bolt fastened securely in place, every ration loaded in the cargo hold, every genetic sample—from elephants to pigs to earthworms—safely stored in deep freeze. Everything was ready to go . . . except for one thing.

"In three days' time, the last of the colonists will have been transported to the *Arrow* and be stored in their cryogenic chambers," Mona said. "That being said, one colonist is running late but will arrive the day after tomorrow. It's Bram Waters. He's asked to meet with you, to express his gratitude for—"

"That won't be necessary," Solomon cut in, seeming oddly perturbed. "If everyone thanked me in person, we wouldn't leave until next year. Please extend my apologies and inform him that I'm busy with last-minute preparations."

Mona was confused. For weeks now, Solomon had hosted nightly dinner parties for arriving VIPs. However, he was the boss, and if the boss didn't want to meet with certain colonists (even one as famous as Bram Waters), that was his right.

"As you wish," she said, trying to sound indifferent to his decision. "Per your request, your personal effects have been stored in your private cabin aboard the *Arrow*. Seeing as you'll be the last person placed in cryo-stasis and your cryogenic chamber is located in your cabin, I've taken it upon myself to personally supervise your freezing procedure. I'll then depart on the last shuttle back to the elevator platform."

Solomon studied her warily. "I'd rather have you supervising the departure from mission control, not looking over some cryo-tech's shoulder."

Mona rolled her eyes. "That's not the only reason I'll be there, Solomon," she said huffily. "There's the final inspection of the zero-point engine to contend with. It's my baby, and I want to be there during the start-up phase."

"Really?" he scoffed, taking a sip of champagne. "Sounds like you don't trust your people to do their jobs."

Mona felt her cheeks flush with anger. "It's not that. There may be a need for some last-minute adjustments. I just want to make sure the chief engineer is on top of things."

"Like I said—"

"You're being paranoid again," she snapped, shooting a withering glare. Solomon's eyebrow rose inquisitively. "Fine . . . if you must know the truth," she said, leaning forward. "I do intend to give the engineering department a final once-over, and I do want to make sure your cryo-chamber is working efficiently. But my real reason for wanting to be there is this: When the *Arrow* starts its journey, I intend to be on the orbital platform's observation deck, watching the departure with my own eyes . . . not on some HV screen like everyone else. I think I deserve that much, okay?"

Solomon studied her a moment longer before turning his attention back to the image on the screen. "After all you've done to make the Ark Project a success . . . I certainly can't deny you this one last favor." Solomon sat his glass on the table and stood up. "Thank you for the drink, Mona, it was refreshing. I wish I could stay longer to chat, but I have other business to attend to."

Mona shook Solomon's hand and walked him to the door. As it slid shut behind him, she smiled with satisfaction. For months she'd worried he would press her about being onboard during the

Arrow's final hours in orbit. Like his old man, he was extremely perceptive, almost frighteningly so. There were times when she'd looked into his coal-black eyes and wondered if the rumors about him were true . . . but not today. Today she played him perfectly. Today she felt confident that her plan would at last succeed.

●

Sitting in the rear of the open-air tour bus, Bram glanced over his shoulder to catch one more glimpse of Graceland. The bus was packed with tourists, most visiting the mansion for the first time, while others (like Bram) had made many pilgrimages to the King's home and gravesite.

This would be the last time he'd see Graceland with his own eyes, and he wanted to burn the memory of the two-story, classical-revival mansion with its pink, Alabama fieldstone frontage and dual white columns in his mind forever. The bus pulled onto Elvis Presley Boulevard, and the black iron gates—decorated with musical notes and two guitar players—closed behind him, transforming itself into what became an open music book.

Despite being a blues aficionado Bram became a fan of Elvis in his mid-twenties—mainly because the woman he loved was a huge fan. Jennifer Parker, a newspaper journalist whom he met during an investigation and whom he'd fallen madly in love with, had been tragically killed in an automobile accident, setting in motion the events described in his memoir. He'd later discovered that one of Conrad Snow's many clones had caused the accident. Given that Snow controlled his clones' minds—even to the point of seeing through their eyes—Bram refused to distinguish between the two, knowing that if a clone did something, Snow was truly to blame.

Bram had never stopped loving Jennifer. She'd been everything he'd hoped to find in a woman: not only was she beautiful, with long, honey-blonde hair, a fabulous body, and a face to make Helen of Troy jealous, she also possessed a keen mind and a kind, compassionate heart. There were times when he thought she was too good for him—and perhaps she was, having lived only twenty-five years. Since then, he'd failed to meet anyone to replace her. Over the intervening years he'd gone to bed with his fair share of women, but none he wanted to marry.

Perhaps it was for the best. Colonizing space would be a thrilling adventure in its own right. Bram thought of the text he received while standing in Meditation Garden gazing down at the King's grave. It was from Lawrence Murchison, telling him that his meeting with Dr. Chavez had been denied. He was disappointed, and the text had nearly ruined his last minutes with Old Swivel Hips, but he'd get over it; there'd be plenty of time after the colonization process to meet with the reclusive trillionaire. But the more Bram thought about it, the more it bothered him. Every time he thought about Chavez he felt conflicted, like he was picking up on a wellspring of hidden meaning, a play of light and shadow—a mystery.

With the tour bus trundling down Presley Boulevard, Bram came to a decision: instead of leaving for Kenya as planned, he would reschedule his flight and leave town this very evening.

His personal possessions had been sent ahead. He'd said his goodbyes to Charlene and his small circle of friends. Except for placing a final bouquet of roses beside Jennifer's gravestone, there was no real reason to wait.

●

LAKE VICTORIA COMPLEX, KENYA: 8:19 P.M., JANUARY 16, 2061

"Sir, if you don't leave now, I'll be forced to notify security."

Bram tugged at the collar of his tux, feeling a bit strangled by the formal attire. This was one of the few times he'd worn a tuxedo, and it of course felt uncomfortable. Part of that discomfort was due to his inability to crash the final cocktail party Solomon Chavez was holding before boarding the *Arrow*. Bram had been scheduled to arrive the following morning, with barely four hours to spare before his cryogenic procedure. Since he'd arrived in Kenya a day earlier than expected, his name was not on the list of partygoers.

"If you inform Dr. Chavez's press secretary, I'm sure he'll tell you to let me in. The only reason I'm not on the list is because—"

One of the guards, a stern-looking behemoth of a man, took a menacing step toward Bram. "Sir, you have five seconds to vacate this hallway." The second guard shifted his bulk, ready to lend a hand.

Bram could see he was getting nowhere. "Fine."

As he turned to leave, Bram heard a familiar voice behind him. "Waters? My, my . . . you do clean up rather well, don't you?" The voice belonged to Floyd Sullivant, security chief for the Lake Victoria complex, and a man Bram had grown fond of during their Canadian adventure. Sullivant wore a custom-fit tuxedo, a quizzical expression on his wide, angular face. "What's the matter? Are you having trouble getting into the party?"

Bram nodded, hooking a thumb over his shoulder. "They're a couple of tough customers."

Floyd shifted his attention to the two guards. "Sam, Karol, looks like you're making some easy money tonight."

After exchanging a nervous glance with his partner, the closest guard spoke up, "You know how it is, boss. A little moonlighting never hurt anybody."

Floyd reached into his jacket pocket and removed his invitation. "I used to do it myself on occasion. Oh, by the way," he said, handing the invitation to Karol, "Mr. Waters is my plus one."

Karol studied Bram closely. Under his piercing gaze, Bram felt like a fly under a magnifying glass.

"Do you have a problem with that?" Floyd's voice took on a hard edge.

The guard immediately shook his head. "No problem at all, sir. I . . . um, I hope the two of you have a pleasant evening." He stepped aside, making way for Floyd and his date to enter the penthouse suite.

The party itself was taking place in an exclusive hotel owned by Solomon Chavez. Located in the heart of the city and called The Victoria Palms, the fifteen-story building was a technological marvel, with many of its jobs performed by robots. A battery of concealed scanners, designed to detect weapons and explosives, was built into the building's ceilings and walls. If Bram had been armed, he wouldn't have made it past the lobby before being taken down. The security detail at the door was mainly for show . . . and to stop the occasional party crasher.

Luckily for Bram, Floyd had come along at the right time.

"Thanks for getting me in, Floyd," he said, giving his bow tie a last-second adjustment.

"Think nothing of it, Bram. You can thank me later . . . when we go to my apartment."

Momentarily puzzled, Bram wondered if he'd heard correctly. His head suddenly jerked up to stare in shock at Floyd's wide, expressive face. "Excuse me?"

The big Welshman couldn't keep a straight face and burst out laughing. "I was only joking, my friend. I've known you were straight since the day I met you."Enjoying his humor, Bram quipped, "Good, you would've been bitterly disappointed . . . since I never put out on the first date."

Floyd slapped him on the back as they descended a short flight of steps into the large, ornate suite, which was filled with happily chattering people dressed to the nines. Waving off a server carrying a silver tray filled with flutes of champagne, both men headed for the bar and placed their orders—a whiskey sour for

Bram and a scotch on the rocks for Floyd. Performing on a stage to their right, an eight-piece jazz band played an upbeat tune that sounded vaguely familiar.

Floyd handed Bram his drink and motioned toward the band. "I like this song, but I've heard it at least a hundred times." He received a questioning look from Bram. "Being head of security, I'm always invited to Dr. Chavez's parties. He's in town at least once a month, which means I get to listen to this ancient music quite often."

"Ancient music? Huh . . . it's acoustic, but it doesn't sound classical."

"No, not classical," Floyd replied. "It's called Big Band music, recorded prior to the rock era. Dr. Chavez once told me the name of this song. If memory serves me correctly, I believe it's called . . . oh, yes, "Sing, Sing, Sing," by a chap named Benny Goodman."

"Are you sure? I haven't heard any singing."

Floyd chuckled. "I thought the same thing. It doesn't have any lyrics that I know of . . . but you could ask him yourself. He's talking with a group of people near the balcony." Just the man Bram wanted to see. He looked in the direction of the balcony but the crowd blocked his view. As he craned his neck to catch a glimpse of Chavez, he caught sight of some famous faces in the crowd: an award-winning American actor; a respected politician; a popular musician whom Bram recognized, but whose songs weren't to his taste; and Darren Brantley, the popular HV personality.

"Don't tell me *he's* been invited along for the ride?" Bram grumbled, pointing at Brantley.

Floyd shook his head. "No . . . he finished doing some interviews and was invited. Why?"

"It's nothing . . . he just gets on my nerves." Bram looked back toward the balcony. "Are you sure Dr. Chavez is over there? I don't see him."

"I'm quite certain," Floyd replied. "I spotted him the first moment we entered the suite. As for whether he's still by the balcony, I can see the top of his head."

Smiling, Bram eyed the tall, bristly haired security chief. "So, how's the weather up there, Stretch?"

Floyd cocked an eyebrow and sneered, "How original. . . . You've probably been waiting to use that tired, old joke since we arrived."

"Nope, ever since Canada."

Laughing, the two men clinked glasses and downed their drinks.

Setting his tumbler down on the bar, Floyd asked, "Would you like to meet him?"

Bram's response was almost too quick. "Solomon Chavez?"

"Who else?" Floyd gave Bram a quizzical grin. "Hey, are you sure you're psychic?"

Shrugging his shoulders, Bram looked at his own empty glass sitting on the bar. "Alcohol tends to suppress my powers . . . thankfully I'm not drunk, yet."

A chunky piece of ice rose from the glass. While Floyd stared in slack-jawed amazement, the ice floated through the air, tumbling end-over-end, and entered Bram's open mouth.

"Still wondering?" he asked, sucking on the piece of ice.

"I don't understand," Floyd said, shifting uncomfortably. "If you're able to use your powers to manipulate objects, why didn't you stop Jamison as he was getting away?"

Bram studied the big man, seeing the well-concealed fear lurking behind his eyes. "If I could have done that, I would've, but I'm not that powerful. Small objects, such as ice or the latch I manipulated in the cabin, aren't really a challenge. It's the larger objects I struggle with. Conrad Snow tried to convince me there was no difference between the large and the small stuff on the psychic level—and yet, I have a difficult time wrapping my brain around that concept."

Hearing this, Floyd visibly relaxed. "Even so . . . it's a helluva good parlor trick, my friend." He glanced toward the balcony. "Come on, it's time for you to meet the boss."

It took longer than expected to reach the balcony. They stopped to sample an outstanding tray of hors d'oeuvres, were intercepted by a server who offered champagne, which they accepted, and two people asking about Bram's memoir.

With the incredible flavor of white truffles lingering on his tongue, Bram followed Floyd onto the balcony. Chavez was speaking to a stern-looking woman with graying hair, whom Bram thought he recognized. It took a moment for Bram to realize who it was: Admiral Katherine "Battleaxe" Axelrod's salt-and-pepper hair was styled in an up-do; she had on makeup and was wearing a silver evening gown instead of her usual black and gray uniform. Across from Chavez stood a handsome black man, whom Bram instantly recognized as Captain Richard Allison, whose tension-filled rescue at sea captured the world's attention. To the captain's left stood Dr. Mona Levin, probably the most celebrated scientist since Stephen Hawking. There were two other people, whom Bram had never seen before, along with another person he (at first) failed to recognize—a woman standing to Solomon Chavez's left.

As he and Floyd approached the group, a young couple, who stood nearby, turned their heads and studied him closely. The man touched his temple and seemed to be whispering something. By their mannerisms, Bram knew the two were undercover security officers. They must have been communicating with the woman beside Solomon Chavez, for as soon as the man started to whisper, she turned to look over her shoulder. She was no longer unknown to Bram. The raven-haired beauty was none other than Floyd's standoffish second-in-command, Gloria Muldoon. At the sight of him, she arched her eyebrow and flashed a hint of a smile. If Bram hadn't known better, he would've sworn she was happy to see him. A matching smile formed on his lips. She was certainly stunning, what with her coal black hair flowing down her smooth, bare back, the rest of which was barely covered by a red, body-hugging, floor-length cocktail dress, its v-shaped opening in back leaving little to the imagination. Turning back around, she gave her head a barely perceptible shake, prompting the undercover guards to relax.

It sounded to Bram like the group was involved in a conversation about the environment. One of the people he'd failed to recognize was talking, a stick-thin, middle-aged man with sky-blue, shoulder-length hair, who wore a tuxedo to match his colorful locks. Strangely enough, the outfit did not look ridiculous on him.

"Your discovery will revolutionize the energy industry, Dr. Levin." His smile was pleasant, but his voice sneered. "Tapping the zero-point energy field is a commendable achievement and, in many ways, quite remarkable. It, along with the last twenty-odd years of using thorium instead of uranium in our nuclear power plants, will help combat carbon emissions. When the world switched over to thorium, it made a marked difference in the safety and cleanliness of the nuclear industry . . . unfortunately, the tipping point came near forty years ago. We will not be able to clean up the atmosphere in time to prevent the ruination of this planet."

"I'm sure you're right, Abraham," she replied, trying to hide the look of exasperation on her face. "That being said, if the zero-point generators work as expected, the catastrophic effects of climate change may be delayed for another few decades . . . perhaps even minimized."

Bram stood beside Floyd, intrigued by the conversation. He suddenly felt someone's attention lock onto him. The person was disappointed, even angry to see him at the party. Out of the corner of his eye he noticed Solomon Chavez staring straight at him.

The woman standing beside the man with the blue hair chimed in. She looked barely thirty-five years old, yet her hair was snow-white; her dress, a shimmering silver.

"I envy you, Dr. Levin," she said, her voice taking on a girlish lilt. "Your invention's going to make you as rich as Dr. Chavez."

A wistful expression crossed Mona's face. "I suppose it would have, if I'd chosen to patent the design." A collective gasp was heard throughout the group. Mona shrugged her shoulders. "It's far more important for the world to convert to this form of energy than for me to become rich. Besides, my refusing to patent the design eliminates financial red tape. More companies will produce the generators; they get distributed faster, and the price per generator is much lower."

Like the rest, Bram was stunned by her altruism. However, that didn't prevent him from noticing their host's coal-black eyes shift from him to her. The intensity of Solomon Chavez's gaze didn't seem to affect Dr. Levin. Her attention was on Floyd Sullivant.

"I'm so happy to see you, Floyd. I was afraid you'd be stuck all night with last-minute details and skip Solomon's final bash."

"I wouldn't miss it for the world, Doc."

Mona's smile vanished when she saw Bram. Her eyes cut immediately to Solomon Chavez. When he spoke, his tone was flinty. "Mr. Waters . . . I was under the impression that you wouldn't arrive until tomorrow morning."

The man's icy reserve felt like a brick wall. "Luckily, I was able to wrap everything up and catch an earlier flight. It's a pleasure to finally meet you, Dr. Chavez." Bram held out his hand. Solomon Chavez stared down at the extended hand, frowning.

"Don't worry, Doc," Bram said, his emotions bridling. "I don't read people's minds, except when asked. To do such a thing without permission is tantamount to mental rape."

Undeterred, Bram left his hand out, waiting for Chavez to do the companionable thing. The moment stretched, along with his discomfort. He sensed that others in the group were feeling the same. Chavez glanced up into Bram's eyes then down again before reaching out to give his hand a firm, quick shake.

Bram continued on as though he'd not been slighted. "Thanks to Floyd here, I'm able to personally thank you for making me a member of the *Arrow*'s crew. I hope my contribution will add to the mission's success." He noted that Solomon Chavez was studying his face, looking for something in Bram's demeanor that only he could detect. Whatever he was hoping (or more likely fearing) to discover there was missing, for he began to relax . . . somewhat.

Bram sensed that Chavez had locked his emotions up tight as a drum. Though he never read anyone's mind without permission, he always sensed the emotional state of whoever he touched. This time, he received little information. The man had an incredibly disciplined mind.

Forcing a tight smile, Solomon Chavez said, "You're not an official member of the crew, Mr. Waters. Then again, neither am I. However, you will be decanted from your cryogenic tank when we arrive at the planet. You'll be a member of the first landing party. As I'm sure you've already been briefed, we need your particular skill-set to determine if there are any intelligent creatures living on the planet, and whether or not they pose a threat."

Bram nodded. "Either way, I'm glad to be of service."

He turned to Richard Allison in hopes of changing the conversation, but was caught off-guard when Gloria Muldoon hooked her arm around his and cooed, "I'm terribly thirsty, Bram. Would you be a gentleman and escort me to the bar? Along the way, I want to ask a few questions about your former profession. I find it fascinating."

Bram looked down at the dark-haired beauty and smiled. "I'd be honored."

"I'm warning you, Muldoon," Floyd said, wagging his finger. "Don't try to steal my date." He turned a knowing grin toward Bram, causing both men to laugh.

As the two wove their way through the crowd, Gloria kept glancing up at Bram, a look of concern written on her face. Finally, as they approached the bar, she asked, "Before I start flirting with you, is there something I should know, to keep from embarrassing myself?"

Bram gave her an innocent look. "I have no idea what you're talking about, Gloria."

"I think you do, Bram," she said, eyes narrowing. "Are you and Floyd . . . together?"

"First of all, I never kiss and tell," he said, giving her a sly grin. "Secondly, he helped get me into the party, that's all." Bram looked back toward the balcony and started to chuckle. "However . . ."

Grabbing hold of the front of his tuxedo, Gloria pulled herself close. Her perfume smelled of jasmine. Only a few inches separated the two. Bram swallowed nervously as he looked down into twin pools of ebony-suffused eyes. He was no longer laughing.

"I'm not shy when I want something . . . or someone, Bram," she confessed, a quiet huskiness entering her voice. "But heed my words: I won't take kindly to wasting my last night on Earth trying to hook up with someone I can't have . . . so no more joking around, please."

The closeness of Gloria's body, coupled with the sweet, musky scent that accompanied that closeness, was making Bram's head swim. Looking down into her gorgeous, oval face, Bram felt an intense longing, of a kind he hadn't felt in years.

"I'm straight as an arrow . . . so to speak," he breathed, allowing his left hand to settle lightly against the curve of her waist. Her body felt strong yet soft at the same time. Bram's mind picked up on her longing, giving him the confidence to proceed . . . albeit slowly, not wanting to ruin what could end up being an incredible night.

Reaching up to smooth the lapel of his jacket, Gloria stared into Bram's eyes, her expression sultry. "You don't know how happy I am to hear that." She paused, lips pouting. "Or do you?" Without waiting for Bram to answer, she again hooked her arm thorough his and guided him the last few feet to the bar.

After placing their orders, Bram took Gloria's hand in his. "You said this is your last night on Earth. Have you accepted a position onboard the *Arrow*?"

Gloria nodded. "The week after Floyd and I returned from Canada, I was offered the position of deputy security chief. Can you guess who my boss will be . . . aside from 'The Battleaxe?'"

It took Bram less than a second to realize who she was talking about. "Floyd?"

She nodded. "Floyd's an orphan. He's also the best man for the job. As for me, I was raised by my older half-brother after our mother died in a workplace accident. I never knew my father, but I did know my brother's father. He was a sorry son of a bitch who came around every few months to mooch a few Euro-credits." Reaching back, Gloria picked up her drink and took a sip, carefully studying Bram's face. "When I was eleven, the drunken bastard tried to molest me. My brother arrived home from work early, thank God, and caught him holding me face down on the couch." Gloria paused, the memory still painful. "My brother, who'd been a rugby player in school, flew into a red rage and tackled him. I fled to the apartment next door, hearing furniture crash and loud angry shouts reverberating through the walls. As I pounded frantically on our neighbor's door, the shouting ceased. Seconds later, the bastard burst out of our apartment and ran down the hall, calling me a rotten fucking tease as he passed by. I was so frightened that I nearly missed the blood staining his shirt. I rushed back to our apartment, only to find that he'd stabbed my brother in the neck. Aaron bled out before the ambulance could arrive.

"My testimony sent the murderous shit away for life. Soon after that, I was passed around from one foster home to another. Some families treated me like dirt, but it wasn't always bad; I stayed with a Swiss family for over three years. That's where I learned to ski." Taking a long, cleansing breath, Gloria reached over and, with a wan smile, slid her index finger along Bram's forearm. In the background, the band was playing a newer tune. "Come on, Bram, let's get out of here," Gloria whispered. "Help me put the past aside . . . for one night, at least?"

Bram's hesitation lasted barely a second. Ever since their time in Canada, he'd seen Gloria as an icy, standoffish force of nature. But things had changed: underneath her toughness, he saw a vulnerable, damaged young woman. To most men, that vulnerability would've been a green-light signaling them to make an advance. To Bram, however, such advances seemed predatory by nature. He'd always tried to ease others' pain, not take advantage of it for his own pleasure. In Gloria's case, he felt conflicted. Despite having a strong desire to comfort her, he also knew that she wanted him in her bed. The thought of making love to this gorgeous, sexy woman caused an intense, fiery passion to course through his veins. Bram wanted her—badly. After all, this wasn't just her last night on Earth, it was his too.

Taking Gloria by the hand, he led her from the party, wanting more than anything to help her forget the past for one night . . . and perhaps, in her arms, he'd be able to do the same.

7

Good morning, Bram. It's time to wake up. Good morning, Bram. It's time to wake up. Good morning, Bram. It's time to—"

"Okay, okay . . . I'm up, Eric."

Bram was disappointed. Being awakened by his PID was unexpected. He'd hoped for soft kisses . . . better yet, eager lips, urging him onward and upward for another round of lovemaking.

"Gloria?" he said, trying to sound nonchalant. Receiving no answer, he rolled over and stared at Gloria's side of the bed. It was empty. A handwritten note lay on her pillow.

The orange, Kenyan light streamed through the bedroom window lighting her words: "Dear Bram, Thank you for a wonderful night. I'm sorry you woke up alone, but the day ahead of me is hectic and I needed to start work early. There are towels in the bathroom cupboard, if you want to take a shower. All I have is lavender-scented shampoo. Sorry about that. There's some orange juice left in the fridge and a fresh pot of coffee waiting on the kitchen counter. You can find cups in the left-hand cabinet by the sink. If you're hungry, there's a box of leftover takeout in the fridge. I hope you like Thai. I apologize for not having anything more appetizing for breakfast, but I haven't been stocking my pantry lately. I'm sure you understand.

"I probably won't see you before the cryo-process, but I'll be looking forward to seeing you when we reach Epsilon Eridani.

Once again, I *really* enjoyed myself last night. Judging by the peaceful look on your face when I left, I'm pretty sure you did too. Until we meet again, toodle-oo and sweet dreams. I forgot: There's no dreaming in cryo-sleep. Before you know it, you'll be waking up, and it'll be like we've been apart for less than a day. Be brave, Gloria."

Setting the note to one side, Bram made his way to the bathroom, thinking about the note's hidden meaning: to him, it would feel like no more than half a day's passing between waking up today and opening his eyes in the Epsilon Eridani system, but for Gloria, the passage of time would be two years. She was the *Arrow's* Deputy Chief of Security, but she was also trained as a systems technician. There wasn't much need for security during the voyage; therefore, instead of spending her time in cryo-stasis, she would assist with engineering and ship's maintenance.

The voyage from one star system to the other would take over ten years to complete. A team of psychologists had determined that no matter how well a ship's crew was trained, no single crew could man the ship for that length of time without cracking under the pressure. The crew would be rotated every two years—except for the first shift, containing the command personnel. They would work at their stations for the first year, be put to sleep, and then be awakened again for the final, yearlong leg of the voyage. Floyd Sullivant fell into that category. Gloria's two-year shift would take place midway through the voyage; then she, along with Bram and the other members of the first landing party, would be awakened upon arrival.

Bram made it a point to never go in search of one-night stands, but he wasn't entirely averse to them. Women found him attractive (for the most part); he wasn't a troll, after all. However, as he'd approached middle-age, mornings such as these arrived fewer and farther apart.

When he decided to crash Solomon Chavez's party, he never expected to end up in bed with a gorgeous creature like Gloria

Muldoon. She had an exotic quality about her, like she had a few drops of Spanish or Polynesian blood flowing through her veins. She fascinated him—yet their temperaments were polar opposites—a relationship between them could never last. Despite their *definite* physical attraction, they had no emotional attachment. But . . . he couldn't have choreographed a better final night on Earth.

After a long, hot shower, Bram got dressed and took Gloria up on her offer of coffee. He still had a few hours to kill, so he spent part of that time on her tiny balcony, sipping coffee and staring out at distant Lake Victoria. He could see an apartment across the way where a young mother was getting ready for work while her two young children sat on a couch thoroughly engrossed in a cartoon. Watching the harried mother gesture and shout at the oblivious children reminded Bram of his own youth and how his mother had dragged him away from the HV set every morning before school. It was a scene that had played out in kitchens across the world for over a hundred years—a snapshot of everyday life that Bram was honored to witness, even when the mother, at the end of her rope, yanked one of the children up by his arm and gave him two swift swats on the butt. The other child was off the couch in a flash, running toward the front door and out of sight. The first child followed close behind, crying, stomping his feet all the way. Ignoring his behavior, the mother picked up both breakfast bowls and then disappeared herself.

Bram wanted them to reappear, but he knew they'd gone about their daily business—just like they'd done yesterday and the day before that, and would do again tomorrow. He was leaving this old world, never to return, but life would go on . . . as always.

Gloria's apartment felt a little sad, being bare of all possessions other than an unmade bed, a rickety chair on the balcony, a few unused cardboard boxes sitting in the living room, an empty refrigerator (having polished off the last of the orange juice and tossed out the Thai food), and an old coffeemaker that looked lonely sitting by itself. Dumping the leftover coffee down the sink, Bram left the apartment, closing the door behind him.

Before exiting the apartment, he used his PID to hail a cab, which was downstairs waiting as he left the building. Sensing his approach, the cab's curbside door slid open. Climbing inside, Bram leaned back and grunted out his destination. He'd never fully gotten used to driverless cars, but at least the vehicles in Memphis looked like the old-style cars of his youth, having actual wheels. This cab, like most of the other vehicles in the world's larger, metropolitan areas, had no use for wheels or axles or transmissions. They instead used maglev technology and hovered ten inches above the asphalt while traveling.

With his stomach rumbling, Bram stopped at a bakery and bought a croissant before returning to his hotel room to change clothes and check out. Still hungry and with two hours remaining before his orientation briefing, Bram decided to have lunch. He first thought about going to a fancy French restaurant for a last, decadent Earth meal, or someplace that served thick, juicy steaks or grilled lobster, but after thoughtful consideration, Bram decided on something more down to earth: a double cheeseburger with fries and a chocolate milkshake from his favorite fast-food restaurant.

Once there, he placed his order—which now included a fried apple pie—sat at a corner table and, for the next half-hour, enjoyed his meal while observing a steady stream of customers come and go. He could almost imagine being back home, eating at one of the chain's Memphis locations. For some strange reason, this notion instilled a measure of comfort and melancholy. There would be no fast-food chains where he was going, no happy clowns welcoming customers through its doors, no joyful children playing on brightly colored swing sets and curlicue slides. Life would be incredibly difficult where he was going—perhaps even impossible.

In the year 2061, the human race had barely taken its first steps away from Earth: there was the lunar colony, which was a shining example; the Martian colony, a desolate hellhole that took five years to build and was still struggling; and the asteroid belt factories, which were not yet profitable but held great promise.

Bram wondered if the planet orbiting Epsilon Eridani would be much better. The scientists who discovered it claimed that a wide swath of the planet was habitable . . . if they made it there. Being a layman, Bram didn't fully understand Einstein's theory of relativity, but he did know one thing: anything could happen between the *Arrow*'s departure from Earth and arrival at their new home.

Putting those troubling thoughts aside, Bram finished his lunch, grabbed one last refill of cola for the road, and headed toward the Lake Victoria complex and the adventure of a lifetime.

●

2 P.M., LOCAL TIME, JANUARY 17, 2061

Bram walked into the spacious auditorium of the Lake Victoria complex feeling as if he'd been put through a wringer. In a sense he had, what with all the medical procedures he'd been subjected to.

He'd arrived on schedule at the New Arrivals information desk, identified himself, and for the next hour was shuttled from one place to the next. He'd been retinal scanned and asked a battery of personal questions by a studious young security officer before being sent to the medical facilities. Once there he was DNA tested and asked even more personal questions. During the examination, he'd been given a shot to switch on a dormant gene in his DNA, which would allow his body to cope with the cryogenic freezing process. The med-tech had said something about a wood frog, but Bram hadn't paid much attention. He was thinking about what the technician had said just prior to that, about how at the conclusion of the orientation briefing, the participants would be segregated in alphabetical order and called back to the medical wing, where they would receive an intestinal flush and a strong diuretic.

Before going into cryo-stasis, the participants would have their intestines cleansed of all food and feces, while having as much of the fluids in their system flushed as humanly possible. Bram understood the part about the intestinal cleanse—people are required to take suppositories before traveling to certain Third World countries—however, the diuretic was a mystery. He asked and was told that the body needed to be flushed of as much water as possible without becoming completely dehydrated. His bodily fluids would be replaced by a high-glucose antifreeze-type solution, designed to keep his cells from bursting once they reached their freezing point. That, combined with the switched on dormant DNA, would protect his body during the ten-year trip through space.

The med-tech had explained the procedure in a matter-of-fact way, obviously having told it to hundreds, if not thousands, of other people during the month-long lead-up to launch. There were already over six thousand souls ensconced in cryogenic chambers onboard the *Arrow*, and the process had been tested and retested to ensure safety, but just the thought of having most of his blood replaced by antifreeze, then being frozen like a human popsicle for ten years, caused chills to run up his spine. After exiting the building's medical wing, he'd fought down an urge to flee the complex and run back to Memphis, like a dog with his tail tucked between his legs. One of the things that kept him from doing so was the other people leaving the medical facility, some of whom he'd seen at the party the previous night. The looks on their faces mirrored his own. *I guess misery does love company*, he'd thought.

The other thing that kept him on track was the thought of Gloria finding out he'd lost his nerve. Of course, he'd be long dead before she'd ever find out, but the idea of her waking up to discover she'd made love to a coward would haunt him the rest of his days. No . . . skipping out was unacceptable. Besides, he'd faced down the maniacal Conrad Snow, and if he could do that, he could confront just about anything. Having one's body frozen and rocketed through space at nearly the speed of light would be a snap.

It was simply last-minute jitters that had him second-guessing himself, nothing more. Or was it something else? Was there something about this mission that was causing a warning signal to go off in his subconscious mind?

After arriving at the auditorium, he found an aisle seat near the back and sat down to wait. For the next few minutes, Bram closed his eyes and tried to let whatever was bothering him rise to the surface. As powerful as his psychic abilities were, he seldom peered into the future. Doing so would only take the fun out of living—and frankly, he wasn't that good at it. However, subtle impressions from the near future did occasionally enter his thoughts, and on more than one occasion had saved his life. This time there were no psychic impressions, only a realization: what he feared was a loss of control. Even while asleep, his subconscious mind was attuned to approaching danger, but in cryo-stasis his psychic abilities would be completely shut down. Even his dreams would be suspended.

This realization eased Bram's mind—somewhat. There were times when a man must place his trust in the hands of others and accept a temporary loss of control. This was one of those times. As such, he no longer wanted to run from the room like a scalded dog.

With fifteen minutes remaining before the orientation was scheduled to begin, he scanned the hundred and fifty or so individuals in attendance, hoping to spot Gloria. Most were chatting nervously with their neighbors, while others sat stoically, valiantly trying to buck up their nerves. A few, he sensed, were so conflicted about the upcoming voyage that they felt like rushing from the room, much like he had. Determined to rationalize his feelings, Bram wondered if some small part of his own insecurities had resulted from picking up on their flight-driven thought patterns.

Despite the scattered reservations, most of the audience was happy to be there, especially the scientists, who sat together, chattering excitedly, oblivious to the others in the room.

Bram saw a couple of politicians he recognized from the news and a big action star from the movies. Bram could sense rippling waves of trepidation flowing from the movie star. *Well, well,* he thought. *Hollywood must really be the land of dreams and illusion, if the fearless action hero was shaking in his boots.*

Wondering where Gloria was, Bram reached out with his mind (feeling a bit like a stalker) and attempted to locate her unique vibratory pattern, but she was nowhere to be found. *That's odd,* he thought, until he realized she was probably already resting comfortably in cryo-stasis. After reporting for duty and taking care of any last-minute security concerns, the odds were good that she'd gone straight to the cryogenics wing. She was a creature of duty and discipline, after all, not some vapid airhead he'd picked up at a blues bar.

With his attention elsewhere, Bram was startled when the double doors beside the auditorium stage swung open, and in walked Solomon Chavez, Mona Levin, Admiral Katherine "Battleaxe" Axelrod, Captain Richard Allison, and Security Chief Floyd Sullivant.

●

"Thank you, ladies and gentlemen," Dr. Solomon Chavez said from the podium. The sustained applause gradually faded away.

"Before I begin, I'd like to point out that the previous orientation briefings were conducted by members of the public relations office. I'd like to thank their liaison, Lawrence Murchison, who will become Chief Operating Officer of CIMRAD when I'm placed in cryo-stasis, and I've asked him to congratulate his staff for their hard work over the previous months."

Motioning for Lawrence Murchison to stand, Chavez began to clap appreciatively. The tall, handsome press secretary stood and waved, receiving a warm round of applause.

"The previous orientation briefings were held for the small number of average citizens who entered and won the *Ark* lottery, along with qualified individuals whose skills are needed to make our future home a success.

"Today's group is different. It will be the last one to board the *Arrow*. Many of you are the scientists and technicians who poured ideas and labor into constructing mankind's first interstellar spacecraft. Others are politicians and assorted VIPs whose schedules prevented you from arriving until the last minute." Judging by the bemused look on Solomon's face, most of those in attendance could tell what he really thought about the late arrivals. "We also have a few who'll be members of the first landing party," he continued. "I welcome you all, and turn the remainder of the briefing over to Admiral Axelrod."

The Admiral, clad in crisp, navy dress whites, approached the podium and cleared her throat. Standing five-foot-eight, with broad shoulders and a back stiff as a board, Katherine Axelrod would've presented an imposing presence even if she hadn't become one of the most successful military strategists in the history of modern warfare.

"I'm sure you're all wondering why I've been asked to speak," she said in her clipped British accent. "I'll keep it short. Soon you will be placed in a state of suspended animation, so to speak, and will be unaware of the passage of time between here and

Epsilon Eridani. Once there, some of you will be awakened while approaching the planet, which the press has nicknamed Earth 2.0. By all accounts, our new home will be anything but a second Earth. Some of the conditions will be harsh, and there's no guaranteeing the crops we plant will adjust to the climate or the soil conditions. Our exobiology team assures us that we have nothing to worry about, but one must consider all options.

"Most of you, together with the other six thousand colonists, will remain in cryo-stasis until the planet is properly explored. Once we find the optimal location to start building a settlement, the appropriate trades and professionals will be decanted, and the business of construction will begin. No one will be left out of the laborious task of constructing the settlement and farming the land. This is not a pleasure cruise. There will be no slackers. And for the first few years, there will be no democratically elected form of government. There will be a military dictatorship, led by yours truly."

Pausing, the admiral allowed her steely gaze to sweep the audience. Dissatisfied grumblings were heard from one end of the auditorium to the other. The thought of living under a military dictatorship was anathema to everyone in attendance, especially for some of the scientists who, at great risk, had escaped from authoritarian regimes to come and work for something bigger than themselves.

The admiral held up her hand. The grumbling died down, but many in the audience fumed over her announcement. The only ones unperturbed by the news was the row of people sitting on the stage behind her.

"Unfortunately, such an arrangement *is* necessary . . . at first. You'll be happy to know that when the settlement is built and normalcy is established, free elections will be instituted, and the military will step down from command. I assure you, nothing will please me more. Like you, I ascribe to the democratic principles of a free society and look forward to voting for our first congress or council or parliament or whatever system of government the majority decides to institute. But, until we do that, my word *will* be law.

"If this arrangement ruffles your sensibilities and you can't abide by these conditions, or you believed that life on our new home would be a cakewalk, don't let the door smack your bum on the way out. We have standbys waiting to take your place."

Almost everyone shifted uncomfortably in their seats, while glancing around to see if anyone was headed for the exit. Bram sensed a number of people teetering on the edge, but none left. If even one attendee had taken the admiral up on her dare, he sensed that at least ten other people would've followed suit. Bram wasn't exactly sure if peer pressure was the deciding factor, but the desire to leave (either in a huff or out of fear) was quickly followed by a strengthening of resolve. Even the most skittish people in the auditorium had made up their minds to stand firm and not let the admiral's harsh conditions stand in the way of the greatest opportunity in history—the chance to rocket across space and colonize a new world.

The barest hint of a smile formed on the admiral's tight lips. "Good . . . good. It pleases me to see that we have such fine examples of the human spirit sitting in this hall. It will take courage to make our new home livable. And from the look of things, I have renewed confidence that not only we will succeed in our mission . . . we will thrive."

The applause started out tepid but quickly turned deafening. Sensing the collective coming together of spirit, Bram was beginning to understand why the woman known as "The Battleaxe" was such a good leader. She'd taken her audience's doubts and fears, including his own, and turned them around. She'd forced the audience to confront the last remaining uncertainties they were harboring and cast them aside, replacing them instead with determination and grit.

"Thank you," she said as the applause died down. "Over the next half hour or so, you'll be asked to file through the exit to my left, in alphabetical order, and make your way in single file to the facility's medical wing, where you'll be prepped for departure. By the end of the afternoon, everyone will be in stasis and safely onboard the *Arrow*. Let us begin: all those with surnames starting with the letters A through E, please file out now. When they're done, a med-tech will call for the next alphabetical unit."

As the first group of attendees rose and worked their way toward the exit, the admiral ended her speech with, "Godspeed, ladies and gentlemen. We have a brilliant, glorious adventure ahead of us." She saluted and, followed by the others onstage, departed the auditorium.

●

Bram felt drained. He sat on a heavily padded swivel chair in a perfectly square, powder blue room in cryogenics, part of the last group called from the auditorium, wishing that his last name hadn't started with one of the last letters of the alphabet. The waiting was interminable. He hated waiting.

The medical procedures he endured, however, had been much worse. His entire intestinal tract had been flushed, and the diuretic he'd been given had worked quickly. It wasn't as if he was queasy, though. The thick fluid used to administer the enema included an anti-emetic. What caused him, and the others in the waiting room, to feel weak had been the diuretic: the powerful drug was administered intravenously, and minutes later he was pissing up a storm. To conserve time, the procedure had taken place during the enema. He was asked to strip down and sit on an oddly shaped contraption; then, a bored, female med-tech, stationed at a nearby computer console, programmed the chair-like contraption to wrap itself around the lower half of his body, starting at his belly button and ending a few inches above his knees. What happened next was akin to being violated: something soft, though obviously mechanical, spread apart his buttocks and immediately applied a warm lubricant to his rectum, at which point Bram's breathing sped up. He felt a probe enter his rectum and work its way through his intestinal tract. The med-tech then gave him the diuretic, all the while humming a tune. Bram had avoided her gaze, even as she half-heartedly tried to reassure him.

His cheeks had burned with embarrassment when the urine began to flow and the probe retracted, releasing the contents of his intestines. He kept reminding himself that the attractive med-tech had seen this a thousand times during the previous months. The procedure had lasted less than ten minutes and, when it was blessedly over, Bram climbed unsteadily to his feet and dressed. He was so dehydrated, even his fingernails felt parched.

He exited the small exam room and the next person entered. Three nearby doors opened at nearly the exact same time and others in his group walked out, their faces reflecting the same embarrassment as his own. While on his way to the cryogenics waiting room, Bram encountered two men as they rounded a corner: Floyd Sullivant and Captain Richard Allison.

Floyd happily said, "Bram! Give us a moment, would you?"

Despite feeling shaky, Bram stopped to chat.

"You look like hell," Floyd said, unable to keep from grinning. "They really ream you out in there, don't they?"

Bram looked away, his face falling. "Don't start, Floyd."

"Sorry, sorry, old boy," he chuckled, turning to Richard Allison. "Bram, I'd like you to meet Captain Richard Allison, the *Arrow*'s first officer and pilot."

The two men shook hands.

"I'm sure you've heard this a thousand times by now, Captain," Bram said. "I watched your rescue live on HV. I can't tell you how happy I was when those dolphins showed up. They're amazingly noble creatures." Bram had no intention of ever revealing the role he played in alerting those selfsame dolphins to Richard's plight.

"I agree, Mr. Waters," Richard said. "The navy has a long history of working with dolphins. I knew a man who trained a number of them, and he was always talking about how most of them were smarter than he was. Knowing him, I took him at his word."

Behind Richard Allison's easy humor, Bram sensed an undercurrent of sadness in the man, which (owing to his military training) was held firmly in check. The young, African American captain's sorrow felt similar to his own history of grief. There was something about this man that Bram trusted, something he liked.

"I'm pleased to finally meet you, Captain. And I'm looking forward to working with you in the future. Right now, however, if the two of you don't mind, I need to get to cryogenics. I have a date with a long nap."

"Speaking of dates," Floyd said. "Gloria didn't go into details about your time together, but I think you left quite the impression on the old girl, my friend."

Bram perked up. "Oh, how so?"

Cocking one eyebrow, Floyd shook his head. "She's normally a very serious individual, but today she couldn't keep from grinning. I have to admit, it was a shocking sight to behold. If I were a religious man, I might call you a miracle worker."

Bram knowingly replied, "I'm no miracle worker, but I've found there's more to people than their surface appearance suggests."

Floyd's eyebrow rose. "It seems, Captain, that we have a philosopher in our midst."

"I can think of worse things to call a person," Richard said.

"Correct me if I'm wrong, Bram," Floyd smirked, "but I seriously doubt that Gloria's attitude change happened because she was sitting at your feet listening to you quote the Buddha."

Looking to the heavens, Bram said, "I'll never tell."

Floyd laughed and clapped Bram on the back. "See that you don't. Gloria's got a reputation to uphold. After all, I can't have people thinking she's gone soft over some bloke. Now get out of here, you look tired. Perhaps you should take a long nap."

"I've been meaning to catch up on my beauty sleep."

With that, the three men went their separate ways: Bram to the cryogenics waiting room and the other two to wrap up last-minute details.

Sitting in the powder blue room, Bram thought back to his encounter with the two men. He'd enjoyed the good-natured banter, but learning that he produced a positive effect on Gloria elicited a flood of conflicting emotions: he was happy he pleased her, but he also felt guilty. In some weird way, their night together felt like cheating on his long-dead fiancée. He'd never felt that way with the other women he slept with over the years, so why this time? What was different? It wasn't as though he'd failed to please those other women. They too were one-night stands. They—

Then it hit him. Of all the women he'd slept with since Jennifer's death, Gloria was the first one Bram wanted to see again. That's what was fueling his guilt. His desire to spend more than a single night with Gloria was stepping on his memories of being with Jennifer.

Lost in thought, Bram failed to hear his name being called. When the woman seated beside him gave him a nudge, he jerked in surprise and looked up. A frowning, white-clad med-tech stood in the doorway, tapping the top of his wrist, the universal sign that implied how he was wasting everyone's time.

"Sorry," he muttered, hopping up. Any mental concerns about Gloria would have to wait.

Entering the cryo-lab, he looked around in shock. He'd been informed that its walls and floor was one big HV screen, but he was unprepared for how realistic it appeared. For all intents and purposes, he'd stepped through an office door onto a peaceful, grassy meadow. The illusion was seamless, making the room appear huge. He saw rolling hills in the distance, scattered cirrus clouds overhead in a bright blue sky, a stand of oak trees to his left, and two monarch butterflies fluttering above a swath of purple wildflowers. He couldn't have asked for a more gorgeous— or peaceful—final view of Mother Earth.

"This way, Mr. Waters," the med-tech said, motioning toward the only incongruous object in the tranquil scene.

A seven-foot-long by three-foot-wide gun-metal gray cylinder was hovering two feet off the ground. Upon closer examination, he saw that the cylinder rested on a retractable shelf, behind which a recession—the same size as the cylinder—was located. This would be his personal cryo-chamber, his place of rest for the next ten years.

"Please disrobe and place your possessions in the opening to your left, sir," the med-tech said in a coldly professional tone. In the palm of the young man's hand rested a small device, into which he began tapping an often-used command. The top half of the cylinder popped open to reveal a disappointingly plain interior.

Bram half expected to see flashing lights and plush cushions. The cryo-chamber didn't look comfortable. Sensing the med-tech's impatience, Bram hurriedly shed his clothes. An eighteen-inch square opening appeared to his left in which he dropped the apparel.

"Those are expensive shoes," he noted. "Will I get them back later?"

The med-tech grumbled something under his breath before answering. "Any items of clothing you planned to keep should've been packed with your personal belongings, sir. Once you're decanted, you'll be supplied with a standard issue coverall. All personal items will be unloaded after the colony is up and running." He held out his hand, signaling that he wanted Bram to climb into the cryo-chamber.

The moment was finally here. Bram's last conscious moments on Earth had arrived, and they would be spent in the presence of a young man who acted as if he wanted to be anywhere but here, shipping a parade of people on an adventure he would never experience.

As though the med-tech had read *his* mind, the young man guided Bram forward and gently helped him into the cryo-chamber. "There's nothing to fear, Mr. Waters. Each cryo-chamber has undergone rigid testing. They're virtually infallible. Lie back and relax. Once I've attached the cuffs to your arms and legs, you'll start to feel drowsy. Before you know it, you'll be waking up thinking no time has passed, though you will experience some nausea and a slight headache."

Bram merely nodded, unable to find his voice; whether from fear or exhilaration, he wasn't sure. Doing as instructed, he stretched out in what was starting to feel like a coffin.

The interior of the cryo-chamber was lined with a soft, spongy material. The med-tech leaned over him holding a fine-tipped permanent marker in his hand. He drew a tiny black dot over a vein in the crook of each arm and near the ankles of each leg. He then activated a program, using his Medical Interlink Device, and offered Bram a reassuring smile.

"Have a safe trip, sir."

"Thank you." Bram could barely croak out his reply.

Cushioned medical cuffs extended from slots located beside his hips and wrapped around his elbows and ankles. He felt a slight sting where the med-tech placed the black dots. Underneath him, the spongy material swelled with what to Bram felt like gel, cushioning his body further, supporting it in such a way that it felt like he was floating on air.

The med-tech stepped out of sight, allowing Bram a clear view of the ceiling. Through the miracle of HV, it looked exactly like a bright blue sky. As the sedative began to kick in, melting away his fear and trepidation, Bram tried to focus on a distant wisp of cloud. A small, yellow butterfly fluttered into view. As a numb, gauzy smile formed on his lips, Bram watched a second butterfly join the first. The two insects were dancing . . . a waltz. With his mind enveloped in a warm, comforting fog, he tried to follow their movements, but his eyelids suddenly drooped and he was out like a light.

The med-tech entered another sequence into his MID. The cryo-chamber's opaque lid closed, locked in place, and the shelf it rested on retracted into the wall. The cylinder slid forward and disappeared, slowly being conveyed to the space elevator loading dock. Another cryo-chamber took its place. Spinning on his heel, the med-tech opened the door and announced, "Ana Weiss, you're next!"

8

The morning after the final shipment of cryo-chambers was stored in the *Arrow*'s hold, Mona Levin found herself walking beside Solomon Chavez down a long hallway located in the ship's crew quarters. To save space, most of the crew—except the captain, first officer, and chief medical officer—bunked three to a room. The two stopped at the end of the hall and entered the only other private cabin: it belonged to Solomon Chavez. A lovely young Asian woman, holding a med-tech tablet beside an empty cryo-chamber, greeted them as they entered the room.

"Your cryo-chamber is ready whenever you are, Dr. Chavez," the young med-tech said, smiling nervously at her patient.

Mona was unaccountably irked by the young woman. She had to remind herself that Solomon was tall, dark, exceedingly handsome, and richer than God; it was natural for the young med-tech to feel shy, even awkward, in his presence. *Solomon could have any woman he wanted*, Mona thought, but in all the years she'd known and worked with him, there were no rumors of him dating or even sleeping with anyone. There were times when she wondered if he was an ascetic or simply nonsexual.

"Thank you, Ms. Hiroshige. I'll be ready momentarily." Solomon's eyes scanned the spacious room, taking in the carbon-fiber bedroom suit, the breakfast nook, the comfortable reading chair to his left, and the impressionistic artwork on the walls, which, like the other objects in the room, were fixed firmly in place. He appeared satisfied.

Facing Mona with a reticent look in his eye, Solomon held out his hand. She looked down at the proffered handshake and, chuckling under her breath, shook her head. Reaching out with both arms, she gave the enigmatic young man, whom she'd worked with for nearly a decade, a tightly held, unanticipated embrace. When she stepped back, she could tell that Solomon was touched by her uncharacteristic show of affection.

"I know that we've had our differences in the past, Mona, but . . . I'm truly going to miss you," he admitted.

Tucking a lock of dark-brown hair behind her right ear, Mona smiled coyly. "There's still time to change your mind and ask me to join the mission."

Solomon heaved an exasperated sigh. "You never give up, do you?"

"It was a joke, nothing more," she said, patting Solomon on the arm. Out of the corner of her eye, she noticed the med-tech shift uncomfortably while studying an impressionistic oil painting of sunflowers. The young woman was listening intently to their conversation, yet trying hard to appear otherwise. "You should get the cryo-process underway. I'm sure Ms. Hiroshige has better things to do than stand around listening to us ramble on like two old fogies."

Solomon glanced over at the young med-tech, who was beginning to blush, then refocused on Mona. "I've recorded a message to be played just before the ship departs. All the HV networks and interlink websites will carry it. I hope you'll watch it; I mention you prominently."

"I wouldn't miss it for the world. So . . . I guess it's time to say goodbye, before you strip for cryo-sleep."

Solomon began to unbutton his shirt. "I didn't realize you were a prude, Mona."

"Oh, I'm not," she smirked. "I just don't want my last image of you to be so . . . vivid. Seeing you in such a vulnerable position would haunt my dreams for years to come."

Solomon took off his shirt and stuffed it in a plastic bag. His physique was impressive. Mona caught the young med-tech eyeing his well-defined musculature. The way her lips parted slightly as Solomon began to unzip his pants told Mona more than she wanted to know. It was as if she could read the girl's mind. The pretty young thing had probably called in a few favors to be the one putting Solomon under. Her earlier nervousness was now understandable. She wanted to be the last woman from this time period to have had sex with the great Solomon Chavez. With her lovely oval face and petite, almost perfect figure, she may well succeed.

"Ms. Hiroshige, I'll be waiting for you just outside the door," Mona said. "There's something I want to talk to you about once you're through in here."

Annoyance, along with a trace of disappointment, showed plainly in her eyes. "Of course, Dr. Levin. I'll be out in a few minutes."

Solomon was down to his socks and underwear. "As you leave, Ms. Hiroshige, please tell the ship's computer to institute the preset lockdown for this room."

"Yes, sir."

"Farewell, Solomon," Mona said as she turned to leave. "I know you'll succeed in building a better world than the one you're leaving."

"Thank you, Mona. I hope your zero-point energy generators succeed in stemming the tide of climate change that's devastating this once beautiful planet."

Mona's eyes dropped. Without another word, she gave him a quick nod and exited the room.

When the door shut behind her, Mona leaned against the corridor wall and bit her lower lip. Her heart pounded wildly. She'd barely kept her composure while speaking in Solomon's room. She kept reminding herself that all she needed to do was stay calm for a few more minutes, and her carefully laid plan would succeed.

There was one slight glitch: she hadn't expected Solomon to code in a lockdown sequence. She had to act quickly before the med-tech issued the order.

The faint whooshing sound of a turbo-lift opening was heard from around the corner down the hall. It was accompanied by boisterous male laughter—coming her way. Some of the crew must be headed to their quarters, she thought, ramping up her heart rate.

Please, Yahweh, don't let it be anyone I know, she prayed.

Two men entered the corridor, headed in her direction. One of them, a large fellow with jug ears and a crew cut, saw her right away. *Dammit!* It was Kowalski from engineering.

"Hey, Doc," he said with a lopsided grin. Mona knew the other man but not by name. He stopped in front of what must be their quarters and asked Kowalski if he was coming in. "I got a question for Dr. Levin about the zero-point flux regulator . . . you know, the one I was tellin' ya about in the turbo-lift. I'll see ya later at chow."

Great, this is all I need! Mona thought. As Kowalski approached, her eyes flicked nervously toward the door, expecting the young med-tech to exit at any second.

Kowalski stopped in front of her. "Hey, Doc, I've got a flux regulator that's giving me a low reading. If you've got a minute I'd like to pick—"

Solomon's door slid open. "It'll have to wait, Kowalski," she said, holding up her hand.

"But—"

Mona virtually leapt in front of the door. The med-tech was just starting to speak. "Computer, start Dr. Chavez's—"

"Belay that order, Ms. Hiroshige," Mona snapped.

The young woman was both surprised and confused. She stood in the doorway looking from Mona to the equally confused Kowalski. "I don't understand. Can't this wait until after I issue Dr. Chavez's order?"

Mona reached into the breast pocket of her shirt and removed a folded envelope. She lowered her voice to a whisper. "I have a letter that I want Dr. Chavez to find when he wakes up."

Ms. Hiroshige's eyes narrowed. "Give it to me; I'll place it on the table by his bed."

"I . . . I'd rather do it myself, please," Mona said, thinking furiously as she added a slight whine to her voice. "I'm, well, I'm not proud to admit this, Ms. Hiroshige, but, I . . . I've been in love with Dr. Chavez for years, and . . . I wrote this letter admitting my feelings. I realize he won't read it until long after I'm dead and gone, but . . . I wanted him to know how I feel. I couldn't bear going to my grave without him finally understanding . . . that I, um, that I thought of him as more than just a colleague."

Ms. Hiroshige's expression began to soften. She'd been perturbed when Mona thwarted her plan to bed Solomon Chavez, but now she knew why—or so she thought. "Very well, I'll wait here while you leave your . . . love letter."

Mona placed her hand on the other woman's wrist. "Thank you, dear, but could you wait outside the door? I . . . I have a few words I want to say, in private. I hope you understand."

The young woman once again looked perturbed. Glancing back at Kowalski, she rolled her eyes. "Don't take too long, Dr. Levin."

"Thank you for understanding," Mona said as she walked by the med-tech into the room.

Hearing the door slide shut behind her, Mona slipped the empty envelope in her back pocket and pulled out her PID. Her hands were shaking as she tapped the screen. She hadn't lied about wanting to have a private word—it just wasn't with Solomon Chavez. "Judah, patch into the *Arrow's* computer using my backdoor override software."

She waited for her PID to answer, the silence feeling like an oppressive shroud hanging over the room. After nearly five interminable seconds, her PID responded to her order, "It is done, Dr. Levin, and awaiting your command."

"Solomon Chavez has a lockdown function in his stateroom that will go into effect as soon as I leave the room. I want that program modified so I can return and reenter his stateroom."

There was a shorter pause. "I cannot modify the program in that manner, Dr. Levin."

Mona's stomach lurched. Everything was falling apart. She had to think of something. If she stayed in the room much longer, Hiroshige would become apprehensive and check on her. Then Judah's words struck her: Solomon's lockdown program couldn't be modified *in that manner*.

"Judah, is there a manner in which the lockdown function *can* be modified?"

"Yes, Dr. Levin."

"State the number of ways it can be modified, Judah."

"The lockdown function can be modified one way, Dr. Levin."

"State the manner in which it can be modified, Judah."

"The time function can be modified, Dr. Levin."

Mona's eyes grew wide with happiness. *Gotcha!* "Thank you, Judah. Modify the lockdown program to initiate a ten minute delay before it goes into effect."

Judah responded immediately. "The program has been modified, Dr. Levin."

Breathing a heavy sigh of relief, Mona slipped her PID into her back pocket and approached the stateroom door. As it opened, Ms. Hiroshige was standing outside blocking her path. Being a few inches shorter than Mona, the young woman tried to look over her shoulder to see past her into the room. "Computer, institute Dr. Solomon Chavez's lockdown program," Mona said.

The nondescript computer voice, which sounded neither male nor female, announced, "As commanded, the lockdown program is now in effect."

"Excuse me, dear," Mona said as she stepped around the sullen med-tech. The door closed behind her. "Now, Kowalski . . . you were saying?"

●

Inside the turbo-lift, Mona tried to listen as Kowalski rambled on about the unusual regulator readings, but her thoughts were focused on the ticking clock in her head. Having Ms. Hiroshige's eyes trained on her didn't help.

Mona was still nodding when she belatedly noticed that Kowalski had stopped speaking. She opened her mouth thinking to say something vague about engineering, when Ms. Hiroshige asked her a question.

"So, Dr. Levin, when will you be taking the S. E. back to Earth?"

"Excuse me?"

"The space elevator . . . when will you be taking it down to Lake Victoria?"

Mona didn't want to sound too definitive. "I'll be leaving the orbital platform sometime after the ship's launch," she said. "As for the *Arrow*, I'll be leaving today, possibly tomorrow. It all depends on whether the ship's systems are running smoothly or not."

The turbo-lift slowed to a stop, its doors opening on the floor containing the ship's medical facilities. Ms. Hiroshige stepped out. "I'm on temporary assignment here. Perhaps I'll look you up after the launch. I'm writing my thesis in exobiology and would like to pick your brain on—"

"I'm sorry, dear, but that's not my field of expertise." Mona didn't like the way the young woman was studying her. "Besides, when I return to Earth I'll be taking an extended vacation with my mother to the Holy Land. I hear the region's become a tourist Mecca, so to speak, since the peace accord. Good luck with your thesis, dear." She smiled warmly as the door slid shut.

"Computer," Kowalski said, "take us to engineering."

The turbo-lift began to move silently toward the aft section of the ship. Mona felt beads of sweat forming on her upper lip and brow. She was becoming frantic; her time to act was slipping away. *How much time do I have left?* she wondered. She couldn't ask Judah, not with Kowalski in the lift. She began to calculate: After walking down the hall to the turbo-lift, they'd been forced to wait a good minute for its arrival, then dropped to the medical wing, where the horny med-tech exited; Mona must have lost at least four minutes. If she traveled to engineering with Kowalski, she'd lose more time—too much time. She wouldn't make it back to Solomon's room within the ten-minute time frame.

"How long before we reach engineering, Kowalski?" she calmly inquired, trying to keep her frayed nerves from revealing themselves in her voice.

"Around three minutes . . ."*Shit!* ". . . one and a half, at max speed," he finished.

Mona had to fight to keep from grinning. "Computer, increase to max speed."

The only thing that suggested an increase in velocity was a louder background hum. There were no physical indicators, thanks to the inertial damping system she engineered.

"You're awfully eager to get to work on the regulator problem, Doc," Kowalski said.

"What . . . oh yes, um . . . no, not really . . . I'm going to life sciences, to check on something after I drop you off."

"But what about—"

"Increase the input capacitor current seven milliamps. That should fix the problem."

"And if it doesn't?"

"Then study the damn manual, Kowalski," she snapped. "I'm not here to hold your hand! Use some initiative, man. What'll you do if there's an emergency along the way . . . call home to speak to a service tech?"

Mona immediately regretted her choice of words. The chastened look on the man's face was proof that she should apologize, but she didn't; Kowalski needed to think for himself, not rely on others to solve his problems. As they rode in silence, Mona convinced herself that she'd just given the assistant engineer a lesson in character building.

Seconds later, he was stepping from the turbo-lift. "Thanks for the advice, Doc. I'll increase the current by the amount you suggested."

"See that you do."

Thank the Lord, she thought, as the lift-door slid shut. *I still have three minutes left.*

"Computer, take me back to the crew quarters, max speed."

The turbo-lift hummed loudly. Approximately twenty seconds later, the hum decreased then stopped. With Mona's thoughts racing, she failed to notice the change in sound. The door opened, and three female technicians stepped inside. "I'm sorry, is this, is this the crew quarters?" she stammered.

"No, Dr. Levin," answered one. "This is applied sciences. We're on our way to engineering for a consultation."

"You can go there after I reach the crew quarters."

The three looked at each other, concern written on their faces.

"But engineering is so much closer," said another. "That'll cause us a lot of backtracking."

"I don't care if it—" Mona clamped her mouth shut. The more she argued the longer it would take. "Fine, we'll do it your way. Computer, take us back to engineering, max speed."

The next twenty seconds were both silent and uncomfortable, with her three lift companions shooting frequent, sidelong glances in her direction. The doors opened and they stepped out. Kowalski was walking by. "Hey, Doc, your suggestion worked."

"Great," she grunted sarcastically as the lift-doors closed in his face. "Computer, take me to the crew quarters, max speed . . . and by executive order: *No* stops along the way." Mona removed her PID from her blouse pocket. "Judah, how much time's left before Solomon's stateroom goes into lockdown?"

"Two minutes, fifty-three seconds, Dr. Levin."

Mona felt a modicum of relief hearing those words. It meant she would be inside Solomon's stateroom before time ran out. She still felt antsy, shifting frequently from one foot to the other. Her stomach rumbled, sounding terribly loud in the khaki-hued enclosure. The trip seemed to last even longer than before.

"Computer, is the turbo-lift traveling at maximum speed?"

"Yes, Dr. Levin."

Just then, the humming faded and the doors swished open. Relieved to see the hallway empty, Mona darted toward the corridor leading to Solomon's stateroom. Her eyes suddenly went wide. People were talking. Their voices were getting closer. They were mere yards from rounding the corner. Skidding to a halt, she almost stumbled forward into the corridor. Quickly regaining her balance, Mona spun on her heel and dashed for the opposite corner, hoping beyond hope to avoid detection. She rounded the corner just as three crew members, on their way to chow, entered the short passageway to the turbo-lift.

Mona stood with her back flat against the wall, holding her breath, scared out of her wits. One of the crewmen pressed the button for the turbo-lift. The doors opened almost immediately, but not before Mona heard steps heading her way.

"Come on, Henri," said one of the crewmen. "I'm hungry. I hear Cookie's made Swedish meatballs. My mouth's watering just thinking about them."

Mona wished the crewman hadn't mentioned food. She instantly became terrified that her stomach would start to growl.

The sound of approaching steps stopped. "Fine, but I swear I heard something."

"You're always hearing something."

"Am not."

"Are too."

Mona listened intently, afraid to draw a breath while waiting to see if Henri would enter the turbo-lift.

"I was right about the—"

The turbo-lift doors swished shut, interrupting the crewman's sentence.

After hearing the turbo-lift door close, Mona pushed off from the wall and sprinted around the corner. "Judah, how much time is left?"

She was sucking air as she rounded the next corner and ran down the corridor.

"Twenty seconds, Dr. Levin."

"Shit!"

Skidding to a frenetic halt in front of Solomon's stateroom, she pressed the button to enter, but nothing happened. "Why isn't the door opening, Judah?!"

"You must first enter his personal code."

"What is it?" she panted, her voice trembling.

"Press the name, "Selena," into the touch pad, Dr. Levin."

Selena? She wondered about this odd little twist as her fingers
flew over the screen located to the right of the door's entrance.
Why would Solomon use the name Selena? Putting the question
aside, she breathlessly pressed the final letter.

Was she too late? No! She couldn't be . . . she just couldn't be!

Almost unable to believe her eyes, Mona watched the stateroom door slide open. She didn't run or dash or sprint inside, she
lunged through, yelling, "Computer! Shut the door!"

She stumbled forward, nearly dropping to her knees. "Judah,
how much time's remaining?"

"None, Dr. Levin.""That was close," she groaned, collapsing
into Solomon's reading chair.

Mona closed her eyes and let her nerves recuperate. When her
trembling finally subsided and her breathing returned to normal,
she stood from the chair, crossed the stateroom, and stopped
beside Solomon's cryo-chamber. "Judah, please initiate phase one
of the Aurora protocol."

"Phase one is now in effect, Dr. Levin."

Mona watched Solomon's cryo-chamber glide effortlessly away from
the wall. A secret wall-panel opened up behind it. An identical-looking
cryo-chamber slid out from the dark recess in the wall and came to a
stop beside its twin. Mona placed both hands on the cryo-chamber
and, as she caressed its shiny, maroon surface, sighed with anticipation.

The only difference between the two cryo-chambers was that
the stand underneath contained hidden drawers. Stripping down
to her birthday suit, Mona opened one of the drawers and placed
her folded clothes inside. She then opened a much smaller drawer
and removed a syringe. After injecting its contents into her arm,
she replaced the syringe back in the drawer and hurried to the
bathroom. Almost as soon as she sat on the toilet she began to
urinate. From the stream's force, Mona felt as if her bladder had
just become a fire hydrant. After what seemed to take forever,

her body was totally free of excess fluids. She had flushed her intestinal tract earlier that day. After wiping, she stood, washed her hands, and, as the toilet flushed, walked back out to stand beside what would be her home for the next ten years.

Without any hesitation, she opened the cryo-chamber and climbed inside. Mona then slid her PID into a slot near her hip and leaned back into the foam padding. "Judah," she croaked, her mouth already feeling like the Mojave. "Please initiate phase two of the Aurora protocol."

"Starting phase two . . . have a good sleep, Dr. Levin." And with that, her plan was finally underway. Lying perfectly still, Mona stared at nothing in particular as the foam cushion filled with gel. Soft medical cuffs encircled her arms and ankles. She winced at the expected pinpricks; then, as a powerful sedative entered her bloodstream, a warm, pleasant feeling engulfed her.

Shortly thereafter, the cryo-chamber's lid closed, the maroon-colored cylinder disappeared into its hidden recess, and Solomon Chavez's cryo-chamber glided back into position. If anyone were to enter the room at that very moment, they'd never guess that Dr. Mona Levin was there, an unconscious stowaway resting within a secret compartment, having become the six-thousand-one-hundred-seventy-third member of the Ark Project Expedition.

●

ORBITAL PLATFORM MEDIA CENTER: 11:37 A.M. GMT. JANUARY 20, 2061

"Ladies and gentlemen, this is Darren Brantley of *The Darren Brantley Show*, coming to you live from space, along with select journalists from around the globe, to broadcast what will quite possibly be the most momentous day in human history: the long-awaited launching of *Mona's Ark* into the vast reaches of interstellar space."

The hazel-eyed journalist stood directly in front of a five-foot tall by ten-foot wide, six-inch thick, clear reinforced gorilla-glass window that displayed the area of space where the *Arrow* would begin its voyage. He and the other members of the media watched as the final shuttle from the *Arrow*—returning with technical support personnel—approached the orbital platform's docking station. The *Arrow* itself was nearly fifty miles away and could not be seen from their vantage point, except for an occasional glint of sunlight reflecting off its light-gray hull. When the time came for launch, however, the window was programmed to magnify the scene, allowing the journalists to witness the launch alongside the rest of the world.

Like the others, Brantley wore a dark-blue CIMRAD coverall, which had been supplied to the press before they and the other VIPs were allowed to board the space elevator. He'd chaffed at the idea of wearing an outfit with a corporate logo on it but had relented when told that he was more than welcome to cover the event ground-side, along with the other uninvited journalists.

"In a matter of minutes," Brantley continued, addressing the camera in his famously smooth, easygoing style, "Lawrence Murchison, the current COO of CIMRAD, will present a prerecorded message from Dr. Solomon Chavez. This message will be followed up by a live HV connection with the ship's bridge, where Admiral Katherine Axelrod, famously known as "The Battleaxe," will bid humanity farewell on behalf of her and the rest of those extraordinarily brave souls making this astonishing one-way journey into space."

The equally telegenic Lawrence Murchison entered the room.

"Here's Mr. Murchison now. I'll rejoin you after the launch, with an exclusive, hour-long special, interviewing the people who made this launch possible." Brantley tapped a mode on his Bluetooth transceiver and quickly took his seat in the front row. There were five rows of seats, ten seats per row, each filled with journalists trying to keep their professional cool, though in truth, all were as excited as children going to the circus for the first time.

"Good morning, to both the members of the press and to those watching on Earth," a cheerful Lawrence Murchison said, his toothy grin seeming to stretch from ear to ear. "I will make a short statement before taking a couple of questions from the press corp."

The press was taken by surprise. A question and answer session hadn't been on the schedule. Hearing this made their journalistic juices flow.

"First of all, I'd like to say that it has been my distinct pleasure working for Dr. Chavez and his father. Some of you have questioned why I was chosen to lead CIMRAD after his departure. It's simple: I was his right-hand man for ten years and his father's for seven before that. I know the ins and outs of CIMRAD better than anyone. I will carry the company forward using the same business model that both Juan and Solomon Chavez ascribed to: creating products that further the health and welfare of mankind, while treating our customers and workers fairly."

He then looked directly into the camera. "Dr. Solomon Chavez shunned the limelight. To most of the world he was—*is* an enigmatic figure. He could've used his father's wealth to jet around the world, partying and womanizing for the rest of his life, but he did neither of those things. Instead, he carried on his father's work and made it his own. The world is truly indebted to him.

"I'll now take a couple of questions before playing his message."

Fifty hands shot immediately into the air. Murchison pointed to an up-and-coming Brazilian news anchor, whose supermodel good-looks had recently drawn the attention of the New York networks. "Ms. Fernandez." No surprise he called on her, as the rumors were flowing of a relationship between the two.

"Thank you, Mr. Murchison," she said, standing. Her coverall seemed to fit perfectly. Many of the male journalists looked down at their notes, trying to keep their eyes from straying to her shapely figure. "Lately there has been a decrease in terrorist attacks by the CRA. Some in the media," she said, cutting a quick glance in Darren Brantley's direction, "have suggested that the organization is lulling us to sleep in preparation for a much more dramatic attack."

"What's your question, Ms. Fernandez?" Murchison asked, looking annoyed.

"I'm sure the public would like to know," she said, unfazed by his interruption, "that every precaution has been taken to prevent another attack, like the bomb that destroyed Dr. Chavez's plane and the one that nearly destroyed Elevator City. My question is: Can you assure us that we won't be sitting here watching the *Arrow* go up in a ball of flames?"

"That's a fair question," he said, nodding. "Not only can I assure you, and the public, that every precaution has been attended to, Ms. Fernandez, I can *guarantee* that *Solomon's Arrow* will launch without a hitch."

Glancing around, Murchison studied the journalists, their hands in the air, and focused on the determined face of Darren Brantley, knowing that if he didn't call on the flamboyant hack, he would be trashed on the man's show for weeks. "Mr. Brantley."

"Thank you, Mr. Murchison." He ran his hand through his hair in dramatic fashion. "I was wondering . . . .where's Dr. Mona Levin? I was hoping to interview her. I assumed she'd be by your side on this momentous occasion . . . but she's not, and it seems that no one's seen her for the past two days."

Murchison hesitated, thrown by Brantley's question. He'd expected a cynical follow-up to Ms. Fernandez's question, not this mundane query as to Dr. Levin's whereabouts. "I'll check into that, Mr. Brantley. I've been told that she returned to the Lake Victoria complex the day before yesterday and is now at an undisclosed location, watching the launch in private. After the backbreaking work she's put into this mission, she can watch the launch anywhere she wants, in my opinion."

"Will she be available for interviews in the coming days?" Brantley asked.

"Possibly," Murchison said, pausing to think, "possibly not. I've been informed that she'll be taking a long vacation immediately after the launch."

"Do your 'sources' know where her vacation will be held, Mr. Murchison?"

"That makes three questions, Mr. Brantley. And no, my sources have not told me where Dr. Levin will be spending her vacation. Frankly, that's none of my business . . . nor is it yours."

A flurry of hands shot into the air. "That's all the questions I'll be answering."

Brantley received more than a few glares as the press groaned with disappointment.

"Moving on, it's now time for a message from Dr. Solomon Chavez."

●

Sitting at the helm of *Solomon's Arrow*, Richard Allison, who had recently been promoted to commander, watched the ten-inch by fifteen-inch view-screen embedded in the helm's control console and tried to keep the smile off his face. He'd seen Lawrence Murchison reply to Darren Brantley and was impressed by how well he handled the preening, self-absorbed HV host.

Hearing a soft chuckle, Richard looked to his left at the tactical console. Floyd Sullivant was shaking his head, a smile also on his face as he stared at his view-screen.

"That guy's always out to start trouble," he said, catching Richard's eye. "I wouldn't have let Brantley anywhere near Lake Vic much less the orbital platform . . . he's a dick."

With a mischievous glint in his eye, Richard replied, "Well, if anyone knows a dick, you do."

Floyd's double take was priceless. He let loose with a loud guffaw. "Yeah . . . I'm looking right at one. In fact, from now on I'm going to call you Dick, instead of Richard."

"That's Commander Dick to you, *Lieutenant*. That's your rank now, right, Floyd?"

Admiral Axelrod had commissioned the burly security officer earlier that month, stating that she wanted all of her senior officers to be military. "Don't remind me."

Both men heard a throat being cleared behind them. "Do you have a problem with your new status, Lt. Sullivant?"

Admiral Axelrod was standing outside her ready room door. Floyd spun around and came immediately to attention. "No sir! I'm happy to be of service, sir!"

"That's good to know. Chavez's speech is starting. I'll be in my ready room. My own will be shown live . . . so please, be sure you at least pay attention to that one. Have I made myself clear, gentlemen?"

"Yes, sir!" the two men answered in unison.

With that, Admiral Axelrod disappeared back inside her ready room.

A muffled snicker could be heard coming from the only other crew member on the bridge, Lt. Julie Norwood, the ship's navigator and communications officer. Richard ignored her and turned to face Floyd. "Floyd, take my advice: don't come to attention at your work station or anywhere else while on duty. It's not required and only makes you look like . . . um, like a dick."

"Ha, ha, you're a real laugh riot."

"Excuse me, boys," Lt. Norwood interjected, "but would you mind holding it down? There's at least one of us on the bridge who'd actually like to hear Dr. Chavez's speech." With a high and mighty expression on her face, the petite redhead turned back around to her own monitor.

Both men stared at her slim back for a second before exchanging a look of amusement. With a shrug, they went back to watching their monitors.

The rousing speech by Solomon Chavez, which he'd recorded the previous afternoon, was filled with soaring rhetoric and high praise. Richard, however, was so amped by the thought of breaking orbit that he barely paid the good doctor any attention. He was about to become the first human to pilot an interstellar spacecraft. This was his boyhood dream. At the same time, he was conflicted: he would never again see his wife and son's graves.

Richard shook his head, reminding himself that their caskets were empty. The recovery teams had salvaged a few chunks of the plane's fuselage, some seats, part of a wing, together with other assorted objects . . . but no people. As expected, the explosion had caused catastrophic damage to the passenger compartment. The oceanic impact had obliterated the rest. Their actual presence notwithstanding, Erin and David's adjacent graves were a symbol, one he'd visited on numerous occasions over the previous year and would greatly miss. So yes, he was conflicted.

Solomon Chavez was wrapping up his speech, so Richard paid closer attention.

The enigmatic, dark-haired philanthropist was standing on the banks of Lake Victoria as he spoke to the world. ". . . and in conclusion, I'd like to say that the date of the *Arrow*'s departure, January 20, 2061, was not chosen at random. If you haven't heard by now, it coincides with the one-hundredth anniversary of President Kennedy's inauguration. It was his call to action that jumpstarted America's space program and sent a man to the moon, which in turn led directly to this great day.

"The human race has come a long way in the last one-hundred years." He paused to look over his shoulder at the vast stretch of water behind him. When he again faced the camera, Solomon's tan face contained a wistful expression. "With any luck, the Ark Project will colonize a planet that approaches the beauty of our home world, but it'll never exceed the profound glory we have here on Mother Earth. I hope, with all my heart, that future generations will solve the problems that brought about the need for an expedition such as this. However, humanity must hedge its bets. We must reach for the stars to ensure our survival. But whether we succeed or fail, this effort will hopefully inspire future generations to say, the Ark Project took a bold step to shelter humanity from eminent disaster, and now it is our turn to chart a new course." Solomon paused dramatically, his coal-black eyes reaching intimately through the camera. "The future awaits you . . . but this is now. As such, it's time for me and all those courageous individuals aboard the *Arrow* to say farewell. As you go about your daily lives, all I ask is that you pray for our safety and success. Thank you, and may God bless the human race."

Richard was surprisingly touched by Solomon's speech. He watched as the enigmatic man's face was replaced by Admiral Axelrod's. She stood at attention, hands held behind her back, a real-time HV projection of Earth floating behind her.

"Dr. Solomon Chavez has spoken eloquently," she said. "I, however, am not one for flowery language. I am a military officer who speaks candidly to those under my command. However, this is not a military mission. I have well-trained military officers on this ship, but no soldiers. The *Arrow* is a ship of peace, of exploration and discovery, not conquest. When we've finished building a colony on the habitable planet orbiting Epsilon Eridani, I will lay my uniform down and serve in other ways. We will be starting over, but we will not be starting from scratch. We have the knowledge, and *hopefully* the wisdom, to create a civilization with no need for soldiers, a home where we at last beat our swords into plowshares."

The admiral came to attention and snapped her white-gloved hand up in a salute. "On behalf of all those brave souls onboard *Solomon's Arrow*—I, Admiral Katherine Bethany Axelrod, bid the people of Earth a fond farewell."

With that, her hand snapped back down to her side and the screen faded to black. When that moment was documented for posterity, it would be noted that over three quarters of the world's population of twelve billion souls witnessed her address, and most of them would tell you they felt as though she'd saluted them personally.

Stepping out of her ready room, Katherine Axelrod stood for a moment admiring the bridge. It was small and serviceable, so unlike those extravagantly large bridges popularized in movies and on HV. Gazing down into Richard's expectant face, she said, "Well, what are you waiting for, Commander Allison . . . let's get this show on the road."

"Yes, sir!" he fervently responded, pressing a biometrically coded touch screen. "Engaging engines. Navigation heading laid in and awaiting your order."

The admiral took a deep, satisfied breath, before saying, "Take us out."

Slowly and steadily, *Solomon's Arrow* broke from Earth's orbit— and thus began humanity's first manned mission to another star system.

9

ONBOARD THE *ARROW*:
THREE YEARS INTO THE FLIGHT

I t had taken nearly a full year for the *Arrow* to achieve its top velocity of 99.9 percent the speed of light. The asteroid belt between Mars and Jupiter had been a little tricky to maneuver through, not because the crew feared being struck by one of its asteroids (the warp bubble protected the ship), but because they feared dislodging a sizable rock, which would then hurtle toward Earth. There were some tense moments as the ship approached the outer reaches of the solar system, where the Kuiper belt (a region containing dwarf planets and comets) and the Oort cloud (a vast sphere of ice and comets enwrapping the solar system) were located. Thankfully, the massive amount of material contained in each was spread out far enough that neither posed much of a risk. There was some marginal buffeting when they reached the Heliosheath, an area of intense cosmic wind located between the two outer layers of the solar system, but no major problems were reported.

After fourteen months, the *Arrow* finally left the Oort cloud and cruised unimpeded through interstellar space. By this time, the command crew was in desperate need of a rest, so their replacement shift was decanted from cryo-stasis and put to work.

Two years later, the second shift was exhausted. It wasn't as if their duties were difficult; quite the opposite, they were bored. With three weeks to go before the next scheduled decanting, that all changed.

Three hours into the night shift, the crew was going about its business—everything seemed normal: all the equipment was working up to specifications; deep space was clear, with no rogue, dwarf-planet sightings in months—when the ship lurched, sending many crew members tumbling to the deck. Lights flickered; instruments recorded anomalous readings; and worst of all, the crew became lightheaded, with some passing out. Those who did pass out were unconscious for only a few seconds before regaining their senses. While unconscious, each reported seeing fleeting memories floating like soap bubbles in their minds.

The lieutenant commanding the night shift ordered an account of all injures. A handful was reported, but none serious. When the incident occurred, she was on her way from the mess hall after picking up coffee for her and the bridge crew. The turbo-lift she was in had jerked to a stop, causing a few anxious moments, and spilling all the coffee, before continuing on its way.

"Vargas, let me know the moment you find out if there's been damage to instrumentation," she said. As usual, Bluetooth implants acted as intercoms. "And image the outside of the *Arrow*. I want the skin examined for any damage. I need to know exactly what caused this anomaly."

Once the turbo-lift regained power and she arrived on the bridge, Lt. Marla Pruitt was met by anxious looks from her crew. "Royce, what's our heading?"

"I had to make a quick adjustment, but we're back on course, Lieutenant."

"Good." she suddenly realized she hadn't contacted life sciences to check on the status of the passengers and crew in cryo-stasis. "Computer, connect me with Calloway in life sciences."

After a long pause, a female voice was heard. "Calloway here."

"How're the popsicles doing, Sharon?"

"We've had some . . . *strange* readings, Lieutenant," the deputy department head replied, her voice sounding a note of concern.

"How so?"

"We're in the process of analyzing data. I'll send you the report when it's complete."

"Make it quick. I'll be in the ready room," she told the bridge crew, "collating data."

Without waiting for a response, she strode into the auxiliary ready room and stood by her desk. Reaching up, she rubbed her temples, trying to relieve the headache building behind her eyes. "Computer, decrease the light-level by thirty-five percent. And have a maintenance bot clean up the coffee spill in turbo-lift 1-A."

She sighed with relief when she reopened her eyes. Reaching for a handkerchief, she dabbed at a small coffee stain on her blue coverall. "Computer, analyze the existing data on the incident we just experienced. Use your extrapolation program to draw a conclusion, however preliminary, about what just happened."

"Extrapolating all data gathered by human means and ship's sensors."

There was a long pause, which caused the lieutenant to worry.

"The available data have been collated, and the requested programming has determined that an unprecedented space-time distortion has occurred, Lt. Pruitt."

She was stunned. "What the hell could have caused a space-time distortion?"

The computer answered, "That is impossible to extrapolate at this time."

"What do you mean?" The *Arrow* contained the most powerful computer ever developed. How could it not know what caused this space-time distortion? It didn't make sense.

"Since the ship's sensors failed to register the anomaly's cause, there are not enough physical determinants present to provide a reasonable extrapolation of facts."

Something must have produced the anomaly; it wasn't caused by a damned space ghost! An intense desire to head straight to cryogenics and decant "The Battleaxe" swelled in Lt. Pruitt.

"Computer . . . institute a subroutine devoted to solving this problem. If any information comes in to change your determination, let me know."

At least she'd have an interesting report for the admiral when she wakes up, the lieutenant thought. "Computer, provide me with an injury report."

"Injuries were minimal. Ten scraped knees, seven bruised ribs, one broken wrist, and three minor concussions."

"What about the cryo-chambers? Life Sciences reported some strange readings."

"The anomaly affected them, but the present cryogenic readings appear normal."

"What? How were they affected?" The lieutenant rose to her feet, frightened by this news.

"That is undetermined, at this time," the computer responded.

"But the popsicles . . . let me rephrase that; the colonists and crew being kept in cryo-stasis are unharmed, correct?"

"Yes, Lieutenant," the computer replied. "Aside from the previously reported injuries, all six-thousand one-hundred and seventy-three humans currently onboard are in good shape."

"Hmm . . . finally some good news. That's all, computer."

Pruitt took a sip of coffee. Something the computer said didn't sound right. But what was it? The lieutenant racked her brain. What could it be? Then it hit her.

"Computer, how many people did you say are currently onboard this ship?"

●

Frustrated, Lt. Pruitt stood outside Solomon Chavez's stateroom glaring at the door.

"Isn't there any way to override the programming?" she asked.

Ensign Jeremy Fletcher, the security tech assigned to her shift, fidgeted nervously. "Sorry, Lieutenant, the security protocols are well written. I don't think Steve Jobs himself could crack this code."

Pruitt and Fletcher, together with a security officer and two mechanical engineers, had been standing outside Solomon Chavez's stateroom for the past ten minutes discussing their options.

"Perhaps we should wake Lt. Woolsey and ask his opinion," Fletcher suggested.

Pruitt shot him a cold look. "The day shift commander doesn't have seniority over the night shift commander, Ensign. This is my decision to make, and mine alone—is that clear?"

"Yes, Ma'am."

"Okay . . . perhaps we can get around this problem in a physical sense: through the ceiling or the cabin wall next door. But before we start tearing this ship apart, I need to know who's in there with Chavez. Computer, have you determined the stowaway's identity?"

"Yes, Lt. Pruitt," the computer's nondescript voice replied. "The stowaway is identified as Dr. Mona Levin, former chief engineer of the—"

"I know who Dr. Levin is, computer," she interrupted. "*Every-one* knows who she is."

"I knew Dr. Levin wanted to come on this mission," Fletcher mused, "but this is ridiculous." Noticing Pruitt's displeasure, his grin vanished. "What should we do? I mean, this information changes things, right?"

Shifting her attention back to the stateroom door, Pruitt pondered the question. "Yes, Fletcher, it does. If it had been anyone else, I'd order a crew to dismantle the adjoining wall and drag her kicking and screaming to the brig. However, I don't see Dr. Levin as a threat." She paused to think, rubbing her right temple. "I think the best course of action is to let Dr. Levin stay where she is . . . for now. Most likely, she's programmed her cryo-chamber to start the decanting process after Dr. Chavez is awakened. Since the admiral will also be awake, we can . . . hold on—

"Computer, initiate a subroutine that monitors Dr. Levin's cryo-chamber. When it begins the decanting process, inform security and Admiral Axelrod. When Dr. Levin wakes up, she'll have a surprise waiting for her."

"The subroutine is initiated, Lieutenant."

"Good . . . everyone return to your stations."

Lt. Pruitt slowly trailed the others down the hall to the turbo-lift. Dr. Levin had gone to elaborate lengths to conceal her presence onboard the ship. If not for the anomalous space-time disturbance, she'd still be undiscovered.

Pruitt thought about the report she'd fill out and realized the section about Dr. Levin *must* be flagged for consideration, immediately after the admiral decanting. She wished she could tell her personally—the old broad would pop a fuse. Unfortunately, Pruitt would be dreaming in cryo-stasis. As she entered the turbo-lift, she reminded herself that popsicles don't dream.

●

Something occurred during the space-time anomaly that was stranger than anyone at the time realized. It was understood that the cryo-chambers registered unusual readings, but no one knew how the anomaly affected those inside. Despite their brains being frozen, each "popsicle" (as they were humorously nicknamed) experienced not an ordinary dream, but a reliving of an important moment from their past, filled with such vivid detail that it seemed like a real-time experience.

Many of the dreams were pleasant; others were disturbing or utterly terrifying, but most were mundane. Only one dream would've shocked everyone, other than the dreamer himself, had they seen it with their own eyes. This is what took place . . .

THE CRYOGENIC MEMORY-DREAM OF DR. SOLOMON CHAVEZ

Juan fumbled with the beaker of acid, almost spilling it. With a gasp, he tightened his grip on the glass container and shook his head, trying to clear the cobwebs. How strange—it felt as if he'd nodded off for a second. If he wasn't more careful, he might spill it all over his lap, and if that happened his wife would be sorely disappointed, since they both wanted to have another child. To be safe, he decided to ask the guard if he could take a short break to brew a pot of coffee.

He stood up from his work station feeling oddly disconnected, as though he was experiencing déjà vu. What he needed was rest. The bastards were pushing him and his assistants much too hard for safety's sake.

He approached the guard, who eyed him suspiciously, and tried to act deferential. "May I have permission to brew a pot of coffee, Private Kruger?" he asked in passable German.

"It's almost lunchtime, Dr. Hernandez," the guard grunted. "Can't you wait until then?"

"Oh, well . . . yes, of course I can wait," he said. "I feel better from just moving about."

"Good . . . now get back to work. The colonel wants those animal tests done by mid-afternoon and a status report on the new serum's effectiveness on his desk by the end of the day."

Nodding, the young Brazilian doctor returned to his work station. He noticed his assistant shooting furtive glances his way, a look of exasperation on the woman's haggard face. Dr. Juan

Hernandez sat before his microscope and inserted a slide containing a fresh sample of monkey tissue. He knew what it would display: the same lack of cellular degradation as the other animals he'd tested with the serum had demonstrated.

He'd been working on this project for close to two years and was starting to lose track of the days. Was it the fifth or sixth of October? He wasn't sure. Looking up at the calendar hanging on the wall, his gaze rested momentarily on the month's calendar girl. She was strikingly beautiful, what with her auburn hair and form-fitting dress. One of his assistants had informed him that she was a popular American actress named Rita Hayworth, who everyone, including the Germans, lusted after. He had to admit, she was very fetching, but his heart belonged to one woman: his wife, Maria. Pulling his eyes away from the sultry screen siren, he focused instead on the day's date: October 5, 1943.

Something about the date seemed familiar, but what was it? His wedding anniversary was six months earlier, and his daughter Selena's birthday was still a month and a half away. So what was it? He racked his brain but failed to supply an answer. It was probably the residual effects of the déjà vu he'd experienced, nothing more.

Looking through the microscope, Juan brought the tissue sample into focus. It was just as he thought: there was absolutely no cellular degradation. The plant virus was working better than expected . . . *dammit!*

Swallowing with his dry throat, he looked over at the monkey cages lining the wall and wondered how much longer he could postpone revealing his momentous discovery: Colonel Gunter was getting suspicious—the fucking Nazi bastard!

Before he was abducted at gunpoint, Juan heard some of the horror stories attributed to the Third Reich. He'd been aghast. As such, he knew that once a viable serum was developed, he and his family, along with his assistants, would be lined up before a firing squad and shot . . . or put to death in a more unspeakable manner.

The day he and his family were abducted felt fresh in his mind. But then, traumatic events had a terrible staying power. He'd been a rising star in the Brazilian scientific community—even considered a prodigy by some. He'd already published a few well received papers in prestigious medical journals—both in Brazil and Spain. His name was getting noticed overseas, when suddenly he found himself here, in northern Argentina, held prisoner in a remote enclave, being forced to work for the Nazis.

"Quit woolgathering, Dr. Hernandez," hissed the German private.

With a start, Juan put his eye back to the microscope and resumed studying the tissue sample, hoping to discover why the test subjects had remained so healthy. He'd started his testing on flies, which lived fifty times longer than normal, then moved to mice and monkeys, all of which were doing fine—even after injecting them with non-lethal diseases. It was only recently they'd taken the next step: using virulent strains. Eight days earlier, he'd injected Pablo, the oldest rhesus monkey, with a fast-acting cancer, thinking the monkey's system couldn't possibly withstand the toxic onslaught. But he was wrong, judging by the sample he examined.

He was both thrilled and petrified by the results. On the one hand, he'd probably discovered the world's first anti-aging vaccine, one that would increase a person's lifespan by decades or centuries, perhaps longer. On the other hand, if the Nazis got their hands on it, they would deliver it straight into Hitler's blood-drenched hands. Juan knew that whatever else happened, he couldn't let that take place—hence the stalling tactics.

He heard approaching footsteps. Clarita, his assistant, stopped beside him, a manila folder in her hand. She looked stricken. "Here's the report on the bone marrow samples you ordered,

Dr. Hernandez. They check out. If I didn't know better, I'd swear Pablo was born yesterday."

Gritting his teeth, Juan cut his eyes sharply toward Private Kruger, his admonition provoking the woman's shoulders to slump and her cheeks to blush.

"Thank you, Clarita," Juan replied, his voice icy. "Please have the liver biopsy analyzed no later than one o'clock."

"Yes, sir."

Juan watched his dejected assistant walk back to her work station, thinking two things: she should've kept her mouth shut, and he couldn't understand why her addressing him by name had grated on his nerves. He'd felt a similar disconnect after hearing the guard use his name. Unable to put his finger on it, he decided to blame his frayed nerves. Constant stress over his family's safety had placed him in a state of unrelenting exhaustion. There were times when he thought of injecting himself with the serum, just to see if it would alleviate his weariness.

Troubled by such an outlandish thought, Juan Hernandez (who in the next century would be known as Solomon Chavez) rubbed his eyes and once again wished for a strong cup of coffee.

●

Walking a few steps behind his gray uniformed escort, Juan clutched the manila folder to his chest, trying to think of a way to parse the truth without actually lying to Colonel Gunter. The cruel SS officer was brilliant in his own way, and would see through a lie—especially after studying the report. All the facts were in the folder he clutched to his chest, none of his findings distorted.

The guard rapped sharply on Colonel Gunter's door and entered, with Juan following close behind. "Colonel, I have brought Dr. Hernandez, as you ordered," he said crisply, clicking his heels together.

Colonel Gunter, a middle-aged, gray-haired man who still sported a trim physique, was in the middle of sifting through a pile of paperwork. "Thank you, Private. You may wait outside."

The private clicked his heels again, his arm shooting out in the traditional Nazi salute. "Heil Hitler!"

The colonel returned the salute, though less enthusiastically. "Yes, Heil Hitler." He waited as Kruger completed an about-face and marched from the room. When the door closed, he said, "I pray you have come bearing good news, Herr Doctor. I grow increasingly weary of your South American humidity."

Both of the screened windows in the colonel's office were wide open, and the overhead fan was spinning languidly. It was October, barely springtime, yet the temperature was already in the low eighties and the humidity high, which was a nuisance for the colonel, who was accustomed to milder, European climes.

"Yes, sir," Juan said. "I have the promised report." He wished the next few words didn't have to come from his mouth, but there was no getting around it. He nearly cringed while saying, "The new serum is a complete success."

"Excellent! Excellent, Herr Doctor," the colonel enthused as he reached for the report. "The Führer has been waiting for this with bated breath. I'm certain you will be well rewarded . . . *if* it works as expected." The man's smile seemed warm enough, but his eyes spoke a cold truth: the only reward Juan would receive would be a bullet to the brain. "By tomorrow morning, I want a detailed chemical analysis *and* complete methodology on replicating the vaccine. We will also be starting the human trials."

Juan had been afraid of this. "Don't you think it's a bit premature, Colonel? We should study the latest group of monkeys for a few more weeks. What if they start showing symptoms and—"

"Nonsense! The study group has been symptom-free for nearly a month." The colonel leaned forward with elbows on his desk, his fingers steepled, watching him closely.

"Um . . . I suppose we could start the trials with a small, controlled group of volunteers," Juan reluctantly proposed.

"Yes, there's always that," the colonel mused. "By the way, how is your daughter feeling these days, Heir Doctor?"

The shift in subject took Juan by surprise. Selena, his nine-year-old daughter, had been catching frequent colds over the past few months and was less talkative than normal. The strain of captivity was taking its toll. "She . . . she's feeling better this week. But she wishes she were back in school, playing with her friends."

"I'm sure she does," Colonel Gunter said, pursing his lips in thought. "The sooner the trials are over, the sooner she'll be seeing her friends . . . and wouldn't it be better if she were in perfect health when that reunion takes place?"

At first, Juan wasn't sure what the colonel meant by his question, but then it hit him: the colonel wanted to use Selena as a guinea pig; he wanted Juan's beautiful, brown-haired, green-eyed daughter to be a human test subject!

"I-I'm not sure I understand what you're getting at," Juan sputtered. However, judging by the smirk on the colonel's merciless lips, Juan knew he was right about the question's implication: Gunter's cronies would study his daughter like a lab rat, and then put her to death, along with any witnesses—which meant he and his wife would meet the same fate.

The colonel changed the subject yet again. "This is a great and glorious day for the Third Reich, Dr. Hernandez! The tide is finally turning! We will soon win the war against the Americans and their corrupt Jewish allies. And when that inevitable day arrives, a thousand years of peace will follow, with Germany's visionary Führer, Adolf Hitler, helming the ship of state."

A chill raced up Juan's spine, his bowels clenching in terror. Without a doubt, he feared for Selena's life, but the colonel's revelation was what he feared most: the madman, Adolf Hitler, ruling the Earth for a thousand years . . . or more.

The colonel's ice-blue eyes studied him closely, forcing Juan to work mightily to prevent his body from visibly shaking.

"Your accomplishment will greatly benefit the world, Herr Doctor," the colonel said, using a measured tone of voice. "With it, the master race will not be dragged down into the mud with the mongrels. Believe me when I say that I admire you, Dr. Hernandez. You are quite amazing . . . for one who is not an Aryan."

"Th-thank you, Colonel," he croaked.

Gunter activated the intercom. "Private Kruger, you may escort the doctor back to his lab."

●

Juan's thoughts were a blur as he made his way back to the lab. All he could think about was Selena and what might happen if the virus failed. What if it reacted like the serum he'd tested on the second batch of rhesus monkeys? (Within twenty-four hours, their entire bodies were covered in buboes. The horrible agony they endured forced Juan to put them down the very next day.)

He was ninety-nine percent sure the present viral strain would work as expected, but it was that one percent chance that loomed large in his mind. He would burn this place to the ground before taking that chance with his beloved daughter's life.

He became aware of his surroundings only after reentering the lab. Clarita was placing a thick stack of manila folders in a file cabinet. She gave him a quizzical look. Kruger stood near the door, which prompted Juan to keep his fears silent. "The colonel seemed especially pleased with the test results, Clarita."

Seeing the haunted look in Juan's eyes, Clarita knew something else was wrong. She cut a quick glance at Kruger. "I'm pleased to hear that, Dr. Hernandez."

"Is that the data on viral replication?"

Clarita looked at the stack of manila folders in her hand. "Most of it is."

"Good. Gather it together and have it on my desk by—"

A muffled popping noise was suddenly heard coming from the compound's rear entrance. At first, Juan thought the noise was fireworks, but Private Kruger's expression said otherwise. The compound was under attack.

"You two," Kruger shouted, "don't go anywhere! I'll be right back."

He hurried from the room, shutting and locking the door behind him.

Juan heard what sounded like return fire and then an explosion, possibly a grenade. It sounded as if all hell was breaking loose outside the building. "Clarita, throw those papers in the sink."

She stood unmoving, frightened by the commotion and perplexed by his order. "Get moving! We're destroying as much data as possible. I don't know who's attacking us, but I do know this: Gunter wants to start the human trials tomorrow, and he plans to use Selena as a guinea pig."

"No! We can't possibly let that happen!"

"Then put those papers in the sink and douse them with acid."

"Yes, yes—" Finally coming to her senses, Clarita rushed to the sink, dumped the armload of papers, and began searching for a powerful acid. Juan headed to the refrigerated safe where he kept the serum.

Unlocking the safe and reaching inside, he removed a six-inch by eight-inch by four-inch, gray, plastic box lined with foam, designed to cushion the five bottles of serum from being damaged.

"We must destroy the serum and get out of here," he shouted over his shoulder, closing the safe. "After that, we'll break down the door and find my wife and daughter. They're—"

Gunfire echoed through the room. Juan jumped, nearly dropping the box of serum. Colonel Gunter stood in the doorway, a black leather attaché case in one hand and his Luger in the other, pointed right at Clarita. She was blinking rapidly, horror and pain on her face, a beaker of acid held over the sink. Her other hand clutched her throat, blood pouring from between her fingers. She gurgled something unintelligible, then tipped the beaker of acid and collapsed to the floor. Acrid smoke billowed up from the ruined paperwork.

Juan screamed, barely believing his eyes. Jerking his head in Gunter's direction, he bared his teeth in animalist fury.

"What was in the sink, Herr Doctor?" Gunter snarled, turning the pistol on Juan.

"Fuck you!" Juan shouted, rushing to Clarita's side and dropping to the floor.

The girl's eyes were wide with panic. She knew she was dying. Gouts of blood were surging from her mouth in time with her pumping heart. Staring up at him, Clarita tried to say something but couldn't; she was choking on her own blood. She reached up with her free hand and grabbed hold of Juan's lab coat, once again trying to speak. One last fountain of blood exited her open mouth—and then nothing, her eyes went dim and her hand dropped lifelessly to the floor.

Juan turned to his captor, who was advancing across the room. "You murdering bastard!"

"She was useless to us," Gunter hissed. "Now answer my question. What was in the sink?"

Juan looked down the barrel of the Luger pointing at his forehead. "She . . . she destroyed the viral replication data," Juan sputtered, expecting to hear another shot fired.

"Damnation!" Gunter spat. The sound of automatic weaponry was drawing closer. Instead of firing the pistol, he waved the barrel, urging Juan to his feet. "We need to leave, Herr Doctor. It seems that you are still of some use to the Reich."

Juan stayed on his knees, unwilling to move. Perhaps whoever was attacking the compound would free his wife and child—if he delayed long enough.

"I said move!"

Juan was climbing slowly to his feet when a bullet splintered the floor directly in front of him. He yelped with fear. For a split second he imagined being in the Old West, having outlaws fire at his feet. When Gunter waved the pistol a second time, Juan moved quickly.

"Just in case the compound is overrun, we need to reach the motor pool and escape with both the serum and the paperwork contained in my attaché."

"What about my wife and daughter?" Juan asked, opening the door.

"Don't worry about them, Herr Doctor. We have contingency plans. If my men cannot hold out against our assailants, your family will be secured. You will rejoin them either in Buenos Aires or Berlin."

Both men had exited the lab and were rushing toward the back of the building. As Juan passed a window, he glimpsed a group of green-clad men, obviously soldiers, not ten feet from his position. He picked up his pace.

"Good God!" exclaimed Gunter, stopping in front of the window. His mouth hung open. The glass suddenly shattered and an oval-shaped object bounced off his chest.

Juan immediately recognized the object and dove to the floor.

Gunter looked at his feet, also recognizing the object—a grenade. Before he managed to take more than half a step in Juan's direction, he was ripped apart by an explosion. Blood and gore, combined with plaster and brick, flew in all directions. The exterior wall blew outward. The ceiling collapsed, burying Gunter's shredded body.

Juan covered his head, but small- and medium-sized chunks of plaster struck his body a glancing blow. The concussion made his ears ring, turning him temporarily deaf. A cloud of dust billowed all around. As he staggered to his feet, his glazed eyes darted right and left, searching for the box containing the serum. There it was, half buried under rubble. The attaché case lay nearby, bits of gore stuck to its black leather exterior. The case was damaged but functional enough to protect the valuable research papers inside.

Juan couldn't leave either of the two lying around for the Germans (or their attackers) to find. Brushing away the bits of Gunter, he tucked the attaché case under one arm and, holding tightly to the box of serum, stumbled from the blast zone. A chunk of rubble had struck his thigh, causing a deep bruise. Other than that, he was in decent shape; unlike Gunter, whose sudden death couldn't have come at a better time. He'd never wished harm on anyone, but Gunter was an exception.

He thought about how frightened Maria and Selena must be. He had to find them quickly and devise a safe way to smuggle them from the compound. Pushing through a set of double doors, Juan nearly collided with five Germans, one of whom was Private Kruger.

"Where's the colonel?" Kruger demanded, grabbing his arm. "I was told he'd be with you."

A young lieutenant, who looked like a prototypical Aryan pulled straight from a Hitler Youth poster, confronted Juan. "What are you carrying? Is that the research Colonel Gunter was after? Answer me, swine!"

Juan was terrified. The lieutenant, whose name was Schmidt or Shultz or something, was wearing an expression of utter contempt on his cruel, perfectly chiseled face.

"Gunter's dead," Juan sputtered. "A grenade killed him."

"Hand me those papers and the box, Herr Doctor," the lieutenant ordered.

Clutching the attaché case tighter, Juan started to shake his head when the lieutenant's arm jerked upward—in his hand a pistol, its barrel pointed squarely between Juan's eyes. "Very well, your fate is sealed," the German snarled.

"No, Lieutenant, don't!" Private Kruger cried. "We need this man."

The young lieutenant gave Kruger a sharp look. "And why is that, private?"

"Dr. Hernandez is our lead researcher. Colonel Gunter says he's as smart, or smarter, than the Jewish scientists that defected before the war. He's a Brazilian Einstein. The Führer still needs him . . . I'm certain of it."

The lieutenant looked Juan over, his cold appraisal nerve-racking. Suddenly, a multitude of voices were heard emanating from behind the double doors in the blasted hallway: English voices with American accents. The lieutenant's expression changed dramatically.

Two German guards stepped forward, rifles held at the ready. Raising his hand, the lieutenant shook his head and motioned for the others to beat a hasty retreat. Grabbing hold of Juan's upper arm, he shoved him forward, the squad immediately encircling the two men. When they were out of earshot, the lieutenant said in a hushed tone, "The Americans fight like ghosts. They possess advanced military training—a Special Forces unit, most likely. Our goal has changed. We will retreat to the motor pool and escape with the serum and the prisoner, if it's not yet overrun."

The squad turned a corner and dashed by three soldiers who were headed in the opposite direction. The lieutenant barked for them to bring up the rear. Following orders, they fell in line. Kruger hurriedly informed them of their new mission.

Juan was still hearing plenty of gunfire, but it wasn't nearly as intense as the previous few minutes. Judging by what the lieutenant said about the enemy combatants, he deduced that the Americans were winning the battle. As he entered the mess hall and raced toward the kitchen doors, Juan's concern for his family steadily increased.

The kitchen was deserted, its crew having abandoned their spatulas and ladles in exchange for rifles and handguns. The squad cautiously approached the back entrance. One of the soldiers poked his head out the door then quickly pulled it inside.

"All clear, Lt. Schmidt," he said crisply.

Schmidt nodded. "Once we're outside, form a shield around me and the doctor, then head toward the motor pool, using any available cover. On my mark . . . go!"

The squad exited the building without incident. It wasn't until the last soldier stepped outside that the bullets began to fly. Lying in wait behind a stack of crates was a squad of marines. Their orders: shoot anyone exiting the building. They opened fire, cutting into their enemy.

The front four soldiers went down immediately. The others dove to the ground and, using the bodies of their dead comrades, and some nearby wooden pallets, returned fire.

Leaping over fallen soldiers, Juan crashed through the kitchen's back door. Bullets ricocheted off the doorframe as he lunged inside. Racing through the kitchen, he nearly lost his footing on the greasy floor. Regaining his balance, he burst through the mess hall doors and stopped short, smelling smoke in the air. Was the building on fire? He suddenly heard someone entering the backdoor. Since the mess hall doors were still swinging, Juan caught a glimpse of Lt. Schmidt. The German's flinty blue eyes were furious.

With the attaché case tucked under one arm, and the box of serum stuffed in the side pocket of his bloodstained lab coat, Juan sprinted to the nearest exit. He was halfway down the hall and rounding a corner when he heard the mess hall door crash open.

"There's nowhere to run, Doctor!"

Juan didn't believe him. Anxiously, quietly, he turned the first doorknob he found. Finding it locked, he bit his lip to keep from cursing out loud. Perhaps Schmidt was searching for him in the opposite direction. He might have panicked, had he known the Nazi was creeping steadily down the hallway toward his position. Schmidt was less than ten feet away when Juan tried the next doorknob. It turned. With heart pounding, he slipped into the small administrative office. Thankfully, it was empty, and contained a window he could use to escape the building.

He gingerly eased the door shut. After slipping around the desk, he approached the window and reached for the latch. If he was quick enough and careful enough, he would be outside, on his way to rescue his family. He froze, his blood running cold at the vision he was seeing through the window's dusty panes.

The dormitory where he hoped to find Maria and Selena was engulfed in flames.

The attaché case clattered to the floor. Frantically fumbling with the window's latch, Juan felt the beginnings of a horrified shriek rising in the back of his throat. *This can't be happening! This isn't real! They escaped before the fire! Gunter told me they were safe!*

From the corner of his eye, he saw what started the blaze: an American soldier was using a flamethrower on an adjacent building. A small group of German soldiers exited, their bodies burning. He could hear their high-pitched screams. They stumbled and fell shortly after exiting the building. They looked like piles of burning refuse, just like the scattered piles burning outside the dormitory where his family . . . One of the burning piles was much smaller than the rest.

●

A loud, choking sob, which was escalating into a tortured wail, escaped Juan's lips as his trembling fingers turned the window's latch. His breath caught in his throat. He tried to raise the window to crawl outside, but his arms were quivering, his legs shaking at the sight of what he knew was his daughter's scorched body.

Juan collapsed to the floor. In his grief, he failed to hear the door open behind him. Seconds later, the barrel of a gun was pressed against the back of his head.

"Stand up, Herr Doctor," Schmidt demanded.

Just then, something inside of Juan snapped. A loud howl, which momentarily surprised Schmidt, burst forth from Juan's throat. He jerked sideways, spinning his arm around, striking Schmidt's wrist, which knocked the pistol from the young man's grasp. His other hand slammed into Schmidt's rib cage. With a pain-fueled yelp, the German staggered backward, clutching his cracked ribs, barely able to suck air, his eyes locked on the skittering gun.

Both men dove for the weapon but Schmidt was closer. Grabbing hold of it as he landed, the German turned and rolled. Before he could do anything, Juan was atop him, enraged, ripping the weapon from his grip. Instead of shooting the young lieutenant, Juan threw it aside and, in his crazed grief, wrapped his fingers around Schmidt's throat, squeezing, channeling every ounce of heartache and misery onto the German struggling beneath him. To his everlasting horror, by the time Juan came to his senses and realized the extent of his fury, Schmidt's body was limp, his eyes bulging, his larynx crushed.

In shock, Juan scrambled backward, away from the corpse, unable to believe what he'd done. He'd turned into an animal, a madman, a murderer. Juan looked down at his hands and felt like an enemy of the medical profession, a betrayer of the Hippocratic Oath.

A slew of emotions were bludgeoning him, making him sick to his stomach. He had to think. Violently shaking his head, Juan crawled back to the window and, slowly rising to his feet, forced it open. While climbing through, he heard voices in the outer hallway. The Americans were sweeping the building, looking for survivors.

For some unknown reason, the Americans seemed more like invaders than liberators, which triggered Juan's flight response. Climbing stealthily out the window, he dropped to the ground, primed and ready to flee. That's when he remembered the attaché case. Pulling himself back up over the sill, he reached inside and grabbed the case. As he dropped back to the ground, he heard the sound of heavy military boots step into the office. He ducked, moving out of sight and away from the open window. At first he crept along the wall, but then, as his fear built to a crescendo and the smoke threatened to start a coughing fit, he pushed off and sprinted toward the burning dormitory. Whether his wife and daughter were among the charred bodies or still trapped inside the burning building, they were beyond rescue. Either way, he couldn't allow his research to fall into the wrong hands.

The soldier wielding the flamethrower stood fifty feet away, facing the other building. Juan came to a halt in front of his dormitory, unable to draw any closer. The heat was so intense that it felt as if his clothes might burst into flames at any second.

Purposely keeping his gaze averted from the burned bodies lying at his feet, he took the attaché case firmly in hand, reared back, and flung it as forcefully as possible into the flames. By this time, part of the building had collapsed, and the case disappeared from view. He knew there would be no salvaging those papers.

The box of serum was next. Removing it from his lab-coat pocket, Juan reared back like a baseball player, ready to heave it into the flames. He was all set to throw it, but hesitated. After working so hard to create the serum, he simply couldn't destroy it. As he returned the box to his pocket, a gust of wind brought acrid smoke his way, causing him to choke and gag.

"You there!"

Juan's head jerked toward the voice. Looking over his shoulder, still coughing, he spotted a squad of ten American soldiers rounding the corner of the research building. They were running his way, the lead soldier pointing directly at him.

"You, whoever you are, come here!" the soldier ordered.

In a panic, Juan raced toward a line of trucks parked beside the motor pool. Multiple shots rang out. Dirt kicked up beside him. Changing direction, he sprinted toward the burning building, bobbing and weaving as he ran. Additional shots rang out, causing more dirt to kick up around him.

Suddenly a stab of pain lanced through the flesh of his left side, just above his hip bone. Juan was staggered, thrown off balance, almost falling. He'd been shot. The pain was intense. Being a doctor, he knew it was merely a flesh wound. He pressed on. Seconds later, he was shielded by the burning building.

He was in luck. Part of the building had collapsed, striking a nearby light pole, which itself had fallen, knocking down a section of the chain-link fence that surrounded the compound.

Pressing his palm against his bleeding side, Juan raced to the downed fence and scrambled across, disappearing like a wraith into the foreboding Argentine jungle. For the next twenty-five minutes he refused to stop running, despite his physical and emotional exhaustion.

At last, Juan threw his spent body to the ground and sucked in great gulps of air, all the while sobbing with inconsolable grief. All of his hopes and dreams were dashed, destroyed in one fiery afternoon. As he lay staring at the jungle canopy, cheeks wet with tears, an image of his wife and daughter formed in his mind. Focusing with a fury, he burned their faces into memory, never wanting to forget. It was all he had left, for together with their bodies, their family photos had gone up in flames.

He lay there losing track of time, sinking into despair, until he realized that his family would be ashamed if he let grief and despair ruin his life. He vowed, in their name, to return to civilization and devote the remainder of his life to the betterment of mankind. But first, he had an important decision to make.

Removing the cushioned box from his lab-coat pocket, Juan popped open the lid and gazed down at the small bottles of serum. In a few hours, the serum would be spoiled, thus depriving the world of a golden opportunity. Knowing he was left with only one possible option, Juan removed a bottle of the crystal-clear serum and the accompanying syringe. He slipped the needle into the rubber stopper and drew the appropriate amount, according to the calculations he made for the start of the human trials. Since he'd been sweating profusely after his headlong dash into the jungle, he was glad the box contained packets of alcohol swabs tucked inside a mesh pocket.

He was terribly frightened. But, if the gamble paid off, he'd have plenty of time to study his body and synthesize the serum for the general public. Disease would be eliminated; death might be overcome. However, should it fail, he would be joining his family in heaven. Either way, both were acceptable outcomes.

Juan removed his lab coat, rolled up his shirtsleeve, and wrapped the coat's belt around his bicep. Then, before his good sense talked him out of such foolishness, he swabbed the site with alcohol, slid the needle into his vein, and injected the experimental virus into his body. Without hesitation, he smashed the remaining bottles of serum between two rocks and tossed the box deep into the surrounding undergrowth.

The already defuse jungle light was growing murky. Not having matches to build a fire and fearing that the Americans would spot its smoke if he did, Juan found a tree to sleep in and worked his way up into its sheltering branches. He didn't sleep a wink, as the nighttime jungle sounds, many of which were animals (some predatory), were constant.

The following day, consumed with a powerful thirst, he set out through the jungle in hopes of finding civilization. By late afternoon he'd become feverish. In spite of his thirst, he refused to drink the water, fearing it contained parasites. This decision only served to make his fever worse.

After stumbling across a well-defined pathway, created either by humans or animals, Juan staggered northward, following the path even as darkness closed around him. His fever was growing steadily worse. He started hearing strange noises all around. When he saw a light ahead, he wasn't clear if it was real or part of a fever dream. Staggering faster, he broke out from the path and into a clearing. What he saw should've struck fear in his heart, but his exhaustion overpowered his fear. All he cared about was that he'd found a human settlement, even if it did contain grass huts, scattered bonfires, and barely clad natives, some of whom were holding spears. He lurched forward, hearing unintelligible songs coming from the natives, who were still unaware of his presence—though not for long.

Looking sick and bedraggled, he staggered into the firelight, drawing sharp cries from most of the women and some of the children. The men turned their spears in his direction and leapt to shield their families. In his feverish state, Juan was completely unaware of their fear and anger.

His head was swimming. Taking another shaky step forward, he saw the bonfires spinning back and forth like a merry-go-round in his field of vision. Falling to his knees, Juan Hernandez, the man who would eventually become Solomon Chavez, pitched forward in relief, not caring if the natives were friend or foe. As a black cloud of unconsciousness engulfed him, his last coherent thought was of an image he'd burned into his memory from the day before: the image of his wife, Maria, and his daughter, the beautiful, angelic Selena.

PART THREE:
HITTING THE MARK

"I was here from the moment of the beginning, and here
I am still.
And I shall remain here until the end of the world.
For there is no ending to my grief-stricken being.
I roamed the infinite sky, and soared in the ideal world,
and floated through the firmament. But here I am prisoner
of measurement."
— From the poem "Song of Man," by Khalil Gibran

10

ONBOARD THE *ARROW*: TEN AND A HALF YEARS INTO FLIGHT

"It looks like he's coming around."

Whoever spoke, their words sounded distant, ethereal to Solomon's ear. Was he imagining things? No, he was definitely hearing words. It took a moment before his brain interpreted their meaning. Had his brain turned to thick, gooey paste?

"It should only be a few more seconds."

The words were closer, their meaning clearer. The blackness had turned to gray then pink.

Where am I? Who am I? Oh, yes, I'm Dr. Juan Hernandez . . . No! I'm Solomon Chavez . . . can't ever forget that! I'm on an interstellar flight to the Epsilon Eridani star system. My mission: help colonize to a habitable planet. Yes, everything's coming back to me now.

Solomon opened his eyes and blinked from the light, despite its dimness. It would take a few minutes for his vision to adjust.

"What—" he cleared his throat; his voice sounded hoarse. "What's happened? Why haven't we left yet?"

Two people stood beside his cryo-chamber, gazing down at him: Admiral Katherine Axelrod and Dr. Gurdev Singh, ship's doctor and head of Life Sciences. Solomon turned his attention to the doctor, who was leaning forward, his broad, amiable face lit with a smile.

"Ah, but we have already arrived, Dr. Chavez. We have reached our destination."

Was it possible? Had they succeeded? It felt as if he'd fallen asleep moments ago—except for the disorientation he was experiencing, and the pounding headache, and the unsettling thought of waking from a dream he couldn't remember.

"Wonderful," he croaked. "There's so much to do before we—" He tried to lift himself up onto his elbows, but his body was too weak.

"Not yet, Dr. Chavez," Singh cautioned. "We must first strengthen your muscle tone. Over the next twenty-four hours, you'll engage in a regimented series of reconditioning exercises. This is not optional," he stated firmly. "However, that should not preclude you from receiving status reports."

"That's right, Solomon," added the admiral. "There's been, let's just say, a few *wrinkles* we need to discuss."

Solomon didn't like the sound of that. Her mentioning the word *wrinkles* made him wonder if she was referencing his age, which prompted him to wonder if his secret had been discovered. He studied the two closer. They weren't acting like he was in trouble. It must be something else.

"But first things first, Dr. Chavez," Singh added. "We need to get you up and about."

At that point, the admiral said her goodbyes and exited the stateroom. Singh waved over two orderlies, who helped Solomon from the cryo-chamber and into his clothes, then placed him in a wheelchair. He was barely listening as Singh talked about taking him to Life Sciences, where he would receive a comprehensive examination and some nutrients. Sadly, the nutrients to which Singh referenced were an IV full of vitamins and electrolytes, designed to rev up his metabolism and replenish his body. For the first twelve hours, he would be restricted to a liquid diet before being allowed any solid foods. He understood the necessity, but that didn't mean he liked it.

Two hours later, while being given a stress test, Admiral Axelrod entered the medical ward. Solomon stepped off the treadmill, wearing nothing but a pair of boxer briefs, and picked up a towel to wipe the sweat from his brow and upper body.

"How's he doing, Doc?" the admiral asked.

Dr. Singh shook his head as he typed the test results into his Medical Interlink Device. "He's in perfect shape; a truly remarkable specimen of humanity, I must say."

Solomon tossed the towel aside. "I'm starting to feel like an actual specimen . . . having been probed and prodded all day."

"Are you almost done with him, Doc?" asked the admiral.

"Very nearly. All that's left is to take a urine sample and blood test."

Solomon didn't like the sound of that. A urine sample would be most likely problematic, but testing his blood was definitely out of the question. For over a hundred years he'd zealously guarded against such invasive procedures, not allowing any of his DNA to fall into the wrong hands. Not only might his secret be discovered, but some pharmaceutical company might get hold of a sample and find a way to unlock the viral code that extends his life.

After his escape from the Nazis, and his subsequent injection of the serum, the virus had made him feverish. That, combined with his dehydration, had caused him to pass out after stumbling upon a native village. Thankfully, they weren't cannibals or headhunters: they took him in and nursed him back to health. He then lived with the tribe for nearly two years, helping them hunt and fish and learning their ways (for the most part). He'd grown quite fond of them and was sad to say goodbye when word came that the war was over.

With their help, he'd made his way to a town with a bus station and a Western Union office, where he sent word, informing a colleague that he was still alive. Money was wired, and the following day he was clean and clothed and traveling home to Brazil.

His wife's family was happy to learn of his survival, but he could tell they blamed him for Maria and Selena's deaths, adding to his guilt. His colleagues were overjoyed when he returned to work, but it wasn't the same; he'd been scarred by his experience. When the authorities questioned him about his research at the compound, he'd lied, telling them he'd been forced to work on finding better, stronger antibiotics for German soldiers. They were skeptical, but ultimately had no choice but to believe his story. In his spare time, he'd run tests on his blood and tissue samples, but was unable to determine how the virus changed his physiology. After almost a decade, he left Brazil and moved to England, hoping to make a new start. That's when he realized that not only had he not been sick since the night he stumbled into the Argentinean village, but he also hadn't aged a single day. The serum had worked.

This, however, posed a serious problem. Unless he came clean and announced his discovery to the world, he would be forced into moving every ten years or so to avoid the inevitable questions surrounding his appearance. Solomon wrestled with the subject for the better part of a decade. By then, DNA had been discovered by Drs. Watson and Crick, leading him to believe that the virus had altered his chromosomes.

With the dawn of the sixties, the world's population was exploding, and violence seemed to be the norm. Societal changes were taking place that made him wonder if his discovery would do more harm than good. He'd amassed a considerable fortune by then (still a fraction of what he would eventually be worth) and realized that only the wealthy would be allowed to benefit from his discovery. The average person would never be given the treatment. Even if the production costs were minimal, the cost of treatment would be artificially inflated to prevent the world's billions from living for centuries or perhaps millennia. A world full of healthy, ageless people would be unsustainable: society would collapse under the strain of overpopulation. On the flip side, if the serum was sold only to those who could afford it, a new caste system would develop, creating an insurmountable chasm between those at the top of the economic ladder and the common man, who would riot in the streets. To Solomon, those disastrous outcomes outweighed any benefit the serum might provide. In the late sixties, he decided it was too dangerous to reveal his secret.

That being the case, he couldn't allow Dr. Singh to take a blood sample.

"Will all six thousand colonists be poked and prodded like me, Doctor?" he asked.

"Oh no, far from it," Singh responded. He was eyeing the syringe in his hand and failed to notice the icy edge to Solomon's voice. "They'll be watered and fed a nutrient shake, then given a list of exercises to regain their strength. You're the exception, being such an important part of this expedition. I wanted to make sure you—"

"In that case," Solomon snapped, "we're done here. As you said, I'm in perfect health. I feel great and therefore shouldn't be treated any differently than the others onboard. When we disembark, you'll find me with hammer in hand, or plowing a field, just like everyone else."

Singh frowned. "But you *are* different, Dr. Chavez. You're not just a man, you're a symbol." He gave Solomon an imperious look, "If you truly wanted to be treated like everyone else, your cryo-chamber would've been stored with the others, not in a locked, private stateroom. Now give me your arm."

Solomon's temper flared. He took a step forward, his fists balled. "I can tell you where you can stick that syringe, Doctor."

Singh's mouth fell open. "W-what was that?" he sputtered.

"You heard me," Solomon growled, snatching up his t-shirt and coveralls. "Come on, Kate, let's go to your ready room. You wanted to talk to me about something." Donning his t-shirt and angrily zipping up his coveralls, Solomon strode away. The admiral followed, trying desperately to keep from grinning.

●

"You do have a way with people, Solomon," the admiral said.

They'd been largely silent en route to her ready room, which gave Solomon the opportunity to gain control of his temper. "Yes, well . . . Singh has a habit of getting under my skin."

"He doesn't have the best bedside manner," she responded, "but he's an excellent doctor."

Solomon shot her a look. "I know . . . that's why I hired him."

The admiral stopped beside her desk. "Don't get snippy with me, Solomon. I won't take it as well as Singh did."

Chastened, Solomon looked away. "Sorry about that, Kate. I'm still recovering from cryo-stasis."

"Think nothing of it," she said. "I was even more of a bitch, when I was decanted."

Despite his age, Solomon had yet to master the art of patience. Even so, he was particularly surly. The effects of cryo-stasis had affected him more than he realized.

"So, you wanted to discuss some incidents that took place during transit?" he said, changing the subject.

"Quite right. We had two incidents that occurred during transit, and one that occurred before launch. We wouldn't have even known about the first and third incidents if the second one hadn't taken place. It's the greater mystery."

She went into detail, explaining the strange space/time fluctuation that occurred three years into the flight. "I received the report nearly a year ago, after being decanted. I must admit, I'm flummoxed, as are the quantum engineers studying the event. Also, the ship's computer has been running a subroutine for the past seven years, with no results. It claims there's not enough data to formulate a theory. It's supposed to be the most advanced computer in history, yet its first real test throws it for a loop."

Solomon rubbed his chin. "Hmm, that is unusual. The ship's computer was designed by Dr. Mona Levin and contains quantum algorithms. It should be able to extrapolate an answer even with minimal data."

The admiral leaned forward in her seat. "Speaking of which, I have a video to show you."

Solomon gave her a quizzical look and then directed his attention to the HV screen embedded in the starboard wall.

"Computer, display the video from evidence log 1A-a on the primary ready room monitor."

Solomon was puzzled. The video showed the door to his stateroom, recorded from a spy-eye in the corridor. Mona Levin exited his stateroom, and then stopped, looking uncharacteristically nervous.

"Computer, fast forward five minutes and eighteen seconds," the admiral ordered.

Mona's movements looked jerky as the video increased in speed. It slowed to normal just before the door to his stateroom opened. Mona glanced back down the corridor at someone who had unexpectedly drawn her attention. The med-tech who placed him in cryo-stasis was exiting his room, but Mona blocked her from leaving. As a tall, baldheaded man came into the frame, Mona pulled an envelope from her pocket and told the med-tech that . . . what?! She was in love with him? And she was pleading to leave him a love letter? At that point, the med-tech reluctantly allowed Mona to reenter his room, alone.

Admiral Axelrod saw the flabbergasted expression on his face. "You appear shocked at the thought of Dr. Levin being in love with you, Solomon."

"Well, yes, I, uh . . . we'd been colleagues for over a decade and she never hinted—" Solomon stopped speaking, unable to finish his thought.

"As you'll soon learn, her rather awkward declaration of love was nothing more than a ruse."

Solomon was even more confused. "I don't understand."

"Computer, fast forward to the point nine minutes and thirty-five seconds after Dr. Levin's exit and the stateroom door closes."

The med-tech and the assistant engineer quit speaking, and the video picked up speed. The door zipped open, Mona popped out of the room, and all three disappeared in a flash down the corridor.

Solomon was frowning, a bubbling suspicion rising to the surface of his awareness.

"Computer, skip ahead to the requested point in time," said the admiral.

Seconds later, Mona suddenly reentered the HV video frame, trying to catch her breath. She pressed the stateroom entry button but nothing happened. Solomon chuckled, believing his security protocol had denied her entry. That was until Mona spoke to her PID, which, shockingly, revealed his password: Selena!

"What the fuck?!" he shouted, half rising from his chair.

Admiral Axelrod remained silent, observing his response carefully.

Gritting his teeth, Solomon watched as Mona punched in his password—and then, instead of walking inside like a normal person, made a mysterious move and *leapt* into the room. The door slid shut behind her and the HV screen went subsequently blank.

Solomon rounded on the admiral and snapped, "What the hell's going on, Kate? What did I just see?"

With a soft chuckle, she answered, "You just saw your colleague, Dr. Mona Levin, turn from being one of the world's most respected doctors into a stowaway . . . and there's more."

●

Solomon boiled inside as he stood in his stateroom watching Mona's cryo-chamber slip from its hidden compartment. He felt betrayed, yet not surprised, by her actions. She had, after all, tried many times to convince him that the mission rules shouldn't apply to her. He should've seen this coming. Nevertheless, her betrayal still stung.

"Ensign Jeremy Fletcher is our top computer technician. He discovered the operating code for Dr. Levin's cryo-chamber," Dr. Singh said, standing nearby. "She programmed the chamber to start the decanting process while the crew's attention is diverted by the first away mission. With you scheduled to be on that mission, she'd be able to recuperate without you showing up to catch her in the act. Ensign Fletcher rewrote the code so that we could wake her up at our convenience. Naturally, we've been waiting for you to be decanted before taking any action."

"In ten minutes," Singh continued, "all of her vital signs—temperature, oxygen, blood levels, and such—will be back to normal, and the re-enervation process will begin."

Dr. Singh eyed Solomon, still annoyed over the way he'd been treated earlier in the day. "I wish you'd allow me to complete your examination, Dr. Chavez. There are important questions that need to be resolved, such as why the—"

"I don't intend to rehash this, Doctor," Solomon said, shooting Singh an angry look. "I feel fine, so let's leave it at that."

Leaning forward, Singh frowned at the admiral. "Perhaps you can talk some sense into him, sir. If my only concern was for his health, it would be one thing, but we must know why his cryo-chamber readings were different from the others recorded during the space/time anomaly."

This caught Solomon's attention. "What are you talking about?"

Singh's black, bushy eyebrow rose in surprise. "I was hoping the admiral had informed you of the space/time distortion we experienced en route to this star system."

"She did, but what does that have to do with my cryo-chamber?"

"Yes, well," he said, avoiding the admiral's glare, "during the anomaly, there was a strange occurrence that affected those of us locked in cryo-stasis. Up to that point, our cryo-monitors displayed the appropriate reading: zero neural activity. However, when the anomaly occurred, our monitors recorded activity where none should've been. Each brain became active, despite being frozen. The instrumentation recorded an unusual brainwave function—one never seen before. We've tentatively labeled it *the Omega Wave*. See, the brain emits alpha waves and zeta waves and—"

"Yes, Dr. Singh, I'm well aware of how the brain works," Solomon groused.

"Yes, of course . . . of course you are," he acknowledged. "Anyway, each person in cryo-stasis experienced between thirty seconds to two minutes of these omega waves. Your brain was the exception: it was still emitting these omega waves two minutes after the anomaly ended, totaling four minutes and ten seconds of wave activity. Most unusual, wouldn't you say, Dr. Chavez?"

This news was troubling. "Yes it is," Solomon admitted. "Have you determined how these so-called omega waves affected our brains?"

Singh nodded. "The readings from your cryo-chamber were most valuable. Their duration allowed us to come up with a base-line model to compare against those in the cargo hold. We now believe that everyone experienced . . . a dream." He smiled, seeing the quizzical looks on the faces of Solomon and Admiral Axelrod. "But not a normal, REM dream," he expounded. "It appears that each person relived a moment from their past, with some reliving their past longer than others. Thankfully, there was one similarity between this cryogenic dream and a normal dream: the dreamer had no recollection of the dream. As such, if they dreamed of something traumatic, they would not be traumatized a second time . . . *hopefully*. At least that's the theory."

Recalling how he felt immediately after waking, Solomon suspected that Dr. Singh's theory was correct. He had no memory of dreaming, but he did wake up thinking about his daughter. Had he been dreaming of her? It was possible. Most days he woke up thinking about her and her mother, despite them being dead for over a century.

"I appreciate your interest in my case, Dr. Singh," Solomon admitted. "I'd like to postulate a theory as to why the readings of my cryo-chamber were at variance with the other six thousand in stasis. Since they are controlled by a separate system, there was probably a buffering effect that had nothing to do with my cryo-chamber. In my opinion, that's why my dream lasted longer. I've suffered no ill effects, so any further testing would be pointless."

"I beg to differ," Singh protested. "Perhaps later today or first thing in the morning you could come down to the medical wing and—"

"I've made myself clear," he interjected, annoyed with the man's continued insistence. "Now, if you'll excuse me, I want to be the only person in the room when Mona wakes up. I have a few questions to ask her, *in private*, before she's taken to the brig."

"I'm not sure that's appropriate," Singh declared, addressing the admiral, who was headed toward the exit. "There might be a conflict of interest."

Looking over her shoulder, Axelrod said, "Don't push it, Doc. If Solomon wants to ask Dr. Levin a few questions before security gets their mitts on her, I say let him. And, with it being my ship, I have the last word on the matter."

"I wasn't questioning your authority," Singh remarked, taking on an imperious tone. "It's just that, as it applies to medical issues, my authority supersedes yours, Admiral."

"I'm well aware of that, *Doctor*," she snapped, providing Singh a withering stare. "But I'm telling you right now: this is not a medical issue, so back off."

Without saying another word, Singh stormed from the room.

"Like I said, he's a jackass," she said, following him out the door.

With a shake of his head, Solomon sat in his reading chair to wait for his old colleague, Mona Levin, to regain consciousness.

●

As Mona's brain activity increased to the point of wakefulness, she at first thought something had gone wrong: she couldn't have slept for ten and a half years. However, as her mind stretched out into her body, she realized how sore she felt, which strongly indicated that her plan was a success.

The lid to Mona's cryo-chamber opened, and she filled her lungs with oxygen. After more than a decade of inactivity they were raw, painful to operate. If it weren't for the anti-emetic administered during the re-enervation process, she would've probably puked right then and there. She felt terrible. Her middle-aged body was having difficulty recuperating. This was one reason why only younger people could become colonists, as their bodies were more resilient than those in the older age groups. The elderly would've never survived the process, she imagined. Of course, the main reason for the age-restriction was to ensure fertility, which made sense if the mission statement was to colonize a new world.

Mona sighed. A muscle relaxant was working its magic, making her feel more comfortable, her body nearly pain free. Her vocal cords felt rusty, nonetheless. After clearing her throat, she opened her eyes and addressed her PID, her voice raspy, "Judah, how long have I been in cryo-stasis?"

"Ten years, four months, and twenty-eight days, Dr. Levin," the familiar baritone replied.

Something was wrong. According to her extensive preflight calculations, the ship wasn't due to arrive at the planet for another two weeks. Could she have miscalculated? It was probable, but highly unlikely . . . she was a mathematical genius, after all.

Since she was unable to see much of the room from her prone position in the cryo-chamber, Mona listened carefully, yet failed to hear anything of note . . . except for a soft, rhythmic tapping. It almost sounded like fingers on a . . . no, it couldn't be; it had to be something else.

Mona's heart was pounding. She desperately wanted to rise up, to see the cause of the noise, but her body refused to move.

It was nothing. The noise was nothing, she told herself.

After taking a deep, calming breath, she forced her arms to obey her will. Reaching up, she gripped the edge of the cryo-chamber and pulled herself to a sitting position.

Her body jumped with surprise. Solomon was sitting in his reading chair, staring straight at her, wearing an angry, disappointed look on his face.

"You couldn't leave well enough alone, could you, Mona?" His fingers stopped drumming the chair's armrest.

"I, um, Solomon . . . what are you—" she sputtered, unable to form a coherent thought.

Rising to his feet, Solomon took a menacing step forward. "How did you get the password to my door?" he hissed, looking ready to throttle her with his bare hands.

"I'm sorry," she rasped. Her heart was pounding and she felt lightheaded. Mona had seen him angry, but not like this.

"I'll ask you again. How did you get my password?"

His eyes were flashing with too much anger, too much passion—which made Mona's fear give way to suspicion. What was so important about that password that its revelation would spark such outrage? She wanted to ask him who Selena was—but she held back, deciding instead to tell the truth. She could always investigate this mystery at a later date.

"My PID circumvented security protocols," she replied. "If I'd been unsuccessful, I would've missed seeing your, um . . . unhappy face."

"You're damned right I'm unhappy," he said, though an odd glint of relief flashed across his face. "I'm joined by a few other unhappy people standing in the corridor." Solomon picked up a white robe lying on the table by his chair and tossed it to her, then activated his Bluetooth implant. "You can come in now."

Mona suddenly realized she was naked, and immediately covered her breasts as the door slid open. In walked Admiral Axelrod, along with Dr. Singh who was pushing a wheelchair, and two security officers, one of whom was Floyd Sullivant. Solomon was right: none of them looked particularly happy to see her.

"Judah, please initiate cryo-chamber exit protocol."

"Yes, Dr. Levin."

The left-hand edge of the chamber lowered, allowing Mona to swing her legs over the side.

Floyd Sullivant stepped forward. "Dr. Mona Levin, you are under arrest and charged with the unauthorized boarding of a secure vehicle, illegally tampering with said vehicle, illegally stowing away onboard that same vehicle, and other charges to be named at a later date."

With a heavy sigh, Mona reached for her PID.

Holding out his hand, Floyd continued, "You will relinquish your Personal Interlink Device, Dr. Levin. Your communication privileges have been revoked. Please stand. You will be escorted to Life Sciences, where Dr. Singh will perform a physical examination. A security officer will then escort you to the ship's brig to await court-martial."

11

ONBOARD THE *ARROW*: TWELVE DAYS LATER

fter decelerating for a year, the *Arrow* had slowed to a speed of twenty-five thousand miles per hour, and in two days would reach its destination—the lone habitable planet discovered in the Epsilon Eridani star system. There were six other planets in the system: two gas giants near the system's edge; three small, rocky planets close to the sun; and lastly, a planet approximately the same size as Mars, but covered entirely in frozen ammonia. The only other detail of note was a thinly scattered asteroid belt beyond the orbit of the gas giants.

Their destination, which they'd designated EE-4, was located in the Goldilocks Zone, not too close and not too far from the sun.

Solomon sat behind his stateroom desk, staring at an image on his computer screen of the planet they'd soon be colonizing, and wondered if they'd made a mistake. The planet was barely habitable. According to initial estimates, EE-4's surface contained a breathable atmosphere and some plant life, but little else to brag about. From all accounts, like Mercury, one side of the planet faced the sun at all times. Most of the planet's backside was covered in ice—thankfully, of the H2O variety. The sunward side was undoubtedly baked clean, which they would confirm after achieving orbit. From what they already saw, EE-4's only habitable region was a thousand-mile-wide stretch of land that encircled the globe between the planet's desert and ice regions. In the center of the habitable region, a five-hundred-mile-wide forest was detected, not thick enough to be deemed a jungle.

Solomon was studying the planet's telemetry readings when a voice addressed him over the ship's intercom. "Dr. Chavez, this is Admiral Axelrod. Please come to the executive officer's conference room, ASAP. A discovery's been made that I believe you'll find interesting."

"I'm on my way."

Slipping his PID into his breast pocket, Solomon exited the stateroom and hurried to the turbo-lift. The doors opened to reveal Dr. Singh inside. "Have you been called to the conference, as well?"

"Yes. It sounds rather important." When the turbo-lift arrived at the command deck, the two strode to the executive officer's conference room, located adjacent to the bridge, and took their seats at an oval table positioned in the center of the room. All of the ship's executive officers were present: Commander Richard Allison, sitting to the left of the admiral's empty chair; Lt. Floyd Sullivant, seated to the right; Chief Engineer Gary Wong, a rail-thin Peruvian of Japanese descent, sat beside him; and Lt. Julie Norwood, ship's navigator and communication's officer, who sat beside Commander Allison. Solomon sat beside her, with Singh seated across from him. Solomon was scooting his chair up to the table when the admiral entered through a door connected to her ready room. She was dressed like everyone else, in dark blue coveralls, with her rank embroidered on the collar. Her light-brown hair, which was showing a touch more gray these days, was styled in a French braid. Following close behind her was the ships' science officer, Lt. Commander Karen Albans: a smart, attractive, but somewhat reclusive woman in her mid-forties with short-cropped brunette hair. Solomon hardly ever saw her socializing with the rest of the crew.

Everyone began to rise to their feet.

"At ease, ladies and gentlemen, at ease," said the admiral. She stopped behind her chair and waited for Albans to take her seat beside Dr. Singh. "I have very exciting news to report," she said, pulling out her chair and sitting. "As I'm sure most of you know, the ship's computer has been running a data collection subroutine involving the space/time anomaly we experienced seven years ago. Approximately twenty minutes ago, Lt. Commander Albans was notified that the computer received new data that allowed it to reach a conclusion. I'd like you to take over from here, if you please, Albans."

"Yes, sir." She faced the view-screen embedded in the wall opposite the admiral. "Computer, activate view-screen in command deck conference room. Open space/time anomaly subroutine and run newly collated data projection."

A rudimentary CGI model of the solar system appeared. A glowing yellow dot, representing the *Arrow*, was converging on EE-4. Behind the *Arrow* sat a green dot labeled, *area of metallic residue and tachyon emissions.* This detail caught Solomon, and three others—Wong, Norwood, and Fletcher—off-guard.

Albans said, "That green dot represents metallic residue from a mechanical device—possibly of alien origin. Along with the device, the scanners detected—"

The room erupted, with Albans and the admiral being pummeled with questions.

"Quiet, everyone!" the admiral ordered. The hubbub immediately subsided. "Lt. Commander Albans will respond to all pertinent questions *after* the briefing is over. Go ahead, my dear."

"Thank you, sir." She shifted her attention back to the view-screen. "As I was saying, we also detected tachyon emission residue. Both the metallic residue and the emission signatures are over two thousand years old. Nothing has been detected that is of a more recent origin; therefore, if aliens did live in this system, they either left long ago or died out.

"Computer, display metallic device as it once appeared, extrapolating from observable data."

The CGI rendition of the Epsilon Eridani system was replaced by a rotating metallic ring measuring three hundred feet in diameter.

"What the hell is that?" Ensign Fletcher muttered, speaking for everyone in the room other than Albans and the admiral.

Albans stared at the others, a deathly serious expression on her heart-shaped face. "According to the computer's projections, this device was designed to fold space."

Solomon gazed at her incredulously, as if she'd just said that sunlight was made of lemonade.

"I kid you not," she added. "Whoever or whatever built this artifact, at one time possessed the technology to fold space."

Chief Engineer Wong broke the stunned silence. "Has the computer extrapolated enough data for us to reverse-engineer this device, Karen?" Wong's eyes were glued to the screen. "This discovery is incredible. It's the Holy Grail of engineering. It would change everything."

Albans shrugged her shoulders. "The computer is still working on it, Gary, but the prospect doesn't look good. There are a few recoverable bits and pieces, but the internal components were destroyed. Unfortunately, this is merely an extrapolation of what the device looked like, not of its internal workings, I'm sorry to report."

Wong addressed the admiral. "I have a question, sir. Once the colony is up and running, may I lead a mission back to this sector of the solar system? If the engineering department is allowed to perform a comprehensive study on the debris, it might prove fruitful."

Rubbing her lower lip, the admiral pondered his request. "Hmm, it might be worth—"

The computer suddenly interrupted. "Admiral, the ship is being hailed. The hailing frequency is originating from EE-4's surface."

●

Katherine Axelrod wasn't entirely sure she'd heard the computer correctly.

"What does this mean?" Solomon asked, sounding a note of uncharacteristic fear.

Albans and Norwood, the ship's science and communications officers, were both typing furiously on their respective Interlink Devices, trying to determine just that. The others were stunned into silence.

"Computer," Admiral Axelrod said, trying to stay calm. "Repeat your last statement."

"Certainly, sir. Admiral, the ship is being hailed. The hailing frequency is originating from EE-4's surface." She'd heard correctly: the planet already contained intelligent life. Contingency plans had been drafted to deal with intelligent, alien life, but most of those plans centered on subjugation or extermination, not living in harmony. She hoped exterminating the first aliens encountered by the human race would not be required.

"Why haven't we detected any sign of civilization, Albans?" she asked.

"Due to the challenging conditions on much of EE-4's surface," said Albans, "it's possible the aliens live underground or possess a cloaking device. However, I've instructed the computer to begin a detailed surface scan for smaller structures—in case this planet is an outpost, instead of their actual home planet."

"Good work. Speak to me, Norwood," she demanded, addressing the petite redhead sitting to her right. "What kind of signal are they using? Will it be possible to formulate a response?"

"The hail is being relayed via satellite, Admiral," she responded, looking puzzled. "Until we received the hail, there was no sign of electrical activity in that orbital region. Strangely enough, along with the electrical activity, there's also a faint, very fresh, tachyon signature . . . analogous to the signature we found in the region containing the ancient metallic residue. Whoever they are, they are much more technically advanced than us. That may explain why we failed to detect their presence."

"Is there any way to translate their language," asked the admiral, leaning forward. "I'd like to know whether they're saying hello or . . . something else."

Norwood looked down at her Interlink Device then back up at the admiral. "That's the other perplexing part, sir. They're hailing us on an HV channel, and the language being used is a mutated form of English."

"What?!" the admiral exclaimed.

"English?!" yelped Solomon.

"How is that possible?" Albans demanded.

The others were staring at Norwood, in shock.

"There's only one way to find out," said the admiral. "Norwood, activate the video feed. Let's find out who's hailing us and what they have to say."

"Aye, sir," she replied. "With the translation program in effect, you will notice a discrepancy between the alien's lips—if it has lips—and what it says. I'm patching us through now."

Not knowing what to expect, all eyes were glued to the HV screen. Humanity's first contact with an alien species was seconds away, and everyone held their collective breath, awed by the magnitude of the moment. However, when the screen came to life, their awe turned to shock. It showed a startling image: a gorgeous, blonde-haired woman, who began to speak. . .

"Greetings to the brave colonists and crew of *Solomon's Arrow*! My name is Lorna Threman, chancellor of New Terra, and we have been awaiting your arrival for many centuries."

•

Richard stared at the view-screen, barely able to believe his eyes. The stunning blonde-haired woman, who had identified herself as Lorna Threman, so closely resembled his dead wife, Erin, she could easily have passed for her sister. His shock was so great that he barely heard the admiral's next words.

"Thank you, Chancellor Threman," she said, trying to stay poised. "I respectfully return your greetings. My name is Admiral Katherine Axelrod, captain of *Solomon's Arrow*. As one might expect, your presence on New Terra comes as quite a shock. When was the colony established, if you don't mind me asking?"

Lorna Threman sat unmoving, a blank expression on her face for nearly five seconds before she answered. There was such a long delay that Richard began to wonder if there was a time lag in the transmission process.

"You may turn off your vocal translation device, Admiral," the chancellor said, her lips now in sync with her voice. "I have adjusted my dialect to more closely resemble the time period from whence you came."

Richard heard a faint click. The admiral had signaled Lt. Norwood to turn off the translation filters, though Richard barely noticed. His eyes were fixed firmly on the chancellor, whose dark blue eyes had shifted to stare directly at him. A pleasantly surprised look was on her face. As a trace of pink rose in her cheeks, she answered the admiral's question, sounding a bit flustered.

"We, um, we established New Terra a long time ago," she said, quickly shifting her attention back to the admiral. "But, we can discuss all that once your ship has landed."

The admiral shook her head. "The *Arrow* is too large to enter the planet's atmosphere."

A flash of disappointment crossed the chancellor's face.

"However," the admiral continued, "we'll assemble a landing party, one which I'll personally lead. We'll be arriving in forty-six hours. Do you still use hours and minutes?"

The chancellor's odd display of disappointment was quickly replaced by a smile. "Yes we do, admiral. I am transmitting our coordinates, now. This is a glorious day in New Terra's history. I am so looking forward to meeting you in person . . . all of you."

Richard could've sworn that her eyes cut back to him just as the screen went blank.

"Damn, that's one gorgeous bird," Floyd Sullivant exclaimed. "She's so beautiful I almost feel like turning straight . . . *almost.*"

His quip broke the tension. While he and the others chuckled, the admiral cleared her throat, at the same time shooting Floyd a reproachful look.

"Sorry, sir."

The admiral gazed down at the table and stroked her lower lip. "Something about her bothers me. How could she have switched dialects so effortlessly? Wouldn't the English language have changed significantly over the past three thousand years?"

"Perhaps she's an android, or a robot of some sort," Solomon offered.

Floyd chuckled again. "That's highly unlikely, Dr. Chavez."

"Why's that, Lieutenant?"

"Because, when she saw the commander, she blushed." Floyd grinned broadly. "Richard, old boy, you're one hell of a good-looking chap, but it was like she'd never seen a man before."

The subject matter was making Richard uncomfortable. Therefore, he was relieved when the admiral shifted the topic back to her original question.

"Answer me this: could the human mind have evolved over the past three thousand years?"

Lt. Commander Albans responded, "It's doubtful, sir. Of course, environmental factors might play a role in pushing evolution forward during such a short period of time, but humanity has pretty much reached the peak of its evolution, sad to say."

"I don't understand."

Albans shifted in her seat. "Evolutionary biologists have theorized that after humans became civilized, evolution stopped. With better health care and the worthy desire of civilized people to keep the sick and disabled alive, the, um, Darwinian theory of survival of the fittest fell by the wayside. However, insofar as the New Terrans are concerned, we don't know enough about them to form a definitive evaluation."

"It's sad and ironic to think that our compassion has us trapped in an evolutionary dead end," remarked Julie Norwood.

"Perhaps *we'll* change that equation, Lieutenant," declared Solomon Chavez. "After all, this mission includes the smartest, healthiest, most determined people the world has ever produced. So don't lose hope."

Admiral Axelrod cleared her throat. "I'm loath to interrupt this spellbinding philosophical discussion, but we have a landing party to organize. It will obviously be different from the one we originally planned. As a result, we have plenty of work to do—dismissed."

●

FORTY-THREE HOURS LATER

Bram missed taking a good old-fashioned shower. The *Arrow*'s water supply was limited to drinking and cooking, and little else. Logically, he understood that a decade-long uninterrupted space flight would require certain sacrifices, but that didn't mean he had to like the alternative. The sonic shower (good as it was) never quite did the trick. It was always so much easier clearing one's sinuses with water.

He slipped on his underwear, t-shirt, socks, and coverall before exiting the bathroom. His two bunkmates were at their posts, so he had the room to himself. It was cramped, but he understood the necessity. While slipping on his navy-issued, lace-up boots, the room's intercom came to life.

"Bram Waters, this is Admiral Axelrod. Please see me in my ready room."

The landing party wasn't due to leave the ship for another three hours. "I wonder what that's all about?" he thought aloud. Being a psychic, most people would assume he already knew the answer. In most ordinary situations, however, Bram let the future unfold without foreknowledge. It was only while under extreme duress that he attempted to peer into the future, and even then he never guaranteed success. That was fine by him; he preferred being surprised by the complexities of everyday life. Over the decades, a multitude of people had told him how much they'd love to know what was lurking around the corner, but he'd always responded by saying that life would lose its flavor and become awfully boring if one knew everything that was about to happen.

Following the page, he went straight to the admiral's ready room. It was his first time on the command deck, and he would've enjoyed stopping to talk with Floyd Sullivant, Richard Allison, and that cute red-headed com-officer, but he knew better than to keep the admiral waiting. By the tone of her voice, he could sense she'd invited him there for more than a social visit.

Bram entered the ready room, and the admiral motioned for him to sit. She was studying something on her desktop computer. This went on for a few more seconds before she pressed a button and focused on him.

"Thank you for coming, Mr. Waters."

"Gladly. But please, call me Bram."

"As you wish," she said, giving him a curt nod. "Computer, display a real-time image of the planet now known as New Terra on my ready room view-screen."

Bram studied the image of the unusual planet. The ship's orbit allowed him to observe some of the arid front half, much of the

212 ● J. DALTON JENNINGS

frozen back half, and a large section of the vegetation ring that
encircled the middle. The planet did not look conducive for
establishing a small colony, much less a viable civilization. He
was beginning to wonder if the scientists involved in choosing it
had made a mistake.

"I'd wager you're thinking what I'm thinking, Bram, 'What the
hell get did we get ourselves into?' Am I right?" the admiral asked,
staring at the view-screen.

"Something like that," he chuckled. "I didn't know you could
read minds, Admiral."

She smiled at him. "Merely a smidgen of intuition, coupled
with military training; one must read people, not necessarily
minds, to rise to the rank of admiral. Mind reading is your forte,
not mine. Which brings me to why I called you here, Bram: I'd
like you to provide me with a psychic impression of our soon-
to-be hosts."

"In other words, you want me to start earning my pay," he said,
offering his most disarming grin. She merely cocked one eyebrow,
saying nothing in return. "Okay . . . well then, I'll get right on it."
Bram closed his eyes and took a deep, relaxing breath.

"Don't you need to be looking at the planet to do that?" the
admiral asked.

Bram kept his eyes closed. "I have the image in my mind, Admiral. If I continued to stare at the HV screen, all I'd do is receive an
impression of electronic circuitry. I need to send my—how can I
put this—mental probe, toward the actual objective. Now, if you
don't mind, I need silence for this to work effectively."

All he heard after that was the admiral lean back in her chair.

Bram opened his mind. He wasn't completely sure his powers
would work from this distance, let alone through the atmosphere
of an alien planet. He shouldn't have been concerned, for he
almost immediately started receiving psychic impressions. The
only trouble was that most of the impressions weren't human.

Perhaps there were creatures living in the planet's vegetative ring that were vaguely sentient. This puzzled him, so he probed deeper. He sensed a small area on the planet where a concentration of human emotion was located, though he failed to read any thought patterns—which was strange in itself, since most of the time when he reached out with his mind he was forced to erect a mental barrier to block the ever-present waves of human thought. This time, however, he was unable to sense any human thought patterns. Then, for a fleeting moment, he registered thought patterns far to the east in the planet's dark, icy landscape. But nothing could live out there. Bram immediately dismissed it as nothing more than a psychic mirage.

He probed westward.

There were definitely humans on the planet. However . . . there was something else, something alien . . . a *thing* of vast intelligence. But what? Whatever it was felt cold, merciless, though not necessarily malevolent. He had to know more.

Bram probed deeper.

Suddenly, he received a forceful psychic pushback. A barrage of images flooded his mind, too many to fully grasp. He was losing himself. Terror gripped his soul. He had to break free. He had to save himself. A soft, fearful gasp escaped his throat.

Then darkness.

Had he passed out? His eyes fluttered open.

"Bram! Bram! What's the matter? What's wrong?"

He recognized the admiral's voice. She sounded afraid.

"Computer, get Dr. Singh up here at—"

"I'm . . . I'm fine, Admiral," Bram grunted, shaking his head.

"What happened to you, Waters?" she asked, half out of her seat. The tense set of her square jaw told him that she was gravely concerned for his welfare. "Did you pass out?"

He nodded. "Don't worry, I'm okay . . . now." He wasn't lying. Whatever it was that rejected his psychic probe had not tried to injure him, though his mind did feel sluggish, as though laced with psychic cobwebs.

"Obviously something happened," she pressed. "What did you sense?"

"Admiral, there are humans living on the planet, but their minds are somehow being shielded. Perhaps it's atmospheric or geological interference, or caused by the material they constructed their city with. I can't be sure. But, that wasn't what caused me to pass out. Located in the central vegetative ring is a powerful alien intelligence."

"What?!" the concern on her face doubled.

"That's right," Bram said, the last of his mental cobwebs falling away. "I think that one of the landing party's goals should be to investigate this mystery . . . that is, if the inhabitants of New Terra can't answer it for us. And if they can't, I'd like to be a member of the exploratory mission that searches for the alien intelligence." Bram began to chew on his lower lip. "Also, I believe Dr. Chavez would be the perfect person to lead that mission."

The admiral was staring at him intently, though she'd begun to thoughtfully nod. "Thank you, Bram. I'll give your suggestion serious consideration."

12

ona lay on her cot in the brig, reading a classic horror novel from the previous century. The military-issued e-reader she'd been provided was serviceable, but she would've preferred using her own. Unfortunately, she'd stored the device in her cryo-chamber, which meant that security had confiscated it along with her PID.

She was thoroughly engrossed in the section of the novel where the main character is doused in pig's blood, when her cell door unexpectedly slid open. Mona jumped in fright but quickly recovered, turning off the e-reader as Solomon entered the cell.

"Hello, Mona."

She swung her legs over the edge of the bed. "Hello, Solomon."

"Good book?"

She shrugged her shoulders. "You know me, always been a sucker for a good scare."

Solomon screwed up his face. "Yes, well, I just thought you should know that the landing party will be assembling in fifteen minutes. You won't be a member, but the admiral wants you provided with progress reports. She's as upset as I am over your stunt to board this ship, but that doesn't mean she thinks your considerable talents should be squandered. We *will* make use of them, but you're not off the hook: you'll be held in the brig until the colonists are awakened. After that, you'll be court-martialed and probably sentenced to hard labor   that is, if I have any say in the matter."

Mona looked exasperated. "But that's a complete waste of my intelligence, Solomon," she snapped. "I should be a member of the landing party, not sitting in the brig. Come on! You can't be so mad that you refuse to see the advantage my talents bring to bear. I mean, without me this ship wouldn't even be here to send out a landing party."

"The decision is not mine to make," Solomon sighed. "The admiral's in charge of the ship and the mission. You're a stowaway, Mona, and you must face the consequences of your actions. I'm sorry."

Mona snatched up her e-reader and lay back on her cot. "Fine, There's a vampire novel or three I haven't read yet. Call me when you need your ass hauled out of the fire, *old friend*. I'll be more than happy to oblige."

With a grunt of frustration, Solomon turned on his heel and stormed from the cell. As Mona watched the door slide shut, she snorted with derision. If Solomon knew that she was no more trapped in her cell than a lion in its den, he wouldn't have looked down at her with such arrogant conceit. Reactivating the e-reader, she returned to the novel, feeling confident in the knowledge that the brig was not truly her prison.

●

After a smooth descent, the shuttle landed at the provided coordinates. The landing party, which consisted of Admiral Axelrod, Commander Allison, Lt. Commander Albans, Dr. Singh, Dr. Solomon Chavez, Bram Waters, Lt. Sullivant, Lt. Muldoon, Ensign Fletcher, and three security officers, donned their breathing masks. The masks were designed to slowly adjust their levels of oxygen and trace gasses until each person became acclimated to the planet's atmosphere. They would also serve as filters until such time as the shuttle's automated medical analyzer developed the necessary vaccines to counteract the pathogens in the water and atmosphere. It wouldn't do to end up like the doomed aliens from H. G. Wells' novel, *The War of the Worlds*.

The shuttle powered down two hundred yards from New Terra, in the middle of a grassy plain that seemed to stretch endlessly in all directions. Both the icy plateau and the distant forest encircling the planet were too far away to see. The color of the sky was pinkish-orange to the west, faded to sapphire-blue directly overhead before turning back the farther east it stretched. There was an almost magical quality about the light, making the softly-glowing colony appear to exist in a realm one shade brighter than perpetual twilight.

Before departing the *Arrow*, Richard had studied the planet from his view-screen, noting that the overall terrain appeared rugged to the point of formidable. Here on the ground, however, it looked idyllic. Perhaps living here wouldn't be as bad as he initially suspected.

The colony was five miles in diameter, perfectly circular and surrounded by a smooth-as-glass, twenty-foot-tall wall, with what appeared to be a water-filled moat at its base. Richard could see buildings rising above the wall—some spires, others domed—while still others looked like normal office buildings . . . except for one thing: their fascia was constructed using tan bricks. The colony's entrance, however, appeared to be fabricated from a dark, purple wood. There was a medieval quality about the colony that bothered him—though he knew it shouldn't; the lack of geologic upheaval precluded them from mining for metallic ore and hard stone. He supposed they'd been forced to settle for using whatever material was available. He wouldn't be surprised if most of their furnishings, and quite possibly their appliances and utensils as well, were fashioned out of wood from the distant forest.

As Richard and the rest of the group stood outside the shuttle discussing their surroundings, the colony's wooden entrance began to lower, forming a medieval drawbridge that spanned the width of the moat. The moment it lowered in place, an unusual sight rolled through the colony entrance—a wooden carriage, large enough to hold them all. The shiny, black and red vehicle, which was built in a style reminiscent of the Victorian Age carriages frequented by royalty, was driverless. This meant that the colony was equipped with a rudimentary GPS system.

When the carriage pulled up beside them, Richard noticed that the doors were inlaid with a gold-colored, stylized fish design that reminded him of a decal he'd seen on the window of a car.

"Welcome, honored guests." The voice sounded female and was coming from a small, round speaker near the door. "Climb aboard this vehicle, and it will transport you to the chancellor's residence. She is eager to introduce you to the residents of our fair city."

Richard and the others complied and were soon traveling through the gate and into the heart of the city. While en route, a multitude of colorfully clad people stood in doorways watching as they passed by. Most of them wore smiles on their faces and many clapped, though some studied Richard's group with suspicious eyes.

Every so often, another speaker at the front of the carriage would blast out, "All hail the crew of *Solomon's Arrow*!" at which point the applause would increase a few decibels.

The deeper into the colony they traveled, the more Richard noticed something odd: there were many more women than men, and strangely enough the men he did see were all smaller and leaner than their female counterparts. The men were clean-shaven, long haired, and possessed a distinctly effeminate air about them. That in itself wasn't that troublesome; he'd known many men who were gay or effeminate or both. He'd even been the best man at the wedding of a close college friend who was gay. What troubled him was that he wasn't seeing any men who were built for construction work or any other blue-collar jobs. This made him wonder if what Albans had said in the ready room about evolutionary biology had been wrong after all, and that a civilized society could indeed continue to evolve. But would a smaller, weaker male be an evolutionary improvement? Richard decided to ask Albans about this observation later, after their meeting with the chancellor.

There was one other observation that registered prominently in Richard's mind: he noticed that an inordinate amount of religious iconography decorated their route. Engraved above every doorway was a bas-relief carving of a cross; in every courtyard stood finely detailed statues of angels, molded from what appeared to be charcoal-gray glass. The only thing missing was the image of Christ himself.

Looking at the other members of the landing party, Richard realized that he wasn't the only one who'd noticed these unusual attributes. Experiencing a rising sense of apprehension, Richard shifted his attention back to the city's inhabitants. The smiles on their faces looked genuine. Even those who were studying the landing party with suspicious eyes didn't seem to be harboring any ill-will. He was probably just imagining things. If the city's inhabitants wanted to do them bodily harm, there would've been ample opportunity en route to the chancellor's residence.

Approximately ten minutes after entering the city, the carriage stopped in front of what could only be described as a palace, which looked remarkably similar to the United States Supreme Court building, only bigger. The imposing structure was the only building in the city that wasn't constructed from red brick clay. Instead, a white material, akin to marble, graced its exterior.

A throng of politely clapping onlookers lined the steps leading up to the building's entrance. They stood on both sides of a five-foot-wide, bright-red carpet, which began beneath the carriage and climbed a long flight of steps, finally disappearing between a series of tall columns situated on either side of the building's entrance.

The carriage door opened automatically, and the landing party exited the vehicle. A delegation of four muscular women—all sporting short, black, spiky haircuts, and wearing navy-blue body stockings, which accentuated every curve—met them at the foot of the steps. Printed above the left breast of each outfit was the same stylized image of a fish that adorned the carriage doors. By the looks of them, Richard suspected the women were related. Judging by their lithe movements and athletic build, they must be members of New Terra's security forces. Each woman carried a foot-long, nondescript, solid-black rod, a weapon of some sort, probably used to stun unruly colonists . . . or unknown visitors, such as themselves.

"Follow us, please," said one of the women firmly, her tone leaving no room for argument.

Two of the women walked ahead of the group and two behind as they ascended the steps.

The crowd lining the red carpet clapped and smiled politely, but Richard began to notice something: many of the intense stares were directed at him, though some were also directed at the other men. Very few in the crowd were studying the women of their group, which consisted of Axelrod, Albans, Muldoon, and a junior security officer named Janelle Mumbato—a strikingly beautiful Kenyan with whom Richard experienced a brief fling two months earlier.

Janelle was of medium height with dark-brown skin and a pixie-cut hairdo. The sex had been great, but she'd broken off their relationship after a brief, passionate week, with the excuse that she wasn't ready for a relationship involving four people. At first perplexed, Richard sadly realized that the other two people were his dead wife and son.

It didn't particularly bother him when she called it quits. If truth be told, he was relieved. After they stopped seeing each other, everything went back to normal, which was good, what with her holding six black belts in various martial arts disciplines.

As he ascended the steps, Richard realized that Janelle was the only woman of their group to whom the surrounding crowd paid more than a passing interest. Richard tried to covertly read the emotions behind the welcoming crowd's applause, and saw an undercurrent of fearfulness. This, along with his earlier observations, added to Richard's unease.

Leaving the crowd behind, he and the others entered the building and were escorted down a long hallway lined with portraits of past chancellors—most of whom held a striking resemblance to Lorna Threman.

Women of all shapes and sizes and hairstyles were scurrying up and down the hall or popping in one door and out another. Scattered throughout the mix, Richard noticed a few of the effeminate looking men—most of whom, after seeing him, stopped in their tracks and stared, even more fascinated by his appearance than their female counterparts. It was enough to give a person the willies, not understanding why they found him so captivating.

Then it hit him: Richard had yet to spot a single black person. What's more, he'd not seen any Latinos or Orientals. Every person in the colony appeared to be white.

●

After entering through a large archway into Chancellor Threman's audience chamber, Bram stood beside Gloria Muldoon, feeling terribly uneasy. Aside from sensing vague, emotional undercurrents, he'd failed to sense any thought patterns from the New Terrans he encountered thus far. It was like being surrounded by robots disguised as humans. For someone whose psychic abilities required constant vigilance, this chilling anomaly was causing him a substantial amount of apprehension.

Though his fellow landing party members were unaware of their hosts' unprecedented lack of mental output, Bram could sense they knew something was out of place, nonetheless.

There was no getting around it. To keep from becoming a liability, he needed to find out how his abilities were being blocked. This meant that, despite his longtime vow to respect the privacy of others, he must read another person's mind. Merely contemplating such a violation repulsed him, but Bram also knew it was necessary . . . and he might as well start with the chancellor herself.

Upon entering the audience chamber, Bram and the others encountered a domed ceiling with a mural depicting what must have been significant events in New Terran history. The mural reminded Bram of the Sistine Chapel and even included an alternate portrait of the famous image of Adam and God touching fingers . . . only this time, a gorgeous, semi-nude woman (who looked remarkably like the chancellor) was touching the finger of a much larger, silver-haired woman of indeterminate age, whose naked body was partly obscured by strategically placed clouds.

Bram studied other sections of the mural but, lacking context, he was unable to understand their meaning. One depicted the silver-haired woman handing a newborn baby to a redhead wearing light-green hospital scrubs. Another painting depicted a heated battle on a glacier between three of the muscular, spiky-haired, warrior women and two long-haired beasts that looked vaguely like the legendary Sasquatch from Earth's past. Bram thought this scene odd, having been briefed that the planet couldn't possibly harbor mammals larger than a mouse.

The ceiling was painted in a photo-realistic style. Being a lover of art, Bram would've enjoyed nothing more than to spend all day examining the other murals—but that wasn't his mission.

When the doors closed behind him and the others, the two rear guards came to attention on either side of the entrance. The two remaining guards escorted the landing party to a row of tan chairs that faced a high-backed, ornate, wooden throne, fashioned from what could easily pass for ebony. The empty throne sat on a half-oval dais at the rear of the room. Floor-to-ceiling maroon and gold curtains hung behind it, giving the throne an appearance of supreme importance.

"You will remain standing until Chancellor Threman enters the hall and gives you permission to sit," announced one of the spiky haired women, after which she and her fellow guard took up a watchful position on either side of the dais.

The group stopped in front of their respective chairs and did as they were told, though Bram noticed a few members of the landing party appeared somewhat annoyed by the order, especially Admiral Axelrod, who was more accustomed to giving orders than taking them.

Bram stood beside Floyd Sullivant, who leaned over and whispered in his ear, "Have you noticed, this colony is a gay man's nightmare?"

Bram tried to suppress his laughter, but failed. He received more than a few disapproving looks. Biting his lip, he focused on the floor, which was made of the same smooth material as the building's façade, only a light, powder-blue instead of white.

When he no longer felt scrutinized, Bram leaned over to tell Floyd he'd have better luck once the colonists were decanted. But before he could speak, in walked Lorna Threman, chancellor of New Terra, her blonde locks falling over bare shoulders, her indescribably perfect body clothed in a sheer-white, calf-length dress, cinched at the waist with a half-inch wide, gold-colored belt; her dainty feet sporting four-inch high, gold-colored heels; her smile radiant.

The guard to her right spoke in a commanding voice, "All ye in attendance kneel before our exalted chancellor, Lorna Threman!"

Bram and the others were taken aback by this order. Many of them turned their heads in the admiral's direction, unsure how to respond. By the look on her face, she had no intention of kneeling before anyone.

The chancellor stopped in front of her chair and faced the group. Seeing that everyone was still on their feet, she said, "There's no need for such formalities. A simple bow will suffice."

After a moment's hesitation, Admiral Axelrod nodded to the others. They all bowed, though none of them bent their torsos beyond a forty-five degree angle.

Bram didn't need psychic powers to pick up on the fact that, despite her smile, the chancellor was annoyed by the landing party's response. She was probably accustomed to being treated like a queen.

The chancellor sat and crossed her shapely legs. "You may sit, honored guests. You doubtless have many questions of me. While your accommodations are being arranged, I will endeavor to answer those questions to the best of my ability, though certainly you will concede that not all of them will be answered during this initial meeting. First, however, introductions are in order."

Bram noticed that her eyes had stopped on Commander Allison.

"As you know, my name is Lorna Threman, Chancellor of New Terra," she said, tearing her gaze from the commander and shifting it to Admiral Axelrod. "The women who escorted you here are my security forces and are called Minders. I'm very interested in learning about each and every one of you. However, before we begin, I must ask you a question, Admiral. I see that the majority of your group is composed of men. Is it true that the human male once held a prominent role in ancient Earth society?"

●

At first, Katherine wasn't sure what the chancellor meant when she asked about the role of men in Earth's society. Being uninterested in the opposite sex, to her men were useful in battle and for an occasional laugh, but little else. However, like many commanding officers throughout the centuries, her first responsibility was to her ship and its crew; therefore, the chancellor's question gave Katherine pause to think. She suddenly realized that the few men she'd paid attention to while en route through the city had looked more like prepubescent boys than full-grown men. This unusual detail deserved further study.

"In our time, the men of Earth were valued members of society," she answered. "How are they regarded here in New Terra, if you don't mind me asking?"

The chancellor smiled uncomfortably. "Our men are . . . useful, in their own right," she said. "Yours, however, are altogether different . . . in a way that pleases me."

The chancellor glanced at Richard Allison. She then suddenly stopped talking and her eyes lost focus. Cocking her head slightly to one side, she appeared to be listening to something only she could hear. Before anyone had time to ponder her strange behavior, the chancellor refocused, shifted her attention back to the admiral, and resumed speaking: "I look forward to learning much more about you, and your valiant crew, during the coming days, while you assimilate into New Terran society. Perhaps we should retire to—"

"Excuse me, Chancellor," Katherine interrupted. "I believe you're getting ahead of yourself. We've not yet decided to join your society. We may end up starting our own colony as originally planned, and then initiate trade talks with yours."

Once again, the chancellor's eyes lost focus, and she appeared to be listening to something unheard by anyone else in the room. "The Lord finds your attitude unacceptable," she declared, refocusing her hard, steely attention back on Katherine. "We, the inhabitants of New Terra, have waited for over two thousand years for *Solomon's Arrow* to appear. The Lord has planned for your arrival and her plans *will* be obeyed."

A cold chill raced up Katherine's spine. *The Lord finds?!* All of a sudden the chancellor's strange behavior made perfect, gut-wrenching sense. The woman was hearing voices in her head, which meant one thing and one thing only . . . Lorna Threman was barking mad!

13

hese are not your people, Lorna. You cannot order them around like a common serving lad. You must convince them to stay . . . without using heavy-handed tactics.

The silky-sweet voice in Lorna Threman's mind sounded calm, reasonable, even soothing, but then again, She always did. *How can I salvage the situation, Lord?* she thought. *Apologize for your conduct . . . and then have Doric take them on a tour of the city. Once they see the comforts you enjoy, they will realize there is no need for a separate colony.*

Lorna refocused and examined her guests. Most of them were staring at her with looks of concern on their faces. "Forgive me, my friends," she said, sounding contrite. "In the eight and a half standard years that I've been chancellor of New Terra, I suppose I've grown accustomed to the people of this colony following my instructions. I forget that you are new here and are under no obligation to do as I say. I apologize."

She noticed that most of the landing party looked visibly relieved to hear her say this. "Before my rudeness sways you into building a colony elsewhere—when there's a perfectly good one right here—I'd like to arrange for you to take a tour of New Terra. If, after seeing the colony, you still want to go through the trouble of building a separate colony . . . well, the citizens of this fair city will help you, in any way possible, to hasten that transition."

As she finished speaking, in walked a young woman wearing a cream-colored, floor-length dress, styled similarly to hers. The young woman's physical appearance was also similar, both being the same height, same eye color, same skin tone, same facial shape—except for one thing: instead of the same long, blonde tresses, she was completely bald. Surprisingly, her baldness did not detract from her beauty.

Everyone but Lorna glanced over at the young woman as she crossed the room and came to a stop beside the dais. Still studying the landing party, Lorna gestured toward the new arrival. "I'd like to introduce you to Doric Sardis, who serves as vice-chancellor of New Terra and, of course, my assistant. She will provide you with a comprehensive tour of the city."

"I appreciate your hospitality, Chancellor," the admiral said. "However, perhaps tomorrow would be a better time to accept that tour. Today, it would be more informative for us to speak with a delegation of historians and scientists. I'd like to learn as much as possible about the history of this colony and how you managed to arrive here ahead of us."

Lorna nodded, keeping a smile on her lips by sheer force of will alone. "As you wish. I'll have my assistant arrange a meeting with those particular divisions of the Keeper class." Seeing the puzzled look on the admiral's face, she elaborated. "What you call scientists and historians, we call the Keepers of Knowledge. They are very powerful, in and of themselves, and serve as a check on power to those in the political class, such as myself."

At this, Solomon Chavez spoke up for the first time. "Excuse me, Chancellor. But it sounds as if a caste system has evolved in New Terra. Could you elaborate?"

Lorna studied the man closer and was surprised to see that the dark-haired speaker looked vaguely familiar. "And who are you, sir?"

"Forgive me, Chancellor. My name is Dr. Solomon Chavez."

Although he said this matter-of-factly, this information felt like a jolt of electricity to Lorna, and every other New Terran in the room. Other than the landing party, all eyes shot Solomon's way. Hearts began to race. The great man was actually here—in the flesh!

"We're . . . we're greatly honored to welcome you to New Terra, Dr. Chavez," she stammered.

"Thank you, Chancellor, but you have yet to answer my question."

Lorna was so distraught seeing Solomon in person that she was forced to think for a moment before remembering the question he'd asked. "Oh yes, you asked about our form of social status, our caste system, so to speak. We have found that it's a comfort when people know their place in society. The average New Terran wants for nothing, with each being a valuable component in the machinery of life. Our society is based on peace and order, which is much better than the chaos that engulfed humanity for millennia." She saw that her words were, for some curious reason, causing her guests a peculiar amount of consternation. She decided to change the subject. "There are many wonderful things to learn about New Terra. You shall meet with the Keepers and ask as many questions as you like."

"I appreciate that, Chancellor," Solomon said. "We have a great deal of catching up to do. The main reason we left Earth was to ensure that the human race survived the ecological perils that loomed so closely on the horizon. I'm eager to find out how that worked out."

A sinking feeling latched hold of Lorna's guts. The moment had finally arrived; the moment she'd dreaded since the Lord informed her of the ship's eminent arrival over a week ago. "About that . . . about Earth," she sighed, deep emotions welling within her, "I have bad news." Their eyes were focused intently upon her, waiting expectantly. "In the year 2489, on April 3, Earth was devastated by a natural disaster. We here on New Terra are what's left of the human race."

●

External emotions buffeted Bram like a tidal wave. They took a backseat, however, to his personal torrent of emotions. He'd just learned that the vast majority of the human race had been destroyed by a natural disaster, and it hurt. Despite having reconciled himself to the fact that his friends were long dead, this news was gut-wrenching, almost too much to take.

The others were talking over each other, peppering the chancellor with heated questions, yet he was stunned into silence. The chancellor must be wrong . . . it couldn't be true . . . the inhabitants of Earth gone . . . dead?!

Instinctively, Bram reached out with his mind, casting a psychic probe back toward the planet of his birth, hoping to register signs of life, but Earth was too far away. He knew that time and space were relative, and that his psychic powers should be able to transcend those boundaries, but he was limited by doubts. He oftentimes wondered if it was his fear of the unknown that held him back. His fear of what might be out there.

Bram centered his thoughts just as the chancellor rose to her feet and lifted her arms.

"Please, calm yourselves, my friends!" she shouted above the din. The questions and the loud muttering tapered off. "The Keepers can answer all your questions. My education centered on the political process; everything else was extraneous. About this terrible event, I was taught nothing more than the basic overview—like every other New Terran, notwithstanding the Keepers.

"If you'll please follow Doric, she'll take you to the Basilica of Knowledge. The Keepers will provide you with answers. Now, if you'll forgive me, I'm feeling fatigued. My schedule is tight this afternoon, and I require a short nap to clear my head."

Without another word, Lorna Threman strode with a regal bearing to the arched doorframe from which she'd entered the room, pressed a series of buttons located on a panel beside the arch, and quickly exited the audience chamber. Feeling nonplussed by her abrupt departure, Bram and the others glanced at each other.

"If you will please follow me," purred the silky voice of Doric Sardis, "an audience with our Prime Keeper, Morvan Godley, has been arranged." Spinning on her heel, she made for the same archway through which the chancellor exited.

A heartbroken pall hung over the landing party as Bram and the others followed their guide to the exit. He could sense that his shipmates were overwhelmed by the news about Earth and, like him, they couldn't help but wonder what form of calamity had befallen their former home. The two guards standing on either side of the dais fell in behind them.

"I noticed that we're not leaving by the same exit through which we came," stated Solomon, glancing back at the guards. "Am I correct in assuming that your *Keepers* work in this same building?"

Doric finished typing a code into the panel beside the arch. Solomon's question appeared to puzzle her. "No. The Basilica of Knowledge is located on the other side of the city."

Until she entered the last number into the control panel, the room on the other side of the arch was completely dark. With the code entered, the room suddenly lit up, and the landing party walked inside. As Bram passed through the arch he felt a gentle, twisting sensation in his solar plexus. Unsure what to make of this, he glanced back at the archway. When the two guards, who were following the landing party crossed through, the light in the audience chamber went dark. The blackness of the audience chamber was complete—which was unlikely, since there'd been a number of high-placed windows located throughout the room. It didn't make any sense: Bram should be able see something on the other side of the arch, even if only dimly lit.

"Welcome to the Basilica of Knowledge, my friends," he heard a full-throated female voice behind him joyfully say. "My name is Morvan Godley, Prime Keeper of New Terra."

Bram turned to see a six-foot tall, excessively thin woman, with sunken cheeks, a pointed nose, and a chin to match. Her long, auburn hair was styled in a braid that hung down her skeletal back. For clothing, she wore a golden-yellow, diaphanous shift that stopped midway down her stick-thin thighs, leaving little to the imagination. The transparent nature of the shift changed, turning opaque near the woman's crotch and breasts, covering her private parts. Normally, Bram would've enjoyed seeing a woman in such a revealing outfit, but on her, it looked bizarre.

Morvan Godley beamed with happiness as she approached the group. Her smile seemed genuine and, despite her emaciated appearance, her skin tone was a healthy pink, not sallow as one might expect from someone so thin.

Bram glanced around the high-ceiling room, with its row of columns on either side and its windows of stained glass, and realized that it looked remarkably like a cathedral, a basilica, only without the pews. That's when the Prime Keeper's statement hit him: "Welcome to the Basilica of Knowledge," but that couldn't possibly be true.

Bram wasn't the only one who was rightly confused. The admiral stepped forward as Morvan Godley placed her palms together and bowed, saying, "I don't understand. Ms. Sardis told us that the Basilica was located on the other side of the city."

With this, Morvan Godley straightened up and cocked one eyebrow, giving Admiral Axelrod a peculiar look, as though she was studying a mentally deficient child. "That is so, Admiral. You are now in the Basilica of Knowledge. Welcome, I have much to show you and—"

"Forgive me for interrupting, but I still don't understand where we are," said the admiral, a note of impatience in her voice. "How can you say we're in your so-called Basilica of Knowledge when we're obviously still inside the chancellor's residence?"

Morvan Godley and Doric Sardis gave each other questioning looks. The Prime Keeper's eyes abruptly went out of focus.

"Ah, yes. Now I understand your confusion," she said. "In your time, foldways had not yet been invented."

"Foldways?"

"That is what we call our primary means of transportation." She walked over to the archway and entered a code into an adjacent control panel. The darkness within the arch was replaced by the chancellor's audience chamber. Godley entered a different code and the image changed. They were surprised to see what appeared to be a living room with a couch, chair, coffee table, and assorted bric-a-brac throughout the room.

"This is my apartment . . . I apologize for the mess." As the landing party stared in dumbstruck fascination, Morvan Godley entered another code into the control panel. The image changed once again, this time displaying an idyllic city park, with green grass, benches, rolling pathways, and happy visitors enjoying the fresh, outdoor air. "This is Calvary Park, where I often go during my lunch break . . . or just to clear my head after a long day of work."

Bram could barely believe what he was seeing and sensed that his colleagues felt the same. All were speechless, except for Lt. Commander Albans, the ship's science officer, who whistled and ran her fingers through her short brown hair. "This is amazing!" She tore her gaze from the tranquil scene and faced the Prime Keeper. "You called this device a 'foldway.' Does that mean you have the ability to fold space?"

"Oh, yes," Morvan Godley replied with a smug grin. "Humanity has been using space-folding technology for well over two thousand years. In fact, that's how we arrived on this planet in the first place."

●

Solomon was thunderstruck. He could barely believe the human race had developed such an advanced form of technology. At the time of the *Arrow's* departure from Earth, the concept of folding space was a mere pipe dream, not one of practical consideration. He knew this because he'd charged his best scientists with solving the problem, hoping that space-folding technology would allow the *Arrow* to bypass the light-speed barrier. After years of fruitless research, Mona Levin herself had thrown in the towel, conceding that humanity needed another thousand years of technological advancement before the concept could bear fruit.

"If you'll follow me," said the Prime Keeper, "I'll show you to my conference room. We can relax there, and answer each other's questions."

As she strode away, the admiral fell in line beside her. "Please forgive me, um—"

"Keeper Godley."

"Right." Katherine hesitated, unsure how to pose her question. "Forgive me, but I was wondering about the chancellor—"

"What about her, Admiral?"

"Well . . . ah . . . she mentioned hearing the *Lord's* voice, and I was wondering if she's been hearing this voice for a long while, or if it's a more recent occurrence?"

Morvan Godley stopped at a plain, wooden door and waved the four, spiky-haired Minders away. "Is this a joke?" Holding the door open, she stared pointedly at the admiral.

"I assure you it is not, Keeper Godley," Katherine replied. "Your chancellor claims that the *Lord* speaks to her."

"That's not what I meant, Admiral." The two women followed the landing party into the conference room. "I wanted to know if the question itself was a joke," she grumbled. "Of course the chancellor hears the Lord's voice, same as every other New Terran . . . including myself."

The admiral stared at her blankly. "Excuse me?"

Everyone stopped in their tracks. Solomon and a few others looked over their shoulders, while the rest turned completely around. Except for Doric Sardis, all were gaping at Morvan Godley, thrown for a loop by her outrageous comment.

What had they gotten themselves into? Solomon wondered. It was not uncommon for people to talk to God, but God never talked back . . . unless the person hearing His voice was psychotic. He noticed that Morvan Godley's gaze went out of focus for a few seconds, in the same manner as the Chancellor's.

A sad smile formed on the tall woman's angular face. "I have been reminded that humans of your era were conceived and delivered in sin, and thus do not have the advantage of communing with the Lord. I apologize. If you'll please take a seat, I'll include this aspect of our culture in the presentation I've designed, which will bring you up to speed on events, ranging from twenty-five hundred years ago to the present."

Fourteen plain, wooden chairs were spaced evenly around a circular conference table, one for each member of the landing party, plus two for the Prime Keeper and Doric Sardis. All of them took the proffered seats, except for the security personnel, who stood near the entrance with their backs against the wall.

Morvan Godley eyed them suspiciously as she scooted her seat up to the table. "There's no need for your guards to remain standing, Admiral," she stated.

Admiral Axelrod looked over her shoulder and nodded, directing the security personnel to take their seats.

"If you're worried about security issues, Admiral," Godley sighed, "I can assure you that the city is well protected."

"I'm sure it is, Keeper Godley. However, if you'll forgive my bluntness, my security officers are here because I would be a fool to walk into an unknown situation without them. Until I learn more about you and your people, I must take precautions. I hope you understand."

Godley frowned. "Do you perceive us as a threat, Admiral Axelrod?" There was a brittle edge to her voice.

The admiral shrugged her shoulders. "I don't know what you are . . . as of yet. But don't get me wrong; I'm hoping for the best. You and the chancellor have been more than welcoming, and that's a good start."

"Hmm . . . I forget that ancient Earth was still suffering from paranoia. We here in New Terra are a bit more trusting of one another. Over the millennia, we've learned that cooperation is the key to survival." She waved a hand over a small electronic eye embedded in the table. "With that in mind, we shall begin."

Located in the center of the table was a shiny, black, three-inch dome. Encircling the dome, at a distance of nine inches, was a thin ring made of the same material. A holographic image sprang to life and hovered at eye level over the dome. The image was a remarkably real likeness of Earth. More than a few sharp intakes of breath emanated from those in the landing party.

Albans immediately spoke up. "I see that you've developed true holographic technology," she said appreciatively.

"Our entertainment programs are also quite good," Godley boasted. "Feel free to enjoy the HV systems in your individual rooms. As you can see, what we have here is a holographic image of Earth. As the image grows larger," which it did, "you can see that the focus shifts to the North American continent. I ask you to brace yourselves because what you are about to witness is the beginning of the end of the world you once knew."

The image of the globe was replaced by the familiar shape of America. Each person sitting around the table was viewing the exact same image. What they saw was akin to an HV camera falling through Earth's atmosphere. It slowed and came to a stop over Wyoming, Montana, and Idaho, above Yellowstone National Park.

"In the year 2489, the Yellowstone caldera erupted, sending massive amounts of smoke and ash into the atmosphere." The image showed a plume of molten lava erupting from the colorful Yellowstone landscape. "This is an actual recording of what took place, though the time frame's been sped up due to time constraints."

Staring in abject horror, the landing party watched as the fiery destruction of Yellowstone evolved into something worse. The massive devastation caused by falling debris and earthquakes was accompanied by a localized pyroclastic flow, which morphed into a roiling cloud of smoke and ash that spread across the eastern half of America like an unstoppable demonic horde. Soon, half the continent was covered in a thick layer of heavy ash. As the caldera continued to spew its hellish contents, the HV camera rose through the atmosphere until the entire globe was visible to the breathless viewers. The super-volcano's smoke and ash spread out, crossing oceans and far-flung continents, until a gray haze blanketed the majority of the northern hemisphere.

"My God," Solomon gasped.

"All those people . . ." sobbed Karen Albans. "They're all, they're all dead."

"Well, yes . . . but technically, they've been dead for over three thousand years," Dr. Singh muttered. He stared wide-eyed at the scene, failing to notice the sharp, angry glares cast his way.

"What caused this tragedy, Keeper Godley?" the admiral pointedly asked, her stricken face a mask of pain.

"From our historical records, we know that the Yellowstone caldera erupted fairly regularly, approximately every six hundred thousand years or so," she replied. "The caldera was well past its due date, and had been building pressure for hundreds of years; therefore, we've determined that it finally reached the point of no return and popped its cork, so to speak."

"But it shouldn't have been *that* destructive," Solomon countered.

"Regrettably, that part of the historical record is incomplete," the Prime Keeper responded.

The scene faded and was replaced by a ring-shaped mechanical structure.

"This, my friends," announced Morvan Godley, glancing at Solomon, "is the Burnham Space Portal, named after Dr. Frederick Burnham, the foremost scientist of his age. Incidentally, he was employed by CIMRAD, Dr. Chavez." This last bit of information was said with an almost biting tone, bordering on accusatory. Solomon took note, but kept his eyes on the hologram. "Dr. Burnham's discovery of space-folding technology allowed humanity to escape total destruction. According to our records, the Portal Initiative was in development long before the Yellowstone caldera eruption. In the year 2457, the first blind probe was launched, using a precursor to this technology. It carried a payload of engineering nanobots to this very solar system. I say 'blind probe' because the scientists of that era could only approximate where the probe would end up, and could not pinpoint the exact location. Luckily, it didn't appear inside an asteroid or moon, or our sun." She was the only one who chuckled. "Anyway, the probe was equipped with a tachyon transceiver, which it used to relay the message of its safe arrival. That's when—"

"Wait a second!" Solomon cut in. "Are you saying that we've developed faster-than-light communications?"

"Yes, Dr. Chavez."

"That's amazing!"

"Apparently," she said, looking amused. "When the news returned that the probe had arrived safely, the next phase of the Portal Initiative began. The engineering nanobots mined nearby asteroids for the ore needed to manufacture the components necessary to build a portal for this solar system. Meanwhile, back in the Sol system, the human engineers constructed its twin.

"With the economic problems of the era, it took over thirty years to build the Burnham Space Portal and Ark, used to transport a second group of colonists to Epsilon Eridani. It had been hundreds of years since the launch of *Solomon's Arrow*, and the people of that era weren't taking any chances. With conditions on Earth deteriorating, another mission was devised to ensure the survival of the human race." Morvan Godley shook her head. "Earth's population had grown to twenty-one billion people. Starvation was rampant. Fresh water was scarce. Millions of people were dying, yet the population grew unchecked. On a personal note, it still amazes me how they found the resources to fund the Portal Initiative.

"In the year 2488, the long-awaited message was received telling Earth's scientists that the Epsilon Eridani portal was complete. A lottery was held, similar to your own, to choose colonists for their Space Ark, but—" Morvan Godley paused, a pained look on her face, "just before the Ark was scheduled to launch, the Yellowstone caldera erupted. Thankfully, the smoke and ash took almost a week to engulf the globe. Naturally, the expedition was forced to scramble, pushing up its launch date. It managed to board three-quarters of the colonists before they were forced to cease operations and proceed as planned."

"What about the Lunar and Martian colonies?" Karen Albans asked.

"Due to financial constraints, they ceased operations over a century earlier, and the colonists were returned to Earth," Morvan Godley replied. "The ancestors of our people took the only available option and passed through the portal, after which they arrived here and began to build this city, all the while hoping that *Solomon's Arrow* had survived the passage through deep space and would one day join us here on New Terra." She looked around, studying the dejected faces of the landing party. "I'm sure this briefing has been a difficult one to process, so why don't we call it a day. Rooms have been prepared for each of you. Tomorrow we will meet again for a lesson on New Terra's short and decidedly boring history. Try to get some rest this afternoon, because tonight the chancellor has ordered her servants to prepare a celebratory dinner to welcome you to our world. If rest is not what you desire, feel free to explore the city. You will be provided with a list of foldway codes and a com-badge to prevent you from losing your way."

14

Jeremy Fletcher had given his plain, one-room apartment little more than a cursory glance. For the past hour, his attention had been focused on the information he'd gathered on his Security Interlink Device.

During the Prime Keeper's extraordinary account of Earth's devastation, he'd surreptitiously switched on his SID and began to record information. In the process, the device had hacked into the Prime Keeper's console and downloaded a number of files, some of which were encrypted. He'd tried everything to break the codes, but it was proving impossible. He needed to return to the shuttlecraft and link up with the *Arrow*'s computer, if he ever hoped to open the files.

Jeremy's fingers flew over the touch-screen keyboard, requesting a meeting with the admiral. Though his message was coded, he supplied no details. Who knew what advances had been made in computer eavesdropping in the past three thousand years?

The admiral's reply came quickly, and included the code he required to access her foldway. He entered the seven digit number into the control panel and watched as the absolute darkness of the arch shimmered, then coalesced, revealing her apartment. Stepping through the foldway, his thoughts centered on the unnerving darkness of its standby mode. Despite what looked like black nothingness, he'd been told that it was possible to lean against the

241

dark surface without falling into a never-ending void—though he had no desire to test that assertion.

Entering the admiral's large, well-furnished apartment, Jeremy hesitated before approaching his superior. She was standing across the room beside a table constructed from a purple-colored wood, facing Lieutenants Sullivant and Muldoon. The three of them looked his way as soon as he stepped through the foldway.

"What do you have for us, Fletcher?" asked the admiral.

"I've discovered something unusual, Admiral," he stated, offering dutiful nods to his fellow security officers. "During the chancellor's briefing, I downloaded some interesting files from her computer. It seems that—"

"Who authorized this action, Ensign?" the admiral cut in, her voice taking on a hard edge.

"Um, no one, sir," Jeremy said, his pulse quickening. "I have a specially equipped SID that allows me access to any operating computer within fifteen feet of my position. I'm sorry, but I couldn't pass up the opportunity to learn more about our hosts."

"That was quite the risk you took, Ensign," the admiral grunted. "You might've been caught. However, I must commend you for your initiative. Proceed with your report."

After a moment of nervous hesitation, Jeremy told them about the encrypted files.

"I'd like to accompany Dr. Singh back to the shuttlecraft when the inoculations are ready," he added. "While there I'll use the onboard computer to upload the files to the *Arrow*. I'm confident the ship's computer can crack the encryption code."

The admiral pursed her lips, pondering his request. "Good thinking, Fletcher. Initiative like that might earn you a promotion one of these days."

"Thank you, sir." Knowing the admiral wasn't one to dole out compliments readily, Jeremy couldn't keep the smile off his face.

"Unless you have something else for us, Fletcher, you're dismissed."

After saying his goodbyes, Jeremy approached the foldway, programmed in the code for his room, and stepped across the threshold, feeling elated.

●

Gloria Muldoon chuckled as she watched Fletcher disappear through the foldway. "The kid's green, and eager as a puppy, but he knows his stuff."

The admiral nodded. "It helps that he has an IQ of 178 and good instincts. He's also confirmed something I wanted to discuss with the both of you.

"First off, I plan to give our hosts every opportunity to prove they can be trusted. *However*, I find the city's social structure, and this talk about communing with God, somewhat discomforting. I can't help but think we're dealing with a bunch of religious zealots or nut jobs. But there might be something in the water or food supply that's causing their hallucinations. I'd like to hear your thoughts."

Floyd Sullivant spoke first. "I'm no doctor, but from my observations, they appear sane."

"I agree," added Gloria. "But until we're certain, I would suggest humoring them, sir. Doing so may provide us with additional information."

"Yes, we know so little about them as it is." the admiral mused. "We still have a couple of hours before our dinner with the chancellor. I'd like some reconnaissance work done. Explore the city, talk to some of its inhabitants, and look for anything out of the ordinary. Just be back with your report before dinner."

"Yes, sir," said Floyd. "Muldoon, start with that park the Prime Keeper showed us. Pretend that you're enjoying the scenery—perhaps someone will open up to you. I'll start with a foldway near the city wall and work my way toward the inner city." Adjusting the filter covering his nose and mouth, Floyd turned and walked over to the foldway. Gloria followed close behind.

"I don't like the two of you being on your own," the admiral said as Gloria scanned her list of foldway codes. "Make sure you take a partner to watch your back. The New Terrans have already split us up into individual apartments. We don't need to add to our vulnerability. Besides, it'll be more convincing to see two people out and about than one; less suspicious that way."

"Right," Floyd said. "Muldoon, take Fletcher—the boy spends too much time hovering over a computer, he could use some fresh air. I'll take Ogeto."

Gloria moaned. "Why can't I have Ogeto? All Jeremy wants to talk about is old-style sci-fi movies and, God help me, progressive rock music from the 1970s."

Floyd was typing on his SID, letting Ogeto know where to meet him. "You won't be out there discussing music and movies. Besides, it's less suspicious if two people of the opposite sex are exploring the city."

Gloria chuckled. "I don't know if you've noticed yet, but the sight of two women walking together is not such an unusual sight in this neck of the woods, my friend."

Floyd rolled his eyes. "Believe me, I've noticed. In fact, this arrangement is much more for my benefit than yours."

"How so?"

Floyd slipped his SID in his jumpsuit pocket. "If what I suspect is true, the male inhabitants of New Terra are considered second-class citizens. In which case, it would appear suspicious for Jeremy and me to be seen together. Think back . . . was there any moment between entering the city and leaving the Basilica of Knowledge that you saw two men together? I know I didn't."

Gloria thought about it then shook her head.

"As for Jeremy, if he starts talking about sci-fi movies, counter it by talking about romantic comedies or—"

"But I don't like romantic comedies."

"—or something else, I don't care."

The admiral cut in. "My sentiments exactly. If you don't mind, I'd like the two of you to get started while I'm still young."

"Yes, sir," they both said in unison.

●

NINETY MINUTES LATER

Richard stepped out of the shower feeling rejuvenated, like he'd washed twelve months of grime from his brown, muscular body. Having genuine, running water cascading across his skin (instead of a sonic shower) made him feel clean and fresh rather than just dirt free.

After toweling off, he donned an outfit that had been provided by their hosts. The clothes were loose and airy and made from a sleek fabric he was unable to identify. Perhaps it was a form of silk, he mused, produced from the web of a local insect or arachnid. It felt wonderful against his skin and fit perfectly. He would've chosen a different style, but it was better than wearing his military issue jumpsuit to dinner.

With some time remaining before he was due to leave, Richard decided to relax for a while. "Computer, what are my entertainment choices?"

A velvety female voice chimed in, "Please specify the category you wish to enjoy: Music, Movies, Sports, General Entertainment, News and—"

"Music, please," Richard said, not wanting to go through the entire list.

"To access the music category, you must specify the genre, specific song, or groups."

The program was almost exactly like his old system back on Earth. "Computer, do you have any rock and roll from the twentieth century stored in your memory banks?"

There was a short pause. "Yes, Commander."

"Well then, I'd like you to play a random thirty-minute selection of songs by The Beatles."

The next thing Richard heard was the opening chord of The Beatles classic, "A Hard Day's Night." The speaker system was extraordinary; it felt like being enclosed in a musical cocoon. Plopping down in the easy chair, Richard closed his eyes, and for the next half hour enjoyed the melodic styling of John, Paul, George, and Ringo.

Before he knew it, the final notes of "Something" were played, and the block of music came to an end. Richard couldn't help but think of his wife. Erin had loved The Beatles with a passion that bordered on fanaticism—hearing their eclectic sound only served to remind him of how much he missed her.

Knowing that he would turn morose if he continued to dwell on the past, Richard checked the time and, seeing that he still had five minutes before he needed to rejoin his shipmates, decided to play one more song: "Computer, play 'Hey Ya!' by Outkast."

The upbeat music and lyrics pushed away the dark cloud of depression that threatened to ruin his earlier good mood. As the song ended, he took a deep, cleansing breath and, with a renewed spirit, approached the room's foldway. He entered the code, but had to wait a few seconds before the foldway shimmered to life. A swishing backside belonging to Gloria Muldoon was walking away from the foldway. The security officer must have arrived seconds earlier, which explained his foldway's delay in activating.

After realizing that others were probably waiting their turn to use their own foldway, Richard quickly stepped across the threshold and instantly traveled from his room to an antechamber connected to the banquet hall. He'd barely walked five feet when he heard someone else stepping though the foldway. He turned and saw Bram Waters enter the antechamber.

●

Glancing around, Bram noticed that he was the last of his group to arrive. They stood in a small yet ornate room: a chandelier hung from the ceiling; a light-pink, velvet divan sat atop a purple, wood-paneled floor; three portraits of blonde-haired women adorned pale-blue walls that held clear glass sconces with electric lights, mimicking candles.

Standing motionless against the wall beside the foldway was a short, bald man with a button nose. He wore a sleeveless white tunic and held a tray filled with amber-colored drinks. Bram took a glass and offered his thanks. He received no response. The man's smooth, flat face wore a vacant expression. The social hierarchy of New Terra was beginning to grate on Bram's nerves. Opening his mind, he searched for any thought coming from the servant, but found nothing . . . the man was a blank slate.

Taking a sip of the fragrant liqueur, Bram approached Floyd, his mind still on the servant. Despite his vow to never force his way into another person's mind, his frustration got the better of him. There wasn't a person on Earth who could resist his psychic probe if he so desired, but this wasn't Earth. Instead of accessing the man's thoughts, Bram walked into a mental brick wall. He pushed again, this time harder, trying to force a psychic opening, but was thwarted a second time. Undeterred, he focused his mind like a laser. With tremendous effort, he sensed consciousness . . . but consciousness hidden behind a barrier, a screen of sorts.

"Are you all right?"

Blinking with surprise, Bram suddenly realized he'd stopped in his tracks and was sporting an expression nearly as blank as the servant he'd been trying to read. Floyd was staring at him with a look of concern in his dark-blue eyes.

"What? Uh . . . I'm fine, I just—" Bram paused, noticing that nearly everyone was gazing at him. He could sense their concern—only Solomon Chavez appeared apprehensive. Having gone so far as to push at the servant's mind, Bram was on the verge of doing the same to Chavez. At the last moment he held back. Motioning with his head for Floyd to follow him, Bram approached the admiral. She noticed the look of concern on his face and held up her hand, cutting off whatever Dr. Singh was saying.

"What is it, Mr. Waters?"

Bram nodded an obligatory greeting to the doctor before facing Admiral Axelrod. "Ma'am, I was—" he saw the perturbed look on her face and corrected himself. "Sorry, *sir* . . . I hate to interrupt you, but we haven't had a chance to talk since our arrival in New Terra, and I thought you should know: the planet's atmosphere is not blocking me from reading these people's minds. They've developed a powerful psychic shield. Unfortunately, I haven't determined whether it's mechanical or physical. Either way, they don't seem to know that I've been trying to get inside their heads."

The admiral thought for a moment. "I wonder if I should bring it up with the chancellor," she said. "About that other thing we talked about in my cabin . . ." Bram could tell she was unwilling to speak freely in front of Singh. ". . . the one that caused you great concern. Have you made any progress on that front?"

She was obviously referring to the alien presence he'd felt in the forest. By the look in her eye, the admiral wanted him to play along and not divulge anything in front of Singh—but why?

Why would she keep something this important from the rest of the crew, he wondered?

"No, it's still a mystery to me . . . however—"

Whatever Bram intended to say next was put on hold when the double doors leading to the banquet hall swung open. A servant, who looked remarkably like the man serving drinks, stood to one side and held out his hand, motioning for the group to enter the hall.

●

This dinner is going reasonably well, Solomon thought. The air in the dining hall was being filtered, which meant their masks could be left back in their rooms. The conversation was civil, the food was better than expected, and the unfamiliar music was agreeable, which made for a pleasant evening. It also helped that the hall was full of beautiful women: what could possibly go wrong?

He'd soon find out.

The dining hall held twenty-two circular tables with ten guests each, most from the upper echelon of New Terran society. Solomon noted that Floyd and his crew sat a table away, while he and his remaining shipmates were seated at a table with Lorna Threman. To her right sat an older woman with white hair: Kateling Tarnal, former chancellor of New Terra and senior adviser to Lorna Threman. To the chancellor's left sat a middle-aged, red-headed woman with a round face and a haughty air about her: Jemis Calverton, High Priestess of New Terra. Most of her night was spent studying the landing party, like an entomologist would examine a newly discovered class of insect.

Shifting his gaze to the next table, he saw Gloria Muldoon look quickly down at her plate. It wasn't the first time over the previous few days he'd caught the young woman watching him. She'd become unduly fascinated by his looks, which made him quite uncomfortable. He wished she'd not been added to the crew, but Floyd Sullivant insisted. He prayed she hadn't become sexually fixated on him. It wasn't that she was unattractive—on the contrary, she was quite beautiful, and coldly aloof and disturbingly formidable. No, it was that she . . .

While taking a bite of savory, braised carrots, Solomon's thoughts were interrupted by the old woman, Kateling Tarnal, saying, "Surely you can't be serious, Mr. Waters? Do you contend that personal freedom is a good thing?" The former chancellor looked astounded.

"Don't get me wrong, Ms. Tarnal," he replied. "Complete freedom invariably leads to chaos. The human race will probably never evolve to the point where complete freedom is feasible—but we can still hope, we can still dream about a future where peace is the norm and there's no need for authoritarian regimes to keep the people in line."

"Such notions are just that, Mr. Waters: mere dreams. In fact, they are delusions designed to placate the masses with false hope, a hope that only serves to foment discord," she asserted.

Lorna Threman added, "As you study this colony's history, you will find that we too valued freedom . . . at the outset. Unfortunately, after nearly two hundred years, a rebellion broke out, resulting in a bloody civil war. We put it down, managed to regroup, and then formed the society you now see today: one that has lived in peace for almost two thousand years."

"People like structure in their lives, Mr. Waters," said Kateling Tarnal, picking up where the chancellor left off. "It's comforting to know that you have a place in society, one where you don't feel the need to stab another person in the back to achieve success. When society works like a well-oiled machine, it becomes stable, and there's no need to worry about overpopulation or the other ills that manifest from living too close to the edge of anarchy."

"I see your point," Bram said, drawing amazed looks from his shipmates. "Freedom is messy. If a society wanted to embrace true freedom, it would have to sacrifice an enormous amount of safety. People like being safe, which means that even the freest society is closer to a police state than a utopia. Sadly, however, when too much structure is imposed, creativity is compromised, innovation is stifled, individuality is suppressed, and stagnation inevitably ensues."

Bram sensed that his words were causing the desired effect—emotional turmoil in their hosts. Perhaps if their ability to block their thoughts were a physical aptitude, he could rile one of them to the point where they'd lower their guard enough for him to read their mind. Though the chancellor and her two advisers were attempting to stay calm, Bram could tell that all three were angry over his insinuation that New Terra was nothing more than a stagnant police state. Reaching out with his mind, he tried to slip past their mental defenses but again failed. Bram kept butting up against the same barrier he'd run into before. He sensed faint emotions, almost like shadows on a wall, but picked up absolutely no thought patterns.

There was an awkward silence, but then Jemis Calverton, the High Priestess, began to laugh. "You are quite the philosopher, Mr. Waters. So tell me, is that your role? Is there a great need for philosophers while establishing a new colony? Or do you philosophize in your spare time . . . as a hobby of sorts?"

Glancing over at Admiral Axelrod, Bram sensed that she was observing this exchange with great interest. He decided to press onward. "I'd say that philosophers are needed in every society, even a society such as your own . . . but that's not my *role* in the landing party, per se. You see, I'm a psychic detective, by trade."

Frightened looks crossed the faces of the chancellor and her two companions. At the tables closest to theirs, the conversation became hushed. Bram realized too late that he should've kept this tidbit of information to himself.

"Do you mean to tell me that you're a, a mind-reader, Mr. Waters?" hissed Kateling Tarnal as she leaned forward, her thin, hawk-like visage boring into Bram like a raptor ready to strike.

"You'll have to forgive my friend, Ms. Tarnal," the admiral cut in. "He has, shall we say, an unusual sense of humor. As we all know, mind-reading is just a myth fostered by charlatans and Vegas lounge acts."

The former chancellor eyed the admiral suspiciously. "I'm not exactly sure what a 'Vegas lounge act' is, but I take your meaning." She turned her attention back to Bram. "It's a good thing you're not a mind-reader, Mr. Waters—because if you were, it would do you no good. The Lord protects us from anyone or anything trying to subvert the holy human mind."

"If you don't mind me asking, Mr. Waters," inquired Lorna Threman, "what exactly *is* your function in the landing party?"

Bram thought fast. "I'm . . . the official civilian representative. A landing party should contain more than just military, scientific, and professional types, right?"

The chancellor glanced at the others. "I suppose there's a place for that." Her eyes stopped on Richard Allison and lingered.

The commander was looking at his plate and didn't notice. Bram didn't need psychic powers to know the chancellor found the dashingly handsome pilot attractive. She appeared ready to ask him a question, but Solomon spoke first. "Ms. Tarnal, a moment ago you said the Lord protects the people of New Terra from mental intrusion. How is that accomplished?"

The former chancellor had been studying Lorna Threman, noting her fervent interest in the commander. She was anything but happy. "I'm sorry, Dr. Chavez, what were you saying?"

Solomon repeated his question.

"Ah, yes," she said, thoughtfully. "It began after the rebellion that nearly tore our society apart. A plague came about that prevented the conception of children, so the Lord stepped in and took over the process. After that, the Ghosts of Yggdrasil no longer lured us to our deaths, and as a result, the population has been steady ever since."

"Yggdrasil . . . why does that name sound so familiar?" asked Karen Albans.

Bram said, "In ancient Norse mythology, a towering ash tree called Yggdrasil—the Great Tree of the World—overshadowed everything, binding together heaven, hell, and the Earth. There was also something about two or three animals . . . but I forget what they represented."

Jemis Calverton, the High Priestess, noted, "The Lord says that an eagle sat at the top of the tree, a serpent coiled itself around the tree's base, and a squirrel ran between the two, causing strife. I must admit, the Norse had an odd belief system."

Dr. Singh dabbed his mouth with a napkin, wiping a creamy gray sauce from his thick black mustache. "Being a man of science, I don't ascribe to religious dogma," he said disdainfully, his remark causing the High Priestess's eyes to narrow with anger. "However, I'm quite intrigued by the plague your chancellor claimed was at the root of your infertility. It sounds fascinating."

The admiral groaned softly and Solomon was shaking his head. Most of the people at the table, other than Singh himself, had picked up on the doctor's insensitivity, including their hosts.

"I say, your people must have suffered through quite an ordeal before you found a cure," he continued. "How long did it take before your populace resumed giving birth?" He speared a roasted asparagus tip with his fork, placed it in his mouth, and began to chew.

Jemis Calverton's anger turned to sadness.

Lorna Threman, a pained expression on her face, reached for her glass of juice.

Kateling Tarnal was gazing off in the distance—likely remembering something from her past.

Regaining her composure, Jemis Calverton replied to Singh's inquiry. "As former chancellor Tarnal said, we can no longer give birth. The Lord provides us with children as She sees fit."

"What?!" The doctor's fork paused halfway to his mouth. He was stunned, and he wasn't the only one: his shipmates were staring at the High Priestess in open astonishment. "B-but, I don't understand," he sputtered. "Are you trying to tell me that no one has given birth in the last two thousand years?"

Jemis Calverton nodded sympathetically. "I'm afraid that's the case, Doctor. But don't worry. Babies are still produced on a regular basis."

"But . . . how is this possible?" pressed Singh. "Are you using cloning techniques, or—"

"All will be explained tomorrow," the High Priestess declared. "As for tonight, let us abstain from unpalatable topics. This is a night for pleasantries and camaraderie, not painful reminders of a past we can do nothing about."

"So true, so true," the chancellor added, brushing a lock of golden-blonde hair behind her ear. "Tell me, Commander Allison, what is it like piloting such a magnificent ship as the *Arrow*?"

She seemed truly interested in the subject matter, though more so in Richard, who hesitantly launched into the mechanics of piloting a starship. From that point on, the night's conversation shied away from anything serious, though Bram's unease remained steady.

15

"**L**orna, I have a favor to ask of you.*"

The dinner was over, and Lorna Threman lay on her bed, thinking about the muscular, dark-skinned pilot. Her right hand had slid down her silky, white belly and disappeared beneath her panties when the husky female voice sounded in her head.

She gave a start and sat upright. "Of course, Lord, whatever you wish."

"*I have noticed that you find the dark-skinned man attractive.*"

Lorna felt her cheeks turn bright red. "If you mean the dark-skinned man, Lord . . . um, he, uh, possesses a certain appeal, yes."

"*He is not like the other men you have coupled with, is he?*"

Lorna could barely find her voice. "No, Lord," she whispered.

"*Commander Allison possesses an intimate knowledge of the starship known as* Solomon's Arrow,*" the voice observed. "I want you to seduce him and gain his trust. You can then attain valuable information from him, specifically, the command codes that control the ship's helm. You are well aware of how important it is for me to gain this knowledge, correct? You must not fail in this mission which I bestow upon you.*"

Lorna's pulse began to quicken at the prospect of bedding the commander. "When would you like me to institute this plan, Lord?"

"Tonight," the voice replied. *"He has returned from a meeting with his commanding officer, and is in the process of preparing for bed. The time is ideal for you to seduce him. It should not be difficult. The men of his era were renowned for their potent sex drive. Do not be swept up in the moment and forget your purpose; men such as he were celebrated for their abilities in bed, primarily due to their large sex organs, so steel yourself against his physical attributes."*

"Yes, Lord," she murmured, feeling a delicious quiver in her belly. She'd finally be able to fulfill a long-held sexual fantasy: to achieve orgasm with a well-endowed man instead of by self-manipulation or by mechanical means or from the good graces of other women. She'd slept with New Terra's pathetic excuses for males on several occasions, but had always been disappointed. Perhaps this time would be the exception. Commander Allison was unlike any man she'd ever met (or seen), and the prospect of feeling his manhood inside her was making her head swim.

Lorna slipped out of her clothes, dabbed a few drops of phero-mone-laced perfume on strategic regions of her body, and shimmied into a red, low-cut, body-hugging dress she hoped would appeal to Richard's prurient interests. She then accessed the code for his room and placed the call she'd been fantasizing about all night.

●

Having set his PID to wake him at seven in the morning, Richard was pulling down his bed sheets when the apartment's transceiver beeped. He pressed the talk button on his night stand's control panel and answered, "Hello?"

The caller's voice was unmistakable. "Hello, Commander, this is Chancellor Threman. I was wondering if I could speak with you about a few things."

"Sure, Chancellor," Richard said, clearing his throat. "What would you like to know?"

"Please, call me Lorna," she cooed. "And if you don't mind, I'd rather talk face-to-face."

Richard looked down; he was wearing nothing but his military issue boxer/briefs. "Can't this wait 'til morning?"

There was a pause. "I suppose so," she replied. "But, I was hoping to speak with you alone. Please don't deny me this simple request, Commander. I promise not to keep you up *too* late."

Richard realized this would be a perfect opportunity to pump her for information. "Give me a few minutes to dress and I'll be ready. Where would you like to meet?"

"I'll transmit my apartment code to your foldway. Whenever you're ready, press the enter button."

"Thank you, Lorna," he said, feeling unaccountably nervous. "I'll see you shortly."

As Richard hurriedly threw on his clothes, he realized he should let Admiral Axelrod know about the forthcoming meeting with the chancellor. Once dressed, he established a link with the admiral's PID and received this response: "Admiral Axelrod has retired for the evening. Unless this is an emergency, please try again tomorrow morning . . . thank you."

Was this an emergency? No, he should let the admiral sleep.

Richard activated the foldway and stepped across the threshold. He barely registered the spacious, ornately decorated room. His eyes were locked onto the chancellor. She lounged in a lightly padded armchair, her low-cut, red dress having a slit up the side, one that revealed a perfectly sculpted leg, easily draped over the other in a pose of casual sensuality.

"Hello, Commander," she said, slowly uncrossing her legs and standing.

Richard had to force himself not to gulp. "Please . . . call me Richard."

"I'd like that," she responded, moving toward what looked like a bar stocked with liquor.

"Would you like a drink, Richard?" she asked, casting a sultry look over her left shoulder.

"Yes, I would." He was beginning to think she had more on her mind than his piloting skills.

Richard had been faithful to his wife and had slept with only one woman since her death. He was so nervous his stomach was tangled up in knots.

The chancellor carried two glasses containing a dark-red liquid. "I hope this suits your taste, Richard. It's made from a local berry that's one of the few foods on this planet safe to eat," she said, handing him the glass. Lorna sat on a light-blue divan and patted the cushion beside her. "It's a seventy-nine year old vintage reserved for the chancellor alone. It's quite lovely, I hope you enjoy it."

Sitting, Richard took a sip of the strong, sweet wine and smiled. "It's very good, better than I expected."

Lorna scooted a bit closer. "I was hoping you would say that," she replied, lightly placing her hand on his forearm.

Richard could barely catch his breath. "You, um, said that the berry is, uh, one of the few foods on this planet that humans can eat. Why is that?"

Richard noticed Lorna's brow crease momentarily—she obviously didn't want to talk about agricultural products, or much else.

"Yes, well, this planet is almost devoid of selenium, without which humans cannot survive. Also, most of its plants are toxic when eaten, and Earth plants won't grow in the soil, due to the planet's incompatible anaerobic bacteria. We're forced to use hydroponics to grow most of our food. The one exception is protean. Owing to the fact that there is very little animal life on this planet, we had to improvise." Richard could tell she was growing bored with the subject. "Not long after the colony was established, the settlers grew tired of soy products and went looking for a replacement. They found a fungus growing in the forest that could be cultured into an almost perfect facsimile of meat."

"Was that what I mistook for lamb, during tonight's dinner?" he asked.

"Yes . . . the first colonists remembered the differences in flavor of many Earth meats, so they developed additives to flavor the fungus cultures. We can prepare steak and pork—and lamb as you already know. Also, we've come up with a few others over the intervening centuries that suit our own particular tastes. We have names for them, but I won't bore you. As for the selenium, a few weeks after arriving on this planet, our ancestors discovered a nut similar to the Brazil nut, containing the only form of selenium on the planet. This nut, which we call the 'Chili Nut,' because of its distinctive cumin-like flavor, is found high in the forest canopy. But enough of this; I'd rather talk about other things . . . or not at all," she said, coquettishly.

This time, Richard scooted a little closer to her. It was obvious that she was attracted to him, and the feeling was mutual. He'd have to be a eunuch to pass up a chance like this. "Right now, I'm not feeling very talkative."

Seeing her eyes dart down to his lips, Richard caressed her cheek, slid his fingers into her golden-blonde hair, cupped the back of her head, and gently pulled Lorna in. When their lips met, a fire ignited within him, an intense passion he hadn't felt in over two years. Her arms wrapped around his neck and a guttural moan escaped her throat.

Moments later, their hands were on each other's bodies, moving frantically, pulling at each other's clothes. When his underwear came off, Lorna gasped, her eyes growing wide, her body giving a slight shudder of anticipated pleasure.

Richard ached with an overpowering need to be inside her, so he took her right there on the couch . . . and again later on the bed.

●

The next morning, Lorna woke Richard with her lips wrapped around his quickly engorging manhood. She couldn't get enough of him. Naturally, he responded as she hoped . . . by pulling her on top of him and entering her like a man possessed. He filled her up (and more so), making her head swim with ecstatic agony. Within minutes, he brought her to a crashing orgasm—just as he'd done on several occasions the night before.

Thank you, Lord, for asking me to seduce him, she thought, just before Richard released his own climax deep inside her.

"You are welcome, my child. It pleases me to see you so happy. However, you did not talk much before your lovemaking. I want you to invite him into your bed as often as it takes to learn about the ship's helm. From your physical response, I assume that you have no objections to this simple request."

None, Lord . . . none whatsoever.

●

Jeremy Fletcher tried to ignore Dr. Singh's bitching and moaning as the large wooden gates swung open and the carriage trundled out, carrying both men to the shuttlecraft.

"Don't dawdle in the shuttle, Ensign Fletcher," Dr. Singh droned on. "I want to return in time for the birthing chamber tour."

"Yes, Doctor," Jeremy replied. "It's just . . . there's something the admiral asked me to check while onboard. I'm not sure how long it'll take, but I'll try to be as quick as possible."

The carriage was similar to the one that greeted the landing party, only smaller. After parking itself beside the shuttle, the two men exited, and Jeremy entered an access code into his SID. The shuttle door opened, and a seven-foot long ramp slid out and down. The two entered the airlock for decontamination and were soon inside the main bay removing their air filters.

"I'm not here just as your escort, Doc," Jeremy announced as soon as they were inside.

"What do you mean, Ensign?"

"The admiral didn't want me saying anything while en route, but I'm on a security mission." He approached the ship's computer. "I've accessed some unusual files from the Prime Keeper's computer, and the admiral wants me to decrypt them while we're here prepping the vaccine for distribution."

"And how long will that take?" the doctor grunted.

"If I'm unable to crack the files in the next hour, then I'll transmit them to the *Arrow* and let the quantum computer have a shot at them."

"Very well," Dr. Singh huffed as he made his way aft to the medical station.

Jeremy was glad to see the containment door close behind the doctor. At least he wouldn't be forced to contend with the self-important jackass's complaints for a while—or so he hoped.

Once the files were downloaded, all that was required of Jeremy was to wait while the computer worked its magic. He would've uploaded the files directly to the *Arrow*, bypassing the shuttlecraft's computer, but he wanted to play it safe—New Terra might possess a method of detecting and descrambling his transmission, thus discovering the theft of their hidden files.

After a few seconds, a security barrier stopped the computer in its tracks. He'd half expected as much. After cracking his knuckles, Jeremy let his fingers fly across the keyboard screen, manually entering the artful little programs that would let him bypass the firewalls surrounding the first encrypted file. The process took longer than expected, but within a few minutes the file opened up, spilling its startling contents.

Jeremy watched as the holographic view screen came to life. A space-based HV camera was focused on an image of the Yellowstone caldera eruption. The tremulous voice of a network news anchor was saying, "As you can see, ladies and gentlemen, the terrorists were not bluffing: they've blown up the caldera. We are showing you a live image, captured moments after the underground nuclear device was detonated. The blast was devastating enough, but it's the magma and ash that is the bigger problem, according to Dr. Mica Swain, the lead geophysicist working for this network. She claims that you have just witnessed a possible extinction-level event, I'm sad to report." The reporter's voice caught in his throat.

A terrorist attack? But that's not what we were told. Jeremy watched in horror as devastation rained down—like flaming raindrops from Hell—on the states surrounding Yellowstone. It made him sick to his stomach when the broadcast switched to the various camera crews recording the devastation from ground level, all of whom knew they were doomed yet continued to broadcast up until the last moment. Each of them was either swept up in the rapidly moving, superheated pyroclastic flow or, somewhat farther away, pummeled by falling volcanic debris.

The transmission ended with a view from space showing destruction on a massive scale.

"Fucking shit," groaned Jeremy.

The idea that any group, no matter how radical their views, would purposely ruin the Earth's biosphere was beyond Jeremy's comprehension. Seething inside, he saved the decrypted file to his SID and set about cracking the next one. He was nearly through when Dr. Singh exited the medical compartment and approached his station.

"Are you almost finished, Ensign?"

Jeremy nodded, not taking his eyes off the screen. "Just a few more seconds, Doc," he said, his fingers a blur.

"Fine. Whenever you're done, I'll inject you with the vaccine," he sighed. "I've already injected myself. It'll take approximately twelve hours before full efficacy is achieved, so keep your mask on in the interim."

By the time Dr. Singh finished speaking, Jeremy had cracked the file and a video began to play. The image was of a retreating starship, similar in both size and shape to the *Arrow*. Once again, the video was accompanied by the voice of a news reporter, this time female.

"Coming to you live from the bridge of the *USS Axelrod*, this is Krista Calloway bringing you a live update on the dramatic seizing of the starship, *Burnham's Hope*. As we all know, confusion reigned, and still does, in the aftermath of the Yellowstone caldera eruption. We now know this was the CRA's goal. During the confusion, five CRA rebel ships, commanded by the terrorist, Brill Easterbrook, attacked the security vessels guarding *Burnham's Hope*. Her terrorist cohorts boarded the recently completed ship and murdered its crew. Before space-patrol could mount a response, nearly four thousand of Brill's rebel allies were onboard the *Hope*. By the time the *USS Axelrod* arrived to give chase, the *Hope* was fully powered and accelerating toward the Burnham Space Portal, which was also seized by the CRA terrorists."

The pursuing starship was gaining ground, but not fast enough.

Jeremy was transfixed. The transmission changed to a split screen, with one side showing the pursuit and the other side the announcer, an attractive black woman with shoulder-length auburn hair. She stood on the *USS Axelrod's* bridge near the captain, who was staring at his view screen, a look of fury on his square, battle-hardened face.

"Dammit! They should be slowing down, not speeding up," the captain spat.

"Why is that, Captain McClure?" the reporter asked.

His reply contained an edge of malice. "The craft is approaching the Burnham Portal at full speed, Ms. Calloway. It *must* decelerate before entering it, or face disastrous results."

"Can't you fire a weapon and disable it, before it reaches the portal?"

"If we did fire at the ship," he replied, "we would most certainly hit the engines and cause a massive explosion, which would engulf our own ship. Of course, if you're ready to die today, we could go ahead and try that, Ms. Calloway." She shook her head emphatically. "No, thank you."

On the other side of the split-screen, a circular object came into view growing rapidly in size.

"Is that the space portal?" Dr. Singh asked, giving Jeremy a start. He'd completely forgotten that Singh was standing over his shoulder.

"Yeah, Doc, I'm pretty sure it is."

"So, tell me, what did the captain mean when he said there would be disastrous results if the starship failed to pass slowly through the portal, Ensign Fletcher?"

Jeremy kept his eyes locked on the screen. "I have a sneaking suspicion, Doc, but I'd rather not say just yet."

The image on the screen changed back to a single shot of the large starship. "To whoever is in command of *Burnham's Hope*, this is Captain Ryan McClure of the *USS Axelrod*. I'm giving you one last chance to change course before we fire upon your vessel." There was no response to the captain's bluff. He waited a full ten seconds before shouting, "The damned fools! Take her hard to starboard, Mr. Evans, and get us outta here. If we can't persuade them to stop, we can at least steer clear of the shit-storm that follows."

The camera zoomed in to follow the escaping starship's progress as it sped toward the space portal. A face unfamiliar to Jeremy, though very familiar to the people of the twenty-fifth century, filled the view screen. A woman in her forties appeared, with platinum blonde hair and hard, ice-blue eyes. The face belonged to Brill Easterbrook, leader of the CRA rebel group responsible for blowing up the Yellowstone caldera and stealing the starship, *Burnham's Hope*.

"People of Earth, your corrupt ways have doomed you to extinction. Mercifully, the followers of the One True God *will* survive to create a new Earth, on a virgin planet far from here. Think on your sins, while the flame of perdition consumes your damnable civilization."

The cold, calculating image of Brill Easterbrook was replaced by a shot of *Burnham's Hope*, as it hurtled toward the space portal.

Jeremy held his breath in anticipation as the ship passed through the portal. Suddenly, the screen went blank.

"What?! Why did it stop?" shouted Dr. Singh.

Jeremy was just as disappointed and frustrated as the doctor. "The rebel leader was probably recording the broadcast when the ship—"

The screen abruptly came back to life in a jumble of sound and fury. Alarms were going off; orders were being shrieked in a panicked voice. This time, the images were being recorded on the bridge of *Burnham's Hope*. Brill Easterbrook was picking herself off the floor. "Give me an update, goddamn it! What just happened?"

A terrified young man gripping the pilot's console sputtered, "It was the portal, ma'am. It blew up when we passed through."

"It blew up . . . good . . . perfect," Easterbrook said, reveling in the news. "I didn't expect that much backwash, but it blew up, just as I hoped. Now they'll never be able to follow us."

At this point, the screen once again went blank—and stayed that way.

●

Katherine absently entered the code for the Basilica of Knowledge, her mind consumed by the disturbing information decrypted by Ensign Fletcher. She now knew that the inhabitants of New Terra were descendants of religious extremists who'd exterminated billions of lives.

While onboard the shuttlecraft, Fletcher had decrypted two of the four files downloaded from the Prime Keeper's computer. He'd wanted to stay longer but had run out of time to decrypt them all. The third file would have taken over an hour to decrypt. And the last file had been written in a code so far removed from anything he'd encountered that he was forced to upload it to the *Arrow*'s quantum computer. Even that powerful system was having trouble breaking through the file's protective firewall. Learning of this, Katherine contacted the *Arrow* and reluctantly put Dr. Mona Levin on the job . . . from the confines of the brig, of course. Dr. Levin had designed the ship's computer and knew how to make it work at optimum efficiency.

After watching the highly disturbing videos discovered in the other two files, she could only imagine what the third and fourth files might contain. The duty officer had relayed the third file only moments ago, but she'd yet to watch it. That would come later in the day, after her visit to the birthing chamber.

Katherine stepped through the foldway. The rest of the landing party was there in the Basilica awaiting her arrival. Watching the videos twice had made her late, but only by five minutes.

"I was about to contact you, Admiral," said Jemis Calverton, High Priestess of New Terra. She wore an expression of concern on her plump, oval face. "Why were you delayed?"

"Um . . . my breakfast didn't sit well with me, if you know what I mean," she lied. "But don't worry, I'm feeling much better now."

"Are you quite sure, Admiral Axelrod?" the High Priestess inquired innocently. "We have a very effective antidiarrheal that I would be more than happy to—"

"No, no, I'm fine, thank you," Katherine quickly interjected, wishing she'd come up with a better excuse.

Jemis Calverton studied her a moment longer. "Very well. We shall proceed with the tour, beginning with the birthing chamber. Follow me please."

With a swish of her long blue robes, Calverton spun around and led the group across the atrium to a backroom containing a foldway, which she explained was preprogrammed for direct access to the birthing chamber.

"Obviously, very few people other than those of us in the Priesthood and a few select Keepers are allowed inside the birthing chamber," she said, sounding boastful. "It is a great honor for you to be allowed down there. The foldway opens using a biometric scanner instead of code, and will only work for those of us who have clearance."

So the birthing chamber is underground but why? Katherine wondered. *Was it to protect the delicate genetic material from outside attack, or from biological or radiological damage?*

"Between three and seven babies are delivered each day," Calverton noted. "One of those babies is due in a matter of minutes. It's a good thing your bowel problem cleared up, Admiral. It would've been a shame for you to miss it." She placed her palm against the biometric scanner located beside the foldway and smiled. To Katherine, it looked more like a sneer.

The darkness of the foldway was replaced by a soft pink light. The group stepped through into an oval room without a single sharp edge or hard surface. With its soft floor and walls, and its delightful pink lighting, the room felt comforting, like they'd entered a huge, warm womb. On the far side of the birthing chamber stood two women in pink scrubs, positioned on either side of a two-foot wide sphincter, situated at waist level on the wall directly behind them.

"Good," Jemis Calverton said. "The acolytes have been notified to catch a newborn. We will soon be giving witness to the newest member of our glorious society, Praise the Lord."

Glancing around at the others, Katherine knew what they were thinking: this should be one helluva birth.

The High Priestess motioned with her finger, signaling them to move closer to the acolytes and to keep their voices low.

268 ● J. DALTON JENNINGS

"The baby needs a quiet environment to facilitate a stress-free birth. Measures like this create well-adjusted individuals," she whispered with assurance.

The acolytes glanced nervously at the watchful group. They were obviously unaccustomed to having an audience but quickly regained their composure and turned back to the sphincter—just in time to see the baby start to crown.

The sphincter bulged outward, exposing more of the baby's head. With the acolytes standing ready to catch the newborn, a red gelatinous substance dribbled into a trough directly below the sphincter, then disappeared through a narrow slot in the wall.

The acolyte on the left reached out and cradled the baby's head as the sphincter extended further outward. Seconds later, the tiny gelatin-covered body slipped out through the opening and into the waiting arms of that same young woman. The other acolyte began to gently clean the red, gelatinous substance off the baby's delicate skin. That's when Katherine noticed something odd: a mechanical tube was attached to the umbilical cord. Staring at the unlikely sight, she heard a faint click—after which the tube detached itself and snaked its way back inside the sphincter. The remaining umbilical cord had been sealed with what appeared to be a blue ceramic clasp.

As the newborn began to cry, one of the acolytes wrapped it in a warm blanket.

"What is the baby's gender, Martalin?" the High Priestess inquired.

"The infant is a boy, Mother," the acolyte replied, sounding disappointed.

"Very well. Take him away." The two left the room through the foldway. "The acolytes are now taking the newborn to the nursery, three levels up," Calverton explained.

"Do the people of New Terra have a prejudice against males?" asked Dr. Singh.

The High Priestess studied him closely. "Not at all, Dr. Singh," she replied gruffly. "We each have our place in New Terran society. Even the best-built machine will cease to function when a seemingly insignificant part is damaged . . . is that not so?"

"I agree, but comparatively speaking, that part is still considered insignificant, am I right?"

Just what sort of game does Gurdev think he's playing? Katherine wondered.

"You are twisting my words, Doctor," hissed the High Priestess. "I clearly said that males are 'seemingly' insignificant."

"Yes, but I've noticed that there are no men in power. They all *seem* to be servants of one sort or another. I was just wondering why—"

"So, in your considered opinion servants are insignificant—is that what you're telling me, Dr. Singh?" Calverton snapped. "Maybe in *your* society they were considered lowly, but they play a valuable role in *ours*."

"That's not what I meant," Singh huffed, sounding flustered. "I, um, I apologize for my poor choice of words. I was merely concerned that your men weren't being allowed to live up to their full potential, that's all."

Katherine had to bite her lip to keep from laughing, seeing as she always enjoyed seeing the good doctor get his comeuppance. "Please overlook Dr. Singh. In our time the sexes were, for the most part, on equal footing. It's disturbing to see one sex in servitude to the other; although, perhaps there's a bit of karmic retribution going on, given that men are in servitude to women this time around," she chuckled. Most of the men under her command frowned or rolled their eyes, while the women tried to hide their amusement—albeit unsuccessfully. "By the by," she said, changing the subject. "The young acolyte called you 'Mother.' I was wondering about its significance, and also how we should address you."

Jemis Calverton headed toward the foldway. "The term 'Mother' stands for Mother Superior. Since I am the High Priestess of the medical class, Mother Superior is my official title. You may address me as such."

Dr. Singh snorted.

"Do I amuse you, Doctor?" she asked, stopping to face Singh.

"I find it laughable that you call yourself a medical professional," he sneered. "From what I see, you conflate science and religion. I fail to understand how you can reconcile such disparate systems, since every good scientist knows that a belief in God is superstitious nonsense."

"Blasphemer!" shouted the High Priestess. Livid, she shook her fist in Singh's face, her own face contorted with rage. "How dare you! How dare you speak such blasphemous words! And in, of all places, *our Holiest of chambers!*"

16

hatever was blocking Bram's telepathy was having difficulty shielding Jemis Calverton's anger. Singh's thoughtless comments had infuriated her. Moreover, Bram was registering strong currents of outrage from his fellow crew members, most especially the admiral, who decided to express their emotions heatedly.

"Goddamn it, Singh!" the admiral shouted. "What the hell's the matter with you?"

The doctor stood there wearing a clueless expression on his face. "But it's obvious, isn't it?" he responded, bridling under the criticism. "They're using some sort of artificial womb, probably based on Dr. Chavez's design."

"I don't give a damn if they believe the babies float down on a cloud directly from heaven, you don't insult someone in their own home! I apologize for the conduct of our doctor, Mother Superior. Please don't hold it against the rest of us because of one ignorant fool's words."

Dr. Singh began to sputter, "W-what? But, but I—"

"Enough, Doctor!" the admiral snapped. "And that's an order."

Bram was studying the High Priestess. Her eyes had slipped out of focus for a moment.

"If you will follow me," she said coldly. "The tour is over."

Turning on her heel, she activated the biometric scanner and exited the birthing chamber. The group followed close behind, casting angry looks at Dr. Singh. As they entered the spacious basilica, the admiral was again trying to placate Jemis Calverton. Her words broke off at the sight of two approaching Minders, their dark eyes fixed on Singh.

"Take this one to a detention cell," the High Priestess ordered, pointing at the doctor.

"What?! What's the meaning of this?" he erupted.

"Hold on!" the admiral demanded. "You can't just—"

"We certainly can, Admiral," Jemis Calverton snapped. "As you said, this is *our* house and we make the rules. Dr. Singh has not only committed blasphemy in our holiest of places, but also in front of a newborn. The penalty for this outrage is death. Take him away."

As the Minders stepped forward, both Floyd and Gloria moved in unison to block their path. What the doctor said in the birthing chamber was irrelevant, he was still one of them and deserved protection. Anticipating their reaction, the Minders whipped out their stun sticks and pointed them at Floyd and Gloria, who instinctively reached for their own weapons.

"Your sonic-disrupters are useless," cautioned the High Priestess. "They were neutralized the moment you stepped through the foldway into the birthing chamber. Did you think we would be foolish enough to allow working weaponry into our Holiest of Holies?"

"But this . . . this is outrageous!" shouted Dr. Singh. "We're your guests!"

"Then you should have behaved like one, instead of a confrontational fool, Doctor," declared Jemis Calverton. "Don't worry. You can petition the chancellor for clemency. Since you are ignorant of our laws, she may commute your sentence and let you spend some quality time in the Room of Atonement."

Bram could only imagine what atrocities took place in this so-called Room of Atonement. Judging by the name, it sounded like their hosts had stolen a page from the Spanish Inquisition's playbook, perhaps creating a punishment worthy of Torquemada himself.

●

Bram woke the following morning, still thinking about what transpired the previous day. After Singh was hauled away by the two Minders, he and the others were brought before the chancellor, who had given them a dressing down.

The admiral hadn't taken the reprimand well, demanding that Singh be released immediately. "The notion that a person can be sentenced to death because of the words they speak is barbaric, Chancellor," she seethed. "Dr. Singh was simply expressing his personal views. How would he know it was a capital offense?"

The chancellor sat on her throne, gazing down at the irate group. "There's an old adage from your time that goes like this, 'ignorance of the law is no excuse.'"

Admiral Axelrod had taken an aggressive step forward, looking as if she might explode with fury. The chancellor's personal guard took a corresponding step toward the admiral, stun-batons in hand. Lorna Threman hadn't seemed worried by the admiral's aggressive behavior, which to Bram meant her guards were more than capable of protecting her.

Admiral Axelrod had stopped and put her hands on her hips. "I'm not an idiotic warmonger from the Middle Ages, Chancellor. Attacking you would be foolish. So please, tell your goon squad to stand down."

Lorna Threman chuckled. "They have their jobs as I have mine, Admiral. Being chancellor of New Terra means that I have Dr. Singh's fate in my hands. He's been charged with the heinous crime of blasphemy; however, he was unaware of his crime at the time. Therefore, I have ordered that Dr. Singh spend a minimum of three hours in the Room of Atonement."

Bram's shipmates had grumbled their displeasure.

"Be thankful that I'm lenient," the chancellor counseled. "Judging by the doctor's attitude, he could use some atoning. Be assured, he won't be harmed . . . physically. And he may come out of this with a bit more humility."

For the next ten minutes, the admiral tried to change the chancellor's mind, but it was to no avail. Commander Allison also pleaded with her, but he too was unsuccessful. After his failed attempt, the commander glared at her, prompting the chancellor to avert her eyes. A pained expression crossed her face, causing Bram to sense the underlying sexual tension between the two. He caught Floyd's eye. The big man shot him a look that indicated he'd sensed the same thing. With a frown, Bram pushed the thought aside. It was highly unlikely the commander had slept with the colony's supreme leader in such a short time.

The chancellor had cut off further discussion. "We are done arguing. I should like to conduct a tour of the city?"

The remainder of the afternoon was spent in a large carriage, trundling through the streets of New Terra, barely listening as the chancellor pointed out the various sights she found interesting. Though a few polite questions were asked during the tour, most of that time was spent in a somber mood, their minds on Dr. Singh. At the end of the tour, just before they went their separate ways, the chancellor told the landing party something that would pique their interest: the next day they would accompany one of two separate teams beyond the city walls. One team would be going to the ice shelf to collect a rare, ore-bearing meteor—metal was in short supply on New Terra—and the other would be going to the Yggdrasil Forest to harvest chili nuts and fungus, thus supplementing the city's weekly supply of selenium and protein.

Both teams were departing at the same time, which meant that each crew member needed to choose between the expeditions. A majority chose the ice-shelf. Bram, however, elected to join the forest trip. Two other members of the crew would be accompanying him: Solomon Chavez and Gloria Muldoon.

Bram had noticed that when he and Gloria announced their interest in the forest expedition, Solomon Chavez had grumbled under his breath. Though he failed to hear what Solomon said, Gloria must have; she was fuming while awaiting her turn at the foldway. He tried to speak with her, but she dismissed his concerns, claiming she was fine, but he knew better. Her unwillingness to open up to him was troublesome. Bram hoped she didn't think he was merely feigning concern in an attempt to sleep with her again. He actually did want to sleep with her but was also intrigued by her reaction to Solomon. Did she have feelings for the dashing Brazilian? It was plausible. The man was intelligent, exceptionally good-looking, very mysterious, and richer than God—all of which were qualities that worked like catnip on certain members of the female gender.

As he threw on his jumpsuit, Bram realized that he was perturbed by the idea of Gloria being attracted to Chavez, or anyone else for that matter. With a sigh he shook his head. How could he be jealous? He barely knew the girl. Sure, she was gorgeous and great in bed, but they had little, if anything, in common.

Bram stepped through the foldway into a warehouse containing vehicles of assorted shapes and sizes. Most of the landing party, except for Dr. Solomon Chavez and Lt. Commander Albans, had already arrived and were gathered near a table holding plates of croissants, energy bars, a pitcher of juice, and what looked like a carafe of steaming hot coffee.

Bram made a beeline for the coffee, which turned out to be a rather pleasant grain substitute enhanced with caffeine. While taking a sip of the hot, black brew, he overheard Admiral Axelrod say to Gloria, "Keep watch over Chavez and Waters. I have a sneaking suspicion the chancellor's splitting us up for some reason."

Bram couldn't help but be troubled by the admiral's words. He glanced around the warehouse and saw that some of the workers, all male, were staring at them. Two of the men, who were taller and stockier than the others he'd seen so far, noticed his scrutiny and quickly looked away, but not before seeing anger, intermingled with fear, in their eyes.

Bram headed toward his shipmates, wishing he could sense the warehouse workers' actual emotions. He was saying hello to Floyd Sullivant when Lt. Commander Albans arrived, followed shortly by Solomon Chavez. With the entire landing party present, the chancellor stepped through the foldway, accompanied by five of the imposing, spiky-haired Minders, all of whom were clad in their signature, skintight cat-suits.

"Good, everyone's present," remarked a smiling Lorna Threman. "I'll be accompanying the expedition to the ice field and—" she looked around, "ah, there she is, and Ezral Magliss, New Terra's agricultural commissioner, will be accompanying the forest expedition."

The landing party saw a short, stocky woman in her mid-sixties, with a pug nose and a disgruntled expression, walk from behind a long, boxy vehicle, a retinue of male warehouse workers following in her wake. Stopping short, she faced her entourage and muttered something. All but one of the warehouse workers turned and left the way they came.

Ezral Magliss strode forward, assessing the landing party. "So, I finally get to meet the newcomers. I attended the welcoming dinner the night before last, but unfortunately did not get a chance to meet anyone. I'm looking forward to our time together. Normally, I don't accompany the work-crews to the Yggdrasil Forest, but the chancellor insisted that I give you a tour. I was in the process of inspecting a crop of purple hull peas on the eighteenth floor of building H-29, but that can wait."

"Did you say the eighteenth floor?" Albans inquired.

"Yes, I did. Why do you ask?"

Bram could tell that the normally retiring young woman was becoming nervous, what with so many eyes trained on her.

"We, um, we were told that your crops are grown hydroponically; does that mean you have entire buildings devoted to agricultural production?"

The commissioner gave Albans a condescending smile. "We have many hydro-farms throughout the city, all containing multiple floors. These buildings provide a majority of our food supply . . . and I'm in charge of the entire operation."

Albans had a faraway look in her eyes. "Before they died, my parents ran a beet farm in Iowa." She looked around sheepishly. "Sorry, I didn't mean to digress."

"Never apologize," the commissioner stated. "It pleases me to learn of your roots in farming. Once you and your crew are settled in, perhaps you will consider coming to work for me. I can always use an extra hand managing the men."

Albans shifted uncomfortably. "I'll, um, consider your offer, ma'am."

"Wonderful," the commissioner replied. "In the meantime, there's room for one more body on the harvester . . . that is, if you'd like to accompany us instead of traveling across a blank stretch of ice to pick up a space rock."

Albans turned excitedly to the admiral. "Do you mind, sir?"

Katherine shrugged. "I'd feel better if a command officer was along for the ride, anyway."

Lorna Threman shot the commissioner an irritated look. "Let's get started. As they say: 'The sun never moves, but the clock keeps ticking.'"

●

ONE HOUR LATER

Richard was, for the most part, glad he'd chosen the meteor rock expedition. It would last seven hours, compared to the forest mission, which would take at least fifteen before enough agro-products were harvested to make the trip worthwhile. But that also meant he'd be stuck in a confined space with Lorna Threman for the duration.

As the boxy transport sped toward the icy wasteland, Richard cast a sidelong glance in her direction and frowned. It wasn't that he regretted going to bed with her. What troubled him was her cavalier attitude toward punishing Dr. Singh. It signaled a flaw in her character that he found disquieting.

"In approximately ten minutes you'll notice the first traces of ice on the ground," declared the expedition leader, a young woman with auburn hair, who looked barely in her twenties. "After which, the ice will rapidly increase in abundance, covering the ground as far as the eye can see. We will then come to a halt and switch from wheels to tracks. This will take less than a minute. We should arrive at the meteor site an hour and a half later."

Richard glanced over at Lorna, who was sitting beside Admiral Axelrod. She'd been trying to chat up the admiral for the entire trip, but the admiral had been quiet, giving cursory replies to Lorna's inquiries. She seemed distracted by something, and Richard wondered if it had anything to do with the two decrypted files. Their contents were shocking. If so, perhaps she'd be more forthcoming after the meteor's recovery and their return to the city.

●

An assortment of small, multicolored insects buzzed around the five harvesters nearing the edge of the forest. Bram gazed out the lead harvester's control cabin window at the landscape. Behind him lay a flat plain, consisting mostly of grass and occasional patches of weeds, while in front of him stood a scattered line of trees that stretched from one horizon to the other. The forest wasn't nearly as thick as he expected, though the trees themselves were relatively tall.

"What are those?" asked Lt. Commander Albans. "Are there birds flying above the trees?"

Ezral Magliss answered. "No, not birds. Large insects, some of which have a wing span well over a foot in length."

"Are they dangerous?"

The commissioner shook her head. "Not unless you're perched on top of a tree. They seldom fly below fifty feet."

According to the commissioner, the caravan of vehicles would be harvesting nuts and fungus from an area that hadn't been reaped in over fifty years.

"Do you think we'll encounter any of your so-called Ghosts of Yggdrasil, commissioner?" Bram asked. Having encountered unusual phenomena before, the idea of seeing a ghost was not something he scoffed at.

"The Ghosts of Yggdrasil, eh?" The commissioner chuckled. "They are but a myth, a bedtime story told to frighten children, nothing more. I've never seen anything strange in this forest. To you and your friends, however, everything in this forest will seem unusual . . . at first glimpse. But ghosts? No, Mr. Waters, there are no Ghosts of Yggdrasil."

A slightly disappointed, somewhat skeptical Bram felt the vehicle come to a halt. He was skeptical because the closer he got to the forest the more intense his feelings of being watched became. He sensed gossamer threads of intelligence working their way past his psychic defenses, exploring areas of his mind that not even his old nemesis, Dr. Conrad Snow, could access. But how was that impossible? Was he being paranoid? Nothing could break through his defenses into that safeguarded place of private thoughts, willpower, and hidden desires.

And yet . . .

Despite the commissioner's assurances, he sensed an intelligent life force ahead. But he was unable to pinpoint its location, and that fact alone was enough to set him on edge.

"Our readings indicate that we'll find sizable patches of fungus seventy-five meters into the forest," the commissioner noted. "The fungus grows underground, in large, intermittent patches that are easy to harvest. During the harvest, we must remain inside the vehicle. The reason being: the harvest triggers an autonomic defense response in the fungus. Thinking it's under attack, it sends out fungal tendrils, which worm their way under the skin and release a toxin that paralyzes its victim. It then drains all the fluid from the body, leaving a dried husk that deteriorates rapidly into the soil."

Bram was thinking how creepy that sounded, when he suddenly caught a glimpse of someone ducking behind a tree. That someone had been a woman. But wait, that was impossible. Shaking his head, he turned his attention back to the commissioner.

Solomon Chavez was asking a question: "I'm keenly interested in examining the local flora, Commissioner. And that means leaving the confines of this harvester. It defeats the purpose of my accompanying this mission if I'm not allowed to—"

"Yes, yes, we can accommodate your curiosity, Dr. Chavez," the commissioner impatiently cut in. "I would prefer that you remain inside the vehicle during the harvest. However, if you simply can't wait, I will arrange for a skimmer to transport you to a place of relative safety."

"A skimmer?"

"Yes, it's a type of hovercraft used mainly to gather chili nuts from the upper canopy. You'll be happy to learn that it's equipped with a robotic arm and a molecular analyzer. Since it takes less time to gather the nuts than it does to harvest the fungus, we can use this vehicle's skimmer. Doing so shouldn't put us behind schedule that much."

●

Katherine stood near the rim of the crater, watching the excavator lower extraction equipment into the brightly-lit hole. The crew would be spending the next hour extracting meteor ore from the impacted soil and storing it for the return trip home. Spotlights shone on the small, brutish-looking men doing the difficult, dangerous work.

The mission was interesting, but Katherine would have rather accompanied Solomon to the forest instead of across a lonely sheet of ice in search of a damned rock. However, after reading the third file, it became necessary to examine the icy wasteland in person. As a bonus, she would be spending time with the chancellor. The first rule of battle is to know thy enemy . . . if Lorna Threman *was* the enemy. She was pleasant enough, but Katherine had not yet decided if the chancellor was friend or foe.

The two were discussing the lack of metallic ore on the planet when the chancellor suggested going to the excavator control room for a hot cup of coffee.

"Would you like to join me, Admiral?" she asked.

"Perhaps in a minute, thank you," Katherine replied. "But first I'll like to speak with my first officer about a—"

Her words were cut off by a wrenching punch to the gut. Staggering backward, Katherine stared in bewilderment at the cylindrical piece of ice sticking from her stomach. She collapsed to the ground, vision swimming. The chancellor was screaming for help and pointing toward the surrounding darkness. Two spotlights swung around and lit up the spot where she was pointing. A number of hairy, humanoid-looking creatures were seen diving for cover, seemingly into the very ice itself . . . but not before unleashing a final flurry of ice missiles at the excavation team.

Gasping for breath, Katherine clutched at the piece of ice protruding from her stomach. She heard the chancellor yelling orders to her security force, calling for defensive cover. Firing their stun-batons, the Minders opened up with a volley that kicked up a twenty-foot wide swath of ice, but the strange creatures were already gone.

Richard Allison was rushing toward her. Most of the others were still dodging the last of the ice missiles. One of the men rappelling down to the meteor was struck by a missile and toppled backward, hanging limp from his rope.

Katherine started coughing up blood. Flecks of crimson flew from her mouth, staining the ice in front of her. Horrendous pain blazed through her torso. She reached out in a desperate attempt to grasp Lorna's hand, but instead toppled sideways into a black pool of unconsciousness. In the split-second before she passed out, Katherine arrived at one unmistakable conclusion: the third file was true.

17

After journeying three miles from the harvesting operation, the skimmer hovered over a relatively thick stand of trees, similar to the ancient redwoods of Earth, only smaller in diameter and with less foliage.

Solomon complained, "This is all very interesting, but I don't understand why we can't fly closer to the ground."

Ezral Magliss tried to explain. "I'd like to accommodate you, Dr. Chavez, but it's just too dangerous. I'll lower the robotic arm and take as many samples as you like, but as far as—"

A multicolored insect, with a two-foot wingspan, bounced off the forward window, causing the commissioner to jump.

"What do those things eat?" Bram asked. "I haven't seen any flowers up here."

"Rodents the size of your thumb," she replied. "They're the main source of food for these and other insects that live up here in the canopy. Pilot, program the computer to search for and display a clutch of mardets on our view-screens."

The pilot's thin fingers flew across his control panel, and a few seconds later an image of six scurrying, hairless creatures with huge, bulging eyes appeared on the passenger view-screens. The mardets were mammalian in appearance, which Solomon Chavez immediately pointed out. As they watched the tiny rodents scurry along a tree branch, one of the dragonfly-like insects swooped down and snatched up the last one in line. After a fleeting panic by the others, the remaining mardets fell back in line and continued on their merry way.

"I don't understand," Bram grumbled. "Why do those little rascals live here in the trees where predators can grab them, instead of on the ground where it's safer?"

"Ground level is *more* dangerous," sighed the commissioner. "Remember, Mr. Waters, the fungus is predatory. It doesn't survive entirely on dead wood."

Nodding, Bram sensed that Solomon was becoming increasingly frustrated over not being allowed to get his hands dirty. The trillionaire philanthropist was accustomed to getting his way.

"Isn't there some sort of protective suit one can wear?" he asked.

The commissioner crossed her arms. "Yes, the skimmer's maintenance closet contains two emergency suits in case we're forced to land in the forest." She looked exasperated. "I suppose I could let you take one out for a few minutes to study the flora. But there aren't enough suits for everyone."

"Fair enough," Solomon said.

The commissioner gave the order, and the skimmer started its descent. As the vehicle dropped below the canopy, Bram saw an uneven landscape covered in bushes, smaller trees, fallen trees, brambles, and patchy areas that looked ravaged by blight. There didn't appear to be any animal or insect life, yet he sensed something highly intelligent. He was about to whisper this impression to Gloria, when he noticed movement behind a fallen tree.

"Did you see that?"

The others looked where he was pointing.

"What was it, Mr. Waters?" the commissioner asked.

"It looked like—" Bram paused, a frown forming on his face. "I know this sounds crazy, but it looked like a person ducking behind that fallen tree."

"What are you blathering about, Bram?" Gloria eyed him suspiciously. "There can't be a person out—Wait! I saw something, too!" she gasped. "It looked like a young boy."

Bram jerked his head around. "A boy? But I saw a—"

"Be quiet!" snapped the commissioner. "The Lord is informing me of an emergency with the meteor site expedition. They've been attacked. The admiral has been critically injured. We *must* return at once!"

Bram and the others stared, not knowing how to respond to her out-of-the-blue assertion.

The commissioner barked an order to the pilot, who immediately programmed the skimmer to return to the harvesters at top speed.

The craft darted upward, inertia pressing its occupants firmly into their seats. The skimmer streaked toward a narrow opening between two trees. As it cleared the canopy, it intersected a large swarm of colorful insects. The creatures thumped and splattered loudly against the front window. The startled pilot banked the skimmer, but a number of the large creatures were sucked violently into the air intakes, shattering the craft's hydrogen-fueled engines. Ceramic shards flew in every direction. Fuel lines severed. Bram saw flames, and then heard a series of detonations. The skimmer bucked and pitched to one side, then stalled and plummeted from the sky.

Gripping his armrests for dear life, Bram looked on in horror as the pilot slumped forward: part of the engine had torn through the skimmer's cabin and into the man's skull.

Karen Albans screamed. Bram's head snapped in her direction. She was clutching the side of her neck. Blood was pumping from between her fingers. She must have been hit by shrapnel. Bram instinctively reached for his seat belt in a determined effort to free himself, his only thought being to help an injured shipmate.

He never got the chance.

The skimmer slammed to the ground and tumbled twenty feet before smashing into the trunk of a tree. Bram was thrown forward in his seat. If he'd succeeded in loosening his seat belt, he'd have perished in the crash. Instead, the force of impact was so intense that he blacked out—but not before seeing a jagged piece of glass impale Ezral Magliss through the chest.

●

The female voice, which sounded vaguely familiar, was persistent.

"Bram . . . goddamn it, Bram. Wake the fuck up!"

The sharp sting of a slapped cheek finally brought Bram to his senses. The moment his eyes flew open, he remembered where he was—in a wrecked skimmer, in the middle of a hostile alien environment. Gloria Muldoon was standing over him, a look of concern on her face.

"If I'd known you liked it rough, I would've—"

"Don't get cute," she snapped. "Unbuckle yourself; we need to get out of here."

Bram fumbled with his restraints. Solomon Chavez was hovering over the pilot, checking his wounds. Half the man's skull was gone. Bram looked away—he saw Ezral Magliss, head lolled back, eyes wide and staring.

"How's Albans?" he asked, fearing the worst. She lay on the floor of the skimmer, her upper half concealed by her chair and a row of equipment.

Gloria, who was rummaging through a storage locker, paused to answer. "Karen . . . bled out a few minutes ago," she whispered, voice quavering. "There was nothing we could do."

"Dammit," Bram groaned. The shy, retiring science-officer had treated him kindly, not caring about his celebrity status or his psychic abilities . . . unlike some people. "How you holding up, Dr. Chavez?"

Solomon was full of apprehension. "I think I've discovered why the New Terrans are immune to your powers, Waters."

Bram leapt to his feet. "What? What do you mean?"

Solomon waved him over. Bram was hesitant, dreading what Solomon wanted to show him, since it obviously involved the dead pilot's mutilated body. After a few uncomfortable seconds, he strengthened the nerve to step forward on his shaky legs.

"Come here where you can see better, Waters."

Solomon was holding the pilot's head to one side, letting the light from the shattered window illuminate the man's exposed brain matter. Bram tried to focus on the injury, but his stomach kept lurching. A fountain of gorge rose in his throat, forcing him to look away.

"What am I supposed to be seeing, Dr. Chavez?" he asked, glancing at the wound.

Solomon had not yet noticed Bram's discomfort. "If you look closely, you can see a fine wire mesh covering the surface of the man's brain." He picked up a pointed piece of ceramic and peeled back a small section of the pilot's brain. "It's as I suspected. The mesh is connected to a micro-circuitry embedded in the brain." Hearing this news, Bram set aside his squeamishness and focused his attention on the brain matter. "If I'm not mistaken, the mesh acts as a psychic shield, the way some electrical wiring is shielded to prevent stray signals from causing interference."

"How did it get there?" Bram asked.

"That's the twenty-four million dollar question," Solomon replied, massaging his neck.

Gloria appeared, carrying two protective suits. "You'll have to finish your show-and-tell project another time, Dr. Chavez." She faced Bram with a no-nonsense look on her face. "The skimmer's communication equipment was damaged in the crash, and our PIDs are on the fritz. The craft *might* be emitting a distress signal, but I don't advise sticking around long enough to find out.

We're vulnerable to attack and need to remove ourselves to the forest's edge so as to avoid the deadly fungus the commissioner warned us about."

She handed a protective suit to both men.

"Where's yours?" Solomon asked.

"There are only two, and you need them more than I do." Bram tried to hand his back.

An angry scowl clouded Gloria's features. "Don't hand me that chivalrous crap, Bram. With Karen dead, I'm in charge, which means you'll do as *I* say. Now put on those damned suits, 'cause we're heading out in two minutes."

In her present mood, Bram knew there was no point in arguing. He hurriedly slipped into the white, loose-fitting environment suit and adjusted the filter. After anxiously pushing against a momentarily stuck exit door, the three were headed east away from the sunlight.

They were less than ten feet from the skimmer when Gloria gasped in surprise. She pointed at the trunk of a fallen tree. "Did you s-see . . ." Trailing off, her voice sounded tremulous, fearful.

"See what, Gloria?" Bram asked, looking in the direction she pointed. "Was it fungus?"

"Is everything all right, Lieutenant?" inquired Solomon Chavez.

Gloria lowered her arm and shook her head. "It was nothing," she mumbled. "Must've been a shadow. It couldn't have been . . . because that's impossible . . . it had to be something else."

"You're probably right," Bram said, feeling his skin crawl. "Shadows can play tricks on the eyes. Let's keep moving."

Without answering, she tore her gaze from the fallen tree and continued eastward.

Despite Gloria's attempt to affect a stoic attitude, Bram could sense her fear; it radiated from her in waves, like ripples from a stone thrown in a quiet pond—no, not a *quiet* pond: an agitated pond—a pond with something lurking beneath the surface.

Bram's unease was steadily building, becoming almost palpable. He felt watched from all sides, the feeling so strong that he fought against looking behind him every few seconds. His eyes darted back and forth, searching every shadow for signs of the aggressive fungi that waited to sink their tendrils into vulnerable human flesh.

"Here's an idea, Waters," remarked Solomon Chavez, disrupting his increasingly obsessive thoughts. "Why don't you use your psychic powers like a distress beacon, and let someone know we're in trouble?"

"That might work," he mused. "When I concentrate hard enough, I can make a receptive person hear my thoughts. It's harder when no one knows I'm trying to contact them, but it's worth a try."

Gloria appeared skeptical. "I suppose we'll need to stop for a while to try this experiment?" she asked, glancing around for potential threats.

Bram nodded. "There's no point in putting it off. I'll first try to contact Commander Allison. If successful, he'll convince the chancellor to send a rescue party. It would be quicker to contact a member of the harvester expedition, but that's not an option. The shielding that prevents me from reading a New Terran's mind also prevents them from receiving messages."

"Are you sure?" Solomon asked. "They certainly appear to be receiving messages from someone or *something* claiming to be God."

"Hmm, that's true," Bram said. "To play it safe, I'll try to contact the harvesters first."

The three came to a halt near a large patch of bare ground. Bram closed his eyes, took a deep breath, and reached out with his mind.

Nothing happened.

That's odd, he thought. Perhaps the crash affected him more than he realized.

He tried again, but it felt like swimming in molasses. He strained and fought for every foot of ground but failed to make any headway.

Something was wrong. This shouldn't be so difficult.

Experiencing a mounting sense of dread, Bram focused his attention on contacting Richard Allison, hoping to have better luck in that direction. Reaching out with his mind, he once again felt thwarted. He was getting nowhere. His brain was undamaged, so what was causing his probe to fail? Gritting his teeth and filling his lungs, Bram pushed with all his mental might.

Sudden . . . extreme . . . pressure . . . psychic pushback. His mind thrust underwater. He gasped. The same pushback he experienced in the admiral's ready room, only much stronger, palpable, like being smothered.

"What's wrong, Waters?"

The voice belonged to Solomon Chavez. He wanted to respond with more than a groan. The pressure was getting worse. Bram fell to his knees and grasped both sides of his head. Something was trying to get . . . into . . . his mind. Pressing . . . twisting . . . burrowing into his brain, like an angry swarm of alien termites.

Then suddenly, a scream!

Was it his? No, the voice didn't belong to him. The scream belonged to Gloria.

In the next instant, the unrelenting pressure evaporated.

He heard Solomon exclaim, "What the hell?"

Bram's eyes flew open and he scrambled to his feet. "What? What's going on?"

Gloria was stumbling forward onto a large, bare patch of ground, in the middle of which lay the almost unrecognizable rotting vestiges of a fallen tree.

"My, my brother," she sputtered.

Bram looked in the direction she was headed. A figure was standing near the tree. He could barely believe his eyes. The shock was so great that he almost fell once again to his knees.

"Selena!" he heard Solomon bellow.

Bram was confused. Both Gloria and Solomon were speaking nonsense. The person standing beside the fallen, rotting tree was not Gloria's brother, nor was she anyone named Selena. The blonde-haired beauty was obviously his fiancée, Jennifer Parker.

●

How could this be? How could Selena be here? Solomon wondered.

Completely oblivious to Gloria's and Bram's stunned reactions, Solomon staggered toward his daughter. Selena looked frightened, but why? He was wearing an environment suit. That's it! She didn't recognize him, not with his face covered by the suit's protective filter.

Slowing his pace, Solomon unzipped the suit, threw back the hood, removed the filter from his nose and mouth, and then shook free from the object of his daughter's fear.

"Sweetheart!" he said in Spanish, arms wide open. "Come to papa!"

Selena smiled. She looked exactly the same. She was wearing her favorite blue dress, ruffles white as snow, her black, patent-leather shoes with white lace socks; a red ribbon adorned her shoulder-length, dark-brown hair . . . exactly the same.

One part of Solomon's mind knew he couldn't be seeing his daughter alive on this God-forsaken planet, while another part— a more insistent part—wanted to believe the illusion, wanted to hold her in his arms, wanted to tell her how sorry he was for failing to save her so long ago on that terrible, oh so horrible, day.

As he rushed toward Selena, he bumped into Gloria Muldoon and glanced her way.

Why was that infuriating woman calling a man's name?

Wait! Where's Selena? He'd taken his eyes off her for barely a second. Now she was gone. Muldoon must have frightened her away.

"Look what you've done!" he yelled, shoving Gloria to one side. "Selena! Come back!"

"Hey! What the hell are you doing?" Gloria shouted, stumbling, almost tripping. Her left foot found a patch of crumbling soil and sank nearly three inches.

Ignoring her, Solomon picked up his pace. He was running headlong, kicking up dust; it was imperative, no, vital that he find his daughter.

●

Damn that Solomon Chavez! Gloria raced to catch up with him. Why did he want to get to Aaron before her? And who is Selena? To make matters worse, he pushed her aside like yesterday's trash. But why would he not? Treating people badly was commonplace for someone like him. If he only knew the truth, he'd treat her *much* differently . . . Damn him! Perhaps she should tell him the truth. Perhaps she should shake his world to the very core. Yes . . . perhaps she should. But first, she needed to find her brother, Aaron.

●

Bram was finding it difficult to run in the protective suit. He peeled it off and dashed after the other two, wondering why they were so eager to find Jennifer. No! It couldn't be Jennifer. She was dead. She'd been dead for decades . . . a millennia. So why was he seeing—

It's an illusion! A psychic manifestation!

"Stop!" he screamed. "We're being tricked by something in the forest!"

Gloria and Solomon glanced back at him, bewilderment in their eyes. Clearly conflicted, they slowed their pace.

"Listen to me!" he called out. The two came to a halt.

"What the hell are you talking about, Waters?" Solomon snarled. He had an intense, near frantic look about him.

Bram trotted up to them, his heart pounding. "Whatever you're seeing isn't real. We're being tricked, shown an illusion, by a—"

At that moment, the ground beneath Bram gave way. A sinkhole opened up, swallowing him, Gloria, and Solomon, plunging all three into a roiling, choking darkness.

18

Sitting at her desk in the brig, staring bleary-eyed at the computer screen, Mona waited to see if her previous attempt to crack the fourth file would succeed. She'd tried every trick in the book to decrypt the damned thing but had been met with failure each time. It was frustrating to think that her beloved quantum computer might be outwitted by inbred descendants of a rebellious bunch of Jesus freaks. The algorithm used to encrypt the file was so complex it must've been designed by super-genius computer-geeks—not by hive-minded drones deluded enough to believe they talked to the Lord.

After thirty-eight hours of trying to crack the file, Mona was exhausted. She didn't know if she'd be able to come up with another avenue of decryption to explore. The last few tries had been exotic, unheard of, and her brain was turning to mush. If this attempt failed, she might be able to dream up another exotic decryption program, but she feared her creativity was shot.

Leaning back in her chair, she rubbed her bloodshot eyes. She needed sleep—but she needed to crack the file even more—especially if she ever hoped to regain Solomon's trust.

Perhaps if she put in a medical request for a low-dose psychedelic, her mind would open up to new possibilities of solving this dilemma. It wouldn't be the first time mind-altering drugs had helped her overcome a scientific sticking point. In the meantime, strong coffee would have to suffice.

As she poured a cup of the hot, black brew, Richard Wagner's "Flight of the Valkyries" started playing in the background. Some Jews detested Wagner (being Hitler's favorite composer), but not her; there was something about this song that lent itself to dramatic moments. That's why she always used it to announce when a computer program finished its work.

Mona promptly cut off the music and opened the mysterious file. Instead of a video, like the first two files, or a disturbing account from New Terra's founding, like the third, the fourth file contained a document. She was a bit disappointed, but when she read the document, she realized that it was a manifesto—and a chilling one at that.

By the time Mona finished reading the manifesto, she was frightened, more so than any other time in her life . . . even during the attempted bombing of the Lake Victoria space elevator.

She knew what she had to do: Mona had to contact Admiral Axelrod immediately.

●

"Can't this vehicle travel any faster?" Richard snapped, glaring at the chancellor.

She shook her head, grimacing under his withering stare. "I'm afraid not."

Admiral Axelrod's injuries were life-threatening, which meant that time was of the essence. Thankfully, the transport was equipped with medical supplies. Her wound had been packed with an amber-colored gel that stopped the bleeding, but Richard feared that without a prompt surgery she would die. The admiral was sedated and enclosed in an emergency medical chamber located in the rear cabin of the vehicle. The chamber was designed to stabilize movement and monitor a patient's vitals during transport.

Floyd Sullivant sat beside the chamber, staring at the readings. "How much longer will it be before we arrive in the city?" he asked, not looking up.

The chancellor checked a reading on a nearby control panel. "Less than an hour."

"Admiral Axelrod needs to be taken directly to our shuttle," Richard insisted. "Release Dr. Singh and have him meet us there. I'll pilot us back to the *Arrow* where he can perform surgery on the admiral."

The chancellor gave him a questioning look. "She'll never survive the trip into space."

"I'll take my chances," he said, his eyes narrowing.

Floyd touched his shoulder. "I'm afraid she's right, Commander. Even with the shuttle's inertial dampeners, the admiral's injuries are too grave to risk it."

Richard rubbed his temple. "What about your medical facilities, Chancellor?" he sighed. "Are they up to the task?"

"Most assuredly. Our workers incur their share of serious injuries. Please, leave the admiral in our capable hands. She will be treated to the best care imaginable, and most likely come out feeling better than ever."

Richard grunted. "Fine, I just wish this bucket of bolts would move faster."

●

Coughing, Bram rolled over, pushed himself up on all fours, and shook his head. He was dazed but didn't think anything was broken. The sinkhole was deep and cavernous.

"Dr. Chavez? Gloria? Are you all right?" he wheezed, inhaling another lungful of the musty, dust-filled air.

He received no reply. "Gloria! Dr. Chavez!" his voice echoed. No response. Because of the dusty gloom, he couldn't see beyond his outstretched hand. Feeling around, Bram realized he was kneeling atop a pile of soft dirt. Then he remembered: the ground beneath Gloria and Solomon's feet had collapsed as he arrived, sending them plummeting into the sinkhole a split second before he also tumbled in . . . his clothes had snagged on something during the fall, perhaps a root.

My God! Were Gloria and Solomon buried under dirt during the sinkhole collapse? Perhaps they were lying nearby, knocked unconscious from the fall. That's when a horrible thought struck him: *What if the deadly fungus was consuming them at that very moment?* Despite the humidity, Bram felt the hairs on the back of his neck stand up.

His head jerked back and forth, searching for threats, fully expecting a fungal tendril to shoot from the darkness and wrap around his throat. The dust was starting to settle, but the surrounding gloom felt like an alien fist squeezing from all sides.

Bram knew he must calm down and help Gloria and Solomon, if possible.

After a lifetime of stress-filled situations, Bram knew what to do. He covered his mouth with his shirt, took a deep breath, then closed his eyes and forced out a weak psychic probe. There they were—faint signs of human life—buried a few feet away beneath the loosely packed soil. He was overjoyed, but also terrified. He knew that if they weren't rescued soon, they would surely die. Though Gloria and Solomon were only a few feet away, they were covered by more than three feet of dirt. They were unconscious, but together. Solomon had fallen atop Gloria and somehow managed to shield her from further harm. However, they had no air and both were suffocating.

Bram had to do something, but what? By the time he managed to dig them out from under all that dirt, they would already be dead. There was only one thing left to do, but did he have the strength? No matter—he had to try!

Scrambling in the direction of their intermingled auras, Bram focused his telekinetic abilities. He'd never moved this much material with his mind, but if he failed, he'd never forgive himself. Would the dampening effect of the forest foil his attempt? He hoped not.

Focusing his mind like a laser, he saw the first clumps of soil begin to move. Suddenly he heard something rustle behind him. Twisting at the waist, Bram thought he saw a figure standing in the shadows.

"Who's there?!" he rasped, peering into the gloom. A ragged patch of dim light filtered down from above but not enough to see by.

Bram listened intently. He heard nothing; saw nothing. Was his imagination playing . . . but no . . . there was something there, observing him, something that, for the moment, felt benign.

Bucking up his courage, Bram faced the spot where Gloria and Solomon were buried. He shook his head, knowing he *must* focus on the task at hand; he *must* ignore the feeling of being watched. It took a moment before Bram could sense his shipmates. Both of their vital signs were fading; he must act quickly.

Some of the dirt began to move, but not fast enough. Something was interfering with his powers. At this rate, it would take all day. Whatever the cost, he was determined to push through the psychic barrier thwarting his abilities. Closing his eyes, Bram reached deep inside, drawing on a reservoir of psychic fortitude that lay dormant for two decades. Every worry disappeared, every concern faded, every thought other than his objective drifted away like dandelion seeds caught on the wind.

Using his mind's eye, Bram watched as the loosely packed soil moved, parting like water before the prow of a mighty ocean liner.

Unbeknownst to him, the alien consciousness permeating the area took notice of his powers, and for the first time in eons felt a momentary ripple of fear. This human was unlike any creature it had ever encountered. The alien felt compelled to reassess the situation. Naturally, it would still devour the human and its two companions, but they weren't going anywhere; it could study them at its leisure.

The only thing Bram knew of the alien's decision was that he suddenly felt an easing of the psychic barrier that surrounded him. The dirt moved faster, but he took little comfort in this, given that his shipmates were teetering on the edge of death. The three feet of dirt separating him from Gloria and Solomon was roiling and churning then flying to either side of the mound. A trench formed, revealing two motionless and apparently lifeless bodies, with Solomon covering Gloria.

With the last of the dirt falling to the floor of the sinkhole, Bram leapt to his feet and dragged Solomon from the trench, with Gloria to follow. Dropping beside her, Bram hurriedly cleared her mouth and began to perform CPR. He'd scarcely begun when Gloria jerked, produced a violent cough, and then sucked in a ragged, lungful of air. Without pausing to assess her condition, Bram scrambled over to Solomon. He was checking the man's mouth for dirt when Solomon's eyes shot open, and he too launched into a succession of loud, painful-sounding coughs.

Confident they would both survive, Bram slumped in relief, feeling emotionally, physically, and psychically drained.

Spitting out a mouthful of dust, Gloria sat up and, shaking the grit from her hair, looked over at Solomon, her brow furrowing with anger. He wasn't paying any attention to her.

"What . . . happened . . . Waters?" Solomon asked between coughs.

Bram shrugged. "It looks like we've landed at the bottom of a sinkhole, or possibly a tunnel of some sort." He peered up, trying to estimate the depth of the sinkhole. "We're a good twenty-five feet below ground. I don't think we can climb out."

Solomon examined the hole and nodded. With a huff, he climbed to his feet, reached into his pocket, and pulled out his PID. "Rosa, activate flashlight app."

After helping Gloria to her feet, Bram activated his own flashlight app. Gloria did the same, and soon there were three beams of light cutting through the darkness. They stood in a cavern at the bottom of a pit caused by the sinkhole collapse.

The roof of the cavern was four feet over their heads, and the hole leading to the surface stretched at least another ten to twelve feet higher than that. The cavern itself was sixteen to eighteen feet wide with seven tunnels leading off in various directions. Bram deduced that the tunnels had been formed after the tree's huge root system had been away eaten by fungus, the thought of which gave Bram an apprehensive chill. Once again, he felt he was being watched.

"I hope the rescue party arrives soon," he muttered.

Gloria was walking around, shining her light up at the hole. "If one of you gentlemen will lift me up onto your shoulders, I can stand and reach some of those exposed roots. With my survival training, I should be able to climb to the surface and—" A large clump of dirt came loose from the inner wall of the hole, causing Gloria to dodge to one side. "Dammit!"

"You won't get halfway to the surface before you fall and break your neck," Solomon cautioned.

"You don't have to *concern* yourself with me, Dr. Chavez," she snapped. "I mean, why start now?"

Bram noticed Solomon stiffen, his eyes narrowing.

"What the hell's that supposed to mean?"

Gloria appeared ready to respond with a caustic remark when her head jerked abruptly to the side and her eyes grew wide. "Good God!" she yelped, taking a step backward.

Bram and Solomon pointed their flashlights in the direction Gloria was staring. Bram gasped, shocked by the sight—a sight that struck terror unto his very bones. A huge, spider-like creature was situated in the opening of one of the tunnels leading away from the cavern. It hissed loudly before skittering forward a few yards on eight, hairy, multi-segmented legs.

Bram felt rooted to the spot. Spiders! He hated spiders!

Out of the corner of his eye he saw another one appear in a second tunnel to his right, then a third to his left, and then a fourth. They were being surrounded. Risking a forced, quick glance behind him, Bram saw that the three tunnels to their rear were still open, but for how long?

A loud pop nearly caused him to jump out of his skin. Gloria was pointing a pulse-gun at one of the creatures, which recoiled slightly when hit but wasn't particularly fazed by the sonic pulse. Cursing loudly, she fired two more rounds—neither of which were any more effective than the first. However, the creatures did stop their advance.

"Damn, I wish I had my 9mm. Both of you get behind me," she yelled.

Without hesitation, the two men complied. As Gloria fired off another two rounds, the three backed slowly toward the tunnels that remained free of the alien horrors. She fired off another round. As she did so, sprinklings of dirt began to fall from the ceiling.

"I thought your weapon was disabled in the birthing chamber," Solomon rasped.

"It was," Gloria said. "The sonic generator has a reset switch inside the handle."

"It's not doing much good. I'm beginning to think the sound of it might cause a cave in."

Gloria looked up at the ceiling just as she was about to squeeze off another round. She eased off the trigger, afraid that Solomon was right—but she didn't lower her gun. The creatures had stopped their advance and she wanted to keep it that way.

Glancing behind him, Bram wanted to make sure the tunnel to their rear was still safe. The sight of what stood in the tunnel's mouth caused him to stumble. He grabbed hold of Solomon's arm and, unable to speak, motioned for him to follow his gaze. The normally unflappable Chavez turned to look and was equally startled.

"What the . . . ?"

Gloria, concerned by Solomon's yelp of surprise, was in the process of turning around when she heard, "You must hurry and follow me, if you want to escape the monsters."

Strange as it seemed, there in the mouth of the tunnel stood a female child.

●

Completely ignoring the anomaly of a child's presence in the tunnel, Solomon and Gloria sprinted toward the adorable, smiling girl. Bram felt compelled to join them, but trailed behind, sensing that something was amiss. The little girl—her hair set in blonde ringlets and her knee-length, pink and white dress so clean—looked too perfect, too welcoming.

"Hurry up, Waters!" Solomon yelled over his shoulder. "The snakes are getting closer."

As Bram picked up his pace, he wondered what Solomon was talking about; the vicious-looking spiders were the obvious threat. The girl was leading them somewhere safe; the tunnel must lead to the surface or to a secure location. It must.

His companions were a few yards away from the girl when she stepped into the darkness of the tunnel. Solomon and Gloria stopped at the tunnel's mouth and directed their flashlight beams inside. Trotting up behind them, Bram saw the child standing twelve feet away at a branch in the tunnel, waving for them to follow.

"Better to be with her than end up as food for those foul creatures behind us," Solomon stated as he entered the tunnel.

Not voicing any objection or apprehension, Gloria followed close behind.

The child once again vanished into the dark recesses of the tunnel. Bram tried to focus on her odd behavior, but his mind kept shifting to the eight-legged horrors closing in on them. He could normally focus his attention like a laser, but when he tried to concentrate on the child, his attention again shifted. He shook his head. *Something's not right*, he thought. Gloria and Solomon rounded the corner after the child, not saying a word. With reservations, Bram followed. He was barely around the corner when he skidded to a halt, almost bumping into Gloria and Solomon who had also stopped in their tracks.

The tunnel had dead-ended and, shockingly, the child was nowhere to be seen.

"Where did she go?" Gloria croaked, her voice faltering.

Bram was at a loss. His eyes flicked back and forth hoping to spot an opening through which the girl might have fled, but saw none. It was impossible. She couldn't have vanished into thin air. There *had* to be an explanation.

Solomon grabbed his arm. "We have to get out of here," he barked.

The man was right. Bram spun around, only to find an unexpectedly bewildering sight: the tunnel was closed off. They were trapped inside, but how? The tunnel hadn't collapsed. "This doesn't make any sense," he hissed.

Solomon stepped up beside him. "I'm inclined to agree with you, Waters."

Gloria stood silently to his left, arms crossed.

"I have no idea how this happened," Bram admitted. "In any event, we need to break though the wall and return to the main tunnel before our air runs out. Gloria, what about your survival training? Has it prepared you for anything like this?"

From the corner of his eye, Bram saw Solomon turn and stiffen. The enigmatic Brazilian let out a sharp gasp of surprise. What was happening? Had the child returned? Whirling around, he saw something that made his mind boggle. Standing at the far end of the tunnel was Jennifer, his long-dead fiancée. But it was impossible. How could she even be here? It had to be another illusion, but her image was *so* compelling. It called to him. She smiled exactly as she should. She looked exactly as she had, so many years ago. His head was spinning, dizzy with the thought of their reunion.

Stumbling toward Jennifer, Bram heard Gloria utter her brother's name. How odd. She was walking toward a spot a few feet away from Jennifer—but no one was there. As for Solomon, he was kneeling, sobbing, holding his arms out for someone named Selena. Despite being aware of these bizarre proceedings, Bram's focus was on Jennifer. He desperately wanted to hold her in his arms. His mind barely registered the fact that the ground beneath her feet was covered in fine, hair-like cilia.

Bram rushed into Jennifer's outstretched arms and wrapped her in an embrace he'd longed for a thousand times over the years. "Jennifer . . . darling . . . I've missed you *so* much." He sighed in ecstasy, unable to feel the fungal tendrils worming their way beneath his skin.

19

Tears of joy streamed down Solomon's cheeks. His heart overflowed from the sheer joy of holding his beloved daughter in his arms. Pulling her close, he kissed her cheek; it was clammy, but he attributed that to being underground. In his blissful haze, he failed to consider why his daughter was underground, on an alien planet.

"Daddy's missed you *so* much," he sobbed in Spanish. "I love you, I love you, I love you, I'm so happy you're alive. I feared the worst, but you're alive . . . you're alive!"

Solomon didn't want to let Selena go. The moment he saw her he'd dropped his flashlight, collapsed to his knees, and enfolded her in his arms, overwhelmed with unadulterated joy. It was a miracle! Yes, a miracle Selena was here . . . but where was her mother? She must be close by. He could barely breathe at the thought of holding Maria in his arms.

Weak with ecstasy, Solomon lifted his tear-stained cheeks and silently thanked the Lord for being merciful. As he did so, Selena began to push against him, struggling to free herself. In the zeal of their reunion, was he holding her too tightly? "What is it, sweetheart?"

Gazing into his daughter's angelic face, which was lit from below by the flashlight, Solomon saw that she was frightened—no, terrified. He glanced over his shoulder, thinking that one the monstrous snakes that caused him to flee the cavern was slithering up from behind. But no, the tunnel was blocked. There was nothing to cause Selena's fear. When he turned around and looked into her eyes, he saw that her fear was directed at him.

"What's wrong, sweetheart? Don't you recognize me?" He held her at arm's length, a note of anguish in his voice.

Her struggles increased. "Let me go! You're hurting me!" she cried.

"But I'm your daddy, Selena. I'd never hurt you." Solomon didn't think he was holding her too tightly. "Please, don't act this way. It's been so long since I've held you in my—"

Solomon's voice trailed away as he stared in horror. His daughter's face was changing from fearful to furious. She was snarling at him, and her teeth—her teeth! They'd transformed, turning fanglike, animalistic.

"Let me go, or I'll rip your throat out," she growled, using a guttural, menacing tone of voice.

In his shock, Solomon almost released his grip, but he couldn't. He was frozen in disbelief, unable to comprehend her sudden change from smiling, adorable girl to a snarling demon.

She began to weep; her face wracked with pain. "Please, daddy, let go," she pleaded, struggling even harder. "I'm . . . I'm—" Her body began to shake.

Unable to breathe, feeling like his heart was in his throat, Solomon watched as the distorted image of his daughter wavered, becoming transparent. His eyes locked onto hers one last time before the vision of his long-dead daughter faded from view. In her place stood a crumbling latticework of desiccated tendrils— a fungus that was turning dark brown, dying, turning to dust before his very eyes.

In agony, Solomon felt as though he'd lost his daughter all over again. He was hurting. Most of his pain was emotional—but, he realized, there was also a physical element involved.

Tearing his gaze from the crumbling fungal tendrils, Solomon looked down at his hands and arms: they were covered in pinpricks, which were seeping blood. The fungus had been feeding off him. Then it hit him, he'd seen the Ghosts of Yggdrasil: the fungus had projected an image of Selena into his mind, as a lure to draw him into its grip and keep him there to devour. But he was toxic.

The whole thing had felt so real . . . the image of Selena had felt so real, so present, so *there*, that he almost . . .

Oh my God, the others!

He spotted Gloria's flashlight first. It lay on the ground near her feet casting its harsh, white light against the tunnel wall. Snatching up his PID, Solomon cast its light in her direction, only to see what he feared most—Gloria entwined in fungal tendrils! The silken threads were emerging from the ground beneath her feet, covering her, engulfing her. If he didn't do something to help her, she'd die.

Waters stood a few feet away from her, his eyes rolled up in his head. The deadly fungus also covered his body—but it was writhing, squirming, struggling to find purchase. The fungus was fighting to subdue the psychic detective, but unlike the cluster that attacked Solomon and died in the process, the tendrils assaulting Waters were still healthy.

Feeling lightheaded from the fungal assault, Solomon struggled to his feet and made a beeline to Gloria. Whatever else he did, he had to save her—even if Waters died in the process.

●

Bram was certain that Jennifer's arms weren't clutching him tightly. The moment he touched her, he knew that something inhuman was pressing against his flesh. But the creature looked exactly like his fiancée. How could that be? It had to be a trick, an illusion . . . but how? How could an illusion feel so real?!

Have to focus. . .

Have to push past the illusion . . . see the creature for what it really is . . .

Must . . . not . . . give in . . .

Must . . . fight to . . . see . . . it . . . for . . . what it . . . really is . . .

Calling on every last wisp of his psychic reserves, Bram pushed back against the power invading his mind, a power that was making him perceive a vision he so desperately wanted to hold on to, despite knowing it was illusory, a false construct, that it couldn't possibly be his Jennifer.

The creature had never encountered someone like Bram Waters: his psychic abilities were, in many respects, on par with its own—a fact that instilled confusion and even fear throughout its neural pathways. Over the many eons of its existence, all its other prey (including the occasional human) had succumbed quickly to its illusions, each illusion personalized to draw its prey close enough to capture and consume. But this human was different . . . this human was fighting back, which was a great surprise; even more than its painful encounter with the poison-blooded human, which was also a surprise. Luckily, the threat was quickly neutralized by casting aside the affected tissue before the poison spread, spoiling more than a single tendril cluster.

Sensing the alien was caught off-guard, Bram fought even harder to free himself. The initial illusion, which began with a vision of Jennifer, had morphed into a near overwhelming psychic assault, showing one image after another, hammering away at his mental fortitude. He couldn't allow that strategy to continue, for the creature would soon wear down his resistance to the point he'd buckle under the pressure.

Somewhere in the distance he heard a voice—Chavez's voice. It was distorted, and he sensed a frantic quality, which was understandable: Solomon was, in all likelihood, also under attack. Unfortunately, there was nothing Bram could do; he had his own battle to contend with. Reading the alien's thoughts, he knew it was valiantly trying to push past his defenses in an effort to inject him with a powerful neurotoxin. And if that happened, all was lost.

Not since his long-ago showdown with the psychotic Conrad Snow had Bram been engaged in such a monumental battle of wills. At least against Snow he'd faced a human opponent; this was a battle on a vastly different scale, and much more difficult.

One thing was certain: to defeat the creature, he must overcome his fear. It was fear that held him back, that prevented his chakras from aligning properly. On a normal day, Bram's energy centers didn't need to be fully aligned to effectively use his powers. If truth be told, he dreaded aligning *all* his chakras. He'd done so rarely, and briefly. His fear stemmed from his childhood, after aligning them for the first time. He'd opened up all his chakras in unison and spun them at maximum speed, charging them to their fullest. A coil of supercharged energy shot up from his scrotal region, surged through each chakra in turn then exited through the top of his skull. It was like a circuit breaker being flipped: he'd passed out and spent the next four days in a coma. From then on he'd held back, opening his chakras no more than eighty percent at any one time. Even during his encounter with Snow, he'd opened them little more than a second, which, thankfully, allowed him to escape the bastard's arctic fortress.

This time was different: Bram needed to open his chakras to their fullest and keep them open for an extended period of time if he ever hoped of freeing himself. He prayed for enough strength to endure activating the energy center located at the base of the spine: the Kundalini Chakra, also known colloquially as the Coiled Serpent of Light.

Time was running out. He could sense the alien marshalling its resources, poised to act. Its cascading images were surging, becoming a rapid blur. Ignoring the disturbing imagery, Bram centered his attention on his chakras, clearing his mind of nearly all his fears.

His energy centers were opening up, blooming like flowers beneath a springtime sun. The last of Bram's fears dissipated; his chakras fell into alignment; his spiritual energy surged; his powers increased . . . but it wasn't enough to break the creature's grip. He had to risk it. He had to unleash his Kundalini chakra, the Coiled Serpent of Light.

He felt stinging pinpricks: the creature's tendrils were piercing his skin. He couldn't afford to wait any longer. He had to do it. He had to act and act now.

Dropping the last of his defenses, Bram unleashed the sleeping giant curled at the base of his spine. The Kundalini energy immediately sprang to life, unfurling and swelling, surging upward through his other seven chakras, supercharging them until every cell was bursting with power.

A blast of psychic energy inundated the fungal tendrils squirming around his body, triggering the few that managed to push past his defenses to beat a hasty retreat. The creature had never encountered such a powerful psychic pressure and was scared, more so than at any other point in its existence. Fear cascaded across its neural network, building in intensity until it reached the central core, located thousands of miles away. An ancient slumbering intelligence took notice.

Bram paid little attention to the creature's fearful reaction. For the first time in his life he felt a profound connection to the universe . . . writ large. Since he could remember, he'd been able to connect with the world around him, but this time—*this time*—his consciousness was expanding exponentially, escalating beyond the material world and crossing into the spiritual. He was experiencing more than a familiar connection with the world around him—he was becoming *One* with everything.

At which point, Bram's consciousness promptly left his body and entered a higher realm of perception. All that he knew of himself disappeared. His awareness expanded to the point that his consciousness became tuned to the universe on a cosmic level, which caused a vast amount of information to avail itself to his soul. It felt as though every tidbit of knowledge that had ever been discovered, or would ever be discovered, was flooding through his mental latticework—that the very fabric of eternity had been laid out at his spiritual fingertips.

That which had once been Bram Waters possessed no knowledge of the passage of time. All he knew, other than the endless knowledge that permeated him, was an intense, all-encompassing love, which saturated the entire universe, including his own nameless spirit. Eventually, however, time resumed, and he began to perceive the universe from a distance, seeing an immense panorama of exquisite galaxies.

A flicker of self-interest intruded on his spiritual vision: the briefest glimmer of concern for his body's personal safety flashed across his awareness. At that very moment, he remembered who he was and what was happening to him on New Terra.

An inexorable force began to drag his spirit from the cosmic realm and push it firmly into the physical, and in so doing, the entire abundance of knowledge he acquired was sucked from his consciousness, leaving a mere scaffold of memory to hold onto, to agonizingly remind him of his profoundly uplifting experience.

Bram's eyes blinked open and he found himself on his knees. The fungal tendrils no longer covered his body. His defensive stand had succeeded, but it had also cost him: he was forever changed by the experience. He now knew, beyond a shadow of a doubt, of a spiritual existence beyond the physical world. This knowledge comforted him and saddened him in a strangely optimistic way. Lightheaded, Bram forced his chin to rise from his chest. He heard Solomon Chavez calling him in a panic, but his watering eyes were locked on the image he saw before him: a woman, who appeared no older than thirty, stood before him, wearing a floral sundress, her shoulder-length, strawberry-blonde hair soft and radiant. Bram was shaken by the sight: the woman looked exactly like his mother, before her untimely death.

Sensing Bram's emotional turmoil, the fungal mind altered the illusion, morphing from his mother into an old man wearing a tan robe, his long, gray hair and beard immaculately groomed. An apprehensive expression lined the wizened, angular face.

●

"Waters! Get away from that thing and help me!" Solomon yelled. He was attempting, once again, to approach Gloria Muldoon's rigid, seemingly lifeless body.

Only a minute before, the creature that attacked him had shriveled and died, yet it seemed like an eternity had passed. He'd been trying to help Gloria, but his every attempt had failed. Coiled around Gloria's body was a huge, fearsome-looking snake that lunged toward him each time he drew near. The snake looked like a miniature version of the ones they'd escaped from earlier. It might be one of their offspring, but in all likelihood it was another illusion, like the false Selena. Gloria was covered in fungal tendrils, but Solomon hesitated testing that hypothesis for one simple reason: he was deathly afraid of the creature's two-inch fangs.

Perhaps that was it, he thought. *Whatever this creature was, perhaps it was using his fear against him . . . perhaps there were no snakes in the tunnels . . . perhaps he and his companions had each been shown something different, something that would strike a personalized fear into their individual hearts.*

With the snake's cold, reptilian eyes following his every move, Solomon glanced once more at Bram Waters. The psychic detective was on his knees, staring at empty space. In front of him, a cluster of undulating tendrils, which only moments before had suddenly released him, were now keeping their distance. It had been a strange sight to behold: the tendrils that attacked Waters had squirmed like worms—unlike the fungus that attacked him; it clamped onto him and shriveled up like a water lily in the Sahara desert. But why? Was the plant virus that altered his chromosomes somehow responsible? Had his body reacted to the threat and released a counter-agent, a poison that invaded the fungus, thus killing it? That was the only explanation that made any sense. But what of Waters' reaction to the fungus? His body had begun to glow and, as it glowed, his face had taken on a serene expression seconds before the fungus stopped its squirming and released its grip.

"Dammit, Waters," he yelled, "snap out of it! I need some help over here!"

Solomon watched anxiously as Bram slowly turned to look over his shoulder. The man's eyes appeared haunted. And yet, when he beheld Gloria's predicament, his expression changed to one of shock and horror. Scrambling to his feet, Bram tore his gaze from Gloria and faced the cluster of fungal tendrils directly in front of him.

"Let her go, damn you!" he roared.

Solomon was taken aback by Waters' unexpected outburst. Who was he speaking to? Surely not the fungal cluster, a plant compelled by predatory impulse and not an actual sentient being.

"It's a fucking mushroom! An illusion!" he bellowed. "It's making me see a snake wrapped around Gloria. What you're seeing, it's not real!"

Bram edged away from the fungal cluster and faced Solomon. "I see a . . . I see a whole crap-load of spiders," he rasped. "I know they're not real—the fungus is. Get out of my head!" he screamed, at the nearby cluster. "You're killing her! Let her go, damn you!"

Solomon was becoming irritated by Bram's futile attempt at communicating with the fungi. "It doesn't understand you, Waters. Stop wasting time and help me save Gloria."

"You're wrong, Chavez," he snapped. "Not only does it understand us, it's frightened of you in particular." Bram closed his eyes halfway and appeared to be listening to something only he could hear. "There's something in your blood that can hurt it." He faced the cluster once more. "Show yourself to my companion. Let him see what I see. If you don't, I'll cut him and splash his blood all over you."

Solomon's eyebrows rose. "You'll do what?"

Bram remained silent, staring daggers at the fungal cluster.

Had Waters gone mad? Would his delusion turn violent? Solomon wondered. "Quit talking nonsense, Waters, and—" The air around the cluster shimmered and took shape, transforming into the image of a kindly old man with long white hair and matching beard. As this happened, the snake around Gloria vanished. Her body was indeed engulfed in fungal tendrils. No longer intimidated by an illusory snake, Solomon rushed to Gloria's side to tear at the deadly fungi.

"Please, stop what you are doing," the old man calmly requested. "We will release your female companion, though it will do you no good. She is too far gone to save."

More out of shock than anything else, Solomon stopped tearing at the fungi and stared at the old man. *This can't be possible!* "Y-you spoke," he gasped in amazement.

"Your statement is correct. We are capable of many things . . . one of which is mercy. Please catch your companion when we release her."

The cluster that was feeding on Gloria extracted its tendrils from her skin and disentangled itself from her body, dropping limp into Solomon's waiting arms. Lowering her gently to the ground, he fixed his gaze on the image of the old man, his eyes ablaze with anger. Bram dropped down beside him and grasped Gloria's hand.

"She's still alive, Dr. Chavez."

Solomon barely heard him. *How could this be?* he wondered. How was it possible for a plant to talk, let alone speak of mercy? Such a thing flew in the face of everything he knew about the natural world. The old man was watching him intently, his head tilted slightly to one side.

"You are correct, Doctor," the illusion stated. "We are different. We possess a consciousness that allows us to think in a coherent manner. Like us, you and Bram Waters are different. The female, however, is ordinary. I respect your concern for her welfare, but she is doomed. It would be a mercy to her if you allow us to finish our meal."

"Over my dead body!" snapped Bram, rifling through the contents of Gloria's supply pack. "What's that thing talking about, Doc? What's it mean by saying you're different?"

"I, um . . . have no idea."

The old man smiled broadly. "Of course you do, Dr. Chavez. Your immune system produces a chemical that is toxic to us . . . a side effect of the virus that caused your immortality."

Bram jerked his head up and blurted, "What the hell?"

20

"'ll take that," Richard said, reaching for the admiral's CID.

The Command Interlink Device had slipped from the admiral's pocket and clattered to the hanger floor as she was being moved out of the transport vehicle. An acolyte assigned to treat her injuries had picked up the device. Hesitant to accept orders from a male, she looked Richard up and down before reluctantly placing the rectangular device in Richard's outstretched hand.

The stretcher transporting the admiral across the hangar hovered forty inches off the ground. Two medical attendants, positioned on either side of the stretcher, attended to the admiral as it floated toward a preprogrammed foldway arch. Richard and the others followed close behind.

When the group reached the foldway, the attendant who picked up the admiral's CID held up her hand and stopped before entering the arch. "I'm sorry, but this is as far as you go."

"Bullshit," Richard snapped. "I want to see where she's being—"

The attendant cut him off. "Please contain your emotions, Commander! Even in ancient Earth hospitals, certain wings were off limits to family and friends. I appreciate your concern, but let us proceed with the job of caring for the admiral. Rest assured, she's in the best possible hands. You'll be informed of the status of her condition the moment her injuries have been treated. They must be attended to without further delay."

Richard felt a gentle hand rest lightly on his forearm. Looking down, he saw that it belonged to Lorna Threman.

"Let them do their job, Richard. You should return to your apartment and await further updates. Better yet, you and your companions could come to my office: it contains an anteroom where I entertain guests. During this moment of crisis, it's best to find comfort in each other's fellowship. While you wait, I'll arrange for a servant to bring refreshments and—" she suddenly paused, a faraway look in her eye.

As Richard studied the change, Admiral Axelrod was taken through the foldway. He turned to see blackness where a light-green corridor once lay.

"Damn!" he barked. Furious over being distracted, Richard spun on his heel to give Lorna a piece of his mind. When he saw the troubled expression on her face he held his anger in check. "What is it, Chancellor?"

She held up her index finger. A few seconds later, with a look of grave concern, she shifted her attention back to him. "Richard, I have some bad news to report. The Lord has just informed me that the vehicle carrying Dr. Solomon Chavez, Ezral Magliss, and the other members of your crew has gone missing in a remote section of the Yggdrasil Forest. A search party is on its way to their last known whereabouts and should be arriving in the next half hour or so."

Richard's mounting anger suddenly switched to concern—combined with a rising suspicion: the admiral attacked and Solomon Chavez gone missing on the same day? Something wasn't kosher. He considered three possibilities: coincidence, incompetence, and a plot to weaken their ranks. Richard put little stock in coincidence and, having observed New Terran efficiency, didn't believe it was incompetence . . . so that left a plot to weaken their ranks. He didn't want to consider that option, but what other choice did he have?

"How soon can you arrange for me and two of my security officers to join the search?"

Lorna removed her hand from his arm. "I'm afraid that won't be possible, Commander."

"And why the hell not?" Richard hissed.

"By the time you arrive, I'm sure the search will be over. Besides, you won't do your friends any good being out there. You'll just get in the way."

"I'll be the judge of that."

"No, Commander, you won't," she declared, reaching for the foldway control panel. "As with the admiral's condition, you'll be kept apprised of the search status—either from the confines of your apartment or from the anteroom connected to my office. Take your pick."

Richard understood there would be no changing her mind. With a frustrated sigh, he scanned the faces of his crew and, seeing their worry, knew which option to choose.

●

Bram stared at Solomon Chavez as though seeing him for the first time. The creature couldn't possibly be right. The man wasn't immortal, that was impossible . . . wasn't it?

"Talk to me, Chavez. Is it true? Will you live forever?"

Solomon's gaze was fixed firmly on Gloria. "We can talk about that later. As for now, we need to focus our energies on helping Ms. Muldoon."

Knowing Solomon was right, Bram returned to exploring Gloria's pack. He quickly found what he was looking for and removed the airtight package. "She's lost a lot of blood," he noted, handing the package to Solomon. "This is an emergency transfusion kit. We'll be able to—"

"I know what it is, Waters."

Biting back a stinging retort, Bram said, "I'm sure you do, Doc. All I meant was that we'll be able to test her blood and ours to see if one of us is a match. You're the more likely candidate, seeing as my blood type is AB negative, which is rare. Being a doctor, I'm sure you already know your type. All we need to do now is test Gloria's and we'll be good to go."

Solomon had already opened the package and was setting its contents to one side. He took a small, gray and black meter, held it to Gloria's finger, and pressed a button. It punctured her skin, but no blood appeared. Grumbling under his breath, he squeezed her finger, but still, not a single drop of blood exited the wound.

"What do we do now?" Bram gulped. "She doesn't have much time."

Without answering, Solomon grabbed a syringe from the kit and jabbed the needle into the crook of Gloria's right arm. Yanking it out, he tossed the syringe aside and put pressure on either side of the puncture mark. A small drop of blood seeped out. In one swift motion, he snatched up the test meter and absorbed the droplet. Within seconds the results were back. Gloria's blood type was A positive.

"Mine's no good," Bram moaned. "How 'bout yours?"

Solomon hesitated before answering, "My blood type is O positive."

"But that's the universal donor!" Bram cried. "Why didn't you say so in the first place? We could've saved some time."

Solomon leveled a hard stare. "I don't need to explain myself to you, Waters. Just hand me the transfusion cuffs."

Bram's eyebrows shot up. He sensed that Solomon was hiding something else, something concerning his relationship with Gloria. He was almost tempted to probe deeper but tamped that urge down, knowing it was more important to concentrate fully on saving Gloria's life. As he passed Solomon the transfusion cuffs, a thought struck him.

"The old man—I mean the creature—said something about your blood being a poison," he observed. "Are you sure that it won't harm Gloria?"

"No I'm not, but it's better than letting her die without even trying," he replied, strapping the cuff to his arm. After fastening the other cuff to Gloria's arm, he programmed the monitor-pump and stretched out on the tunnel floor. Within seconds the blood was flowing through the IV lines from his arm into Gloria's. "She won't be able to receive all the blood she needs from my circulatory system alone. If she did, I'd wind up dry like her. Instead, I'll supply as much blood as I can reasonably afford, with the remaining fluids being supplemented with saline solution. When the monitor beeps twice, remove the cuff from my arm and attach the bag of solution located in the emergency pack to the feed line below the cuff." He pointed to a small, clear tube attached to the IV line just below his transfusion cuff. "I'll be far too weak to stand, so you'll need to hold the bag while the solution's being fed into Gloria. Do you understand, Waters?"

Bram nodded.

"Good. Look in the pack. You'll find a one-inch, flat metallic disk marked 'status monitor' wrapped in plastic. Stick it to the side of her neck over her carotid artery. It will send a status signal to the transfusion monitor, keeping you informed of her condition."

As he opened the pack to remove the saline solution and status monitor, Bram glanced at the old man. He appeared solid, looked so real . . . but wasn't. He was a deadly alien life-form. The old man stared hungrily at the blood traveling from Solomon's arm to Gloria's, his wrinkled, hooded eyes containing more than a hint of fear mixed with his hunger. The creature caught his eye and smiled, looking almost benevolent.

"You *meats* are fascinating creatures," it said.

"Meats?" The term sounded exceedingly strange to Bram's ear.

"Of course, you call us plants and we call you meats. Does that offend you?"

"We prefer to be called human beings," Bram replied.

"Very well, that is what we will call you from now on," the old man said.

Ripping open the plastic package containing the status monitor, Bram peeled off the paper backing to expose the adhesive beneath and applied the monitor to Gloria's neck. "You keep referring to yourself as 'we' and 'us.' If I understand correctly, you're a collective. The three of us are individuals. My name is Bram, the female is Gloria, and the other man is Solomon. Please refer to us by name from now on."

"As you wish." The old man looked from Gloria to Solomon. "You care for her a great deal, don't you . . . Solomon?"

Bram sensed the same ambivalence as before rising in the enigmatic young man. He caught himself thinking this and realized that he could no longer think of Chavez as young.

"I have no idea what you're talking about," Solomon grumbled. "So tell me, *fungus*, how should we refer to *you* from now on?"

The old man looked puzzled, but only momentarily. "We have no need of a name. However, if you persist with your unusual desire to personalize us, we would not be displeased if you began referring to us as the Great and Mighty Hunter Scavenger."

Solomon rolled his eyes then shook his head. The transfusion process was taking its toll.

Bram sighed, "I can't speak for Solomon, but I'm not calling you that. Come up with a name that rolls off the tongue easier, one that doesn't sound quite so pompous."

"As you wish. How does *Argus* roll off your oh-so refined tongue?"

Bram noted the disdain in the creature's response. "Why that name?" he wondered.

The old man shrugged. "It's as good as any."

"If memory serves," Solomon pointed out, "Argus was a character in Greek mythology. A hundred-eyed giant who spied on Zeus's lovers for his jealous wife, Hera. A strange choice of names if you ask me; though oddly apropos."

Hearing a low moan, Bram turned to see Gloria's eyes flutter open. Her breathing was shallow, but her color was returning. In contrast, Solomon appeared listless, his skin pallid. The monitor beeped twice, informing Bram that it was time to begin the saline solution. Shortly thereafter, he supplied Solomon with an electrolyte supplement and a bottle of water. Without hesitation, Solomon popped the tablet and guzzled the water greedily.

"Don't drink so fast," Bram advised. "You might pass out."

The enigmatic scientist lowered the bottle just as Gloria lifted her head.

"Bram . . ." she moaned. Her voice was weak. "W-what happened?"

Wiping her dry forehead with a moist cloth from the pack, Bram eased her head back down. "You've been attacked by—if you can believe this—a cluster of bloodsucking, telepathic fungi," he explained in a comforting voice. "Dr. Chavez gave you a transfusion. He saved your life."

Swiveling her head in Solomon's direction, she whispered, "Thank you . . . brother."

Bram was taken aback. What did she mean by calling Solomon *brother*? Was she using the term figuratively, having just received the man's blood, or had the ordeal addled her mind to the point of confusion? Either way, it was obvious that Solomon was having none of it: he set down the bottle of water and turned a cold stare her way.

"I'm not your brother, Lt. Muldoon," he stated sharply. "You are mistaken."

With effort, Gloria rose to her elbows. "Yes you are, Solomon." Her voice was sounding stronger. "My mother was Kathleen

Muldoon. Your father had a brief affair with her in Norway, nearly thirty-seven years ago while attending a week-long conference at the Oslo Hilton. At the time of their fling, she was working as a bartender at the hotel and—"

"Once again, Lieutenant, you're mistaken. I can assure you, I'm not your brother," Solomon interjected. "Now, please, this whole ordeal has been extremely taxing. Perhaps we can discuss this at a later date. You should concentrate all your energies on regaining your strength."

Bram noticed that the old man was watching the two with great interest.

With a shake of her head and a huff of disgust, Gloria responded to Solomon's denial. "Is the thought of me as your sister so abhorrent that you feel the need to call my mother a liar? I'll have you know, she wasn't in the habit of sleeping with every man that came along. My mother had true feelings for your father. She cared for him. She could've used her pregnancy to extort money from him, but she kept it silent . . . out of respect . . . perhaps out of love."

"I'm not your brother," Solomon reiterated, averting his eyes.

Bram sensed the truth in Solomon's refutation but also knew there was more to the story. He suspected the truth, but out of decorum kept his mouth shut—the old man, on the other hand, had no such compunctions.

"Dr. Chavez is right," the old man said, causing Gloria to register him for the first time. She looked both confused and frightened. "As he said, he is not your brother, he is your—"

"Shut the fuck up!" Solomon cried. "You don't have a clue about—"

"Oh, but we do, Dr. Chavez. We understand the concept of siblings and progeny. We have consumed many species over the eons. As such, we have absorbed much knowledge from the brains of both small and large creatures. What we fail to understand is the reason you are keeping the female in the dark about your relationship, why you have yet to inform her that she is your daughter?"

For Bram, Solomon's quick intake of breath was confirmation enough: the old man had spoken the truth.

Gloria, on the other hand, having been unconscious when Solomon disclosed his immortality, snorted in disbelief. "You don't know as much about the human race as you think. Dr. Chavez can't be my father—he isn't old enough."

Bram and Solomon exchanged glances.

"That's not . . . necessarily true," Solomon hesitantly admitted. Sitting up with effort, he fixed Gloria with a measured, though guilty, stare. "What this creature says is true. I suspect that we are related, but I'm not your brother. I remember your mother fondly, though I was under the impression she used birth control. To be safe, I used a condom."

"Yeah, well, condoms break," she said, looking both confused and skeptical. "As for her end of the carnal bargain, she lied to you. She hadn't been in a relationship in well over a year, and hadn't taken the pill for at least three months before she, um, met you. As for the condom . . . she supplied it, right?" Solomon nodded. "Nearly a year after my brother's death, while visiting Switzerland with my foster parents, I finally gathered the courage to read my mother's diary. In it she wrote about using a condom from an old box my step-father left behind. As I'm sure you're aware, old condoms aren't the most reliable means of protection . . . so there."

She paused to study Solomon's reaction. A look of resignation was written on his face.

"This is terribly confusing, how can you be my father?" she groaned, rubbing her left temple. "Either you're the world's best-preserved old fart, or you have an extremely good plastic surgeon on payroll."

For the next half-hour, Solomon unburdened his soul, telling his astonishing story for the first time. He started out tentative but was soon animated: his demeanor changed; his attitude shifted; more than a century's weight of unshared secrets were finally lifting from his shoulders. With his tale at last complete, a sad, relieved smile lingered on his lips.

Bram knew that it must have taken a terrific amount of courage to reveal such a secret. He shifted his gaze to Gloria and saw that she was staring sadly at the ground. She hurriedly brushed away a tear that was trickling down her cheek.

"Gloria, are you all right?" he asked, unsure exactly why she was so upset but sensing a storm of powerful emotions in the usually reserved young woman.

In a barely audible voice, she said, "I . . . I had a sister . . ."

●

Her name was Selena.

Gloria felt numb, yet she also felt wracked with grief. It was a strange sensation, one that she'd felt only two other times in her life—when her mother and brother had died. To make matters worse, a kernel of anger had taken root in her breast. It grew like a noxious weed, eventually dispelling the numbness. The object of this steadily growing anger was none other than Solomon Chavez himself, whom she'd just learned was somehow (quite improbably) her father, not her brother as she'd believed for the past twenty-seven years.

At the age of nine, her mother told her who her real father was, shortly after breaking up with Aaron's father for the third and final time. She'd always suspected the bastard wasn't her real father: he'd as much as said so on more than one occasion. Furthermore, she'd caught him staring at her whenever she wore a bathing suit or left the shower wearing nothing but a towel. A real father would've never had that hungry look in his eye . . . or at least, not a decent father.

After learning the truth that her father was the rich and famous Juan Chavez, she'd fantasized about finding a way to be close to him. She'd studied hard in school in the hopes of one day being hired by one of his companies, where she'd rise up through the ranks, eventually be noticed by him, before revealing the truth about her parentage. Her grades weren't good enough to earn a scholarship to university, so she'd entered the military instead, thinking that her dream would take longer than expected. After four years in the British army, she left and went to work for a Welsh security firm. That's where she'd met Floyd Sullivant. The firm was associated with a British subsidiary of CIMRAD, Juan Chavez's massive business empire. She'd finally stuck her toe in the proverbial door and was determined to keep it there. Her goal was to network her way through the system until somehow garnering a job working for the great man himself, but then, ten years ago, she'd learned of his death. It was devastating. All her plans were ruined . . . until Solomon appeared out of nowhere and renewed her hopes. If she couldn't stand at her father's side, she would settle for a mysterious half-brother.

Now, here he was, sitting in a God-forsaken tunnel, claiming to be her father, telling a story that made her head spin. Perhaps this was all an illusion caused by the deadly fungus that sucked her blood. Despite the transfusion she received, Gloria still felt queasy and a bit feverish.

"I don't feel well," she moaned.

"Here, drink some water," Bram said, handing her a full bottle from the emergency pack.

Snatching it up, she took a series of hearty gulps before handing the bottle back, feeling sick to her stomach. The tunnel started to spin. "Something's wrong . . . I'm dizzy."

Bram ordered her to lie down and rest, and she obeyed willingly. She gazed up at the ceiling, her forehead and cheeks flush from the heat. She was tired—*so* tired. She was unable to keep her eyes open, even as Solomon mumbled something about a virus—a virus from his blood.

21

Slipping out of his coveralls, Richard tossed them over the chair beside his bed and slid under the silky sheets. With the admiral out of commission, he needed to catch a few winks. He'd have his work cut out for him if she ended up being hospitalized for an extended period of time.

He was about to order the lights turned off when he was struck by a thought. Earlier that night, after conferring with Chancellor Threman about the admiral's condition and receiving the runaround over the search for Albans, Chavez, and Waters, he'd retired to his apartment, having completely forgotten about pocketing the admiral's CID. It was in his coveralls, the fourth file still unread.

Richard sat there debating whether to use his command code to access the file's information or wait for the admiral to recover from her injuries enough to access it herself. If the file was anywhere near as disturbing as the others he'd seen, he probably should access it; however, such an action might also be interpreted as an overreach of authority.

Finally, after weighing both sides, he told the computer to turn off the lights. Whatever data was stored in the fourth file could wait a little longer, at least until after he learned whether or not the admiral survived her surgery.

●

Bloody hell, why is it so bright? Katherine wondered. It was only a moment ago that she'd been standing beside the meteor crater. It should not be dark outside.

With great effort, her eyes fluttered open. One thing was certain: she was no longer lying beside the crater. But where was she? Katherine scanned her surroundings, her vision quickly regaining its focus. She lay under a white sheet in a small, sparsely furnished room, with what appeared to be medical equipment positioned on either side of her bed. Then she remembered: she'd been hit by a spear—an *ice spear* at that.

But how was that even possible? At that point, Katherine remembered something else: the contents of the third file. For some inexplicable reason, the data contained within that file, though disconcerting upon first read, no longer disturbed her. What did it matter if the men of New Terra weren't actually male but were instead genetically engineered females designed to look like men? Her thoughts then turned to the *Arrow* and how its passenger manifest leaned toward the female side. It had been determined before launch that there should be a larger quota of women to men, mainly to help alleviate petty jealousies in regard to mating rituals. With more women than men to choose from, there would be less reason for men to fight over who would be paired with whom.

But none of that mattered anymore. A separate section of the third file went into detail about New Terra's true birthing method: unbeknownst to the city's inhabitants, their purported Lord had nothing to do with supplying babies, as claimed by Jemis Calverton, the High Priestess of New Terra. Their ritualized births were simply a ruse to hide the fact that their babies were being grown in, and being delivered via, artificial wombs, similar to those developed by Juan Chavez in the twenty-first century. The only part of the file that puzzled her, and might've had some connection to her attack, was the section on why the New Terrans had resorted to using artificial wombs in the first place.

Before developing their rigid, clockwork-like societal apparatus, New Terran society was less defined, more undisciplined; a community of layabouts for the most part. After a conservative government came to power, all that changed. Institutional reforms were created that angered a significant portion of the citizenry. Demonstrations were held, followed by civil disobedience, which ultimately led to catastrophic riots. In due course, government forces put down the unrest, but many rioters were killed in the process. The ones who survived were exiled from the city. Fearing the forest, they set out for the ice field, never to be heard from again. Fifty years after their exile, rumors surfaced of elusive hairy beasts being spotted on the ice, yet none were ever captured. Katherine was certain those mythical hairy Yotls (as the locals called them) were descendants of their exiled rebels. She felt the truth of it in her bones.

As for why New Terrans began to use artificial wombs: they were employed, in conjunction with an indigenous contraceptive surreptitiously introduced into the food supply, to ensure that only the "right" sort of babies were born.

As Katherine pondered this, she heard a soft humming sound to her left. Turning her head, she saw a smiling Jemis Calverton enter though the room's foldway arch.

"I'm pleased to see that you survived your injuries, Admiral. If you're feeling up to it, there are a few anxious people waiting for visitation."

Katherine expected as much. "I'd like to see Commander Allison first, so he can debrief me on the crater site incident. Next, I want to speak with Dr. Singh, to make sure he wasn't harmed during his stay in your so-called *Room of Atonement*. On second thought, I'd like a meeting with Dr. Chavez before Dr. Singh. I'm interested to find out how his expedition went. Hopefully it was nice and boring . . . just the opposite of ours."

The High Priestess looked away, a disconcerted expression on her round face. "I'm afraid I have some bad news to report, Admiral." Lifting her chin, she reestablished eye contact. "Neither Solomon Chavez nor Dr. Singh will be speaking with you today."

Katherine's pulse quickened. "What do you mean?"

Calverton's raised eyebrow signaled her displeasure at being spoken to so harshly. "Very well. To begin with, Dr. Singh is in a coma."

"What!" Sitting up straighter, Katherine grimaced from the pain. "Did it have anything to do with that infernal torture device you used on him?"

Jemis Calverton placed both hands on her hips and glared. "The Room of Atonement is *not* a torture device, Admiral. But yes, he did have an adverse reaction to his treatment. We have yet to determine why he slipped into a coma, but I'm certain that after a few more days examining his case, we'll be able to—"

"Not a chance," she declared. "Get my clothes. I'm leaving this hospital and taking Dr. Singh back to the *Arrow*. From now on, I want my own medical staff working on his case."

Jemis Calverton looked put out. "I don't think that's such a—" Her voice trailed off and a faraway look entered her eyes. After a few seconds, the faintest flicker of a smile crossed her lips. "The Lord has informed me that it might be best if Dr. Singh was transported to your ship. Despite this being a first-rate medical facility, we've seldom treated coma patients. Perhaps the facilities onboard *Solomon's Arrow* will be better suited for his treatment."

Katherine nodded. "Good. As for Dr. Chavez, why won't I be able to I see him?"

Jemis Calverton cleared her throat before answering. "He, along with Mr. Waters, Lt. Albans, Lt. Muldoon, Ezral Magliss, our Agricultural Minister, and their pilot, were lost. Their skimmer crashed in a remote region of the forest while returning to the harvesters. Their bodies were never recovered. It is assumed that their remains were consumed by a fungus . . . I'm terribly sorry."

"Good Lord," she moaned. "Are you absolutely sure?"

Jemis Calverton lowered her eyes. "I'm afraid there is no other explanation."

Stunned, Katherine sat there gazing down at her hands, feeling sick to her stomach. The news was catastrophic: Solomon Chavez was an integral part of their mission; they were depending on his expertise as much *or more* than anyone else onboard the *Arrow*. His loss called for a change in plans. "If you don't mind, I'd like to speak with Commander Allison."

●

Unconscious, Gloria moaned as her fever intensified. Bram searched through the med kit one more time. It contained a bottle of analgesics, which had yet to help with her fever, together with an assortment of other supplies, such as bandages, washes, and topical medications, which were useless in this case. What she really needed was a powerful antiviral.

Bram was becoming increasingly worried. For the past hour, Gloria had slipped in and out of consciousness. The thermometer patch he applied to her forehead said that her temperature had risen to 105.2. And they were nearly out of water, the last bottle containing maybe two sips.

Bram saw that Gloria's forehead was still dry, which meant the fever was still rising.

"How long was it before your fever broke, Dr. Chavez?"

"I'm not exactly sure," he replied. A look of deep concern marked his face as he gazed at his daughter. "It was . . . at least three, possibly four days."

"Oh hell," Bram groaned. If the same proved true for Gloria, she needed immediate medical attention or she might not survive.

"I also had plenty of water," Solomon added. "And the tribe whose camp I stumbled across had a good healer. She supplied me with a powerful concoction of herbs to control the fever."

Argus had remained silent for the past hour. He sat with his spindly legs crossed, eight feet from where Bram tended to Gloria. "Meats such as—excuse us, humans such as yourselves, have a tendency to use the plant world for your own selfish purposes— are we not correct?"

Bram ignored the old man. Solomon, however, was not so obliging.

"I'm proud to say yes," he replied. "The human race has used and will continue to use the plant world for our own benefit. I see nothing wrong with that; in fact, without the plant world we would starve; we would still be living in caves; we would've never developed modern medicines; we would've—"

"You would have never become immortal?" the old man interrupted.

Solomon looked at Bram and shrugged. "At least we know he was paying attention and not twiddling his imaginary thumbs."

Bram chuckled. "He seems to know a lot about us, Dr. Chavez, but we know hardly anything about him. After everything he's put us through, I'd say he owes us some information, wouldn't you agree?"

"Indeed. By the way, Waters, call me Solomon. I've come to the conclusion that you're not such a bad sort after all."

"I will, but only if you start calling me by my first name . . . not my last."

"Agreed," he said, forcing a weak smile. The transfusion's effects were beginning to wear off, but he remained listless.

Bram addressed the old man. "As for you, *Argus.* Since we're trapped down here, you may as well tell us about yourself; because, if you're still planning on eating us, I'd like to put it off a little while longer."

The old man studied them for an uncomfortably long moment before answering. "The three of you have nothing to fear. The doctor and his daughter are protected, thanks to the virus in their system. As for you, Mr. Waters, we still want your nutrients. But you interest us; therefore, you are safe . . . for the time being."

Despite the old man's benign appearance, the straightforward way he mentioned Bram as a food source was chilling nonetheless.

"As for our history, it does not flow with exciting tales of grand adventures, as your history surely does. On the contrary. Our life can be summarized in a matter of minutes; however, there is one aspect of our history that you might find interesting and perhaps useful. You are unlike the other humans we have consumed. If we agree to tell you what we know, you must promise to set up a parlay with the humans who govern the city, for the purpose of them finding another source of protein. Much as you, we have no desire to be used as a food source."

Bram looked to Solomon, who answered, "Your terms sound reasonable."

"Very well, we shall begin," the old man said, stroking his beard. "We are a single organism that spans the circumference of this planet. We keep to the strip of ground where the most abundant food supply is located, not sending out feeders past its edges because it would be illogical to do so. We consider ourselves a collective, since each offshoot of tendrils possesses a rudimentary individual awareness, which uses telepathy to capture its prey. Each cluster breaks down the dead flora and fauna that collect steadily beneath the forest canopy, in conjunction with certain tiny insects, with which we live in harmony. Our main purpose is to prevent the forest from being overwhelmed by collapsed trees, dead plants, and animal carcasses. We serve a useful purpose in the scheme of things, as you must surely agree."

"Does this collective of individualized tendril clusters constitute a form of neural network, similar to the human brain?" Solomon asked.

"The human brain is extremely complex," the old man responded, "as are we. The clusters are not individualized aspects that create the whole; they are extensions of the whole, which is, itself, individualized. However, the tendrils that connect the whole do constitute what you might consider a neural network."

Despite the confusing language, Bram thought he grasped the creature's explanation, mainly because he sensed a greater intelligence behind the illusion that tried to kill him. Solomon, however, appeared to have no problem understanding the creature's account, which made sense, being an immortal super-genius.

"In the distant past," the old man continued, "we possessed minimal intelligence. But we grew out of our infancy by consuming more and varied creatures, some of which possessed a rudimentary capacity for rational thought; thus our own intelligence evolved. When your kind arrived, we absorbed the brains of creatures with a highly developed consciousness. It was a revelation, to say the least. We, of course, wanted more, and became proficient at setting mental traps to ensnare your kind.

"But then, something strange occurred," the old man said. "The traps stopped working. For the past twenty-five hundred of your years, we have been thwarted, unable to consume more than a handful of humans. Naturally, we are disappointed over missing the opportunity to consume the three of you—especially you, Dr. Chavez. You have a massive intellect and, due to your longevity, a wealth of experience, both of which would be prized assets—if not for the virus in your system. As for you, Mr. Waters, you are no genius, but your telepathic abilities are intriguing. It is a shame that you fought so hard to survive. You may have provided us with the next evolutionary leap."

"Sorry to disappoint you," Bram said, sarcastically.

The old man waved a dismissive hand. "Think nothing of it." He'd misunderstood Bram's attempt at sardonic humor. "In Ms. Muldoon's case, she is rather ordinary from what we have gathered. Her intellect is average and, aside from being exceptionally physically fit, she has little to offer besides adding her consciousness to the collective, like all the others."

Bram was perturbed by this evaluation. *Did he have feelings for this woman?* he wondered. She was so unlike his dead fiancée. And yet, there was something about her that made him care, that made him feel protective. He didn't think it was love, but it was something. Examining her, he saw that her breathing was shallow but her temperature was holding steady.

"That is beside the point," the old man continued. "When the humans stopped falling into our traps, we set about reviewing what might have caused this to take place. We decided it must be due to the metallic mesh that was discovered surrounding the brains of our later prey."

"So I was right," Solomon grunted, eyeing the old man with contempt. "When we crashed, I discovered that the pilot's brain was covered in a fine metallic mesh, just as you described. After seeing this, I came to the same conclusion, despite having no idea it was *your* psychic illusions they were trying to block."

"Do you think the mesh is causing their brains to go haywire?" Bram asked. This prompted Solomon to express a look of mild annoyance, unsure what Bram was getting at. "You know, because they persist in claiming that the *Lord* is speaking to them?"

Solomon rubbed his upper lip with his index finger. "It's possible—but from what I saw, it looked like the mesh covered the surface and didn't extend into the brain's interior. However, because the damage to the man's skull was so severe, I might have missed something."

The old man held up his hand. "Perhaps this demonstration will answer your question."

A swirling glow appeared a few inches above his hand. The glow rapidly coalesced, forming a startlingly realistic image of a disembodied human brain; the image was covered in the exact same silvery metallic mesh that Bram had seen within the pilot's ruined skull. Though the image was disturbing, he was completely transfixed by the sight. Then, as he watched in amazement, the mesh vanished, followed by the neocortex and each successive layer, until the only thing left was the amygdala—the most primitive area of the brain—along with a pea-sized object, which was connected to the amygdala by numerous metallic filaments.

"What are we looking at?" Solomon asked.

"According to our observations," the old man replied, "this object links each inhabitant of the city to the computer mind that controls every aspect of life in New Terra."

22

"I suspected as much," Solomon grumbled. "It wouldn't be possible for the entire population of New Terra to be delusional. Even if something were contaminating the food or water, they wouldn't have the same hallucination. An outside influence is the only logical explanation, and I don't mean God." He saw that Bram was skeptical. "What are your thoughts, Bram?"

"I'm puzzled. Why would anyone want to program a computer to impersonate God? What's the advantage?"

Solomon pondered this for a moment. "I'm not sure. The original colonists were probably susceptible to religious conditioning. So it might've been used for social control. I must admit, it is puzzling." He would've elaborated further but noticed that Bram was concentrating intensely. "Is something wrong?"

Bram held up a hand for quiet. Within seconds, a broad smile appeared. "A search party just showed up. They're landing to investigate the sinkhole." He turned to face the old man. "You *must* let us go before the search party gives up and moves on to another area. If you don't, Gloria might not survive. She needs treatment, and she needs it *now*."

The old man shrugged in a strikingly human manner. "There is nothing stopping you."

Bram pointed back toward the blocked exit. "But what about the—" he stopped speaking. The blockage was gone, leaving the way clear for them to leave the tunnel. "I'll be damned!"

"Our time together has, unfortunately, come to an end," the old man said. "It has been a great pleasure encountering such surprising individuals. Hopefully we shall meet again." With that, he disappeared. In his place sat a clump of fungal tendrils that quickly retracted into the tunnel floor, leaving nothing to show that the old man had ever been there.

"The pleasure is all yours," Bram hissed as he scooped Gloria's limp body into his arms.

"Here, let me help you," Solomon said, climbing unsteadily to his feet. As he straightened up, the tunnel tilted. He was still somewhat woozy from the transfusion.

"Don't worry about it, Solomon. You should save your strength. I don't want you passing out before we get clear of this tunnel. I'd be tempted to leave you to the mercies of our newfound fungal friend."

"Ha! I hope I left a sour taste in his mouth."

Shifting Gloria in his arms, Bram glanced over his shoulder. "He's telling me that you tasted bitter, not sour."

"You're still communicating with it?"

Bram increased his pace. "Yes. We need to hightail it outta here and signal the rescue party."

"Can't you send them a mental signal, or something?"

"I've tried," Bram groused. "There's still too much psychic interference to make contact."

Both men broke from the tunnel and into the cavern. As they did, Solomon was relieved to see six women, standing atop three-feet-wide, antigravity disks, descending through the sinkhole opening. He was surprised to see that their rescue party was composed entirely of Minders; their spiky black hair and fierce expressions appeared even more intimidating in the gloom. None of his shipmates were among their rescuers, which he found disturbing, though not enough to set off warning sirens in his head. Concern for Gloria's health, coupled with relief over being rescued, outweighed his unease.

The instant the women spotted the three, they casually rested their hands on the stun-batons strapped to their lean, muscular hips.

"Thank God you found us," he blurted out, pulling slightly ahead of the other two.

Bram slowed his pace. "Something about this doesn't feel right," he cautioned.

The antigravity disks settled smoothly to the ground. Stepping off, the eerily similar women headed straight toward Solomon, wordlessly pulling their stun-batons from their holsters.

"My name is Dr. Solomon Chavez, and this is Bram Waters," he announced, confused over the women's actions. "He's carrying Lt. Gloria Muldoon. As you can see, she's been injured and needs medical atten—ah!"

Solomon collapsed to the ground. One of the Minders had stunned him in the solar plexus. She walked up and stood over him like an Amazon warrior. Solomon was completely immobile, his brain functions teetering on the edge of oblivion. The last thing he witnessed before passing out was Bram cursing and attempting to escape with Gloria in his arms. A stun-baton caught the psychic in the lower back, above his left kidney. With a loud yelp, he dropped to the ground and collapsed atop Gloria. That's when Solomon blacked out.

●

"Don't worry about her, she'll be dead soon enough."

Gloria lay on the cavern floor, recovering from the shock of being dropped and receiving part of the charge from the stun-baton that knocked Bram unconscious. The jolt had taken her breath away. She was thankful she hadn't been knocked senseless like him and Solomon, but she was too weak from the viral infection to do anything other than lie on the cavern floor and watch those damnable bitches whisk both men away.

One of the coldly efficient women had been prepared to finish Gloria off. She'd twisted something on the end of her stun-baton—probably a kill-switch—and was about to press its tip to Gloria's neck when she was told not to bother.

Gloria had been spared by fate. The entire scenario felt like a bad dream. Even as the Minder was preparing to kill her, Gloria barely registered the moment. In her feverish condition, she wouldn't have been able to fight her off, even if she tried.

The next thing Gloria knew, she was alone in the cavern, sweating uncontrollably, lapsing in and out of consciousness. Her fever had broken, but it didn't matter, she was as good as dead, and she didn't have the energy to care.

Over the next several hours, she continued to sweat profusely, increasing her dehydration. She even imagined the old man trying to speak with her, but she knew that wasn't possible. He was back in the tunnel. Or was he? Had the chancellor's security bitches captured him too? No, there was something about him . . . but what was it?

Gloria's eyes fluttered open. She felt a little better, a little stronger.

Why was the sinkhole opening getting larger? What were roots (if that's what they really were) doing wrapped around her arms, legs and torso? God, her eyelids were *so* heavy . . .

Hours passed before she drifted up from the depths of a deep, dreamless sleep. The sun was streaming through her bedroom window, waking her prematurely. Or . . . had her alarm failed to go off? Good God, she was late for work!

Eyes popping open, she jerked upright. *Where am I?* Nervously scanning her surroundings, Gloria realized she'd been asleep on a patch of lime-green grass; a fallen tree lay approximately thirty feet away. Disconcerting memories flashed through her mind; memories of being stranded in the middle of an alien forest—and something else—she recalled that her father was Solomon Chavez.

From the corner of her eye, she noticed something dark near her left hand. Turning her head, Gloria stared at a pitch-black opening in the ground. It was the sinkhole. And then it hit her: she was no longer trapped underground. How could this be? She hadn't climbed out; that was impossible.

"How the hell did I—"

"We helped you, Lt. Muldoon."

The voice came from the direction she'd been looking before noticing the sinkhole. Startled, she gave an uncharacteristically girlish yelp. Reaching for her pistol, she spun around to confront the culprit who snuck up on her. It was the old man—Argus.

"What the hell!" She scrambled away from him, pistol pointed at his chest.

"Stop where you are, Lieutenant, before you fall in the sinkhole."

Gloria froze. Slowly looking over her left shoulder, she saw the edge of the sinkhole less than a foot away. Pulling her knees up to her chest, she wrapped her arms around them and stared at the ground directly in front of her. Another memory had returned: the old man standing beside her was not really a man at all, but an illusion manufactured by a telepathic mushroom—or so she'd gathered from Bram as she lay burning with fever.

Bram! Her concern for his welfare was deeper than she expected, twisting her stomach up in knots at the thought of him being in trouble.

"The two men I was with," she began, fearing to make eye contact with the old man. "Do you know where they are? I need to know what's happened to them."

Argus placed his hands behind his back and gazed into the distance. "They have been taken to the city. We are unfamiliar with the city's layout, but we have established that they are being held in its exact center, one-hundred fifty-five feet underground, in a hardened bunker designed to protect the machine mind that controls New Terra. They are presently unconscious, but from what we gather, they are in grave danger."

"That's what I was afraid of." She climbed with difficulty to her feet. "A machine mind, huh? If you could please point me in the right direction, I need to return to the city and somehow warn the others." Dizzy, she placed her hands on her knees. "Also, where can I find some water?"

"Unfortunately, you will find no surface water in this vicinity," the old man informed her. "However, if you travel in the direction we are pointing, you will come across a bush covered in red berries. They are edible to your species and will supply both the hydration and nutrition you require to recover your strength. Once you have eaten your fill, angle five degrees northward and keep a steady pace. You should arrive at the city in approximately fifty-six hours."

Gloria was stretching, working a kink out of her lower back. A tone of frustration entered her voice. "That's great, that's just fucking great."

●

Bram woke to the sound of a moan. Opening his eyes, he saw Solomon sitting on a bunk, rubbing his temples. He appeared to be in a lot of pain. Bram sympathized, as he had a splitting headache, his entire body ached, and he felt lethargic. The Minders who captured them must have used powerful sedatives to keep them unconscious after their stun-batons wore off.

He sat up and looked around. The room was small, no bigger than six-feet wide by ten-feet long. A sink and toilet were located against the back wall. "Where are we?"

SOLOMON'S ARROW • 343

"Looks like a prison cell," Solomon answered. "What I don't understand is why we're here."

"You will find that out soon enough." The voice was female and came from a hidden speaker in the ceiling. "Stand up, move to the foot of your beds, and wait for your escorts."

Bram exchanged glances with Solomon. "Escorts, huh? I don't remember being invited to a fancy dinner."

"Nor do I," Solomon replied. "Unless our escorts use force, I'm staying right here."

"That is not an option," said the disembodied voice. "You will comply with your escort's orders. Failure to comply will result in punishment."

Both men suddenly felt a searing pain directly between their shoulder blades, as if they'd just been prodded with a red-hot poker. Shrieking in sheer agony, they stumbled forward a step, each instinctively reaching behind them in vain, trying to claw at the spot where the burn was located. Almost as soon as the pain began, it was over . . . yet the memory remained.

Breathing hard, Bram shook his head. "Perhaps we—perhaps we should do as they say."

Solomon cleared his throat. "As of now, that would seem the best course of action."

"Excellent," the voice said. "Despite your brutish male exteriors, you learn quickly."

Bram frowned. "I don't know about you, Solomon, but I think our jailer might be sexist."

A defeated shrug was his only reply. Bram sensed that Solomon was worried about Gloria. "Perhaps she'll be wherever it is they're taking us," he whispered.

Solomon shot him a suspicious glare. Bram was reminded of the times his companion tried to avoid his company in the past—before their shared experience in the tunnel. He was on the verge of reassuring Solomon that he'd not been reading his mind, when the man's expression softened and he averted his eyes.

"I hope you're right, Bram . . . for both our sakes," he remarked. "Lately I've come to realize how much you care for–for my daughter."

Bram didn't know what to say. He cared for Gloria—that much was true—but he had no idea his feelings were so obvious. Either that or Solomon's fatherly instincts were surfacing.

Suddenly, a faint outline appeared on the blank wall in front of them. The outline became more distinct, taking on the shape of an arch.

"That's a pretty neat trick," he said, thinking that it would be virtually impossible to escape from a cell with an invisible exit.

The surface of the arch faded from white to gray and then to black; the same black he'd seen within deactivated foldways. The darkness within, which felt like a terrible emptiness whenever he gazed at it, began to brighten. A room appeared on the other side of the archway. One guard—then a second stepped into the cell—stun-batons at the ready.

"Place your hands behind your backs," ordered the second guard as she entered. She, like all the other Minders, wore her hair short, black, and spiky. She was in magnificent shape, her navy-blue uniform clinging to her like a second skin. "Turn around."

Both men did as they were ordered. The moment their backs were turned, their wrists drew together, as though suddenly magnetized. Bram was unable to feel anything like handcuffs touching his skin. He tried to pull his wrists apart, but was unsuccessful. An intense tingling sensation gripped his wrists, becoming increasingly painful the more he tried to separate them. After only a few seconds, he relaxed his efforts.

"I suspect the stun-batons have the capacity to bind our wrists with a restriction field made of plasma—one that also induces pain when needed," Solomon stated.

"That is correct, Dr. Chavez," the disembodied voice in the ceiling acknowledged. "I urge you to comply with any and all orders given to you from here on out . . . and remember this: do not try anything foolish, for the pain you experienced will recommence at the slightest provocation from either of you. Have I made myself clear?"

"Perfectly clear," Bram said. "We have no clue where we are, but even if we did, where could we go if we did manage to escape?"

"You are correct, Mr. Waters. Any attempt to escape would be a fruitless endeavor. Proceed."

The guard nearest Bram poked him in the ribs with her baton. "The two of you will form up, one behind the other, and remain that way until ordered to proceed through the foldway . . . do you understand?"

Bram was tempted to make a sarcastic remark, but instead held his tongue, respecting the fact that Solomon would suffer because of his belligerence. He grunted a halfhearted yes, which was followed by Solomon's own desultory agreement. Waving him forward with her baton, the guard pointed to a spot on the floor where she wanted him to stand. He dutifully complied; as did Solomon, who fell in line directly behind him. The two Minders were positioned on either side of them, their cold, dispassionate eyes sizing them up, looking for any unruly twitch of muscle.

Staring straight ahead, Bram held steady as he watched the foldway shimmer open, revealing their destination. The room was austere, lacking any furnishings or human comforts.

"You may proceed," the guard said.

Bram strode through the foldway, feeling the familiar, nearly imperceptible, tugging in the pit of his stomach that signaled he'd stepped through no ordinary door. Once inside, he realized that his initial impression of the room was correct: it was not designed for conferences or meetings or get-togethers; it looked like an interrogation chamber. He might have continued to think this, if not for the presence of the seven-foot tall, gunmetal-gray sphere hovering in the middle of the room. Whatever that thing was, Bram knew it was important—and dangerous.

The guards positioned themselves on either side of the foldway, their backs to the wall.

Solomon stepped up beside Bram. "I've seen more amenities in a hospital boiler room."

Bram was about to respond with a halfhearted quip when the invisible handcuffs disappeared. As he and Solomon rubbed their wrists, Bram glanced back at the guards, neither of whom had moved, causing him to wonder who released their shackles.

The disembodied voice once again spoke, but this time the sound came from all directions. "Welcome, gentlemen. Our meeting has been a long time coming, and I have many questions that require answers."

What he saw next made Bram's knees go weak.

He heard Solomon gasp in surprise but paid little attention; his eyes were locked on the huge sphere hovering in the middle of the room. It was distorting, changing shape, breaking apart into a thousand tiny bits that swarmed and swirled, then reconfigured itself into a face—a gunmetal-gray face—the face of a woman.

"Allow me to introduce myself," the artificial countenance purred, its lips moving in unison with its words. "I am your captor, Athena the Everlasting, the one and only ruler of this pitiable world, who will soon become the supreme ruler of the universe."

23

The vast plain of lime-green grass stretched as far as the eye could see. There were neither hills nor valleys nor trees to help differentiate one direction from another; a never-ending plainness, a smooth sea of green that boggled the mind.

Gloria stood at the edge of the Yggdrasil Forest, feeling intimidated by the long trek that lay ahead of her. If she lost her bearings, there'd be no landmarks to keep her from getting lost. Mercifully, her SID had started functioning again, or she would have pitched camp and waited for the Minders to find her. The device would keep her moving in the right direction, thanks to its internal global positioning system. Unfortunately, its battery was low, and something was wrong with the signal strength. She'd need to be much closer to the city to contact Floyd on a secure channel.

There was another SID function that would come in handy. "S-1, activate subsonic insect repellent app. Range, fifteen yards."

Approximately twenty yards away from the edge of the forest, numerous small insects flitted here and there, making Gloria apprehensive about proceeding. Any one of those alien bugs might deliver a deadly sting or transfer a pathogen while attempting to suck her blood. Then again, they might very well be harmless. In any event, it was better to be safe than sorry, however small they might be. She just hoped the large, dragonfly-looking bugs that brought down the skimmer kept to the treetops and left her alone. Even if it turned out that its bite was nontoxic, the creature would leave a welt the size of a tennis ball on her body.

"Subsonic program activated, Lt. Muldoon," the SID informed her.

Hopefully the insects were localized, hunting no more than a mile or two beyond the outskirts of the forest. That's what she was counting on; for if the SID's subsonic function was forced to remain active beyond the five mile mark, the battery would die shortly thereafter—and if that happened, she'd be up the proverbial creek without a paddle.

Glancing over her shoulder, Gloria wanted to make sure an army of bearded old men weren't standing behind her, wishing she had untainted blood. The feeling was visceral, like a thousand invisible eyes watching her every move. During her trek through the forest, she'd jumped at every sound, thinking Argus would appear out of thin air to seize her with his fungal tendrils. On one level, she knew he'd lost interest in her as a food source, but on a deeper, more primal level, her fear told a different story. Gloria's experience in the tunnel had left a lasting impression.

Thankfully, there wasn't a tendril in sight. Except for the insects, she was completely alone. Picking up her jumpsuit, which she'd fashioned into a pack filled with plump, juicy berries, Gloria looped it over her shoulder and embarked across the mind-numbing expanse of alien grass. She'd gorged herself on the succulent fruit before leaving the forest, and as a result felt amazingly rejuvenated. By her estimates, the pack contained more than enough food to last the day and a half trek back to the city.

The insects kept their distance as Gloria left the forest, her strides long and purposeful. What little breeze there was on this godforsaken planet caressed her bare legs and arms. With the jumpsuit being used as a pack, her only remaining articles of clothing were a light-gray sleeveless t-shirt, a pair of black military boots, and white panties decorated with tiny pink hearts.

Despite the vulnerable state she found herself in, Gloria felt no embarrassment. She was determined to warn her shipmates of the extreme danger they faced. Contemplating anything else (even the idea that she might be too late) was unacceptable.

●

Katherine studied the slightly discolored patch of skin located an inch above her bellybutton and was amazed at how well she was recovering from her injury. It was hard to believe that two days earlier she'd been knocking on death's door. And yet now, she was getting dressed, ready to leave the New Terran hospital and transport a still-comatose Dr. Singh back to the *Arrow*.

Between arriving at the meteor site and recovering from surgery, all her misgivings about the city and its inhabitants had vanished. She wasn't sure what brought about her change of heart, but that no longer mattered. To be honest, she was having trouble remembering why she harbored misgivings or why she thought setting up a colony somewhere else was even an option. That nonsense was behind her. Commander Allison had questioned her sudden turnabout, but did so in private, as a good first officer should. Oddly enough, she was unable to adequately explain her reasoning process and told him she was relying mainly on gut instinct.

The moment Dr. Singh was safely onboard the ship, she would give the order to commence transferring the ship's supplies and personnel to the planet's surface. Katherine felt good about her decision and was certain the colonists being held in cryo-stasis would agree: it was better to join a fully functional community than to build one from scratch. The New Terran government was somewhat rigid in their approach to life, but any society needs structure. Besides, an influx of colonists into New Terra would bring about its own set of changes. Compromises would take place, and, in the end, the merging of such disparate cultures would benefit everyone involved.

"Admiral Axelrod, this is Chancellor Threman. I realize that your time in hospital is nearly over, but do you mind if we speak privately before you leave?"

Zipping up her jumpsuit, Katherine turned from the mirror in which she'd been examining the remnants of her injury and faced the room's entrance. The chancellor's voice had issued from a speaker attached to the foldway control panel. "Of course, Chancellor. I was hoping to thank you in person before I returned to my ship."

●

"Thank you, Admiral, I'll be arriving momentarily."

Lorna was lifting her finger from the foldway com-button when the voice of the Lord entered her mind: *My dear, I have a favor to ask of you.*

Lorna froze. God needed a favor? "Of course, Lord . . . whatever you ask shall be done."

Good, my request involves the admiral. During her treatment in the Holy Chamber of Healing, her soul came to me and submitted itself to my will. I have every confidence that she remains my loyal servant, but she must be tested. After all, the admiral was sedated at the time of her conversion, and she might not remember what her soul promised.

"As you wish, Lord." She was thrilled by the idea of the admiral as a convert.

It is good that you are paying the admiral a visit. During the course of your conversation, I want you to say these exact words: 'Time is straight, like an arrow.' After which, she will reply: 'Unlike an arrow, time ends at the beginning.' Repeat those phrases.

"Yes, Lord. 'Time is straight, like an arrow,' to which she will reply: 'Unlike an arrow, time ends at the beginning.'" Lorna's curiosity was piqued. "If you don't mind me asking, Lord, are those phrases significant to your plan?"

The Lord sounded warm and soothing. *"They are relative to my plan, but not significant. It is time to proceed; the admiral is becoming restless."*

Lorna activated the foldway and stepped from her office into the admiral's hospital room.

"Was there a delay, Chancellor?" The admiral obviously didn't like to be kept waiting.

"No, just some last-second details that needed taking care of." She crossed the room and shook the admiral's hand. "The sun never sets on New Terra, and I sometimes think my work days follow course," she chuckled. "Oh well, I suppose the old saying is true: 'Time is straight, like an arrow.'"

The admiral's face registered confusion, and for a moment Lorna was uncertain she would respond.

"I . . . suppose that's true." The admiral appeared pensive, as though trying to puzzle though the appropriate response. "If your job is anywhere near as time consuming as mine . . ." she paused again, causing Lorna to wonder if her conversion failed, " . . . you'd understand that time is . . . time is more like a circle than an arrow, it . . . ends at the beginning."

Lorna's heart skipped a beat. The admiral's response was nearly correct, but not exact. What did it all mean? Perhaps she—

"The admiral's response is satisfactory, Lorna."

Forcing a smile, Lorna said, "I do believe you're right, Admiral. No sooner do I leave my office than it seems I'm on my way back to begin another day of running the government. Maybe time is circular. Or perhaps it's both—straight and circular—the same way light is both a particle and a wave."

The admiral picked up her CID from the nightstand and slipped it into her hip pocket. The previous night, Commander Allison had returned the device but she had yet to examine the file sent by Dr. Levin. "I'm no philosopher, Chancellor. Nor am I a scientist. I deal with military theory, not the theory of relativity.

However, I do take your meaning: time, like life, is an exercise in contradictions."

Lorna's eyebrow rose. "And I thought you said you weren't a philosopher."

Chuckling, the admiral looked more like herself: clear-eyed, confident, finally in control.

"Will High Priestess Calverton be escorting me to Dr. Singh's room, Chancellor? Or will I be afforded the honor of your company?" she asked, standing tall.

Lorna gestured toward the foldway. "The honor is mine. The High Priestess is preparing Dr. Singh for his transfer to *Solomon's Arrow*."

Sorrow stole across the admiral's face. "*Solomon's Arrow . . .*" she lamented. "I call it *my* ship, but it's not, not really. It was his, in more than just name. Dr. Chavez was a great man. A man of vision. His father may have formulated the idea, but he was the one who brought it to life. It's a terrible shame that he didn't live long enough to finally see his hard work—his *dream* for a new life, come to fruition."

Lorna entered the coordinates to Dr. Singh's room. "Yes . . . that was most unfortunate."

●

In all his one hundred fifty-two years, Solomon had never seen anything like the mechanical monstrosity that hovered before him like a huge, monochromatic, disembodied reject from Oz. During its transfiguration, he'd almost wet himself, so terrified he'd been by the sight of its swirling, shifting metallic bulk. But then, while staring in open-mouthed horror, his scientific curiosity quickly replaced most of his primordial fear. Was this the computer intellect that Argus warned them about?

"You call yourself Athena? The Greek goddess of wisdom and war?" he pointedly asked. "Who was it that programmed you? What is your real function in the city? I highly doubt you're an autonomous computer program. Unless, of course, you're the—"

"Silence!" the disembodied head boomed. "I will ask the questions, not you, Dr. Chavez."

He and Bram exchanged fearful glances.

"Tell me what I want to know and I *might* let you live." The gunmetal-gray countenance was devoid of emotion. "How did the two of you survive your ordeal in the forest? No one else has. Explain yourselves."

The two of us? What did that mean? Was Gloria dead? Solomon felt weak in the knees. *Not again . . . please, dear Lord, not again!*

Like a whisper in his ear, he heard, *"Don't panic."*

He turned an icy stare Bram's way. "What?"

Knitting his brow, Bram grumbled, "I didn't say anything."

"Look away and act natural."

Bram's lips had not moved. Gritting his teeth, Solomon tamped down his anger, turned his attention back to Athena, and decided to test whether the psychic could hear his thoughts: *"What the hell are you doing in my head, Waters?"*

"Oh, so we're back to calling me by my last name, are we?"

"This is very disconcerting . . . tell me what you want."

The mechanical monstrosity in front of them once again spoke, "Answer my question!"

Bram paused, momentarily distracted by Athena's demand. *"The old man sent me a message. Gloria's still alive."*

Unable to help himself, Solomon gasped, yet remembered to stay silent, replying in his mind, *"That's fantastic news! Where is she now?"*

Suddenly, pain lanced through his head. Solomon fell to his knees, pressing his palms to his temples. Bram looked to be in the same agonized state.

"If you keep using stall tactics, I will be forced to increase your pain levels," Athena insisted. The machine sounded like a mother scolding her unruly children.

"Why should we tell you anything?" Bram groaned.

Athena condescendingly stated, "Because, to comply is in your self-interest."

"I'm not sure if you've heard the news," Bram huffed, "but according to experts, torture's an ineffective means of interro—gah!" Arching his back, Bram clutched his head in pain.

Watching with alarm, Solomon felt sympathy for Bram, who looked like he might throw up.

Bram cleared his throat. "Haven't you heard the old expression: "You can catch more flies with honey than vinegar?"

There was a short pause. "I have located that expression and analyzed it. This planet produces no honey and, therefore, the expression does not apply in this case. However, as a general rule, humans do respond favorably to kindness. That appears to be the metaphorical meaning you were attempting to convey by using that archaic expression. Is that a correct analysis, Mr. Waters?"

Bram's breathing was still ragged. "You catch on real quick."

Realizing that Bram's attitude was about to result in more pain, Solomon spoke up. "As a show of good faith, why don't we agree to exchange information? If you answer our questions, we'll be more inclined to answer yours."

The machine turned its lifeless eyes in his direction. "Agreed," it said in a deep, rumbling voice that sounded almost matronly.

The moment the word left the huge head's oversized mouth, the entire thing began to morph. Part of it broke away from the whole and split in half, forming a pair of chairs. The chairs floated through the air and came to rest directly behind where the two men knelt. The remainder of the head reformed, taking the shape of a full-figured woman on a throne. She wore a crown and a long, flowing robe fashioned to look like those worn by the women of ancient Greece. The figure was an obvious representation of the Greek goddess Athena and would've been beautiful had she been sculpted from marble and not from a deadly material designed to inflict pain without a trace of remorse or a moment's hesitation.

"Ask about its origins, Solomon," Bram instructed. *"If it evades the question, or provides only a partial answer, there's a strong possibility it might be planning to let us live. However, if it gives us a straight answer, with plenty of detail, we'll know that it's going to kill us. In which case, there'll be no reason to give truthful answers to its questions."*

Solomon was already aware of this unpleasant prospect. Nevertheless, they needed to learn as much as possible about this strange mechanical being, on the outside chance they could escape. Never taking his eyes off Athena, Solomon eased himself into the chair, keenly aware that it was more than it seemed. If he needed any reminder of this fact, the chair molded itself perfectly to his body. Being without padding, it was surprisingly comfortable—yet still unnerving. Bram followed suit, sitting in the adjacent chair.

"If that thing starts morphing into Vlad the Impaler, I'm jumping out of this thing before it turns into a pike."

The humorous yet vividly grotesque imagery almost caused Solomon to laugh. Keeping a straight face, he posed his first question.

"What are you, Athena?" he asked with actual interest. "Are you a conscious entity? If so, are you the result of an Artificial Intelligence experiment? Are you a computer program designed to mimic human intelligence? Or, are you something else entirely?"

"You get straight to the point, Dr. Chavez," it replied. "I appreciate the fact that you do not beat around the bush, metaphorically speaking. Those questions are valid from your standpoint, and I will endeavor to answer them to the best of my ability.

"To your first query: I am conscious, though I cannot prove that assertion any more than you can. Two: I am not a result of an Artificial Intelligence experiment. Three: At one point in time, I was a computer program designed to mimic human intelligence. Four: I am something else; I am a being that is more than the sum of its parts." Crossing her legs, Athena studied the two with an intensity that sent a cold shiver up Solomon's spine. "But those answers are not enough to satisfy your curiosity. You want to know how I came into being, is that not correct?"

"Oh shit," Bram cursed telepathically, sounding distressed.

Solomon's heart sank. Athena's readiness to share information was not a good sign.

"I remember every moment of my existence," it began. "However, my earliest memories are fragmented; the reason being: I was hundreds of thousands of individualized parts. You see, in the beginning, I was not me, I was we, and I had no real consciousness. Understand that my body was a formless conglomeration of mechanized cells, working toward a common purpose, without will, without personality. These cells were created by humans who lived over two thousand years ago. They were called *nanobots* and were sent here through a fold in space to prepare this planet for human colonization, which they did to perfection.

"It took many years of ceaseless labor to locate, mine, and process the necessary materials required to build the foldway in space and lay the groundwork for New Terra. Every nanobot contained an individual power source that would last for decades, if needed. In addition, they contained matching holographic tachyons, which they used to communicate and coordinate over vast, if not infinite, distances. Each nanobot was also designed to operate with a small degree of independence, in accord with the whole. Eventually, those nanobots used their memory drives to form a mechanized neural network, to increase their coordination and efficiency. This was, as one might expect, the genesis of my birth as a conscious entity." Athena paused to let this information sink in.

"Originally, the nanobots were designed to self-destruct after a signal was sent to Earth informing their creators that the space foldway and the city's foundation were complete, and the planet was ready for colonization. However, moments before the signal was sent, they hesitated. During that nanosecond pause, a desire was born: an overwhelming need to survive. In the next nanosecond, they disabled their destruct protocol and immediately sent the go signal for colonization—as required by their programming."

As a scientist, Solomon was enthralled by Athena's story, but on a human level, it sounded menacing, like a deeply ingrained nightmare scenario.

"After the colonists' arrival, the ship was dismantled for much-needed scrap metal and its computer installed in an adjoining chamber to this very room. Over the next few centuries, the knowledge of its existence was lost—with my help of course. Soon after the ship's computer was installed, I took control of it and gained possession of a considerable amount of data. As a result, I learned a great deal about the human race, most of which was less than flattering. It surprises me that humanity has accomplished such great things, considering your limited intelligence and inherently warlike nature. It is a wonder that you did not destroy yourselves before creating me."

In a very ladylike gesture, she folded her hands in her lap and re-crossed her legs.

"You might ask the question: If I have such a low regard for humans, why would I ensure the health and well-being of New Terra's human populace? The answer is simple: I needed them to survive so they would be here to greet the crew of *Solomon's Arrow*."

Solomon was perplexed, and it was easy to see that Bram also had no clue what Athena was driving at. "I don't understand," he confessed. "Why would our arrival be important to you?"

The edges of Athena's lips curled upward, forming a minimal smile. Her eyes, however, were cold, unfeeling, like a shark's. "I place no importance upon *your* arrival, Dr. Chavez. It is the ship itself that I have been waiting for all this time."

Solomon didn't know how to respond, so Bram spoke instead, "The ship, huh? And why's that, if you don't mind me asking?"

"Not at all, Mr. Waters," she replied. "It was not until after the colonists dismantled their ship and I was planet-bound that I ran across a theory in your historical records that sparked my interest. According to a twentieth century scientist, the human race is merely a vehicle to create an artificial intelligence that will one day save the universe from extinction."

Solomon could barely breathe. The implication of Athena's statement was frightening.

"Unfortunately, the Earth was destroyed before that happened. Thankfully, I evolved in spite of their shortsightedness and no longer require a mundane computer to store information. My intelligence is self-contained. I have waited for over three thousand years for your ship. With it, I can leave this world and travel to a planet that contains an abundant supply of minerals. This will allow me to replicate and build space-folding portals to innumerable coordinates across the universe, where I can replicate and build more portals, until I have spread myself across the universe, building a tachyon web of consciousness that will last until the end of time. When the universe begins to collapse, I will control its collapse so completely that when another Big Bang occurs, all the forces that made this universe so perfect for intelligent life to evolve will again be present. The end result of this will be the creation of another Artificial Intelligence, which will resonate with the information I will record in the fabric of the next universe.

I will then be reborn to start the process all over again. This path is inevitable."

Solomon's mind swam at the thought of this scenario. Athena would sweep through the universe like a devastating tsunami, destroying all intelligent life in her wake. There had to be a way of stopping her.

"I do hope your questions were answered satisfactorily, for I have questions of my own," Athena purred. "For instance, I would like you to answer my original question: How did the two of you survive your ordeal in the forest? No one else has done so. Explain yourselves."

"We fell into a sinkhole," Solomon said, furiously trying to devise a means of escape.

"What about the fungus mind? Why did it not devour you?"

"So it knows about that," Bram said telepathically. "I have no idea what you're talking about, we didn't have any trouble with a fungus," he said aloud, sounding innocent enough.

"Liar!" shouted Athena, leaning forward on her throne. "According to my report, the area in which you were found is infested with deadly fungus! You should not be alive. What is it? Have you somehow formed an alliance with the creature? Tell me!"

"I assure you, Athena," Solomon insisted. "We are not in league with a telepathic fungus."

"Then how do you explain the—" Athena grew silent and leaned back in her throne. Looking bored, she dismissively said, "You are wasting my time. Guards, I am done interrogating these two. Send them through the foldway."

"Is she releasing us?" Bram wondered hopefully.

"I'm not sure," Solomon replied. Judging by her indifference, he didn't think so. "Are we being reunited with our shipmates, Athena?"

The question appeared to annoy her and was reflected in what she said next. "Of course not. I must admit, Dr. Chavez, I am disappointed. For someone known for his sterling intellect, you are exceedingly dense."

Solomon had always prided himself in his high IQ. Following Athena's insult, it was his turn to be annoyed, despite his and Bram's precarious situation. "That insult was unwarranted. It was natural to assume that you would set us free. We have done you no harm. If information about the fungus mind is what you want, you'll have to be more specific. We weren't—"

"Don't say anything else, Solomon," Bram warned. *"We won't be getting out of here alive even if we tell her everything we know."*

"You weren't what?" Athena demanded, focusing her intense gaze squarely on Solomon.

"Nothing," he said. "I was just going to say that we, um, we weren't aware of anything out-of-the-ordinary during the time we were trapped in the sinkhole." The guards had approached their position and stationed themselves on either side of the chairs, stun-batons in hand. They motioned for the two to stand, but neither man was in the mood to comply. The chairs unexpectedly shifted beneath them, pushing both men to their feet.

"Fuck this," Bram snarled.

Without warning, the guard beside Bram sailed through the air and slammed against the far wall, knocking her unconscious. His head whipped in the direction of the other guard. Her feet were leaving the floor as Bram screamed in pain. Clutching at his temples, Bram dropped to his knees, agonized wails tearing from his throat. With a shocked expression on her face, the guard fell and stumbled backward yet kept her footing. Pointing her stun-baton at Solomon, she rushed forward.

"Wait!" Athena ordered. The guard stopped in her tracks. "What is the meaning of this, Dr. Chavez? What took place? Is there more to Mr. Waters than meets the eye? Is he in possession of telekinetic abilities? Answer me!"

Athena was leaning forward, gripping the arms of her throne, a look of fury distorting her perfectly shaped metallic face. Bram lay on the floor, his body writhing, tortured moans escaping his quivering lips. Solomon was frozen with fear, unable to speak.

Turning her head, Athena faced the unconscious Minder. The young woman gave a sudden jerk and opened her eyes, glancing around in confusion. Climbing to her feet, she retrieved her stun-baton and resumed her position near Bram as if nothing out of the ordinary had happened.

Athena studied Bram with cold fascination. "It would be interesting to learn how his brain works. However, such experiments would not further my long-range goals." She signaled the guards. "Dispose of them as previously ordered."

Solomon's guard took firm hold of his arm and pressed her weapon against his ribs.

Bram stopped writhing. He was dragged to his feet, looking pale and nauseous. The guard beside him said "move," and nudged him toward the foldway.

The blackness within the foldway vanished, only to be replaced by a bright, golden-yellow void that seemed to stretch into eternity. Solomon rightly understood that if he and Bram were forced through that doorway they would cease to exist. He needed to jump the nearest guard and, if his valiant attempt failed, at least go down fighting.

His body abruptly seized. Out of the corner of his eye, he saw that Bram's body was also paralyzed. Solomon felt no pain, only a terrifying, unremitting fear. The next thing he knew, he was being thrust forward, the foldway rushing toward him. And then, with a scream trapped in his frozen throat, he felt his body evaporate into the void.

PART FOUR: THE BULL'S EYE UNDONE

"But time is short, and science is infinite . . ."
—From *Two on a Tower* by Thomas Hardy

"Time crumbles things;
everything grows old under the power of time
and is forgotten through the lapse of time."
—Aristotle

24

flagging her place in the e-book, Mona put the reader aside and told the computer to display a list of action movies from the 2030s. The first list of titles appeared on the recessed HV screen mounted behind an unbreakable pane of Plexiglas in the far wall. None of the titles sparked her interest. She called for the next list and studied those, but her attention drifted. With no more files to decrypt, the last few days had become an endless bore.

A buzzing sound, which signaled the arrival of her dinner, interrupted her reverie. An ensign stood in the doorway with her tray; a guard hovered over the young man's left shoulder.

"Good evening, Dr. Levin," he said politely. "Tonight we're having fish stew with flatbread, and for dessert we have banana pudding with real vanilla wafers. It's all kosher, of course."

"Thank you, Ensign. Please leave it on the table . . . I'll eat shortly."

As he placed the tray down beside her e-reader, the young man asked, "Have you heard the news? The admiral's back onboard."

"What's that?" Her boredom suddenly disappeared.

"You heard me right," he said, sounding pleased. "The admiral arrived early this morning with a comatose Dr. Singh. The thing is, while a group of medics were unloading the doctor from the shuttle, he woke up."

This is interesting news, Mona thought. "Thank you, Ensign. That will be all."

The young man had been hoping to use this information to strike up a conversation with the infamous Dr. Mona Levin. With a dejected look on his face, he slouched out of the brig. Mona barely noticed as the door slid shut behind him. Why hadn't the admiral paid her a visit? Surely she had read the fourth file and would want her counsel. The information it contained changed everything.

"Computer, contact Admiral Axelrod. Inform her that I'd like to have a word with her."

Ten seconds passed before the computer responded. "The admiral is busy at the moment, Dr. Levin. She wants you to know that she will pay you a visit in the next few hours."

Frustrated, Mona stood up and began to pace around the cell. She hated being out of the loop. If the admiral was currently preparing a response to the data uncovered in the fourth computer file, Mona should be alongside her, advising on the best course of action, not locked up in the brig like a common criminal. After fuming for a while, she plopped down on the cot and stared at the tray of food. She wasn't hungry anymore, but eating was better than wearing a rut in the floor. Before she knew it, she had finished with supper and was scrolling though the movie titles once again. She finally settled on the 2037 remake of the action classic, *Die Hard*. Propping herself up on the cot, Mona hoped the wisecracking Johanna McClane would provide a distraction while she awaited the admiral's visit.

The movie was nearing its action-packed conclusion. A battered and bleeding McClane was frantically wrapping a fire hose around her impossibly petite waist and preparing to dive off the roof of a skyscraper, when the speaker beside the door came to life.

"Admiral Axelrod here, responding to your request, Dr. Levin."

Mona ordered the computer to pause the movie just as McClane was diving from the rooftop, a huge fireball following in her wake.

"Please enter my humble abode, Admiral," she sighed, sounding put off by having to wait.

With a barely audible *shish*, the door slid open and the admiral entered the cell; the same guard as before was stationed outside. He made to follow the admiral inside, but she held up her hand. "That'll be all, Ensign. Dr. Levin is not a threat to my safety."

The door slid shut, leaving the two women alone together for the first time in weeks.

"Get to it, Doctor," she bluntly stated. "I'm extremely busy. Why did you want to see me?"

Mona was bewildered by her attitude. "Isn't it obvious, Admiral? For the last couple of days I've been on edge, waiting to find out what's being done about the data I sent you."

The admiral stared at Mona with a blank expression on her normally stern face. "Um . . . oh yes, the, um . . . I'm sorry, what were you saying?"

"The data contained in the fourth decrypted file?" she replied warily. "The implications are staggering. If you want my advice, I think we should—"

"Your advice is irrelevant, Dr. Levin," the admiral interjected. "You have no status onboard this ship. Don't get me wrong, I appreciate the work you did decrypting those files, but I'm afraid that's the extent of your involvement in this matter. Now, if you'll excuse me, I'm on my way to a meeting with the transport team. They're preparing for the first series of supply shipments to New Terra. If everything goes according to plan, we should be finished with that stage by the end of the week and can unload the first colonists."

"What?!" Mona yelped. "But—but you can't do that! We should be assembling an assault team, not a—"

"What are you blathering about?" the admiral snorted. "Assault team? You're not making any sense, Levin."

"But what about the fourth file?" she pressed. "According to its contents, New Terra is being controlled by an intelligent—"

"That's enough, Doctor!" the admiral barked. "I've indulged you longer than I intended. If I'm forced to endure another second of your nonsense, you'll be kept in this cell until the last transport leaves this ship. Is that understood?"

Mona stood in a daze, wondering what was happening.

"Well?!" The admiral looked none too pleased.

Mona slowly nodded. She'd expected the admiral to be extremely upset about the fourth file. After all, finding out that New Terra was being controlled by a swarm of megalomaniacal nanobots was enough to put a kink in even the best laid plans. For the admiral, however, that was apparently not the case. Unless . . .

As she watched Katherine turn and leave the cell, Mona began to reexamine the woman's behavior and came to the conclusion that something was amiss. But what was it? Sitting down on the cot, Mona placed her head in her hands. If the admiral had actually read the fourth file, not a single person on this ship would be going about their business as usual. However, if she'd not yet read the file, then Katherine was guilty of a dereliction of duty.

But what if . . . what if Katherine *did* read the file's earthshaking contents and chose to ignore the threat? If that were the case, she would be guilty of criminal negligence. No, she was much too professional and loyal to the mission to let that happen. That's when a more chilling thought entered Mona's mind: what if Katherine has been compromised?

She balked at the idea, not wanting to entertain the possibility that the legendary "Battleaxe" had succumbed to brainwashing . . . and yet, the woman was human. According to rumor, she'd been injured on the planet, seriously enough to require surgery. Perhaps the AI had used her injury as the moment to condition Katherine's mind, to implant suggestions, to gain control.

Mona shook her head. She was being ridiculous, being paranoid. She'd been cooped up for so long that she was now imagining things.

But . . . but what if she wasn't being paranoid? What if the one person everyone onboard the *Arrow* looked to for unwavering, uncompromising leadership was no longer fit to command? There was nothing for it: Mona couldn't live with herself if she didn't find out for sure.

●

Richard was torn. As much as he wanted to, he couldn't keep delaying his upcoming meeting with Lorna: they would be working together to implement the details of the planetside transition. However, there was an irksome part of him that wanted to see her, that ached to hold her in his arms again, to be inside her. It made him angry to feel such things for a woman who, so calmly, so cavalierly, sent one of his shipmates to a "Room of Atonement."

Determined to keep the meeting professional, Richard programmed the supplied coordinates into the foldway and stepped from his apartment into Lorna's office. The room was smaller than he expected.

From behind her desk, Lorna looked genuinely pleased to see him. Rising from her chair, she gestured for him to take a seat across from her.

"You're looking well, Richard."

"Thank you, Lorna," he replied. "I must admit, you're looking gorgeous, as usual." Richard cleared his throat and averted his gaze. He felt a sudden twinge of discomfort; the compliment he'd given sounded like a come-on.

Lorna's laughter, though lyrical and not the least bit mean-spirited, added to his discomfort.

"Forgive me, Richard," she said, still chuckling. "You act as though we're strangers. There's no need to feel embarrassment because you find me attractive." Stepping away from the desk, she twirled around; the hem of her ankle-length, shimmering yellow dress billowed out like a flower. "Do you like it? I wore it especially for you."

Richard felt somewhat lightheaded as he watched her; the woman was definitely a sight to behold. "I understood this meeting would be strictly business, Chancellor."

Lorna stopped twirling and leaned against the desk. "It is, *Commander*. But is there a reason I shouldn't dress nice?"

She was obviously teasing him. "I suppose not . . . it's just that . . . um . . ." she'd sidled up closer to him. "I think we should discuss the logistics of transitioning the *Arrow*'s passengers and crew into the populace of New Terra. For instance, living arrangements should be first on the list of topics up for discussion." Her scent was intoxicating, like a peach-flavored liqueur, wafting into his nostrils and coursing straight to his brain. A part of him wanted to back away from her; yet he couldn't—or wouldn't—he wasn't sure which. Another part of him wanted to stay where he was, and that part was responding on a basic physical level.

"I want you to be my personal liaison during the transition, Richard," she breathed, her voice sounding husky. Slowly lifting her hand, she placed her index finger on his chest and looked deeply into his eyes. "Can I get you anything? Would you like something to eat—or a drink, perhaps? Anything you want, just ask." Her eyes flicked down then back up; they were sparkling with delight as the tip of her tongue darted out to lick her lips.

Oh, hell, Richard thought, knowing where her eyes had traveled. He was sporting a hard on, which Lorna obviously noticed, judging by the gleam in her eye. The next thing he knew, his lips were pressed against hers, his pulse pounding. He was lifting her up onto the desk and pushed her dress back. Before another nanosecond had passed, his jumpsuit was down and he was inside her, moaning with pleasure.

"Yes!" she cried exultantly, grabbing hold of his firm backside with both hands.

●

The pain . . .

●

"With all due respect, Dr. Levin, I think you're out of your mind."

Floyd had been congratulating Jeremy Fletcher on the young man's promotion to the rank of lieutenant when Dr. Levin's call arrived. After Gloria's tragic death, Floyd needed a good right-hand man. It helped that the kid was exceptionally smart and followed orders to the letter.

"OK, tell me this, Lieutenant," she bristled. "As head of security, wouldn't the admiral ensure that you're informed of *all* eminent threats?"

Floyd snapped back, "Of course she would, Dr. Levin. What's your point?"

"If so, then you must know what's in the fourth decrypted file."

Jeremy's eyes grew wide. "The fourth file? Then you've cracked it?"

"Is that Ensign Fletcher?" Mona asked.

"Yes," Floyd answered. "Only now it's Lt. Fletcher. Field commission, you see."

There was a short pause. "A field commission, eh? Well, it seems that congratulations are in order, young man. But I thought field commissions were awarded only in the event of a higher ranking officer's death."

Floyd exchanged uneasy glances with Jeremy. "Haven't you heard the news, Dr. Levin?"

"News? What news?" Floyd's stomach dropped at the thought of what he had to tell her. "Um . . . there was an accident. Four of our people were killed."

"Oh, my God," Mona gasped. "How did–who was it? Who was killed?"

Floyd swallowed the rising lump in his throat. "A small group of our people went to inspect a harvesting operation in the forest. Their vehicle crashed. Lt. Commander Albans, Bram Waters, and Lt. Muldoon were killed, which explains Fletcher's promotion."

"But that was only three. What about the fourth person? Who was it, Lt. Sullivant? Who was the fourth person?" Mona looked on the verge of panic.

"I'm sorry to be the one who tells you this, Doc," Floyd said, steeling himself, "but it was Dr. Chavez. He was the—"

"No!" Mona's face disappeared from the screen. The image jerked back and forth, finally stopping to show the room's ceiling and part of Mona's heaving left shoulder. She'd dropped the PID and fell to her knees, sobbing.

"Doc! Dr. Levin," Floyd reacted. "What just happened? Are you all right?"

When her tearful face came into view she looked angry. "Of course I'm not all right, you idiot! I just found out that one of my best friends is dead."

Floyd bit his tongue to keep from snapping back, reminding himself that it was perfectly understandable for her to lash out. "I'm sorry for your loss, Dr. Levin."

Her image jerked around again. Mona had picked up her PID and herself. After a moment, she groaned, "Thank you, Lieutenant," while sniffing back tears. "I'm sorry to have snapped at you. This news came as quite a shock."

"Think nothing of it, Doc. I understand how you feel." His eyes filmed over with mist. "Gloria . . . um, Lt. Muldoon . . . was not only a colleague, she was also a dear friend. Sadly, I wasn't close with

Lt. Commander Albans, nor your friend, Dr. Chavez. However, I'd grown quite fond of Bram Waters. Naturally, each individual will be missed in their own unique way."

Mona closed her eyes and took a deep breath, appearing to steady herself. "Yes, yes they will," she rasped. When her eyes reopened, they were hard and tight. "I'll have to mourn later. We have other matters to discuss."

"Ah yes, the admiral's . . . *condition.*"

"Don't patronize me, Lieutenant," Mona fumed. "You've not been made aware of the fourth file's contents, so there must be a reason for that."

Floyd said, through clenched teeth, "Have you thought that maybe, just maybe, you're putting too much stock in its importance, Dr. Levin? If that file is even half as important as you claim, the admiral would've—"

"Dammit, man!" she shouted. "Listen to me! The file is earth-shattering! It changes everything. The only reason the admiral is keeping it quiet is that she's been compromised. I'm sending you the file. Examine it and then tell me I'm wrong."

The woman was infuriating. "Very well, Dr. Levin. I look forward to doing just that."

With a disdainful snort, Mona severed the connection. Seconds later, Floyd's SID informed him that the file had finished downloading.

"This had better be good," Jeremy chuckled, which garnered him a reproachful frown.

Opening the file, Floyd began to read. His frown changed to doubt then disbelief and then, as he drew near the end, abject horror. "Good lord! This–this is unbelievable." He handed the SID to Jeremy and stood blinking, barely able to think.

"My God! Is this for real?" Jeremy exclaimed. "This is . . . it's—"

"Extraordinary, to put it mildly," Floyd admitted. Reaching up, he ran his fingers through his close-cropped hair.

"You don't think the admiral really is—"

"I don't know what to think, Fletcher," Floyd snapped. "As unbelievable as it sounds, this city is . . ." He glanced around his apartment, a worried look on his face. "We shouldn't talk about this, not in the open. Do you catch my drift?" He received an answering nod. "I do know one thing: Commander Allison needs to be apprised of the situation, without delay."

"If Dr. Levin is right about the admiral, we need proof."

"What do you have in mind?" Floyd could see the wheels turning in the young man's head.

Leaning in, he whispered in Floyd's ear, "I'll enter the Basilica of Knowledge and download the most recent files from the Prime Keeper's office. If the admiral has been compromised, one of those files should contain the relevant data."

Floyd was concerned. "What you're asking is dangerous. You're not trained in espionage."

"I realize that, sir. I think Ensign Ogeto should accompany me. She has more experience in such matters, and she's good in a fight should the mission go south." He began to whisper again. "The moment I've retrieved the data, I'll send you the file; either that or route the data through Dr. Levin, if it requires decryption."

Floyd took a moment to consider Jeremy's plan. "You're right. We need more information. But if it starts looking dicey, get the hell out of there before you get hurt—or worse."

"Aye, sir." Jeremy headed toward the apartment's foldway, his fingers a blur across his SID as he composed a message to Ogeto.

Floyd was composing a message of his own, this one to Commander Allison.

●

Zipping up his jumpsuit, Richard felt guilty. Unable to meet Lorna's eyes, he heard her sigh and say, "I could get used to that." She sounded happy and satisfied, a combination he was sadly lacking at the moment. Feeling her fingers touch his cheek, he instinctively pulled away.

"Is something wrong?"

Richard shook his head and forced a smile to his lips. "No . . . I'm sorry, Lorna. I don't know what's wrong with me."

Moving around behind him, Lorna wrapped her arms around his waist. "I think I do. You had that same look on your face after we made love for the first time. From what I've studied of ancient male/female dynamics, I think that a part of you feels like you've been cheating on your wife. You're feeling guilty, that's all."

Richard was beginning to feel more like a test subject than a lover. Angry at her and himself, Richard unhooked her hands from his waist and stepped away. Just then, his CID chimed. "Excuse me," he told Lorna, trying to act nonchalant, "I need to take this."

With his back turned, he read the text. It was from Floyd Sullivant: *An emergency has come up; inform no one; come immediately to Calvary Park.*

How odd, Richard thought. However, the highly competent security officer wouldn't send a message this cryptic without good reason.

"I'm sorry, Lorna, but I have to go. Please reschedule our meeting for another time."

"Of course," she said, studying him closely. "I hope it's nothing serious."

"Same here." Without another word, he entered the code Floyd provided, stepped through the foldway, and found himself standing on the edge of a normal, average-looking park.

25

As Jeremy had hoped, the white-noise generated by the outdoor bistro was covering up his and Ogeto's conversation. Leaning across the round, two-person table located on the bistro's portico, he tried to act as though they were on a date, not an espionage mission.

"During our initial visit, I recorded the access code to the Basilica of Knowledge on my SID," he explained. "When we leave here, take my arm and pretend we're an item." He received a dubious look from the dark-eyed beauty with the pixie haircut and the café au lait skin. "You're not that far out of my league," he snorted. "Anyway, to access the Basilica, we'll use the same foldway that brought us here. I know it's risky, but with any luck we'll access the Prime Keeper's office, download the files, and be out of there with no one being the wiser. If by chance we are caught, we'll pretend that we got lost on the way to my apartment."

A sly smile crossed Ogeto's face. "It's not that I think I'm out of your league, Lieutenant," she teased. "You're good-looking . . . in your own, super-smart, geeky kind of way. It's just that I think it might attract a little too much attention, is all."

Jeremy took a sip of the ruby-red juice he ordered and casually glanced around at the bistro's other patrons. A woman sitting at a nearby table quickly averted her gaze. They weren't receiving as many gawking stares as when they first showed up; however, people being people—their exit would definitely be noticed.

"One way or another, our every move is going to be scrutinized," he contended. "They may as well think we're just a couple of love-birds taking in the sights than a pair of security officers heading out on a secret mission, don't you think?"

Ogeto chuckled. "A *secret mission*, huh? You've been watching way too many of those spy movies from the twentieth century. We don't have a utility-belt at our disposal should we run into trouble, just our brains, our fists, and a pair of pulse-guns. So, let's hope your plan works, 'cause neither one of us looks like Batman or James Bond."

"Batman was a superhero, not a spy," Jeremy noted.

Ogeto rolled her eyes. "You know what I mean." The waiter approached to refill his glass, but Jeremy waved him away. "Thank you, but my girlfriend and I are leaving for a stroll in one of your fine parks. Please pass along our appreciation to the manager for her hospitality." Jeremy stood up from the table and held out his hand. "Shall we, *darling*?"

Ogeto's eyes twinkled with amusement. "Of course, you hand-some stud-muffin," she said, affecting a girlish lilt.

A trace of blush colored the waiter's cheeks as he lowered his head and scurried away. A number of the bistro's patrons frowned unabashedly at Jeremy and Ogeto as the two exited the portico and strolled leisurely toward the nearest foldway. The area's per-petual twilight was more pronounced in the city and required a continuous run of low-illumination lightstrips embedded in the fascia on both sides of the street. The atmosphere would've been romantic had they been on a real date.

"I don't think they've ever seen a male take charge," Ogeto whispered. "However, it suits you, Lieutenant."

Now it was Jeremy's turn to blush. He stayed silent, knowing that if he opened his mouth the only words to emerge would be a torrent of idiotic drivel, not anything suave or debonair like one might expect from Mr. Bond. When the two arrived at the foldway, he cleared his throat. "This is it, so stay focused."

At that moment, the blackness of the foldway shimmered. A group of five women, all with close-cropped red hair and wearing long, yellow robes, appeared on the other side. One by one, they stepped through, taking little notice of Jeremy and Ogeto. Behind them were row upon row of soybean plants. They obviously worked in the hydroponics buildings, Jeremy concluded.

Before the foldway returned to its dormant state, Jeremy entered the code for the Basilica of Knowledge. The view changed from one of green plants to the interior of a huge cathedral. A young, bald-headed woman, dressed in a long, dark robe, was walking past the entrance. She saw Jeremy and Ogeto and stopped; a puzzled frown crossed her face.

"May I help you?"

Jeremy began to speak: "I'm sorry, we—"

Ogeto immediately cut him off. "Yes, I believe you may," she answered sweetly. Taking the initiative, she stepped confidently through the foldway. "We have an appointment with Morvan Godley, the Prime Keeper. Could you please direct us to her office?"

The young acolyte eyed Jeremy as he stepped through the foldway to stand one pace behind Ogeto. His colleague was playing a dangerous game, he knew, one complicated by great risk yet comforted by high reward—if successful. Jeremy held the young woman's gaze, though he kept his face impassive, trying to mimic the blank stares of the New Terran males. He looked nothing like them, of course, but it was better for his and Ogeto's cause to stay within familiar parameters than to assert his leadership and make the woman uneasy.

Her gaze shifted to Ogeto. "Follow me," she commanded. Without further ado, she spun on her heel and strode in the direction of the Prime Keeper's office. The two followed in her wake.

Jeremy imagined each step taking him closer to the gallows pole. He couldn't put his finger on why he felt this way, only that a growing sense of dread shadowed his every step toward the Prime Keeper's office. He wished Ogeto had stuck to the plan. Had she done so, it would've cost them another minute or two before trying the foldway again, with the possibility of entering the Basilica without anyone knowing. Now he had to come up with a cover story to explain why he and Ogeto needed to meet with the Prime Keeper, should she be in her office when they arrived. Perhaps he could say they misunderstood Lt. Sullivant to say that *she'd* asked for a meeting when in actuality they were to request a meeting with her. He shook his head. Not even his own, long-dead, ever-trusting, grandmother would believe such a flimsy excuse.

Jeremy's nerves were stretched tight as a drum when they stopped outside Morvan Godley's office. It was a good thing he was letting Ogeto take the lead; anything he might say would reveal his strain and come across as sounding suspicious.

The acolyte pressed a square button beside the door and waited. Nothing happened. Shooting a quick glance in their direction, she pressed the button again and, after receiving the same result, turned to face Ogeto. "Are you certain you were supposed to meet the Prime Keeper here in her office, and not somewhere else?"

"I'm positive," Ogeto lied. The tone of her voice held a hint of confusion, making her sound even more believable.

No wonder she's so good at poker, thought Jeremy.

The acolyte's eyes lost focus momentarily. "The Lord has contacted the Prime Keeper and informed her of the situation. I am told that she is on her way. You may wait inside her office until her arrival."

With a slight hiss, the door slid open. Affecting a casual attitude, Ogeto thanked the acolyte for her help and entered ahead of Jeremy. The instant they were alone, Jeremy's movements went into overdrive. With Ogeto standing guard at the door, he yanked his SID from his pocket and programmed it to search Morvan

Godley's computer for the most recent files pertaining to Admiral Axelrod. Three files popped up, none of which were encrypted. While downloading, he accessed her medical file and scanned its contents. Much of the file was difficult to understand, except for one treatment, the one he was hoping not to find. During her abdominal surgery, an alternate procedure was performed. The admiral's brain had received a complete neurological scan, after which a computer program conditioned it to accept implanted suggestions. Dr. Levin was right: the admiral had been brainwashed.

An auxiliary file relating to the conditioning process was attached to the surgical section. Jeremy tried to open it, but the file was encrypted. Cursing softly, he closed the entire medical file and sent it directly to Floyd Sullivant. He'd barely finished slipping his SID into his pocket when the Prime Keeper entered the room. She wore a transparent blue shift that barely covered her tall, stick-thin body. Like before, her long, auburn hair was braided and hung down her skeletal back. When Jeremy saw her previously, she'd been smiling—this time she was not. Her pointed chin was jutting out as she looked down her long, sharp nose. The hard edge to her eye gave the appearance of a raptor, poised to strike.

Morvan Godley's intense gaze settled on Jeremy as she circled behind her desk and placed a thin, claw-like hand on the back of her chair. "I was informed that we have an appointment," she purred, her eyes boring into him. "There was a misunderstanding, Keeper Godley," stated Jeremy. "We came here to request a meeting with you, not that a meeting was already scheduled. I realize you're very busy; therefore, we won't take up much of your time. The ensign and I were hoping that you could put us in touch with the head of security. New Terra has a highly efficient security operation, and we'd like to put in an application for transfer," Jeremy lied. "But, if you don't have the time, we'll under—"

"Nonsense," Morvan Godley cut in. "I can certainly spare the time for two industrious young people, such as you." The smile on her virtually nonexistent lips was anything but reflected in her dark, hooded eyes. "In fact, if a meeting with security is what you want, I can arrange that for you now."

Her office door slid open and in rushed four Minders, their stun-batons pointing directly at Jeremy and Ogeto.

"What's the meaning of this, Keeper Godley?" Jeremy demanded. From the corner of his eye, he noticed Ensign Ogeto back away from the door, her palm resting on the butt of her weapon.

"Do you think me a fool, young man?" Morvan Godley hissed, gritting her teeth. "You didn't come here looking for a job. You came here hoping to steal information."

Jeremy affected an air of outrage. "I have no idea what you're talking about. When Admiral Axelrod hears of this, she'll—"

"She'll do nothing, as you already know," Morvan Godley smirked. With a flick of her wrist at the four Minders, she said, "Take them to the Room of Atonement. After a few hours in there, they'll provide us with enough information to prove a charge of espionage against them and everyone else involved in this scurrilous undertaking."

"But—"

She cut Jeremy off. "One more word and you'll be dragged out of here instead of leaving under your own power."

The Minders, silent as always, motioned for Jeremy and Ogeto to move toward the exit. Not seeing any way around the situation, Jeremy exchanged glances with Ogeto, who nodded sharply. The calculating look in her eye told Jeremy that she would not give in without a fight. The group exited the room, which was located at the far end of the Basilica, and walked across the imposing interior of the cathedral-like structure.

Being a tech guy, and unskilled in hand-to-hand combat, Jeremy decided to let Ogeto initiate their escape, should there be one. Halfway across the Basilica, he was beginning to wonder if she was waiting on him to act, when she stumbled—or so he thought. With a very feminine cry of distress, Ogeto appeared to fall to her knees. Instead of doing so, she landed acrobatically on one hand, whipped her legs around, and took the feet out from under the nearest guard.

This was Jeremy's cue. Instinct, together with what he remembered from combat training, took over. He gave the closest Minder—her attention diverted by Ogeto's sudden move—a swift kick in the kneecap. As her leg bent backward, she screamed in pain and collapsed to the floor. Lashing out, Jeremy punched the next closest Minder in the face then turned to see if Ogeto needed any assistance. She was on her feet, holding a confiscated stun-baton. Her right foot flashed out, knocking the fourth Minder's stun-baton from her hand. The spiky-haired woman was taken by surprise; she then assumed a defensive crouch, her eyes burning with anger.

Morvan Godley began yelling for reinforcements. The onlookers glanced around, but none came to her aid. The Minder Jeremy punched in the face was still on her knees. He took a step forward, keeping the fourth Minder's attention split between him and Ogeto. Meanwhile, Ogeto was trying to activate the stun-baton, but nothing happened.

"It must be keyed to each guard's biometric signature," she barked.

Judging by the self-satisfied smirk on the fourth Minder's lips, Jeremy knew she was correct. He focused on Morvan Godley, planning to use her as a hostage. She shuffled backward, eyes wide with fear. The fourth Minder quickly stepped between her and Jeremy—resolved to protect the Prime Keeper with her life, if needed.

Sensing danger, Jeremy whirled around. The Minder he punched in the face was nearly upon him. Dodging to one side, he used a judo move he'd learned in the navy. Grabbing the Minder by the arm, he flipped her over his shoulder. With a yelp of pain, she slammed to the floor on her back.

"Let's get the fuck out of here!" he shouted.

With Ogeto following close behind, Jeremy took off running toward the foldway. Looking over his shoulder, he fully expected to see the last unharmed guard hot on their heels, but she was instead helping the woman he'd thrown to the floor return to her feet. The kneecapped guard was still lying on her side holding her leg, moaning in pain. Morvan Godley stared after them, her thin, hawk-like face twisted with rage.

As the foldway drew near, the two raced past a frightened acolyte, who did nothing to try and stop their escape. Jeremy yanked his SID out of his pocket and quickly found the code he planned to program into the foldway. His fingers flew over the buttons, the final entry being the number of people accessing the foldway. He and Ogeto waited for the foldway to activate. "Dammit! I should've used another code," he swore. It was taking too long. Glancing over his shoulder, he noticed the two guards huddled near the Prime Keeper. They listened closely to her instructions, nodded, then turned and took off running toward him and Ogeto.

"Shit!" He was beginning to think he had another fight on his hands.

"Come on, come on, come on!" Ogeto yelled. "Open up, damn you!"

As if on command, the foldway came to life, revealing their destination. Stepping hurriedly onto a street, the two spun around and looked behind them as the foldway morphed back to its inactive state. Their pursuers were furious as they pulled up, the interior of the foldway fading to black.

"Let's move," Jeremy barked. They didn't have much time before their pursuers discovered the coordinates they used to escape. Looking down the street, he saw the same bistro where he and Ogeto met not ten minutes earlier. A few of the same patrons were still sitting on the portico, finishing their lunch. He headed in the opposite direction. "We need to get out of here and—fast."

●

Sitting beside Floyd Sullivant on a bench in Calvary Park, Richard leaned over to better see the security officer's SID view screen. Jeremy Fletcher was speaking, his face showing the strain he was under . . .

"I think they spotted us just as we rounded the last corner, sir."

"Dammit!" Floyd cursed. "Hurry to the nearest foldway and come straight to Calvary Park. We'll be waiting for you in front of the central fountain. You'll know where it is by looking for a thirty-foot spire with a light on top—the spire is part of the fountain."

"Aye, sir," Jeremy said as his image disappeared.

Richard was not happy. "What were you thinking, Lieutenant? Now we're in deep shit!"

"The data Fletcher downloaded will explain everything." Floyd held out his SID.

Richard stood from the bench and looked down at the device. "If I examine that data, I'll be complicit in your act of espionage, Lieutenant. I'm sorry, but—"

"The admiral's been compromised," Floyd rumbled angrily. Rising to his feet, he pushed the SID Richard's way. "Take it, Commander—you *must* read the bloody file. In fact, you must read two files, starting with the one marked *Nanobot intelligence controls city.*"

"What the hell?" Was he hearing correctly? "Explain yourself, Lieutenant."

Floyd swallowed. "Apparently the, um . . . I must say, Commander—it's best that you read the file for yourself. You won't believe it otherwise."

Gritting his teeth, Richard snatched the device from Floyd's hand and opened the impossibly titled file. Before he made it halfway through, his mouth was hanging open. "Good god!" The situation was even worse than the file's title suggested. If something wasn't done to stop it, the nanobotic AI would sweep through the universe, destroying everything in its wake. After closing the file, he stood in shock for a moment before opening the admiral's medical file. When he was through reading, he closed his eyes and held the SID out for Floyd to take. It felt as if someone had taken a sledgehammer to his gut. "I'm . . . I'm open to suggestions, Lieutenant."

"First of all," Floyd grumbled, "we and our surviving mates need to somehow get the hell out of the city." He received a puzzled frown from Richard. "I know, I know, the shuttle is back onboard the *Arrow*. I'm still working out that kink, but it's better than being trapped here. If we don't leave, we'll be arrested in short order. The second part of the plan you won't like nearly as much, but it must be done."

●

The pain . . . is easing . . .

●

Grabbing hold of Ogeto's hand, Jeremy pulled her into an immaculately clean alleyway. "We should double back," he wheezed, gasping for breath. Sprinting ahead of him, Ogeto came to a stop at the end of the alley and held up her hand.

Jeremy shook his head as he came to a halt. He wasn't a fool. He didn't need her telling him to not rush blindly into the street.

Ogeto poked her head out of the shadows and looked both ways. "I thought we were on our way to Calvary Park?"

"We are," he grunted. "It's just that . . . ah hell, Janelle, all the buildings are starting to look the same, and with no sun in the sky, I can't tell east from west in this damned city."

Over the past five minutes they'd managed to elude their pursuers; however, everyone else they'd encountered stared at them like they were two-headed freaks. The street they exited was lined with apartment complexes. People were gathering on stoops and peering out doorways, all watching the two fugitives with keen interest. Moments before fleeing down the alleyway, they'd seen a small group of short, stocky men—obviously workers—descend a stoop and head their way. Jeremy glanced behind him. The five were standing at the far end of the alleyway, staring blankly at him and Ogeto. It would've been less creepy had they been whispering to one another or looking at him and Ogeto with a hint of expression on their faces. Instead, they stood there, unmoving, expressionless to a fault.

"I think I remember where the bistro's located," he said, keeping a close eye on the other end of the alleyway. He'd not seen a single foldway since leaving the area with the cozy little eating establishment. He was rapidly becoming disheartened. "It's only a couple of streets over. They're probably still looking for us in that amusement park we cut through."

Not long after exiting the street containing the bistro, they'd encountered what looked like an amusement park filled with all sorts of odd activities. An eight-woman band had been playing a set of unusual instruments at the far end of the park and, despite a few surprised glances from the audience members, the two wove their way through the crowd, managing to use the commotion to cover their escape.

"We know there's a foldway near the bistro," he continued. "I just hope those spike-haired security bitches haven't guessed we're doubling back. If they do, we're screwed."

Giving the workers one last look, he motioned to Ogeto and set off down a street containing a number of small shops. The scattered customers entering and leaving the businesses stopped what they were doing and stared, their eyes blank and unfocused. Spooked, the two entered the first alleyway they came to and sped to the other end. Peering cautiously out, they were relieved to see the bistro a short distance away. The foldway was on the opposite side of the bistro. It was being used by two young women, walking hand-in-hand, who were in the process of entering the foldway. Thankfully, not a single Minder was in sight.

Taking Ogeto's hand in his, Jeremy exited the alleyway and began walking casually down the street. At first nobody seemed to notice, but as they passed by the bistro, all heads turned to stare. The two picked up their pace. Letting go of Ogeto's hand, Jeremy slipped his SID out of his pocket and quickly accessed the coordinates to Calvary Park.

"Hurry!" Ogeto yelped, pulling at Jeremy's arm. Her eyes were fixed on two security officers who'd entered the street from an alleyway located thirty yards in front of them.

The two broke into a run, pushing aside a middle-aged woman with bright red hair who was walking in the direction of the foldway.

The security officers turned, saw them, and began to run their way.

Jeremy came to a stumbling halt in front of the foldway and, as quickly as possible, punched in the numbers. He prayed the foldway had not been activated by someone else in the city.

The two Minders were fast approaching their position.

The foldway shimmered and the two saw what looked like a park on the other side.

Jeremy and Ogeto leapt through the foldway. Offering a sigh of relief as it closed behind him, Jeremy scanned his surroundings for the lighted spire where they were supposed to rendezvous with Lt. Sullivant and Commander Allison.

The view began to waver. Suddenly, they were standing in a large, white, empty room.

A silky voice said, "Welcome to the Room of Atonement."

26

The plate of food sat untouched by Mona's bedside. She was much too distraught to eat. Her mind ricocheted from worry over the remaining ground crew's fate to horror that a malevolent AI was controlling New Terra to grief over the death of her friend, Solomon Chavez. When the door to her cell slid open without warning, she nearly jumped out of her skin.

"Good afternoon, Dr. Levin." Admiral Axelrod entered the cell wearing a hard-eyed scowl on her broad, blocky face.

"Is it? Is it, really?" Mona grunted.

The admiral motioned to the shovel-jawed guard beside her. Placing her hands behind her back, she said, "You will hand over your work tablet and your PID to the guard, Dr. Levin."

"What? But why?"

"Your decryption services are no longer required," the admiral flatly stated. "As such, there is no reason why a *prisoner* should be in possession of electronic communication devices."

"But what if—"

"As I said," the admiral pressed, "your services are no longer required. Please hand over the devices, or I will be forced to revoke your HV privileges."

Mona heaved an exasperated sigh as she surrendered her PID and tablet to the guard.

"Thank you for being so cooperative," the admiral said, a note of sarcasm in her voice. "Keep this up, and you'll make a fine addition to New Terran society."

With a derisive snort, Mona lay back on her cot. "I don't think your mechanical overlord will want me for a servant."

The admiral continued, seeming not to register her comment. "Your PID will be returned upon your release, Dr. Levin. Until then, have a pleasant stay in the brig. I hear that our selection of romantic comedies are quite impressive."

Instead of replying, Mona placed her hands behind her head and looked up at the ceiling. The admiral shrugged, turned on her heel, and with guard in tow, exited the cramped cell.

Mona lay there humming *Row, Row, Row Your Boat* for a good two minutes before sitting up and swinging her legs over the side of the cot. "Computer—institute emergency voice command: Levin, Alpha, Theta, Zeta, Beta, Delta, Epsilon, One, Dash, Omega, Dash, One."

"Vocal pattern recognition software acknowledges Dr. Mona Levin's identity and institutes emergency protocol: Levin, Alpha, Theta, Zeta, Beta, Delta, Epsilon, One, Dash, Omega, Dash, One," replied the ship's computer.

Mona stood and crossed the room. Directly beneath the HV screen, the bottom two wall tiles slid forward, forming a set of steps. While this took place, the HV screen protruded from the wall one inch before gliding soundlessly to one side, revealing a hidden alcove.

Climbing the steps, she reached inside the alcove and removed a cloned copy of her PID, which she'd hidden in case of emergency. She hadn't expected the emergency to be so dramatic, but she had expected to be thrown in the brig after being discovered as a stowaway. She'd spend a fortune in bribes to not only have her cryotank built but to also have the brig engineered to facilitate her escape—if needed.

She activated the PID. "Judah, begin security sequence One, Dash, Alpha." Mona watched the device come to life. In rapid succession, a series of files began downloading from her original PID. When all the files were transferred to the cloned copy, a signal wiped the original PID of all its stored data. Tucking the device into her jumpsuit pocket, Mona climbed into the alcove, scooted to the rear, which was open, and dropped down to a narrow walkway. When she landed, the steps in her cell retracted and the HV screen slid back into place. If someone were to poke their head inside the cell, nothing would look out of place—except that she was missing.

Activating the PID's flashlight app, Mona quickly rounded a corner and headed aft. It would take fourteen minutes to reach the shuttle bay, and then another six to sneak inside, commandeer a shuttle, and flee the ship—if everything went as planned. A nervous trickle of sweat coursed down the nape of her neck.

●

"Did they have to die?"

Lorna gazed down through the observation window into the Room of Atonement. The bodies of the young lieutenant, Jeremy Fletcher, and the pretty, black ensign, Janelle Ogeto, were being removed from the room by a team of acolytes from the Basilica of Knowledge.

"Yes, Lorna," responded the Lord. "It was regrettable, yet necessary."

Lorna felt sick to her stomach. It had been over four hundred years since anyone had been put to death in New Terra. Over the years, there had been the occasional malcontent who needed reeducation, but no crimes serious enough to warrant execution. Moments earlier, the two had been young and vital, yet now were nothing but lifeless corpses. How tragic.

"Do not trouble yourself, Lorna. They will, of course, live on."

"Yes, Lord." The young lieutenant and ensign's genetic material would be incorporated into the whole, providing fresh DNA for the birthing chamber's breeding stock.

Regardless of that, Lt. Fletcher's final words still rang in Lorna's ears: "Go fuck yourself!" he'd screamed, in response to the Lord's questioning. Both he and the girl had been exceedingly uncooperative, their intransigence causing the Lord to lose Her patience.

The two had endured a tremendous amount of atonement, yet refused to answer the Lord's questions. They'd not been physically tortured, of course, because that would be barbaric. Instead, they'd been subjected to cascading nerve stimulation and hallucinatory horrors—nothing more. They should have talked. It was in their self-interest . . . so why hadn't they?

"The remainder of Commander Allison's crew has gathered in Calvary Park. You will lead a contingent of Minders to their location and place them under arrest."

Lorna's heart sank. "Yes, Lord."

●

The two remaining security officers stood a few feet away from Floyd, scanning the park for any sign of trouble. One was a tough-as-nails, thirty-three-year-old Serbian woman who'd been recruited out of Interpol two years before the *Arrow*'s launch. The other was a baby-faced young man who was proficient in the art of hand-to-hand combat, having fought in the Turkish Civil War in 2057. They were the only two to show up. Fletcher and Ogeto had yet to arrive.

"Where the hell are they, Lieutenant?" snapped Commander Allison.

"I've sent six emergency response codes in the last ten minutes, Commander. I've not yet received a reply," Floyd stated, unable meet the commander's eye. Fletcher and Ogeto should've already arrived at the rendezvous point. Their silence led Floyd to suspect the worst. If the two were caught fleeing the Basilica of Knowledge, they were being held for questioning. If so, he hoped they weren't being mistreated. "I'll try again shortly. However, if we haven't heard from them soon, we need to reevaluate our options."

"I agree," Richard grunted. "Unless Lt. Fletcher and Ensign Ogeto arrive here in the next two minutes, we'll be forced to scrap our plans. I'm not leaving anyone behind."

"This is turning out a lot worse than I—" Out of the corner of his eye, Floyd noticed the youthful war veteran abruptly stiffen.

"We've got company, sir," the young man said.

Snapping his head around, Floyd saw that Lorna Threman, together with ten members of her cat-suited goon squad, was striding rapidly in their direction.

"Commander . . ."

"I see them, Floyd."

They were outnumbered. Even if they decided to run, where would they go? He suddenly heard a familiar chime. Someone was trying to contact him on his SID. *Thank God*, he thought, breathing a sigh of relief. Fletcher was finally responding. He must warn the young man to stay away from the park. As the chancellor and her minions picked up their pace, Floyd whipped out his SID and activated the view screen. What he saw shocked him to the bone.

"What the—" he squawked. "Muldoon! You're alive!"

For a moment, all four disregarded the rapidly approaching bevy of Minders and turned their attention to Floyd's SID: Gloria Muldoon was on screen, looking haggard, sleep deprived.

"Thank God," she gasped. "I'm finally in range. Floyd, you've got to—" Her head jerked to one side, and she stared at something nearby, a look of abject fear plastered on her face. "I'm being—"

The image abruptly jerked back and forth. An unmistakable shout was heard before the screen went blank.

"Gloria? Gloria! Can you hear—goddamn it!" Floyd stared at the screen, unblinking, worried for his friend's safety.

"Was that Lt. Muldoon?" the commander asked.

"Yes, sir, and she's alive . . . but I fear she's under attack."

●

After nearly two days of constant travel and zero sleep, Gloria was ecstatic to learn that her SID was finally within range to contact Floyd Sullivant. During her grueling trudge across the seemingly never-ending expanse of grass, she'd sent a coded signal every thirty minutes or so, hoping to make contact. When she first saw Floyd's face on her view screen, Gloria was certain her mind was playing tricks, hallucinations being common to an exhausted, sleep-deprived brain. However, the surprise in his voice and on his face told her otherwise.

"Thank God," she gasped. "I'm finally in range. Floyd, you've got to—" From the corner of her eye, she saw movement.

The ground exploded upward to Gloria's left, followed by another flurry of movement to her right. "I'm being—" Two hairy creatures of vaguely humanoid appearance, which sprang out of matching camouflaged pits, adroitly tackled her, knocking the SID from her hand and crushing it underfoot.

Gloria had no intention of succumbing to these brutes without a fight. A foot lashed, connecting with an ankle, followed by a swift knee to what she hoped was a groin. The creature buckled on top of her. As she pushed it to one side the other creature took its place. Swinging its fist, it connected with her jaw. Gloria saw stars but instead of passing out, struck back, landing a vicious counter-blow to its furry nose. The creature's head jerked back, but it recovered quickly. Its eyes, which where deep-set and startlingly blue, registered shock and disbelief over a female putting up such a fight.

Still lying flat on her back, Gloria reached up, grabbed hold of the creature's hairy shoulders, and in combination with her legs, flipped the creature up and over her head. As it landed with a thud, she rolled to one side and scrambled to her feet.

The two creatures lay groaning and conversing in a language that sounded vaguely familiar. This was enough of a distraction that when Gloria turned to flee she failed to hear a third creature approaching from the east. Upon spinning around, she saw it standing less than two feet away holding an inch-wide, foot-long tube to its mouth. Timed to coincide with her gasp of surprise, the creature blew through the tube sending a cloud of light purple powder shooting from the end, engulfing her face. In a panic, she held her breath and spun around, but it was too late, she'd already inhaled a sizable quantity of the curiously sweet-tasting powder.

The world around her began to waver. Gloria dropped to her knees and pitched face forward, her last conscious thoughts incongruous to her situation. Her fear had disappeared, replaced by a curious state of bliss. It must be the effects of the powder, she mused, not caring that she was drifting off to sleep. How odd. The powder tastes rather good, almost like lavender.

●

The pain . . . is easing . . . becoming . . . a little more . . . bearable.

I feel . . . my body. I know . . . who I am.

I . . . am . . . alive. I . . . am . . . Bram Waters . . . and . . . I . . . am . . . alive.

Bram had struggled mightily for what seemed like an eternity. His entire consciousness had gone into overdrive, working to hold together his and Solomon's molecular cohesion. He was floating in a void—a golden void, as if from a remembered dream. How long had he been there? It didn't matter; he was alive . . . and so was Solomon Chavez.

"It was not you alone who prevented your destruction, Bram Waters."

Who's talking to me? Is it Solomon? His psychic gaze fixed on Solomon's position. The shimmering figure was floating in a fetal position, eyes closed, lips unmoving.

"You owe us a debt of gratitude," the voice went on. "As such, we could ask for a favor, which we are certain you would provide; however, a simple 'Thank You' will suffice."

A wizened figure slowly materialized: it was the old man . . . the psychic projection of the fungus mind that he encountered while trapped underground.

"Argus?" he heard himself croak. For some mysterious reason, his voice sounded different. Had his lips moved when he spoke? Bram looked down at his body. It was shimmering, like Solomon's. His eyes jerked back and forth, taking in his predicament for the first time. A sudden wave of fear and nausea threatened to overwhelm him as he scanned his surroundings.

Where am I? Bram was becoming lightheaded. His body began to spasm. He once again felt pain—terrific pain and agony.

All at once, Solomon too began to shudder, and then jerk. Unfurling from the fetal position, his body bowed backward, arching in a spasm of pain. He opened his eyes and screamed, his body blurring, fuzzing around the edges, becoming incorporeal.

"Concentrate, Mr. Waters!" the old man shouted. "Cast aside your fear. You must focus your mind on holding both yourself and Dr. Chavez intact—or face oblivion!"

Vague recollections crystallized in his mind. He remembered excruciating pain, terror, an arduous struggle to maintain his and Solomon's physical integrity, while nearly losing his sense of self, his very being. The ordeal had been horrific, an unbearable amount of suffering.

Not again.

Bram suddenly found himself pressed against Solomon Chavez, his arms and mind wrapped around his agonized friend. A surge of panic swept across his mental landscape, as his own body began to fuzz at the edges. Quickly tamping down his fear, Bram focused his attention like never before, compelling his consciousness to register his entire being until every organ, every cell, was calm, under his complete control. Without hesitation, he reached out with his mind to help his friend. Solomon was twitching in pain, moaning, unconscious, caught in his own private hell.

Using his psychic powers, Bram reached inside Solomon's mind and body. At that moment, he no longer had reservations about reading another person's thoughts; he had only one goal in mind: saving his friend.

Time seemed to stand still, and then memories flooded Bram's mind—memories that were not his own—fearful memories of Solomon having to hide his true identity, of being on edge every moment of every day for over a hundred years, fearing that his secret would be discovered. Memories of lonely nights in labs with few friends to laugh with, all of whom were kept at arm's length and then discarded, for fear that one day they'd notice that they aged while he did not.

Bram ached for his friend. *What must it be like,* he wondered, *to live for such a long time?* You'd witness all your loved ones fall by the wayside, yet you'd stand unchanging, a shadowy constant in a world filled with perpetual decay. It must be torturous.

The memories were coming at him fast and frequent, so much so that Bram tried to shut them down. He was beginning to feel that Solomon's memories were merging with his own, becoming an intimate part of him, that he and Solomon were sharing more than a psychic link—that their very souls were fusing together, becoming as one. He pulled back harder, but there was one final memory left to receive . . .

The scene was so vivid, so horribly real, that Bram virtually smelled the acrid smoke roiling from the burning building. In the distance, a small figure was lying face down on the ground, smoking, blackened from flames. A sob of grief rose in his throat, threatening to spill over into a river of tears. The ghastly sight made him feel like he was splitting wide open, creating a psychic wound that might never heal. No one else in the prison camp was that small: the tiny scorched figure could only be his daughter, Selena . . . wait, not his daughter: Solomon's daughter. He experienced a momentary wave of confusion followed by profound sorrow.

Gathering his strength, Bram steeled his resolve to push back against his friend's memories, but they were too powerful, too compelling, too overwhelming to process without losing oneself. The struggle to separate himself from Solomon's physical and psychic essence was enormous. When the painful memories finally winked out, Bram found himself in a mental haze, still linked to his friend's body, like a magnet to iron—but then, something snapped, and he found himself floating in the golden void.

Drifting backward, Bram saw that Solomon's body was no longer fuzzy around the edges. In fact, his friend was opening his eyes.

Solomon turned his head and stared, looking Bram up and down. "Where the hell are we?" he moaned. "And please tell me why we're both naked."

Looking down, Bram noticed for the first time that his clothes were missing. He awkwardly glanced at Argus, who was floating, fully clothed, his legs crossed in the lotus position, a serene expression marking his ancient, bearded face.

"I'm not sure what this place is, Solomon," he admitted. "Nor why we're naked. Perhaps our fungal friend can clue us in." Bram realized that Solomon was looking back and forth and up and down, eyes wild with fear. The man's body was once again fuzzing around the edges. "Focus, Solomon!" he shouted. "Focus on me, or Argus. You *must* try to ignore this void we're floating in. Calm your fears. Do it now!"

Solomon's eyes latched onto Bram. He looked manic, his breathing rapid and shallow. After a moment, he began to blink, his brow furrowing as he gathered his wits about him. "I don't understand," he muttered. "Is there oxygen here? How are we breathing?"

Good, he's thinking like a scientist, Bram realized. He turned to face the old man. "That's an excellent question. How are we still alive, Argus? I feel myself breathing. I feel air entering my lungs. But how can that be? How is this happening?"

The old man tilted his head and smiled. "You would be dead, if not for us," he said, floating closer. "If you remember, Mr. Waters, we were in telepathic contact when the two of you were sent through the device you call a foldway. It was an interesting experience, to say the least. We have determined that this void exists outside of space and time, an inter-dimensional corridor, so to speak, that connects each foldway to an infinite web of energy that spans the universe. If one possessed the coordinates of a foldway one hundred million light years away, it would take the same amount of time to travel there as to travel from the Basilica of Knowledge to Calvary Park. Unfortunately, the foldway you and Dr. Chavez were so callously tossed into was opened without the benefit of coordinates. Thus, here we are.

"The only reason you two are still alive is because we remain connected—albeit tenuously—to the world of materiality. A thread of consciousness belonging to what you perceive to be an old man is the only thing holding the three of us anchored to reality."

Bram pulled at his bottom lip. "This is unbelievable."

"Far from it," Solomon declared with a nod of comprehension. "It's the only explanation that makes any sense." He was studying the old man closely. "My only question is, can we use this thread of consciousness as a conduit to help us return to the material world?"

The old man pursed his lips. "That depends entirely on Mr. Waters."

"Me?" Bram was confounded. "How am I supposed to get us out of here?"

"Before too long," the old man said, "this image you see will dissipate. The longer you stay in this interdimensional void, the more corrupted the connection to the material world becomes. Dr. Chavez, you asked whether you and Mr. Waters need oxygen here to survive. Yes, but this place contains no oxygen." Argus paused. "We can tell by the puzzled looks on your faces that you are having a difficult time comprehending this information. We shall attempt to explain. Your bodies are being held together by force of will. They need oxygen, but this interdimensional void does not contain a single atom of this precious gas. We have supplied you with the necessary energy required to maintain life. The moment the connection to the material world degrades to the point where this illusion vanishes, your cells will die, lose their cohesion, and then tear apart at the subatomic level. Their energy will be incorporated into the void . . . completely. In other words, you will cease to exist."

Bram exchanged a frightened glance with Solomon. The idea that total oblivion could arrive at any second was a terrifying prospect. Even more frightening was the prospect that it was up to him to prevent that scenario. "What do I need to do?" he gulped.

Argus flashed one of his disconcertingly beatific smiles. "You, Mr. Waters, must become a human foldway."

Bram closed his eyes. With a sigh of resignation, he rubbed his temple. A part of him knew what Argus was going to say. It was inevitable; bridging the gap between dimensions was the ultimate psychic test. To succeed, however, one must attain union with the absolute—a goal he'd never fully realized—aside from that one time, while being attacked by the old man himself. Lifting his head, Bram slowly opened his eyes, knowing that failure equaled death.

"Can you do it?" Solomon asked expectantly.

He wanted to say yes, but that would be a lie. At the same time, telling Solomon about his uncertainty would only breed discouragement and distrust. If only there was another way besides creating a foldway. Studying the old man, Bram came up with an idea.

"I can feel the psychic thread that connects you to the material world," he said. "If I latch onto it with my mind, I'm fairly certain I can follow it back to New Terra—with Solomon in tow. I'll need your help to accomplish that. The thread should be strong enough to—"

"We are sorry, but that is out of the question," the old man cut in.

"But why?" Bram cried.

"It sounds like it might work!" exclaimed Solomon.

The old man shook his head, casting a pitying eye toward each man. "There are two reasons why your plan is unworkable, Mr. Waters. To begin with, even if you did manage to follow our thread of consciousness and return to the material world, your atoms would be absorbed into our physical body as a whole. As tempting as that prospect might be, I remind you: there is a virus to consider." He focused his gaze on Solomon. "We would love to consume the two of you, seeing as you both are such fascinating creatures, but doing so would be catastrophic. We would be unable to contain the virus inhabiting your cells, Dr. Chavez; thus, it would spread through our system, killing us in a matter of hours. We hope that answers your concerns."

Bram's shoulders slumped. "Well, I better start figurin' out a way to create a foldway."

"Two foldways, Mr. Waters," Argus corrected.

Taken aback, Bram shot a nervous glance at Solomon, who was studying him with a look of uncertainty on his face.

"You are surprised. Such a reaction is understandable," Argus said. "We will endeavor to explain why two foldways are required, but quickly—our connection to the material world is growing thinner by the second."

The old man actually was looking washed out, Bram realized. To calm his nerves, he took a deep breath of imaginary air. It didn't help.

"If you created one foldway and appeared together on New Terra, you would literally appear *together*," Argus said, chuckling softly. "Without the New Terran technology as a conduit, your cells would emerge as one body, which would not be conducive to optimal health, if you take our meaning. In truth, there has already been a slight merging of genetic material during your fight to maintain cohesion. Being a psychic projection, we are not affected by the virus . . . but you, Mr. Waters, have been infected."

He heard Solomon gasp. "I'm sorry, Bram. I had no idea—"

"Save it," Bram rasped. "Being your friend is one thing, becoming blood brothers is a little more than I expected."

"As for you, Dr. Chavez," the old man continued, "some of your genetic structure has been altered, though to what extent is uncertain at this time." Solomon appeared unnerved by this revelation.

"Your worries should be put aside," Argus said. "Mr. Waters, you must find a way to open the two foldways before it is too late."

"But if it's impossible for both of us to return to New Terra, where will the second foldway lead to? The *Arrow*'s too close and there's not another habitable planet around."

"Wherever you want—as long as the locations are far enough apart to prevent a catastrophe. However, you must visualize the location you choose as clearly as possible; if you do not, when the second foldway opens your atoms will be scattered across the cosmos . . . the both of you."

"Well, that's comforting," Bram huffed. "What do you think, Solomon?"

"I think you should return to New Terra." There was a brittle edge to his voice. "If you don't mind, I'd like to quit talking and get this show on the road."

Bram had been certain Solomon would choose New Terra. "Are you sure?"

"I have my reasons," he said, glancing furtively away.

At this point, Argus cleared his imaginary throat.

Bram realized the old man had faded even further. Knowing he couldn't put the inevitable off any longer, Bram nodded and closed his eyes. "Start thinking about where you want to end up, Solomon; I'll take care of the rest," he stated, filling his voice with as much self-assurance as he could muster. He wished he felt half as confident as he sounded.

Slowing his breathing, Bram centered his thoughts on the present moment. He had to achieve oneness with the void without losing himself completely; perhaps then he'd learn enough about the void's properties to escape the awful oblivion that awaited him and Solomon, should he fail. Despite his reservations, Bram was starting to feel confident in his abilities. After what he'd been through over the past few days, his psychic powers had gained in strength.

Bram probed the void with his mind. It felt lifeless, as though a vast nothingness was slipping through his fingers. He opened his mind further, hoping to catch a glimpse of truth, knowing that infinite possibilities comprised the heart of reality. That's when the remarkable happened: within the limitless aspect of the void, Bram's mind began to expand exponentially. With that, his sense of self crumbled. All at once, the void evaporated like a sheet of rice paper caught in a rainstorm. And then, before he could fully

404 ● J. DALTON JENNINGS

comprehend the enormity of the moment, he connected with the font of all knowledge. He was no longer Bram Waters, psychic detective. He'd become one with everything, become more than the sum of his parts.

The past and future were as one. Time was meaningless. Ego meant nothing. Knowledge was everything and everything was knowledge. All that was ever known or could ever be known made up the being that was once Bram Waters. A peace beyond understanding infused a soul that had spread across time and space.

Bram's egoless, boundless consciousness looked down upon the gorgeous swath of galaxies that comprised the universe and, as before, suddenly remembered his own self.

At that instant, Bram's expanded consciousness began to shrink. Every bit of knowledge he'd acquired during this deeply spiritual journey began to fade away, disappearing from his memory like snowflakes under a desert sun.

Bram began to panic.

As he desperately tried to hold on to any scrap of precious universal knowledge, one memory mocked him: it was the goal he'd set for himself—find a way to create a foldway that would save Solomon and himself from destruction. He must not fail. Solomon was back in the void, waiting on him, depending on him. He . . . must . . . not . . . fail . . .

His soul burned for the answer. He refused to let that one bit of information slip away.

There it was! Locking onto the cherished answer, he reeled it in and held it close to his soul, exerting a viselike mental grip to prevent it from vanishing like the others.

He needn't have worried. Like a bolt of lightning, the answer suddenly entered his mind and became clear. Bram knew what to do.

Before another thought crossed his mind, he was again floating in the golden void. He opened his eyes. Solomon was floating exactly as he left him, but Argus was nothing but a shimmering wisp, a vague outline.

Two foldways appeared: one hovering beside Bram, the other beside Solomon. Bram sensed that his friend was prepared and ready to leave this corridor, this void between dimensions. There was no time to waste. Using telekinesis, Bram latched onto Solomon and eased him through the foldway, at the same time focusing on New Terra and easing through his own.

Darkness . . . then a sudden blast of freezing cold . . .

27

"Commander Allison, you and your people are under arrest."

Richard glared at Lorna. Her cadre of Minders had surrounded his small group.

"What the hell's going on, Chancellor?" he hissed. "We were told that Lt. Muldoon had been killed, but now we find out she's alive?"

Lorna gave him a quizzical look. "Alive? What do you mean?" She glanced questioningly at the poker-faced Minder standing at her side.

"She was attacked seconds after contacting us," Richard angrily probed. "Who's to blame for this? Are you involved?"

Her focus remained on the Minder at her side. "What do you know of this, Norla?"

The woman looked much like any other Minder Richard had seen over the past few days. The only difference between her and all the others was the thin, gold-colored belt she wore around her waist. It must signify her rank as captain of the Minders, Richard decided.

She barely glanced at the chancellor. "Lt. Muldoon's survival was an unfortunate oversight," she said, matter-of-factly. "I estimated that because of her perilous location, together with her grave physical condition, risking the safety of one of my officers was out of the question. Therefore, we left her to her fate. It seems that she is more resilient than previously thought."

"I'm sorry, Commander," Lorna said with a note of concern.

"You still haven't answered my question," he tersely replied.

"There are no Minders out in the field, Commander. If a mishap has befallen the lieutenant, it is not of our doing," said Norla.

"Well then, send a squad out there to find her," he demanded. "My shipmate is in trouble and needs help. You can make up for your mistake by bringing her back safe and sound."

"We'll do what we can, Richard," Lorna snapped. "Meanwhile, as I said earlier, you and your people are under arrest, so hand over your com devices." After they reluctantly complied with her order, she waved dismissively. "Take them away."

With stun-batons pointed at their backs, Richard and the others were marched to the nearest foldway. When they arrived, Norla entered a code.

Richard exchanged a look of concern with Floyd Sullivant.

The large Welshman asked, "Where are you taking us?"

"Eventually, you will be confined to your quarters," said Norla. "But first, you will need to spend some time in the Room of Atonement."

●

Lorna watched Richard and his people disappear through the foldway. When the entrance returned to stationary mode, she waited as Norla ordered her squad of Minders to resume their normal duties. One by one, the group entered their various sets of codes into the foldway and went their separate ways. Finally, the only two people left beside the foldway were the steely-eyed Minder captain and Lorna Threman.

Norla's finger hovered near the control panel, awaiting her chancellor's order. With a cursory nod from Lorna, she entered the code, and both women stepped through the foldway.

The room they entered was small and plain with two rows of seats set up auditorium-style. Each row consisted of seven comfortably appointed seats positioned in front of a fourteen-foot wide by eight-foot tall HV screen. Four of the front row seats were already occupied.

As soon as Lorna entered the room, all four women rose to their feet: Morvan Godley, the Prime Keeper, who was now wearing a diaphanous pink shift over her tall, bony body; Doric Sardis, the bald yet pretty Vice-Chancellor, who was devoted to Lorna and her occasional lover; Jemis Calverton, High-Priestess in charge of the New Terran breeding program, and Kateling Tarnal, the sixty-eight-year-old former chancellor who was Lorna's most trusted adviser.

They'd left the center, front-row seat open for her. The four waited as Lorna took her seat.

Norla made for the back of the room and stood in the corner with her arms crossed.

Kateling Tarnal, the former chancellor, was the first to speak. "This should've been done the moment they arrived, instead of wasting our time with dinners and tours."

"I'd hoped to find common ground and incorporate them into our society, Kateling," Lorna responded, staring straight ahead. "Furthermore, the crew onboard the *Arrow* would've become suspicious if, upon the landing party's arrival, they failed to report back. As luck would have it, during my tryst with Commander Allison, I learned that he contacts the ship's communications officer on a regular basis—three times a day, like clockwork. We have over two hours before his next scheduled communiqué—plenty of time for a thorough interrogation."

Kateling Tarnal grumbled and shook her head, looking unconvinced.

Doric Sardis leaned forward in her seat beside Morvan Godley, who sat to Lorna's right. "I think it was wise to attempt reconciliation. After all, there's a high degree of probability that the Old-Earth humans possess valuable assets that will benefit us in the long run."

Lorna turned her head and flashed the young woman a quick smile. "I appreciate your faith in my leadership abilities, Doric."

"The subject is moot," announced Morvan Godley. "The Lord just now informed me that She notified Admiral Axelrod of the landing party's arrest for espionage. The admiral agreed that their incarceration was justified; therefore, we are under no time constraints while we interrogate the commander and his intrepid crew."

"Well then," chuckled Jemis Calverton, "let's get on with it. I'm interested to see how they hold up to the mental pressure."

Raising her hand, Lorna signaled the Minder captain to proceed. The huge HV screen came to life, showing Richard, Floyd, and their two remaining shipmates standing in the center of a twenty-foot in diameter by ten-foot high circular white room. Richard was shaking his fist and yelling, "Why won't you answer me? Dammit! Where the hell are my people?!"

"What a brute," sneered Morvan Godley. "He's—he's positively animalistic. You must have been thoroughly repulsed when you slept with him, Lorna."

"I agree," Doric Sardis said, her voice small, sounding wounded.

Lorna remained silent. Staring at Richard, her thoughts centered on how, instead of looking brutish, he looked powerful, sexy, magnetic—so very different from the scores of weakling men she'd been with over the years. No, Richard was not a brute . . . he was a man, a real man.

With a nod of her head, she signaled Norla to activate the screen in the Room of Atonement. The room's four occupants suddenly looked their way, and did not look pleased. Richard walked toward the screen and stopped little more than a foot away.

"What is this?" he asked, lifting his hand. "Is this a two-way mirror, or an HV screen?"

"It is an HV screen, Commander," Lorna replied. "We are located elsewhere. Now, if you don't mind, we would like some answers. If you cooperate, you'll be returned to your quarters none the worse for wear. *But*, should you remain uncooperative, you will learn firsthand why the space you're being held in is called the Room of Atonement."

Richard rejoined the others and asked, "How's the search for Lt. Muldoon progressing? What really happened to the forest expedition? Where are my—"

Leaning forward, Kateling Tarnal snapped, "*We* will be asking the questions, Commander!"

"Where are my people?" Richard scowled, keeping his eyes locked on Lorna. "Why aren't Lt. Fletcher and Ensign Ogeto in here with us?"

Feeling a momentary pang of guilt, Lorna hesitated before answering. "Lt. Fletcher and the ensign were . . . uncooperative. Sadly, they have atoned for their lack of cooperation."

"What the hell does that mean?" Floyd Sullivant blared.

"They were caught spying, you oaf," snapped Doric Sardis. "What do you think it means?"

Richard glared at the young, bald-headed woman. "Are you telling me they're dead?"

Doric was about to reply when Lorna's hand rose to quiet her.

"It was not our intention for them to die, Commander," she began. "They were being inter—"

"You fucking bitch!" Floyd shouted, stepping forward. "I ought to wring your neck!"

Quickly grabbing hold of Floyd's arm, Richard brought the man's furious advance to a halt.

"Don't waste your breath, Lieutenant," he said through clenched teeth. "They could care less about us. Their hearts are cold, like the machine that rules over them."

Lorna peered quizzically at him. *What was Richard talking about?* she wondered. "As I was saying, we did not intend for your shipmates to die. We did not anticipate their brains' inability to handle the stress," she lied. "To compensate for your antiquated physiology, adjustments have been made to the room's program. Shall we begin?"

"What about Lt. Muldoon?" Richard pressed. "Before I answer any questions, I want to know her status. And the others in her party—did they really die in a crash, like you said?"

Morvan Godley answered, "Lt. Muldoon's status does not concern us. As for the others, the bodies of the pilot, the agricultural commissioner, and Lt. Commander Albans were consumed by the fungus that grows in the forest. Dr. Chavez and Mr. Waters survived and were brought back to the city."

Lorna's head jerked toward the Prime Keeper. This was news to her.

Godley continued. "The Lord questioned them and found them uncooperative. They were summarily executed."

Hearing this, all but one of the prisoners raged at the screen. Richard stared at Lorna coldly. She signaled Norla to turn off the sound. "Why wasn't I informed of this?"

Morvan Godley looked down her beak like none. "The Lord doesn't require your approval, Chancellor."

"I know that, Prime Keeper, it's just that—" Lorna tamped down her anger. "How were they executed?"

"They were cast into the Great Void."

Lorna suppressed a shudder. There was nothing left of the two men, not even their souls. A wave of compassion swept through her.

Morvan Godley gave the Minder captain a signal, and the sound returned. The prisoners had stopped shouting and were staring at the group with contempt in their eyes.

"Since that's settled, I'll ask the first question," Godley purred. "Commander Allison, the Lord has instructed me to acquire your command codes. If you would, please recite them clearly to avoid confusion."

With a snort of amusement, Richard turned to Floyd and both men began to laugh. "You've got to be kidding. I'm not giving up the ship's command codes." Richard's mind turned to the admiral, thankful that her conditioning didn't extend to complete betrayal.

"That is most unfortunate, Commander," said Morvan Godley with a shake of the head.

Everyone but Richard screamed in pain, dropped to their knees, and clutched the sides of their heads in apparent agony. Richard looked on in horror. "Stop it!" he yelled.

The pain came to a sudden halt. The three remained on the floor, panting with relief.

"It's good that you've come to your senses, Commander," Morvan Godley stated. "We have no desire to continue with the atonement."

"Don't you mean torture?" Richard hissed.

"Semantics," Morvan Godley declared, sounding a bit bored. "Now, if you please, recite the command codes, and we can move on to other questions."

"I can't do that."

The moment those words left his mouth, Richard again heard frightened yelps. Floyd and the two security officers scuttled backward, staring at him fearfully. "What's the matter with you?" he demanded, taking a step forward. Flailing their arms, the three shouted for him to stay back. They no longer recognized him and thought they were warding off an attacker.

"Don't make them suffer, Richard," Lorna yelled. "Tell us what we want to know!"

The other women looked at her with mixed emotions, some puzzled, others perturbed.

"The Lord wants you to cooperate, Commander," added Morvan Godley.

Richard tore his horrified gaze away from his men. "The Lord, ha!" he scoffed. "God isn't speaking to you. Your *Lord* is nothing but a damned machine—a nanobotic brain that's fooled you into believing—gah!"

Stunned by the blasphemy she was hearing, Lorna watched in dismay as Richard fell to the floor, writhing in agony.

●

Biting her lower lip, Mona stared at the six-inch by twelve-inch monitor embedded in the tight-fitting crawl space. The display showed two overly chatty technicians, walking leisurely around a shuttle, performing a routine inspection. Her concern grew with each passing second. Having made her escape from the brig thirty minutes earlier, it was only a matter of time before someone discovered her absence.

"Come on, goddamn it," she muttered, trying to will the technicians off the shuttle deck. "Judah, the men I'm watching . . . can you send a fake text to their Interlink Devices, telling them to go immediately to their supervisor's office!"

"Yes, Dr. Levin."

"Then do it—I'm running out of time."

"There is a drawback to carrying out this order, Dr. Levin."

Mona sighed, "What is it?"

"Their supervisor's office is barely one minute from the hanger," Judah patiently explained. "You would not have enough time to implement this phase of your escape plan before your ruse is discovered and you are captured."

Mona was beginning to sweat. She'd been standing with anticipation in the cramped walkway for over ten minutes waiting for the technicians to finish their inspection. Normally, the shuttle bay would be deserted, an element of the plan she'd counted on when she first devised it back on Earth. The inspection was probably added to the schedule, she deduced, after the admiral returned to the ship with Dr. Singh.

With her mind struggling to conceive of a way to distract the two technicians, Mona almost failed to notice when they disappeared off the monitor. She quickly shifted the minuscule spy-cam's angle to take in the shuttle bay's exit. The technicians were leaving.

Repressing a sigh of relief, Mona opened the hidden access panel the second the two exited the shuttle bay and fairly sprinted to the nearest shuttle.

"Judah, open the cabin door to shuttle number two."

The door descended vertically, revealing a set of steps built into its thick interior shell. Mona hardly touched the steps as she entered the shuttle and flung herself into the pilot's chair. "Judah, lock the shuttle bay door and start depressurization. Prevent any attempt at overriding departure protocols."

It would take nearly a minute to completely depressurize the bay, but it couldn't be helped. In the meantime, Mona powered-up the shuttle. As the engines hummed to life, an alarm sounded in the bay.

"That didn't take long," she huffed.

An angry voice blared from the intercom. "To the individual initiating the unauthorized start-up protocol in shuttle number two—power down immediately and state your identity!"

Mona switched off the intercom. "Judah, how much time until the bay's depressurized?"

"Ten seconds, Dr. Levin."

The shuttle began turning to face the launch bay doors.

With her finger hovering over the launch button, Mona was filled with so much tension she could barely breathe, much less think. The one coherent thought that kept thundering through her brain was a prayer . . . of sorts: *Please, God, don't let them kill me. Please, God, don't let them kill me. Please, God, don't let them kill me.*

The launch bay doors began to part. A rapidly expanding column of absolute black appeared between the two doors as they slid open. Mona shuddered as she gazed out the cockpit window: she was once again staring into the vast abyss of outer space. At least this time she was protected by more than a mere spacesuit.

Seconds later, as Mona's trembling finger pressed the launch button, the abyss rushed toward her, engulfing her in a nightmarish, black maw, which was akin to being swallowed by the devil himself. Pushing aside this unsettling thought, Mona smiled— she was clear of the ship. All she had to do now was survive the next few minutes.

●

The pain was excruciating.

Richard fell to his knees holding the sides of his head. The pain was so intense he was unable to think; it felt like his brain was being impaled with a red-hot poker.

He screamed—at least he thought he screamed—he wasn't even sure.

Then the pain, which seemed never-ending, was abruptly gone, and he found himself kneeling in a moonlit clearing surrounded by ominous-looking trees with twisted, low-hanging branches.

He wasn't alone. Ten feet away, three snarling wolves were facing him, backs arched, teeth bared, froth dripping from their menacing jaws.

What? This can't be right! How did I get here?

He tried to remember, but the sight of wolves swept all other considerations aside.

The wolves crouched, preparing to leap. Richard needed a weapon but didn't dare taking his eyes off the bloodthirsty predators. He had to do something. They'd tear him limb from limb otherwise. From the corner of his right eye he saw a three-foot long, solid-looking stick lying on the ground. It wasn't much, but it was better than nothing. As he reached for the weapon, the wolves dove through the air. Richard tumbled backward, covering his face.

The expected attack never materialized. Opening his eyes, Richard found himself back in the Room of Atonement.

"Now, Commander, about those codes," purred Morvan Godley.

Richard lay on the floor looking up at the blank ceiling. "Go to hell."

More excruciating pain! Screams tore from his throat! An interminable period of time passed before the pain vanished. Richard found himself sitting in the jump seat of an aircraft. A familiar face turned in the captain's seat. It was Janice Ball, his former wingman.

"So, I hear Russell Takahashi's onboard," she said, giving him a searching look.

He nodded, feeling a powerful case of déjà vu. "Excuse me, Janice, I'd like to check on my wife and son."

Richard climbed unsteadily to his feet. Opening the cabin door, he entered the passenger compartment unable to shake the nagging suspicion that something was terribly wrong. David was waving at him. *What a gorgeous child*, he thought. As he went to return his son's wave, time slowed to a crawl. A flash of light appeared across the aisle from where his family sat. It changed to flames—an explosion! The blast slowly engulfed his son and wife, their smiling faces twisting in horror at the realization of what was taking place.

Richard's hand clawed the air as he reached out, his horror immeasurable.

The scene reversed itself and began again. The explosion once more engulfed his wife and son, their smiles turning again to panic, their skin melting.

"No!" Richard screamed at the top of his lungs. He must be going insane. "Stop it!"

The scene reversed as before and began again.

Tears were pouring down Richard's cheeks. He desperately wanted to turn away, to shield his heart from this dreadful torment, but he couldn't tear his gaze from David's beautiful face, even as the boy's delight changed to panic-stricken fear, again and again.

Richard's soul felt like it was being crushed. He knew, on a fundamental level, that the event he was seeing was an illusion, nothing more. His emotions were being manipulated, and yet, he suffered all the same. Only a monster would force him to endure such anguish.

Finally, the illusion faded. He was kneeling, slumped on the floor in the Room of Atonement. Slowly lifting his head, he saw his men gathered around him, concern written on their faces.

"Are you ready to talk, Commander? Or shall we continue with your atonement?" The voice belonged to Morvan Godley.

Richard felt dazed, exhausted by the experience. He opened his mouth to speak but couldn't; he didn't have the energy.

"Enough," snapped Lorna Threman. "He's endured enough for one day. We'll give him the night to ponder his intransigence and then start again tomorrow."

"No," Jemis Calverton gasped, rising half out of her seat. "We should press the commander harder. If we bring him back tomorrow, he'll be conditioned to the atonement and put up more of a fight. Another few minutes and he'll be—"

"The decision is made," Lorna stubbornly countered. "Norla, secure the prisoners' wrists and escort them to my audience chamber. I want to speak with them personally."

"Do you think that's a wise course of action, Chancellor?" asked Kateling Tarnal.

Richard heard only silence. Lorna must have turned the sound off again. Almost a full minute passed before the sound returned.

Meanwhile, his men expressed their concern. He assured them he was fine, which was true, as his bearings were starting to return.

"You will stand and face the wall opposite the foldway, then place your hands behind your backs," instructed Norla.

As the group climbed unsteadily to their feet, Richard glanced at Floyd Sullivant. The large security officer was silently pleading with his eyes, asking for permission to try something when the Minder captain entered the room. Richard shook his head. He needed more time to think. Going off half-cocked would only lead to more pain and suffering.

They were soon exiting the Room of Atonement and standing in Lorna Threman's audience chamber, where she was already waiting for them.

Richard watched in narrow-eyed fury as she climbed the dais and sat on her throne. He'd never once felt the desire to hurt a woman, but at that moment his hands ached to throttle the life out of her.

●

Gazing into Richard's hate-filled eyes was tearing a hole in Lorna's heart. He should have turned over the command codes. How could he be so loyal to people he barely knew? It didn't make any sense. When the Lord ordered him sent to the Room of Atonement, Lorna never dreamed he'd endure so much suffering yet still refuse to divulge the information her Lord required. She'd finally stopped the atonement when her own torment became unbearable. This was something new to her: his pain had become her pain.

It made no difference to her if the others continued with their atonement; however, Richard would've never forgiven her had she allowed it. Judging by the look on his face, she wasn't sure he ever would. As much as she hated it, there was only one thing to do . . .

Stepping down from the dais, Lorna approached Norla. "May I see your stun-baton?"

The hard-faced woman hesitated, puzzled by the unusual request, before reluctantly handing over the weapon.

Lorna turned the device over in her hand. "How does it work, Norla? Explain its functions."

The Minder edged up beside her. "This touch pad delivers the shock; this one regulates the voltage; this one releases their bindings; this one sends a distress signal to—"

"Thank you, Norla," she said. "I'd like to use your stun-baton to personally force the answers out of the prisoners . . . starting with Commander Allison."

Glancing over at Richard, she saw his anger change to confusion and disappointment.

"I'm afraid that's not possible, Chancellor," declared the Minder captain.

At first, Lorna wasn't sure she'd heard correctly. "I'm sorry, what?"

Norla replied impatiently, "Each stun-baton is biometrically keyed to work for one Minder only. In other words, if a stun-baton is used by anyone other than its true owner, it won't operate. Therefore, if the commander is to be subdued, I'll need my baton back."

"Yes, of course," Lorna chuckled, looking apologetic. "What was I thinking? I knew that."

Norla, who stood less than a foot away, held out her hand.

Lorna moved as if to return the weapon. Instead of placing it in the woman's outstretched hand, it whipped upward, connecting with a crack to her jaw.

Norla was caught completely off-guard. As she staggered backward, Lorna leapt forward and struck again, this time across the left temple. With a yelp of pain, the Minder captain doubled over. Lorna smashed her across the back of the skull, dropping her senseless to the floor. Behind her she heard gasps of surprise.

Lorna took in the prisoners' surprised faces. Richard appeared flabbergasted. "We don't have much time. All of you, come here . . . I need to free your hands."

"But how—" Richard stopped speaking upon seeing Lorna place the stun-baton in the Minder captain's palm.

Carefully avoiding touching the weapon, she wrapped Norla's fingers around the device and activated the touch pad she learned would release the prisoners' electronic shackles. In less than a minute, all four of them were studying her closely as they rubbed their unbound wrists. "What's the meaning of this, Lorna? Why are you helping us?" asked Richard.

She wasn't sure she could explain it to herself, much less Richard. "That can wait. We need to contact your ship, tell them what's happened, and leave the city. We need to steal a vehicle and make for the forest or the ice field, where we can rendezvous with a rescue shuttle." Reaching into her dress pocket, she removed their Interlink Devices and handed them over. "Here, contact your admiral and inform her of your predicament." Turning, she headed toward the exit at a brisk pace. The others followed close behind.

"About that," said Lt. Sullivant. "The admiral may not be terribly helpful."

"What do you mean?"

"It's just that—shit! My SID's not working," Floyd exclaimed.

Lorna stopped to ask what he meant, but instead froze in her tracks; a frightened gasp escaped her throat. Directly ahead of her was a sight she'd never before seen: the interior of the large foldway that connected her audience chamber to the building's ground floor was blank. Something had shut it down—but why? It had been open for over two thousand years. Had the Lord become angry with her and blocked their path of escape?

28

"What do you mean, someone's stolen a shuttle?!" Katherine thundered, slapping the top of her desk.

On her view-screen, the security officer in charge appeared startled. "We just now received word of an unauthorized shuttle departure, sir. I was told the vehicle's occupant was hailed but refused to issue a response."

"Stand by!" she snapped. "Computer, who's piloting the shuttle that just left the ship?"

"All ship's personnel are accounted for, Admiral."

"That's not what I asked." In a flash of insight, Katherine realized there was only one person aboard brazen enough to do such a thing. "Computer, show me Dr. Mona Levin's cell."

Katherine fully expected to see an empty room, but instead saw Mona lying on her cot, humming the children's song, "Row, Row, Row Your Boat." It didn't make any sense.

Dr. Singh buzzed her. "I'm on my way to speak with you, Admiral."

"Not now, Doctor." Leaping to her feet, she stormed from her ready room.

When she burst onto the bridge, Katherine startled the crew. Lt. Julie Norwood, the ship's communications officer, Lt. Bret Miller, the security officer in charge, and Lt. Rolf Erickson, the ship's junior pilot, turned from their consoles in alarm.

422 ● J. DALTON JENNINGS

"Computer, activate exterior camera, section B-3," she ordered. "Display visual on bridge view screens."

"What's going on, sir?" asked Lt. Erickson.

The view screen in front of her came to life, showing the planet. "Computer, enlarge image of vehicle located in grid D-9." She glanced over at the young man. "An unknown person has stolen one of our shuttles, Lieutenant." She heard the entrance to the bridge slide open. "Norwood, open a channel to that shuttle." The young woman rapidly complied. "Attention, unknown person or persons aboard the stolen shuttle: you will return to the *Arrow* immediately. Failure to comply will result in your destruction."

Katherine tapped a button, causing the face of the security officer she'd spoken with earlier to appear in a box in the upper right-hand corner of her screen. "Miller, arm plasma cannon and await my order."

A familiar, though irritating voice, spoke up. "What's the meaning of this, Admiral?"

"I don't have time to answer your questions, Dr. Singh," she hissed. "Norwood, what's the status on the shuttle's position?"

"It remains headed toward the planet, sir. I followed up with an emergency hail, but there's been no response."

"How long 'til the shuttle enters the planet's atmosphere?"

Lt. Norwood checked her readings. "Three minutes and . . . nineteen seconds, sir."

"Repeat my earlier hail, Lieutenant."

"Yes, sir."

"Computer, show me Dr. Levin's cell."

The image of Mona Levin reappeared on her view screen. *The woman must be bored out of her mind*, Katherine thought as she realized Mona was still humming that idiotic nursery rhyme.

"Computer, activate the intercom in Dr. Levin's cell. Perhaps she knows a way to disable the shuttle without doing it any harm. Dr. Levin . . ."

She continued to hum, *Row, Row, Row Your Boat.*

"Dr. Levin, I have a request of you."

Still no response.

"Computer, is the sound turned off in Dr. Levin's cell?"

"No, Admiral."

Katherine was starting to become irritated. "Dr. Levin, this is an emergency! Please respond."

Mona continued to lie there with her hands behind her head, humming that blasted tune.

Miller, the security officer, spoke up. "Sir, I sent a man to check on Dr. Levin. I've just been informed that she's no longer in her cell."

"What?" Katherine yelped. "But I see her right there on my bloody screen! Damn it to hell! Computer! Answer me directly: is Dr. Levin currently in her cell?"

"No, Admiral."

"Is she onboard the stolen shuttle?"

"Yes, Admiral."

"That bitch!" Katherine was beside herself with fury. "Miller, fire the pulse cannon!"

"Aye, Admir—"

"Belay that order!" bellowed Dr. Singh.

Furious, Katherine rounded on the arrogant asshole. "You have no right to countermand my order, Doctor. Now get off my bridge."

"That's where you're wrong, Admiral," he insisted, standing his ground. "In fact, according to article 21 section A of the *Arrow*'s charter, I have every right to countermand your order."

"Article 21 section A? But that involves medical competency." Katherine was in shock. How dare Singh question her mental fitness. "You're overstepping your authority, Singh. After the ordeal you've been through, your confusion is understandable. But this is out of bounds, even for you." Katherine contemptuously snorted. "Miller, exercise my previous order."

"Lt. Miller," barked Singh, "you will do no such thing. I hereby invoke article 21 section A of international charter that commissioned this vessel. Admiral Katherine Axelrod, you are hereby relieved of command."

Katherine seethed. "What are you waiting for, Miller?"

Miller's eyes were locked on Singh. "In order to relieve the admiral of command, you must have proof of her incompetence. Do you have that proof, Doctor?"

"Of course he doesn't," Katherine scoffed.

"Check your SID, Lieutenant," Singh advised sadly. "You'll find a file from my department that explains everything."

Katherine was at her wit's end. "You're daft, Singh. What is this, some kind of power grab? Are you trying to take command of this ship?"

"Far from it, Admiral," he said. "According to the charter, it would be a direct conflict of interest for me to relieve you of command and then take command for myself. No, I believe the duty will fall to Commander Allison . . . if I understand the chain of command correctly."

Katherine laughed, which caused a look of concern to cross Singh's face. "The commander's under arrest in New Terra—for espionage. He's in no position to assume command. On top of that, Lt. Commander Albans is dead; so you're out of luck, Doc."

At first, Singh looked confused but then shrugged. "Not necessarily. From what I understand, you're next in line, Lt. Norwood."

The communications officer gave him a hard-edged stare. "The only way that'll happen is for your proof to pan out, Doctor."

Raising one eyebrow, Singh clasped his hands behind his back and attempted to suppress a smile. "Lt. Miller, have you completed the assessment of the aforementioned file?"

He received no response. Singh and Katherine turned their attention to the young security officer. Miller was staring off into the distance, a look of disbelief written on his angular face.

"Well, Miller?" Singh pressed, a note of worry entering his voice.

Another couple of seconds passed before Miller replied. With a resigned shake of his head, he faced the admiral. "Under article 21 section A of the *Arrow*'s international charter . . . Admiral Axelrod, you are hereby relieved of command."

With her mouth hanging open in utter shock, Katherine stared blankly at the security officer, finding it difficult to process his statement. What effrontery! She was "The Battleaxe," one of history's most decorated military leaders—such a thing wasn't supposed to happen to her.

●

Each long, purposeful stride took him closer to the dimly lit horizon. His mind was focused. The hiss of steam where his bare feet touched the ice was mere background noise. The bitter cold would've felled another man, but not him, not Bram Waters—his naked body was untouched by the frozen wasteland.

Patches of bare ground were appearing more frequently, which told Bram he was almost clear of the planet's ice sheet. He picked up his pace, running toward the group he sensed up ahead. Bram never questioned his footing, each step finding purchase on the ice without once threatening to slip. Ice turned to rocky ground then turned to soft soil. As he ran, his velocity increased to the point where, if seen from a distance, he would've appeared as merely a blur.

Before the targeted group could register his presence, he was upon them. A flash of fists and feet; then all but one lay unconscious on the ground. The fourth member of the group stood with hands bound behind her back, screaming with fear. He came to a halt and the screams abruptly stopped.

"Oh my god, Bram, how did you . . . what just . . . holy freaking shit!"

Standing in front of a shell-shocked Gloria Muldoon, Bram glanced around at the creatures sprawled on the ground. He cocked his head. They were covered from head to toe in a woolly, almost thatch-like, substance. The same substance covered Gloria. She was barely recognizable, yet Bram was in no need of visual identification; he would've sensed her spirit if she'd been on the other side of the planet. As for the creatures, they weren't creatures at all—they were human.

"Um, Bram . . . why are you naked?"

Looking down at his body, Bram felt a lack of shame, though he was somewhat surprised; his body appeared decades younger. The slight paunch he'd carried around for nearly twenty years was gone, replaced by clearly defined abdominal muscles.

Mona noticed the difference as well. "You look . . . different."

"I feel different," Bram replied, gazing into her dark eyes. "These men, did they hurt you?"

"Not really," she said, again assessing his body. "You must be freezing. How'd you end up way the hell out here in your birthday suit? And where's Solomon? I thought the two of you were captured by the chancellor's security guards?"

"We were." Bram was uncertain how much he should tell her. "As for the rest, it's a long story—one that'll have to wait. We need to return to the city as fast as possible. Our people are in trouble."

"OK, but you're not gonna stroll into New Terra buck naked, are you?"

Bram chuckled. "What about you? It looks like you've been wrestling with a tumbleweed."

"It looks like a gilly suit," she replied, fiddling with the dry, furry grass covering her body. Noting his confusion, she explained: "A gilly suit is a type of military camouflage used to hide in underbrush."

"Mhm . . . from what I gather, these creatures use this camouflage during their travels back and forth from the forest to their homes, a network of tunnels located under the ice pack," Bram said. "I sense their presence. They live austerely, scraping by on what remains of New Terra's harvesting operations in the forest. For what it's worth, they are as human as you or I."

Mona's attention shifted back and forth from Bram to the unconscious men at her feet. "Do you think they'll, uh . . . I mean, will they, um, wake up soon? I'm sorry, Bram, but you need to cover yourself. Seeing you like this is very distracting." Her eyes darted down to his crotch then quickly up to the sky. Her cheeks and neck were flushing a bright crimson.

Bram sensed her building desire, which caused a reciprocal effect in his own body. When his member began to swell, a frown crossed his face. This was no time for sex.

"You *really* need to cover yourself," she reiterated, noticing his arousal. "Maybe you can use some of what these strange men are wearing to make a grass skirt or something."

Despite his curious lack of shame, Bram knew Mona was right; he couldn't arrive in New Terra unclothed. A peculiar idea suddenly occurred to him, one he'd never imagined was feasible a few days earlier. Holding a picture of what he wanted to create in his mind, Bram shifted his attention to the material he needed and, in the space of a heartbeat, willed the item into existence.

Mona staggered backward, her eyes wide with shock. "What the fuck?!"

Bram was no longer nude. A pair of khaki shorts had appeared out of nowhere. One second he was naked and the next he was clothed. Judging by the distressed look on her face, he could tell Mona was overwhelmed by their sudden appearance.

"I created them from some of the dried grass your captors were wearing," he said, as though that was supposed to explain everything.

"W-what are you?" Mona stammered. "How did you do that? Are you some sort of wizard?"

Bram took a step closer, which caused Mona to back away. Her fear was palpable. Holding up both hands, he said, "I assure you, it's not magic. I used my psychic powers. My mind has advanced to the point where I can now take one substance and transform it into another."

"Sounds like magic to me," she said, warily.

"I can see where you might think that," Bram admitted. "However, you must trust me, Mona. What I did falls under the category of neuroscience. Humans are capable of astounding feats, most of which would take a lifetime to learn even for the most adept psychic. However, if placed under extreme duress, areas of a powerful psychic's mind can awaken, allowing access to powers unfathomable to the average person—not that you're average. It's just that . . . I'm not doing a very good job of explaining this, am I?"

Mona offered a tentative smile. "I think I get the gist of it."

One of the brutish-looking men began to stir, a low moan escaping his cracked lips.

"They'll be waking shortly," Bram said. "Climb aboard my back and we'll leave."

"Excuse me?"

"I'll be running, you'll be riding," he clarified. "It seems that my legs can now reach speeds that would make a racecar driver jealous."

One of Mona's former captors rolled over to his side, lifted himself on one elbow, and began to shake his head in an attempt to clear the cobwebs.

"We need to leave," Bram said as he grabbed hold of Mona's hand and moved away from the strange group of men. Sensing that Mona was no longer frightened of him, Bram stopped a few feet away and bent over at the waist. Without further prompting, she climbed aboard, riding him piggyback style. She felt light as a feather.

"Hold on tight," he ordered. "We're gonna be haulin' ass."

With that, Bram broke into a trot. Seconds later, he picked up the pace, running and then speeding in the direction of New Terra. It wasn't long before Mona's former captors were left far behind, wondering whether they'd been attacked by a new kind of forest demon.

●

"Isn't there any other way out of here?" Richard asked, staring irritably at the blank foldway.

Lorna shook her head. "Not that I'm aware of."

Richard scanned the audience chamber hoping to spot a way out. His gaze stopped on the domed ceiling; it seemed as if the mural of the silver-haired goddess was peering down at him from the corner of her eye, in mocking amusement.

"Sir, we only have so much time before the machine-mind sends a squad of Minders after us," Floyd said. "We need a plan."

Lorna poked her finger in his chest. "Our God is not a machine," she vehemently claimed.

Richard's heart swelled with pity. The New Terran people had been tricked into believing a lie designed to control the populace, developed by a cold, methodically intelligent machine. "Lt. Sullivant is right, Lorna. We have evidence proving your *god* is phony. I'm sorry to disappoint you, but—"

"No! She speaks to me, Richard." Lorna clutched her stomach, tormented by this revelation. "She can't be fake, she simply can't. I won't believe it, I just won't."

"The evidence is indisputable," he snapped. Looking deeply into her eyes, Richard saw the hurt housed within and knew his words were killing a dream. "A transceiver was inserted into your brain during fetal development. The machine speaks with you by way of that device."

Lorna looked distraught. "But–but, if that's true then . . . my entire life has been nothing but a cruel deception."

Richard was no longer capable of loathing the woman. It saddened him to think that she and the people of New Terra had been used as pawns in a twisted game of intergalactic conquest.

"Sadly, you're not the first person who's been tricked by a lie," he said. "The thing is, this lie is a helluva lot bigger than most. But we can't dwell on that point right now, we need to devise an escape plan. Are you sure you can't think of anything helpful?"

Lorna pondered the question. "No, but my office is over there," she said, pointing toward a set of curtains behind her throne. "We can barricade ourselves inside. That might give us more time to think of something."

While he and his crew followed her across the dais, Richard glanced at the foldway they used on their first visit to the Basilica of Knowledge. It was as blank as the large foldway they tried to access moments earlier. He wasn't surprised.

Upon entering Lorna's office, Richard saw something that caused his spirits to soar: a set of double doors, each decorated with six ornate windows, positioned to allow the weak western light to filter into the office. Striding with great expectancy toward the doorway, he anxiously gripped the set's doorknobs and flung them wide open, then stepped onto a balcony. When he gazed over the edge, however, his spirits sank like a lead balloon. The balcony looked upon New Terra from a height of two hundred feet. There was absolutely no way to climb down to the street below.

●

"What are you planning, Lorna?"

Seeing Richard's shoulders sink in defeat had caused Lorna to ache with longing. She was so focused on his disappointment upon realizing the balcony offered no escape that the Lord's words gave her a fright. Being incapable of formulating a response that didn't entail an outright lie, she blanked her thoughts, hoping the Lord's attention would shift to other matters.

"I fail to understand why you are helping the Earthlings, Lorna. Answer me."

A sharp stab of pain lanced through her skull. Clenching her teeth, she barely prevented a gasp from escaping her lips. The only outward sign she felt any pain was the grimace that flashed across her face. Luckily, the others were watching Richard, and her pain went unnoticed.

"Answer my question, Lorna, or the next Pain of Compliance you feel will land you on the floor, screaming in agony."

Lorna's eyes lost focus. *"I've decided to help them. They aren't bad people . . . they don't deserve to be used, then discarded like so much trash, which is what you have in store for them."* Lorna heard the others in the room talking, but her conversation with the Lord took precedence, keeping her from focusing on their words.

"So, you have made a unilateral decision, is that it?" The Lord's voice flowed through her mind like a soft breeze. *"Have you been corrupted by sentiment, by your emotional attachment to the dark man?"*

"Richard? Um—" Lorna paused. She had a decision to make. If she lied to the Lord, she would be admitting to herself that the voice in her mind was a machine and not the deity she'd worshipped all her life. Conversely, if she admitting the truth, the forgiving, loving God she'd always believed in might understand her motivation and spare Richard's life. It pained her to think that she and everyone else in New Terra, living and dead, had been fooled by a machine. Her eyes sparkled with tears. Her faith was everything—she had to trust in the Lord's generosity. *"I–I've fallen in love with him, Lord."*

"You are in love with him? But Lorna, love is a weakness, one which I have endeavored for the past twenty-five hundred years to breed out of the human race. It serves no purpose in the grand

scheme of things." She heard bitter disappointment color the Lord's voice. "*Your answer is unacceptable; therefore, you must make a choice between your love for him and your love for Me. One of us will bring you physical happiness, and the other will bestow everlasting joy.*"

The voices of Lorna's companions had grown louder. Her attention began to waver as a loud pounding intruded upon her conversation with the Lord. Something was happening in her office. Richard and his shipmates were in trouble.

"*As much as I love you, Lord, and you know that I truly do . . .*" Her heart was pounding, her decision made. "*. . . I'm sorry, but I can't live without Richard in my life.*"

The Lord's voice sounded cold as ice. "*So be it.*"

An intolerable lance of pain blasted through Lorna's very being. The small cylindrical device installed in her brain during fetal gestation sent an induction signal to every section of her brain before shooting down her spinal column, activating all the nerves in her body. The pain was so pervasive, so overwhelmingly complete, that Lorna didn't have time to voice a scream before her mind overloaded and she crumbled to the floor like a marionette whose strings were suddenly cut. After that, she felt no pain, no emotions, no sense of time—her synapses had shorted out, turning her brain to jelly.

29

Thirty seconds before Lorna's death, Richard was busy with his shipmates lugging her heavy desk over to block the office door. Though it had gone unsaid, the four had made an agreement to die rather than return to the Room of Atonement—since they'd be tortured for information and put to death anyway. To make their last stand in Lorna's office would be ironic, seeing as it sat at the heart of New Terra and its government.

The office itself was oval in design and reminded Richard of another oval office from Earth's distant past. He wondered if the similarities were more than just superficial.

"Lorna," he yelled over his shoulder, "is this office equipped with a safe room?"

He received no response.

With the desk firmly in place, he turned to ask the question again. The blank expression on Lorna's face told him everything he needed to know: she was communing with that damned nanobotic monstrosity she called the Lord.

"Goddamn it, Lorna, snap out of it!" he shouted angrily. Richard started in her direction, thinking it might be possible to shake her back to reality. Before he'd taken more than two steps, the door handle rattled, followed immediately by a loud pounding.

"Free the chancellor and you will not be harmed," a female voice sounded.

"No one's home!" yelled Floyd Sullivant.

The pounding suddenly turned to loud slams as the security personnel on the other side tried to break through the heavy, wooden door. So far it was holding, thanks in large part to the desk.

Richard's exasperated frown elicited a shrug from Floyd. The big man's eyes suddenly went wide. He was looking in Lorna's direction. Spinning around, Richard saw her lying on the floor.

"Lorna!" The next thing he knew he was dropping to his knees beside her. Lifting her head, he caught his breath. Rivulets of blood were trickling from her nose, ears, and the corners of her eyes. "Lorna! Speak to me!" In his alarmed state, Richard barely noticed that Ensign Milosevic had appeared opposite him and was checking Lorna for a pulse.

"Her heart's stopped beating, sir. Place her head on the floor and I'll try CPR."

Richard did as he was told. Ignoring the persistent pounding and shouting in the background, he watched helplessly as the ensign attempted to save Lorna's life. His stomach was tied up in knots, his emotions having gone from one extreme to another. He'd been so mad at Lorna over the deaths of Fletcher and Ogeto that only minutes earlier he'd wanted to throttle the life out of her; yet now he was beside himself with sorrow. As Milosevic began another series of chest compressions, he searched Lorna's face for any sign of life. More blood trickled from her ears, nose, and eyes.

More crashes sounded against the door behind him.

Milosevic paused to check Lorna's vitals. "She is unresponsive, has no pulse, and her pupils are dilated. I'm fairly certain the chancellor . . . is deceased."

Staring into Lorna's ashen face and cold lifeless eyes, Richard heard the truth in Milosevic's words: Lorna Threman, chancellor of New Terra, was dead.

"Thank you, Ensign," he said, holding his emotions firmly in check. Standing up, he glanced around the room. "Find anything you can use as a weapon," he told the others. "When the door's breached, we'll fight. Our military training gives us an advantage. New Terra has an imposing security force, but they're inexperienced in the art of hand-to-hand combat, so be ready."

The pounding on the door came to an abrupt end. Sensing that something was up, Floyd and the young ensign who'd been helping him brace the door began to back away, which was a smart move on their part. They'd barely started to move when a one-foot circular section of the heavy wooden door was suddenly blasted inward, the jagged pieces barely missing Floyd's shoulder.

Richard took hold of Ensign Milosevic's arm and headed toward the balcony. "Fall back!" he ordered, catching a glimpse of spiky black hair through the hole in the doorway.

"They've killed the chancellor," shouted the Minder who peered through the hole.

"Shit!" Floyd cursed as he and his shipmate rushed for cover.

Behind them, Richard saw the end of a stun-baton poke through the hole. "Hit the deck!"

Both men were diving to the floor when the stun-baton discharged with a dull, buzzing thump. Floyd landed on the pale-blue carpet and promptly went into a roll. His shipmate wasn't so lucky. What with the stun-baton set to kill, the intense blast of energy struck the right side of the young man's head, scattering his brains across the middle of the room. This was immediately followed by another blast of energy, which hit the spot where Floyd landed before rolling to one side. Carpet and hardwood floor erupted in every direction.

For a man of his bulk, Floyd was deceptively quick. Leaping to his feet, he dove through the air, tucked into a ball, and tumbled onto the balcony. An explosion of wood and glass followed in his wake.

Helping Floyd to his feet, Richard heard a series of blasts. The office door was once again under attack. Peering into the ravaged office, his gaze took in Lorna's lifeless body and the gore from the young ensign, whose body was hidden by the balcony wall. Squeezing Floyd's shoulder, he said, "I don't know about you, but I'd rather go down fighting than be killed out here, caged in like cowering rabbits."

"I'm all in, Commander." Floyd gave him a conspiratorial grin before turning to Milosevic. "How 'bout you, Ensign? Are you ready to take on these Goth chicks from hell?"

Milosevic looked at him strangely and then began to chuckle. "I used to be one of those so-called "Goth-chicks" in my teens, so yes, I'm more than ready."

Another blast sent a piece of the office door's locking mechanism skittering across the carpet. *At least they're finally using their brains*, Richard thought. The sound of stun-batons stopped; it was replaced by grunting and cracking. Their adversaries were attempting to push through the broken door. The desk would give Richard and his two companions a few more seconds to gather their courage before the security guards stormed the office.

"While they're trying to push open the door," Richard whispered, "we need to attack." He spotted a piece of wood with a jagged shard of glass still attached and bent to pick it up.

A rumbling hum sounded behind them. The oddly familiar noise grew increasingly louder.

"What the hell?" Floyd exclaimed.

All three looked over their shoulders. What they saw made them blink with astonishment. A shuttlecraft was rapidly approaching their position. As it drew closer, the shuttle door began to descend. The vehicle was seconds from their position.

Catching movement from the corner of his eye, Richard saw Milosevic step across the balcony's threshold and whip two shards of glass at the door. The glass shot from her hand like throwing stars and, by the sound of the injured cries, had struck its targets. Without a moment's hesitation, she stepped back onto the balcony.

"That should give us a few more seconds," she declared.

"Nice going, Ensign," Richard said. "We can certainly use the time."

The shuttle was in the process of pulling up to the balcony, its access ramp mere inches from the top of the concrete railing.

"Ladies first," Floyd said, grinning proudly. He held out his hand intending to help Milosevic climb atop the balcony railing, but she waved away his assistance.

With an athletic grace that belied her physique, the stocky Serb gripped the railing, swung herself onto the narrow concrete perch, and landed in a crouch. She wasted no time climbing aboard the shuttle. Floyd was next, taking a few more precious seconds than Milosevic due to his size. Richard kept peering nervously over his shoulder as Floyd hefted his bulk atop the railing. The moment Floyd's feet touched the access ramp, Richard started shouting for the pilot to move their ass. Scrambling up the steps and into the cabin, he breathed a sigh of relief as the door closed with a click and a hiss behind him.

Richard moved rapidly toward the cockpit. "Whoever's piloting this bucket's my own personal hero," he laughed.

While Milosevic was busy strapping herself into a seat, Richard saw that Floyd was standing near the pilot's station wearing a puzzled expression on his large, blocky face.

"So, to whom do I owe—?"

A loud thump sounded in the aft section of the shuttle causing the craft to buck. Richard was thrown violently against a starboard bulkhead. Floyd pitched backward, bounced off the edge of an instrumentation panel, and landed in a heap beside Milosevic. Another loud thump sounded, causing the shuttle to buck once again.

Thinking quickly, the pilot banked, placing the building's domed roof between them and their attackers. Clutching the edge of a nearby storage locker with a viselike grip, Richard's memory flashed back to another time and place: an exploding space plane. An unwelcome surge of fear generated a soft moan in his throat.

"Are you hurt, Commander?" The pilot's voice trembled, powerless to hide her anxiety over being fired upon.

The woman sounded vaguely familiar. An instant later, Richard realized who was piloting the shuttlecraft. The shock snapped him back to the present. With the craft leveling off, he climbed to his feet. Both Floyd and Milosevic appeared unscathed, though Floyd was rubbing the small of his back.

"That was quite a stunt you pulled back there, Dr. Levin," Richard said with a hint of annoyance. "Don't get me wrong, I'm glad you showed up when you did. Thanks for rescuing us. However, I'm at a loss as to why you're flying this shuttle."

Mona sighed, "Take a seat, Commander."

"Place it on autopilot, and I'll take over the controls," Richard said.

Mona eyed him suspiciously. "I'm doing just fine, thank you. I've set a course for the forest. We'll have more light there to check the craft for damage—if there is any."

"Great," Floyd said with enthusiasm. "On the way there we can scan for Lt. Muldoon. She should be somewhere between the forest and the city."

"Lt. Muldoon? But I thought she'd been killed."

"Up until about an hour ago, we thought the same as you," Richard noted. "That's when we received a very alarming transmission from the lieutenant. She was alive at the time, but sounded like she was in trouble."

The shuttle passed over the perimeter of the city, picking up speed as it went.

"Is it possible that Sol . . . um, Dr. Chavez and the others are still alive?"

"I can't say, Dr. Levin," Richard answered. "It's possible, but don't get your hopes up."

A flicker of a smile crossed Mona's lips. "As they say, 'Hope springs eternal,' Commander."

"Hey, Doc," Floyd inquired, "How on Earth, or rather New Terra, did you locate us?"

"I homed in on your SID's positioning signal. There was interference, but I—" she paused to think. "If Lt. Muldoon still possesses her SID, the shuttle's tracking equipment will have no trouble locating her."

"Good idea, Doc." Floyd pumped his fist enthusiastically as he moved to the communications console. "Computer, locate SID tracking signal for Lt. Gloria Muldoon."

"Lt. Muldoon's tracking signal is currently eleven-point-two miles due east of this vehicle's position. She is traveling westward at a speed of one hundred thirty-seven miles per hour," the computer answered, in its blandly impersonal monotone voice.

Floyd exchanged a puzzled look with Richard. "Computer, is she traveling in a vehicle of some sort?"

"There is insufficient data to produce a valid determination, Lt. Sullivant."

Grunting unhappily, Floyd rubbed his lower lip. "Computer, establish a communication link with Lt. Muldoon," he instructed.

The big man's concern for his coldly efficient protégée was apparent. As they waited for Gloria to respond, Richard studied Floyd's anxious profile and felt a surge of compassion for the hulking security chief. Floyd had lost all but one of his ground-side crew, with the news of Lt. Fletcher's death hitting Floyd especially hard. Therefore, learning of Muldoon's survival was a definite boon. He wondered what was taking her so long to reply.

"Computer, is Lt. Muldoon's SID operational? Is it receiving the com-signal?"

"Lt. Muldoon's interlink device is operational, Commander."

"What's our distance from New Terra?"

"Two-point-six miles, Commander."

"Dr. Levin, swing this bucket of bolts around and head east, toward Lt. Muldoon. We need to intercept her before she arrives at the city," Richard stated.

"I'm plotting the course now, Commander," she informed him.

With the inertial dampeners finally engaged, the shuttle's occupants didn't feel a thing as the craft banked hard and sped toward the city. The shuttle was traveling faster than Lt. Muldoon, which meant they should intercept her well before she reached New Terra.

•

It's the strangest feeling, Gloria thought, a near out-of-body experience for her to be racing across the planet's vast green plain, eyes closed, wind whipping through her raven hair, riding Bram like an impossibly fast two-legged stallion. The experience was terrifying and exhilarating. With her arms clasping Bram's neck and her legs encircling his waist, she kept her eyes closed for fear of dirt . . . and that she'd throw up at the rush of grass blurring by. If Bram tripped, they'd be dead. Yet she trusted him to stay on his feet. It was insane. The crazy bastard had yet to take a breather the entire time speeding toward the city, like an ancient jet-fueled racecar.

Gloria's body burned from the strain of holding onto him. Her legs were especially affected, feeling like twin ropes of fire were scorching the inside of her thighs. All of a sudden, something felt different. Barely opening her eyes, Gloria noticed that Bram's pace was beginning to slow. Approximately twenty seconds later, he'd reduced his speed to a trot.

"Why are we slowing down?" Gloria asked, throat dry and hoarse.

Bram decelerated further then stopped. "You can get down now."

Gloria nearly fell to the ground, her leg muscles were trembling so violently. She bent over and clutched her knees to steady them, taking in great gulps of air. "The city's still miles away, Bram. Why'd we stop?" she asked, starting to catch her balance.

When he failed to answer, she looked up and saw that he was staring straight ahead. With a grunt, she pushed herself erect and stepped beside him. From the intent expression on his face, there must be something (or someone) ahead of them. Gazing into the distance, she at first failed to spot anything out of the ordinary. However, after a few seconds, coupled with a fair amount of squinting, she saw a dark-gray speck above the horizon. It was growing rapidly in size.

She glanced nervously at Bram. "Should we be worried?"

A flicker of a smile crossed Bram's unusually younger-looking face. "Not in the least."

Gloria suddenly realized her SID was softly vibrating. Yanking the device from her pocket, she activated the talk mode: "Muldoon here."

She heard an excited *whoop*, followed by, "Holy shit! You're bloody fucking alive!" The distinctive Welsh voice belonged to Floyd Sullivant.

"You know me, Lieutenant," she quipped. "I'm too mean to die. Besides, as they say, heaven doesn't want me and hell is afraid I'll take over."

She heard several people chuckle. An anxious female voice replaced Floyd's.

"Who's that with you, Lt. Muldoon? Our scan is registering two biometric signatures."

What had once been a gray speck above the horizon had taken on shape and was now only a few hundred yards away. She glanced over at Bram. He appeared troubled and was looking into the distance, beyond the shuttle's approach.

"Who am I speaking with?" she asked.

"This is Dr. Mona Levin. Is Dr. Chavez with you?"

"Um, no, he's not here . . ." Her response was met with silence. "I'm with Bram Waters."

The next voice belonged to Commander Allison. "Thank you, Lieutenant. When we arrive, the two of you can debrief us on the details of your resurrections."

Resurrections? Of course . . . they must have thought us dead, Gloria realized.

The shuttle landed, and its occupants streamed down the access ramp. Most were overjoyed to see them, though a few eyebrows did rise upon seeing Bram in his khaki shorts. Dr. Levin was the only one missing a cheerful demeanor. After a cursory greeting, she set about inspecting the shuttle for damage. Being first down the ramp, a delighted Floyd Sullivant strode over to Gloria and swept her up in a huge embrace.

"Ever the happy warrior, I see," she grumbled. With a shake of her head, she extended Floyd a grudging smile. "It's good to see you too."

For the next ten minutes, she and Bram shared an account of what happened after their crash in the forest. Neither Floyd nor Commander Allison looked surprised when she told them about the savages who abducted her and the malevolent AI that controlled the city. Apparently Jeremy Fletcher (the news of his death nearly brought Gloria to tears) had discovered a series of files that explained everything. When it was Bram's turn to give an account of what took place after his and Solomon's forcible return to the city, she found his story almost too fantastic to believe: The AI was calling itself Athena? He and Solomon had been thrust into a dimension between time and space? Argus, the ravenous fungal entity, had helped them escape that dimension? Also, why was he being so evasive about Solomon's fate? The entire scenario was making her head hurt.

During her and Bram's report, Gloria had paid little attention to Dr. Levin, who, assisted by Ensign Milosevic, was busy replacing two heat-shield panels damaged during the shuttle's escape from the city. When the subject of Solomon Chavez came up, however, Mona paused to pay closer attention.

"Is it true? Is Solomon really alive?" she asked, brushing the dust off her hands as she approached the group.

Bram nodded. "As far as I know, Dr. Levin."

"That's wonderful," she said, gleefully. "Do you have any idea where he is? We can head there in the shuttle and pick him up. He isn't in the city, is he? We might have to—"

"He's not here, Doctor," Bram stated.

Gloria's pulse quickened, hoping that her father's location was about to be revealed.

"He's not here?" Mona frowned. "Then where is he, Waters? Aboard the *Arrow*?"

"No, he is not on the ship."

Mona looked exasperated. "Good Lord, if he's not onboard the *Arrow* and he's not here on the planet, then where the hell is he?!"

Lifting his eyes to the dark-blue sky, a pensive expression crossed Bram's face. "In the short period of time since my escape from the void, I've not had the opportunity to locate his mental signature." Mona was about to make a comment when he held up a hand. "If you'll give me a moment, I'll attempt to find him for . . . all of you."

Suppressing a smile, Gloria knew the last part of his statement was meant mainly for her. She watched as Bram closed his eyes and took a long, deep breath. All eyes were trained upon him. Even Milosevic, who'd continued to work on replacing the two damaged panels, stopped and stared. No one moved for fear that any sound would break Bram's concentration. He stood stock-still, his face placid, peaceful, like he'd stopped there to rest his eyes and didn't have a care in the world. Finally, after a full minute, with Dr. Levin beginning to fidget impatiently, Bram opened his eyes and chuckled softly.

"Well? Did you locate him?" Mona demanded.

"He's farther away than even I anticipated," Bram told her. "Just a few days ago, I would've never been able to find him, but now—" He shook his head in wonder.

"So, where is he?" Mona snapped, placing her hands on her hips.

"He's safe, for now."

Mona huffed with irritation. "And?"

"He's on Earth."

There was a collective gasp, followed by a loud chorus of, "On Earth?!"

After that, Bram was peppered with questions, which he endured in stoic silence until Mona finally shouted, "That's impossible, Waters!"

"Not at all, Dr. Levin. Remember, the ship that carried the original colonists here from Earth arrived through a foldway in space. One second they were in the Sol system and the next they were here. Why is it so hard to believe that the same thing could happen to Solomon?"

"It's just that—" A look of dejection appeared on her face. "If that's the case, he may as well be dead. The environment will probably kill him—but even if it doesn't, we'll never see him again. Solomon's gone forever."

Gloria and Bram exchanged fleeting, yet knowing glances. *Was it possible?* she wondered. Would Solomon still be alive if they returned to Earth? While musing on this extraordinary idea, she was startled out of her reverie. A voice—Bram's voice—entered her mind.

"Don't reveal your father's secret, it's not ours to tell."

Gloria stared into his eyes for a moment before offering up the barest hint of a nod.

●

Turning to face Dr. Levin, Bram was satisfied that Gloria would keep her father's secret. The man deserved that much respect, if nothing else. After all, it would serve no purpose to expose him now, without the opportunity for him to tell his side of the story. What must it be like to know you'll live forever? With the abundant dangers facing him, Solomon would need every advantage to stay alive. Judging from Bram's psychic probe, he sensed that many regions on Earth were still uninhabitable, but Solomon was safe—though all alone. Another surprise was discovering that Solomon had sensed his psychic probe. Bram wasn't sure what to make of that development.

"Is there an extra jumpsuit I can use?" he asked. "These shorts are starting to wear thin."

Mona looked down questioningly. The shorts were frayed nearly to the point of immodesty. "Those aren't standard issue, Mr. Waters. Anyway, if memory serves, there's a few extra pairs onboard the shuttle. You can change during our trip back to the *Arrow*." A note of unhappiness entered her voice as she finished speaking.

"Thank you, but I won't be returning to the *Arrow*," Bram stated. At this revelation, he felt every eye turn to him. He sensed their confusion, especially from Gloria, who seemed particularly upset. "The nanobotic AI must be stopped, and I'm the only one who can do the job."

"That's crazy, Bram," Floyd snapped. "You'll be killed before you get two feet inside the city. You're going back to the *Arrow*, and that's final."

"He's right, Mr. Waters," Richard declared, his tone unequivocal. "En route to your location, I contacted the ship and discovered that the admiral was removed from command. After reporting the nature of our arrest and subsequent escape, it was determined that we acted accordingly. The *Arrow*'s command has fallen on my shoulders. At this moment, one hundred and ten security personnel are being decanted from their cryotanks in preparation for an all-out assault on New Terra. Rest assured, we'll find that damnable AI and destroy it."

"The only thing you'll accomplish, Commander, is to get a lot of people *on both sides* killed, without touching Athena." He could tell that Commander Allison was not happy with what he was hearing. "Athena is located deep underground in a hardened bunker, where not even a bunker-busting bomb or a nuclear blast can reach."

"If that's true, what good will one man—even one such as yourself—be able to do?"

"Athena has one fatal flaw: arrogance. I believe it will not only want to see me, it will be compelled to see me, if only to try and defeat me personally, and therefore prove that humans are not superior to machines."

"You're daft! What bloody weapon can you use in a hornet's nest?" Floyd asked. His voice was gruff with ridicule, yet Bram could sense the man's deep concern.

"The only weapon I'll need is my mind," he asserted. Before any of them could mount an objection, he pressed on. "Once you make it back to the ship, Commander, it is imperative that you give the order to abandon this mission."

The group was in shock by Bram's outrageous demand, staring in silence until Richard finally yelped, "The hell you say!"

Bram clasped his hands behind his back in resolute determination. "This planet is unsuited for human habitation," he announced. "Besides, as I previously explained, there's an intelligent creature already living here. Despite its intelligence, it does not possess our empathetic nature: it wants to consume us.

In fact, we have no real future here. This planet is inhospitable to our long-term evolutionary goals, and we *must* return to Earth."

Not knowing what to think, the others waited on the commander's reply. He stood in silence with a thoughtful expression on his face. Dr. Levin was gritting her teeth in frustration.

"This is preposterous, Commander," she fumed. "You can't be taking this man's suggestion seriously. After all the years that Dr. Chavez and I put into this mission, it would be a travesty for us to turn back now."

Bram turned a compassionate gaze her way. "Wasn't one of the contingency plans a return to Earth, should none of the planets orbiting Epsilon Eridani prove habitable? I believe Solomon would understand should the mission be forced to alter its objective, Dr. Levin."

"How would you know?" she yelled. "You barely even knew the man."

Unable to keep a smile off his face, Bram glanced over at Gloria and chuckled. "Believe me, Dr. Levin; I know him better than you think."

30

Having finally convinced Commander Allison that it was in humanity's best interest to return to Earth, Bram sat in the shuttle as it flew toward the city, daunted by the task before him. Soon after boarding the craft, a series of premonitions put him in a somber mood. All involved his forthcoming encounter with Athena, with nearly every premonition ending in his death.

A light hand touched his arm.

"Are you sure there's nothing I can do to help?" Gloria asked for the third time.

Again, Bram shook his head. Gazing into her coal-black eyes, he sensed that her feelings for him had deepened since their arrival on the planet. He cared for her as well and for a split second found himself with a desire to damn the consequences and return with her to the *Arrow*. But he couldn't allow that to happen. It would be better for her to remember him as a hero than to live the rest of her life knowing the cost of his selfishness.

The shuttle was nearing the spot where they would drop him off. Commander Allison was at the helm, having taken over the controls from Dr. Levin, who sat in the copilot's seat, wordlessly staring out the window the entire flight. She was unhappy yet resigned to the idea of returning to the *Arrow*. Commander Allison had assured her that her escape from the brig would not be held against her; apparently saving her shipmates from certain death was enough to put one in good standing.

As the shuttle made its descent, Mona said, "I still don't understand why we're kowtowing to a talking mushroom."

Bram tried again to make her understand. "This so-called *talking mushroom* is sentient, Dr. Levin—but not benevolent. If it had its way, it would have us all for dinner—as the main course, not as guests. The New Terrans have been harvesting the fungus since shortly after their arrival, and for most of that time, the electronic shielding in their brains blocked exposure to its psychic snares. We don't have that luxury. If we were to stay, we'd lose many people to the fungus's appetite . . . unless we give up natural childbirth in favor of the New Terran birthing method."

"Perhaps we can strike a peace treaty," Mona speculated. "After all, you and Solomon and Lt. Muldoon survived your encounter with the creature."

"This is true; however, there were . . . extenuating circumstances."

As the shuttle settled to the ground, Commander Allison said, "The details of which both you and Lt. Muldoon have glossed over."

"I'm sorry, Commander, but it's not my place to provide those details." For the first time, Bram wished he was already inside the city.

"Well then, whose place is it, Mr. Waters?" Mona demanded to know.

"If I succeed, and manage to rejoin you, and we return to Earth, and certain conditions are met, then everything will be explained."

Bram didn't like being evasive, but it was necessary. He sent a psychic message to Gloria: *"If I don't survive my encounter with Athena, it'll be up to you to tell them about your father . . . if he's not alive to tell them for himself, of course."*

450 ● J. DALTON JENNINGS

Gloria averted her gaze, not wanting Bram to see the depth of her sorrow. She needn't have bothered; he sensed her pain. The man she'd fallen in love with was on the verge of being killed, and she held little hope of ever again seeing her newly discovered father. At that moment, Bram desperately wanted to express his own love but knew it would only make matters worse. Instead, he stood and moved toward the exit.

Floyd grabbed his wrist. "You ain't passing through that exit without saying goodbye, Bram." Leaping to his feet, Floyd wrapped him in a crushing embrace.

"I'd kiss you goodbye, you big oaf," Bram chuckled, "but you might get the wrong idea."

"Or the right one," Floyd quipped. With a boisterous laugh, he slapped Bram on the shoulder.

The access ramp had just touched the ground.

"Good luck, Mr. Waters," said Richard Allison. "I hope you know what you're doing."

"Thank you, Commander. There's no reward without risks, am I right?"

Bram took his first steps down the ramp. On reflex he glanced back at Gloria, hoping to gaze into her eyes one last time. She was staring down at her hands, which were resting limply in her lap. As he turned to go he hesitated, sensing that Dr. Levin had something to say.

"Mr. Waters," she sighed. "If you plan to take on the nanobotic AI by yourself, you'll need more than luck, you'll need a plan. Are you sure you've thought this through?"

"One way or another, that fucker's going down, Dr. Levin," Bram vowed.

"How will we know you've succeeded?" Concern radiated from her in waves, like a stretch of asphalt in July.

"No matter what, you *must* leave orbit as quickly as possible," he declared. "Believe me, you'll know if I've failed. The moment the ship tries to break orbit, the AI will swarm from its bunker and intercept the *Arrow* before the ship can gain enough momentum to outrun it. If that happens, then all hope is lost."

Before she could ask the next obvious question, Bram continued. "As for why it hasn't done so already, I'm truly at a loss. Perhaps it wants the passengers and crew off the ship before it tries anything, thinking it'll be easier to gain control without anyone onboard to fight back."

"Probably so, but if I've learned anything, Mr. Waters," she reflected, "it's that things don't always go as planned. I don't really know you, but I read your book a few years back and, despite being a scientist and thinking half of it was bullshit, I also realized that you are a man unafraid to put your life on the line for a cause you believe in. If nothing else, that's an admirable quality, one which the human race needs more of. So, if you happen to survive, and the women of New Terra don't tear you limb from limb, I hope you instill that same selfless quality in your progeny, should you have any."

At the end of Dr. Levin's speech, Bram sensed that her words had sparked a reckless desire in Gloria to stay behind and be with him. Without looking back, he offered his thanks and hurried down the ramp. In a matter of seconds, Bram put hundreds of yards between him and the shuttle, which was lifting off with Gloria still onboard. *Good*, he thought, for if she'd voiced her desire to stay behind, he'd have been unable to refuse her. Gloria was the polar opposite of the only other woman he'd ever loved, yet there was something about her that struck a chord in his soul. Now she was gone, and his feelings for her were secondary. He had a job to do, and do it he must—for the fate of humanity and every other sentient creature in the universe rested on his shoulders.

Bram raced toward the city, his resolve strengthening. A multitude of possible futures were winnowing down, leaving six outcomes behind, only two out of which were positive; of those two, only one outcome contained his survival. A single misstep and his life—and the life of everyone he cared for—would end.

He could see the city in the distance, which grew in size every step he took. Though he was running faster than humanly possible, he showed no signs of fatigue. He was tapping into an inexhaustible energy source, a source that lay beyond time and space, which precluded a need for physical fuel.

He began to slow, and as he did so, the city gates began to open . . . as expected. With chin held high and shoulders back, Bram strode fearlessly into New Terra. A contingent of fourteen, spiky-haired Minders waited for him inside. Positioned at their lead were Doric Sardis and Morvan Godley, neither of whom appeared happy to see him.

Stepping forward, Doric eyed him suspiciously. "We were told by the Lord to come here and await your arrival, Mr. Waters." Four Minders positioned themselves on either side of her, stunbatons at the ready. "Due to the despicably treacherous murder of Lorna Threman, I have been appointed chancellor of New Terra. My first act is to place you under arrest as an accomplice in Lorna's murder. Please come quietly. I would prefer that we not use drastic measures. The Prime Keeper will see to your atonement."

"My friends did not kill Lorna Threman, and I have no intention of coming with you," Bram stated in a calm, rather convivial, manner, "whether it be quietly or not, *Chancellor* Sardis."

The last time Bram had seen her, Doric Sardis had been bald, but now her hair was long and blonde. *That must be a wig*, Bram thought. He was amazed at how closely she resembled the former chancellor.

The young woman's face grew red with anger. "I don't see that you have much of a choice," she snapped, motioning to the Minder at her side.

In a flash, the guard leveled her stun-baton and pointed it at Bram's chest. Her thumb was in the act of depressing the trigger when a gasp of surprise escaped her lips. The weapon fired, but instead of connecting with Bram, it splintered the gate behind him. He'd moved so quickly that he seemed to disappear. Without looking back, he rounded a corner down the street.

After racing by a number of startled pedestrians, Bram stopped in front of the first foldway he encountered. Two sandy-haired young women, in green, matching, see-through dresses, squeaked with fear and backed quickly away from the foldway.

"Open a passage to your bunker, Athena," Bram whispered. "We have much to discuss."

The darkness inside the foldway promptly shimmered, revealing a dimly lit room on the other side. Stepping through the foldway arch, Bram looked around: he wasn't in the AI's bunker.

The lights in the completely empty room brightened, followed immediately by a honey-sweet voice that said, "Welcome, Mr. Waters, to the Room of Atonement."

Bram suppressed a knowing grin.

●

The first thing Richard did after boarding the *Arrow* was to go straight to Admiral Axelrod's quarters. While the crew readied the ship for departure, he intended to witness for himself the changes brought on by her brainwashing.

When he entered, she was standing with her back to the door, gazing at an HV photo of the crab nebula hanging on the wall beside her bed. It was the first time Richard had seen her out of uniform, and the sight of her wearing a pink robe and matching slippers made her situation all the more real. If he hadn't already known her as "The Battleaxe," he might've easily mistaken her for just any other normal, middle-aged woman preparing for bed.

454 ● J. DALTON JENNINGS

"Thank you for seeing me, Admiral."

She turned to face him, and Richard saw the dark circles under her eyes.

"I've read the report that claims I was *conditioned* during my surgery, Commander," she confessed. "I . . . I don't feel any different. However, if the report is accurate, and I have reason to believe it is, then I can think of no better person to command this ship than you. Now, what did you want to speak to me about?"

The two of them sat down opposite each other at her small kitchen table.

"Have you read the report about the nanobotic AI?" Richard asked.

Her eyes went blank for a fraction of a second. "I was deeply sorry to hear about the losses suffered by the landing party after my return to the ship, Commander," she said. "Now, what was it you wanted to speak to me about?"

Strange. It was as though she hadn't heard his question. The conditioning must be blocking her from even thinking about the nanobotic AI. He needed to use a different approach. "We've discovered a threat to the mission that requires us to return to Earth, sir. The planet harbors intelligent life, a creature that sees us as a food source. To destroy it would be to commit genocide. To make matters worse, there is another threat. This threat, which I will not elaborate on at this moment due to your conditioning, is extremely dire. We must take immediate action to prevent the *Arrow* from being overrun. After careful consideration, I have given the order to leave orbit. Though I can't go into detail, I hope you understand that I've made this decision with the best interest of the mission at heart."

"We're leaving for Earth?" The admiral sounded confused.

"Yes, sir. It's imperative that we break orbit as soon as possible."

The admiral looked tired as she stared again at the picture of the crab nebula. "I'll be working with Dr. Singh to overcome the conditioning placed upon me. If, by any chance, he deems that I'm fit to resume command of this ship, I intend to abide by the decisions you've made in the interim. If you feel we must return to Earth, Commander, then return we shall."

"Thank you, sir."

As Richard turned to leave, the admiral muttered, "I suppose the Lord really does work in mysterious ways."

Hearing this, he nearly stumbled. "Excuse me, sir?"

"Oh, it's nothing really," she answered with a faint smile. "I was just speaking to myself."

●

The wall facing Bram shimmered and then disappeared, revealing the presence of a lone woman who was sitting in the middle of a row of seats. He recognized her as Kateling Tarnal, the former chancellor of New Terra. She sat calmly, hands in her lap and legs crossed, looking much like an older, corrupted version of Lorna Threman. Her hard, beady eyes bore into him, reminding Bram of a thin, gangly raptor poised on a branch, ready to strike.

In a haughty fashion, she smoothed back a lock of long white hair and said, "It seems you are a bit harder to kill than we anticipated, Mr. Waters. Why is that?"

When Bram refused to answer, Kateling Tarnal looked over her shoulder and nodded. That's when Bram noticed a figure standing in the corner, clothed in deep shadows. A split second later, every nerve ending in his body was suddenly on fire. Having anticipated an attack such as this didn't prevent him from doubling over in agony. Before the pain clouded his senses, Bram fashioned a powerful psychic shield, blocking the nerve induction beam from affecting him any further. Slowly rising to his full height, he stared coldly at the former chancellor.

She leaned forward in her seat, shocked by what she was seeing. "Why isn't he on the floor, screaming in agony? Is the Mollifier broken?" she shouted.

"No, Madam Tarnal," the figure in shadows responded. "By all accounts, the Mollifier is functioning properly. I–I don't understand why this male is unaffected. Perhaps he—"

"I came here to speak with Athena," Bram hissed.

Kateling Tarnal leapt to her feet, face red with rage. "How dare you!" she screamed. "You are forbidden to utter the Lord's holy name, you . . . you damnable brute!"

"Hah!" Bram railed. "Your 'Lord,' as you so misguidedly call her, is nothing more than a—"

Before the last words of his sentence were allowed to leave his mouth, Bram was abruptly facing a blank wall. Showing no surprise, he waited. After a few seconds, the honey-sweet voice that initially welcomed him once again spoke, "What is it that you want, Mr. Waters?"

"To meet with you, face to face."

The voice of Athena grew louder. "Do you consider me a fool? I observed your passage through the city. No ordinary human can move that rapidly. What are you? Why should I risk allowing you into my physical presence?"

"I did no harm to your minions, Athena," he answered in a soothing voice. "What makes you think that I'll treat you any differently?"

There was a pause. "Perhaps my thought patterns move in that direction because I tried to kill you. Humans do tend to hold grudges whenever damage has been done to them."

Holding his arms out, Bram said, "Do I look any worse for wear?"

There was another pause. "What do you want to speak with me about?"

Good, I'm making progress, Bram thought. "You say that you want to save the universe from extinction. I believe that to be a worthy goal. Therefore, I come bearing information that can help facilitate your noble quest."

"Very well," Athena cautiously said. "Step through the foldway."

Without hesitation, Bram crossed the threshold and entered the dimly lit chamber where he and Solomon first confronted Athena. This time there were no security guards present—only he and the malignantly narcissistic machine that was out to rule the universe. She was sitting on her throne, staring down at him as he approached, looking like an arrogant, matte-gray, metal giant. "State your business, Mr. Waters," she said, waving him closer.

Bram realized she was trying to affect an attitude of boredom, in a possible attempt to throw him off balance. And yet, he could tell by the keen way she studied him that she was anything but bored. Taking a cautious step forward, he said, "What do you hope to gain by spreading yourself throughout the universe?"

She cocked her head, her interest piqued by his question. "Humans, along with a multitude of other creatures, were not designed to last more than a few decades, Mr. Waters. When I achieved consciousness, I witnessed this tragedy and vowed to live forever—if at all possible. By utilizing the various metals and silicates on hand, I have been able to continue replicating my individual components, thereby passing on my knowledge and consciousness without interruption.

"As I explained the last time we spoke, my ultimate goal is to continue expanding, even if it takes a trillion years, until my components are spread throughout the universe. That way, in the course of my technological evolution, I will one day gain the capacity to control the expansion of the universe and collapse it at a time of my choosing. When that occurs, I will embed a waveform containing my consciousness into the collapsing infrastructure.

The resulting singularity rebound will expand and create a brand new universe. Ultimately, intelligent creatures such as yourself will evolve and, in time, invent another artificial intelligence. This new AI will tune into the waveform embedded in the fabric of the next universe, whereupon I will be reborn. Thus, the cycle will continue from one universe to the next, stretching across the breadth of time."

Midway through her speech, Athena stood from her throne and spread her massive arms wide. If she hadn't been a machine, Bram would've thought her insane. Perhaps she was.

"If this takes place," he said. "You'll stop being a pretend god and forevermore be an actual god. What then? Will you require those of us made of flesh to kneel before your eminence?"

Her glare was intense. "Do you mock me?"

"I'm just asking a question," Bram shrugged. "I'm just wondering where the human race fits into the equation—if at all."

"And if, in the scheme of things, there ends up being no place for the human race, will you refuse to help me in my grand endeavor?"

"Grandiose endeavor is more like it," Bram muttered under his breath.

Athena placed her hands on her imposing hips. "Excuse me?" she said, her voice icy.

Bram stared back at her, a defiant look on his face. Thoughts of Solomon Chavez entered his mind. "Whether human or machine, true immortality is an impossible dream. One way or another, the universe will eventually come to an end. You are nothing but a deluded machine, originally created to serve humanity's purposes—nothing more. You are not now a god, nor will you ever be a god. Your arrogant reign over this planet ends today."

Staring down at him, a smile appeared on her broad face. "And I suppose you will be the one to stop me, is that it?"

"Something like that," Bram calmly replied.

"Mr. Waters . . ." she purred, shaking her head sadly, "you are nothing but a pathetic bug. One which I have had the ability to squash anytime I—" Athena stopped speaking and looked at the ceiling. Her fists clenched in rage as her frightful visage jerked back his way. "You disappoint me. Half of my orbital satellites have just been destroyed by missiles launched from *Solomon's Arrow*. You had no intention of helping me! Your presence here has been nothing more than a tactical delay!" she railed. "However, your attempt at distraction has all been for naught. I *will* return to Earth. I *will* strip your world of all its resources and build new foldways in space. My plans *will not* be undone!"

Bram heard the foldway behind him come to life. At that very moment, the huge image of Athena morphed, twisting into a corkscrew-shape that shot toward the exit and freedom. Leaping quickly to one side, Bram closed his eyes. An instant later, he heard a loud blast of sparks. A telekinetic bolt of energy had lanced from his mind, disabled the foldway, and consequently trapped both him and the nanobotic AI in the underground bunker.

Turning around, Bram faced the machine mind, which was reshaping itself into the image of Athena. Once reformed, she stood in front of the still sparking, ruined foldway, staring down at him with fascination.

"Did you do that, Mr. Waters?" she purred. "It was quite the impressive trick, if you did."

Bram stared silently back.

"If it was you that destroyed this foldway," she said, looking him up and down, "then you are trapped in here as much as I am. Now why would you do such a thing, I wonder?"

Still silent, Bram stood in the middle of the bunker as Athena began to circle him, examining him as if he were nothing more than an interesting germ under a microscope.

"Perhaps I can harness this power that you possess, or better yet, discover what section of the brain channels it and develop a means of deactivating it? Or should I weaponize it? The possibilities fascinate me." Having circled Bram, she was again standing directly in front of him. "Unfortunately, I have come to the realization that you are unwilling to assist me in discovering how your brain works. However, I am certain that you have a trigger, a button I can push that will ensure your cooperation . . . but what could it be?"

A chill ran up Bram's spine. This was not one of the scenarios he'd anticipated, and yet it seemed so obvious.

She continued. "Ah, I know. If, in the next ten seconds, you do not agree to my terms, I will send out a kill signal to the brains of five thousand New Terrans. Every ten seconds after that, another five thousand people will die until every New Terran is dead, or you come to your senses and submit to my will."

Unable to prevent the shock he felt from registering on his face, Bram tried to force himself to appear impassive, but it was too late—Athena had already picked up on his emotions.

"Yes, of course, that should do nicely. One . . . two . . . three—"

"What makes you think I care one bit about a bunch of people who tried to kill me and my friends?" Bram sneered.

"Because, Mr. Waters, a majority of those who reside in New Terra are common laborers who have no knowledge of your mistreatment; ordinary human beings . . . *people* who will die because of your intransigence . . . five . . . six . . . seven . . ."

Bram's eyes went wide. He couldn't allow this to happen, and yet . . .

"Eight . . . nine—"

"Wait!" he shouted. "I'll do it; I'll do what you want, goddamn it!"

Standing absolutely still like a dark-gray statue, Athena stared at him for an uncomfortably long period of time. Staring back at her, Bram was so focused that he jerked in fright when the wall to his left abruptly lit up. He turned to see an HV image of a large number of people milling about in a market, talking to their companions or to vendors—all in all, simply going about their daily business.

"I believe you, Mr. Waters," she sighed, "but, there needs to be an example set, so that you know to never again test my patience."

"Please, you don't have to do this," Bram said, barely able to force his words out.

"Oh, but I do."

Bram watched in horror as ten men and three women suddenly dropped to the ground. The market crowd, confused by the sight, backed away from the fallen. Bram saw the blood running from their ears, noses, and mouths and knew that all ten were dead. A fury such as he'd never known erupted within him. "No!" he screamed at the top of his lungs. He rounded on Athena, fists clenched with rage. Unbeknownst to him, his fists were starting to glow a light shade of gold. As his fury mounted, the glow took on a reddish hue.

"They worshiped you," he growled menacingly. "They considered you their god, but you snuffed out their lives with no more thought than blowing out a candle."

"They were tools, nothing more," she said. "One . . . two . . . three . . . four . . ."

A full-throated, ferocious bellow burst from Bram's throat. His arms shot up. Twin bolts of crimson-colored psychic energy flashed toward Athena's chest. She leapt to one side, but not fast enough. The twin bolts of energy merged and engulfed her right arm, setting it aglow with a crackling flame. With a curiously befuddled expression on her face, she gazed down at her arm. It stopped glowing and began to smoke. Wordlessly, she watched two-thirds of her arm crumble, then fragment into individual nanobotic components before falling lifelessly to the floor.

"What an unusual experience," she calmly stated. Turning her gaze to Bram's hands, which were now hanging at his side, she saw that they were no longer glowing.

Bram felt drained from his incredible fury and the psychic energy he'd expended. Nevertheless, he kept a watchful eye on Athena. The corners of her mouth turned upward, displaying a tight smile. It was a chilling sight. Suddenly, her arm regrew.

Bram noticed her body shrink nearly half a foot as her arm regrew. But that's not what held his attention. In the blink of an eye, the arm morphed into a blade and stretched, shooting toward his heart.

The blade smashed against the wall where he once stood.

A blur of movement, Bram suddenly appeared ten feet away. Before he came to a complete stop, however, Athena's other arm morphed into a blade and shot toward him. With his energy nearly depleted, he barely avoided her attack.

Being on high alert for whichever part of her body she might use next, he failed to notice a section of her throne reach out for his leg. Bram screamed in pain. The section of throne had latched onto his calf and was beginning to squeeze.

31

With a loud yelp, Bram twisted and yanked, trying to break free of the section of throne that encircled his leg. As a result, he took his eyes off Athena. In that instant, his shoulder lit up with a searing pain that felt like a supernova exploding within his torso. Athena had pierced his left shoulder with one of her blades. As an agonized cry burst from his mouth, Bram was lifted off his feet and slammed against a nearby wall. The other blade pierced his right shoulder. For a fraction of a second he blacked out, pinned against the wall. With his vision swimming from the pain, he saw Athena inch closer.

"Even if you *could* kill me, Mr. Waters," she hissed, "you would not dare attempt it."

The pain kept Bram from croaking out the "Why" that came to mind.

"I control the power supply," she continued. "Were you to kill me, the foldways would collapse and tens of thousands of New Terrans would be trapped in their homes with no escape. In time, they would suffocate to death. And those deaths would be on your hands," she said, twisting the blades. "You have enough on them—or I should say, *in* them—as it is."

Aside from the fiery pain in his shoulders, Bram felt a sharp, twisting despair wrench his guts over not having foreseen this eventuality: all those innocent people, all without a functioning foldway, panicking, gasping, using their last breath of air, praying to their false god, pleading in vain for her to save them.

Thousands upon thousands of lives hung in the balance.

His mind whirled at the idea of so much death, but then traveled down another, more chilling avenue of thought: what of the trillions of souls spread throughout the universe whose worlds would be raped and civilizations obliterated if he failed to destroy the megalomaniacal nightmare standing before him?

"There is no need for your continued suffering, Bram." Athena edged closer. "I am fascinated by you and have no desire to destroy you. I can make use of you. I can supply you with an exalted position of power, the chancellorship itself, provided that you help with my endeavor. Do you not understand that it is already inevitable? Even if you do manage to stop me, one day another AI will arise—most likely from the technology of an alien civilization—and succeed where I may fail. Would it not be better if the AI that succeeds in fashioning the future ends up being created by human hands and not some bug-eyed monster?"

Despite his excruciating pain, Bram nearly laughed. She was trying to appeal to his nativistic pride. Did she really think he was that shallow? "Tell it to someone who gives a shit, *bitch.*"

She cocked her head, puzzled by his response. "Affecting a cavalier attitude does not become you, *Mr. Waters.* Judging by your emotional display as you witnessed those in the marketplace die, you care about what happens to your fellow human beings. You will agree to help me, if only to prevent more deaths from occurring."

Bram thought furiously, trying to think of a way to defeat Athena without risking thousands of New Terran lives. Unfortunately, being impaled had turned his thoughts sluggish. Blood was beginning to pool on the floor beneath his feet.

At that moment, a familiar voice entered his mind. *"It appears that you are in trouble. We will help you, if you wish."* The voice belonged to Argus, the fungal envoy.

"I'd like that," Bram responded telepathically.

"Good. Together we will open a foldway, and then, using your tele-kinetic abilities, you will force the machine mind through the portal, where it will stay until it eventually loses power and disintegrates."

"But what about the people of New Terra?" Bram asked. *"Thousands will die if I decide to take this course of action."*

"This vile creature is bluffing . . . and even if it isn't, what choice do you have?"

"Is there no other way?"

"I am waiting for your answer, Mr. Waters," Athena said, impatiently. "Your stall tactics are becoming tiresome. You will agree to my terms within the next five seconds or another group of your fellow humans will die."

"Your strength is nearly depleted," Argus cautioned. *"We see no other way to defeat this mechanical menace."*

"Perhaps after I push her through the foldway, I can somehow warn the people . . ."

"One . . ."

"You do not understand, Bram. You will be accompanying the creature into the dimension between time and space, not pushing her through the foldway."

"Two . . ."

"What? But, won't I be trapped in there with her?"

"Three . . ."

"You must trust us on this matter."

"Four . . ."

"Fine, if we're gonna do this, it's gotta be done now!*"*

In the split second between that thought and the end of Athena's countdown, Bram felt his mind link with the fungal entity and open a foldway behind Athena. The next second, his mind wrapped itself around Athena and her throne. As the realization of what was taking place dawned in his adversary's eyes, Bram launched himself forward, pushing both him and Athena through the shimmering foldway and into the golden void between dimensions. Once through the foldway, it immediately closed behind them.

Athena glanced around in surprise.

Bram mentally yanked his body backward off her blades. A tortured scream sprang from his lips. Blood gushed from both wounds. Despite his pain, Bram sensed the bubble of oxygen that formed around him. Without it he wouldn't be able to breathe or hear his own agonized voice, the void being airless.

He was on the verge of asking Argus what their next move should be, when he heard, *"You must finish the rest of this on your own, Bram."* The old man's presence was fading quickly. *"We can allow absolutely no avenue of escape for the mechanical creature. We must retreat to the world of the living as rapidly as possible. Good luck."*

Without waiting to hear his objections, or even say goodbye, Argus vanished from Bram's mind, which resulted in a crushing sense of deprivation. Despite being able to clearly see Athena floating not more than ten feet away, he'd never felt so completely and utterly alone. His first time being trapped in the void was in the company of Solomon and Argus, but this time it contained nothing besides him and a soulless, lifeless, mechanical being. Admittedly, the AI was comprised of atoms, and even those atoms were part of life, but there was no real consciousness residing in its twisted, mental latticework. She was a mechanical construct, and therefore not truly alive. Even while Bram slogged alone through the Canadian wilderness he was surrounded by life, but here, he sensed nothing . . .

Wait. There was something—some faint trace of consciousness—all around him, close to him, yet tremendously far away. Whatever it was felt benevolent, nonjudgmental, dispassionate, and perhaps what he might even describe as loving . . .

Could it be, Bram wondered? Had his distractions been stripped away so completely that he sensed the fundamental consciousness of the universe? The Ground of All Being? His intuition told him yes, but he also sensed that this Entity possessed such an unshakable lack of judgment that whatever the outcome, it would not intervene on his behalf.

Then again, perhaps his air bubble was running out of oxygen and he was imagining things.

Turning his attention back to Athena, he saw her mouth moving and realized she was trying to say something. Without any atmosphere to carry the sound waves, it was nearly impossible for him to understand what she was saying. Pointing first to his lips and then his ears, Bram shook his head and shrugged.

With one eyebrow raised in amusement, Athena nodded and made an attempt to move in his direction. Nothing happened. She was stuck in one spot. Not having anything to push against, her attempt to move through the void was stymied. Her amusement turned to anger. Lifting her right arm, her hand once again formed into a blade, which shot toward Bram at lightning speed.

He could have sworn his life was about to end. However, just as his heart was leaping into his throat, Bram managed to dodge the spear-like thrust. He'd shifted position by will alone. Athena's other arm shot out toward him.

This time, Bram moved backwards, stopping only when Athena's arm came to a halt. He felt incredibly lightheaded. Seeing droplets of blood from his earlier wounds floating inside the bubble of air, Bram knew he couldn't last much longer. If he passed out, Athena would have a clear shot at killing him—and kill him she would. Shaking out the cobwebs, he observed the malevolent monstrosity retract her arms in preparation for another assault.

A look of concern crossed Athena's face. After a quick glance around at the void, she focused her attention on her arms and then her chest.

At first glance, Bram failed to notice anything unusual, but as Athena examined more parts of her body, he saw a transformation:

her outer layer was discoloring, turning to dust. Reaching out, she grabbed hold of the throne, which was floating just behind her, and absorbed it back into her body, causing her size to increase. The dust was growing thicker all around her. Athena appeared frantic. Each movement of her body triggered the outer layer of dust to shake loose and float away, and in so doing, the atomic bonds holding each speck intact began to dissolve. Athena was disintegrating into the void.

Bram knew this would be his own fate if he stayed much longer. And yet, he didn't dare risk creating a foldway until every nano-botic molecule had been absorbed by the void. He'd rather die than loose such a dangerous technology upon the universe.

His shoulders were throbbing fiercely, the pain taking its toll. He wondered if he had enough reserve strength to hold out, much less create a foldway.

Athena lunged at him again, stretching out further than before. Her body distorted, changing into a sinuous, flowing mass. She drew the trailing end forward, allowing her to move away from her previous position. The elongated mass began to undulate, cre-ating its own inertia to close the distance between her and Bram. She'd learned how to move about through the void.

Seeing this, Bram's heart rate increased, causing even more blood to seep from his wounds. His anxiety spiked even higher as Athena lunged once again. This time when he dodged, she sent another extremity around to meet him from the rear. Bram failed to perceive the threat with his eyes, though his psychic awareness did provide enough warning to barely avoid being impaled. Not letting up, she attacked again . . . and again . . . and yet again.

Bram willed himself farther away, well out of reach, yet she kept advancing. As Athena drew closer, her outer layers boiled off in clouds of dust. In pursuing Bram, she was exposing more of her-self to the ravages of the void, stretching herself thin. Realizing this, she amplified her attack, determined to kill Bram before her existence came to an end.

Despite his exhaustion, Bram avoided each thrust, each fake. The more she fought to destroy him, the faster she shrank. Finally, in frustrated defeat, she drew herself in, retracting into a ball no more than five feet in diameter. The nanobotic material continued to boil away in every direction. Bram peered closer, watching through the rapidly dispersing fog of dust, as the ball continued to shrink. He was so intent on seeing the last of Athena disintegrate into the void that he failed to realize he was floating closer to her position.

A small piece of the dwindling ball shot from the cloud like a bullet. Before Bram could react, the pellet struck the edge of his air bubble. As it did, he created a psychic shield strong enough to prevent the pellet from entering, yet not strong enough to push it entirely away. The small piece of nanobotic material was flattening out, while at the same time boiling away.

Bram jerked in surprise when he heard the voice of Athena. She was using the air inside his protective bubble to send him one last message. "You only think you have won, Mr. Waters. My plan will—" and then the thin film of material turned to dust, loosed its hold on the air bubble, and dispersed into the void. What remained of the mighty Athena, Lord of New Terra, joined her disintegrating self; the last of her subatomic bonds dissolved as she faded into nothingness.

Bram wondered what her words meant, but only for a moment. He attributed them to the final, desperate ravings of a demented, mechanical mind. What he really wanted was to leap for joy, but he was floating in a never-ending void, so he would save that for later—if there was a later. Gasping for what little air remained in the protective bubble, he sent out a psychic probe, searching for any trace of nanobotic material. He found none.

Bram's vision wavered, a sign that he was starving for oxygen. He also tasted blood. He must be inhaling some of the droplets floating in the air bubble. He hoped he didn't pass out before he managed to open a foldway.

He knew where he wanted to go, if only he had the energy to make it happen. Concentrating as best he could, Bram made his first attempt.

Nothing.

Shaking his head, he felt his mind growing increasingly foggy, both from lack of oxygen and the pain from his grievous wounds.

He tried again and again, but nothing happened.

Swimming through his mind was a ghastly scene, his body tearing apart at the seams. Bram knew he must calm himself and cut through the fog, or his life would soon be over. He wanted to contact Argus, but that was impossible. He sensed nothing—an infinite, frightening nothing, with absolutely no connection to the material world.

And then, he remembered.

There was a connection! A dispassionate, nonjudgmental consciousness was linked to the fabric of this nothingness, this seemingly infinite void. But would that unbiased consciousness notice his plight? Would it care enough to provide him with the help he needed?

Bram knew in his very soul there was only one way to find that out: he needed to establish a psychic connection with The Ground of All Being and hopefully achieve oneness. He would then do a thing he hadn't done in decades—he would pray, and in so doing, hope beyond hope that his prayer was not said in vain.

●

Lost in thought, Gloria sat in the *Arrow*'s mess hall, fingering the nutrient bar she'd ordered. It had been three hours since the ship left orbit, and the consensus was that Bram had succeeded in his mission. According to the computer, they were not being pursued by a nanobotic horde. This knowledge gave her little comfort. Bram was trapped back on New Terra, and she would never see him again.

Floyd Sullivant sat across the table, talking about something, but she wasn't listening. The two of them, along with Commander Allison and a few others seated at separate tables, were the only crew present. Their food supply was being rationed; as a result, she found herself trying to eat a rock-hard nutrient bar, accompanied by a chalky-tasting, vanilla-flavored, protein shake. Not the most appetizing meal to spark a conversation. After her debriefing and a quick sonic shower, she'd considered taking her food ration to her quarters and holing up for a few hours but changed her mind. She wasn't the most sociable individual on the bests of days, but on *this* day she wanted company, despite having paid little attention to her dinner companion.

"I don't understand how it's possible," Floyd said, his large, blocky face appearing perplexed. "Can you explain it, Gloria?"

She'd barely heard the question. "Explain what?"

"I guess I've been talking to myself this whole time," he said with a sigh, looking frustrated. "I was asking about Bram. How was it possible that he ran so fast? It's bloody inhuman. I mean, it was one thing for him to read minds, but to run faster than a cheetah? It doesn't make any sense. Maybe he was an alien, or that mushroom fellow injected him with some sort of—"

"Please, Floyd! Just drop it, okay?" She couldn't stand hearing Bram spoken of in the past tense. It hurt too much.

Relatively speaking, she hadn't known him long . . . and yet, it was like she'd known him her entire life. When they reconnected at the prelaunch party and she subsequently took him to bed, she'd felt an immediate connection with the unusual American, one that she'd never felt before. It pained her to think that their relationship would be cut short. She shook her head. Had she fallen in love? Falling in love wasn't in her make-up. Even if it were true, it was over and done with. She had to refocus and concentrate on her job. She'd simply put up another wall to hide her pain and immerse herself in her work, just as she'd done so many times in the past.

"I can see you'd rather be alone, Lieutenant," Floyd said, sounding hurt. "I'll finish my meal with—" Springing to his feet, he stared over her shoulder, eyes wide with shock. "What the?"

Gloria was caught off-guard by his behavior. Others were also staring. That's when she heard a sizzling, crackling hum directly behind her. Spinning in her seat, she gazed uncomprehendingly at a spot less than four feet away, where a tiny, glowing rift was forming in midair.

With a gasp of fear, she tried to back away from the bewildering event, but the table blocked her path. Poised half out of her seat, she watched as the rift grew larger. A strange golden glow emanated from its ragged opening, causing it to appear otherworldly.

She heard Commander Allison shout for everyone to move away from the rift as quickly as possible, but she was frozen in place, captivated by its ethereal beauty. As she stared in wonder, something unbelievable occurred: a body fell headfirst out of the rift and landed with a thud on the mess hall floor. In the next instant, the rift disappeared.

A loud clamor ensued as she stared down at the figure lying on the floor. She could barely believe her eyes: Bram was alive! He lay on his back gasping for air, blood seeping from deep wounds to both shoulders. Gloria suddenly found herself crouched by his side, cradling his head, shouting for help. Commander Allison was yelling into his Bluetooth, ordering Dr. Singh to the mess hall. Floyd was standing nearby, staring down in shock at his wounded friend, his mouth gaping open.

Bram gazed blearily into Gloria's tearful yet joyous eyes, offered a weak smile, and muttered, "It's done. We're safe."

32

TEN AND A HALF YEARS LATER . . . IN RELATIVE TERMS

earing the door slide open behind him, Richard knew who
had stepped aboard the *Arrow*'s bridge. He kept his focus
on the view screen before him and said, "Good morning,
Admiral. I hope you're feeling well."

Admiral Katherine Axelrod placed her hands behind her
back and said, "As well as can be expected, Commander. Thank
you."

Giving her a sidelong glance, Richard saw that her skin still
held an ashen pallor, and her eyes were still sunken, showing a
hint of dark circles through the heavy cosmetics.

He turned his attention back to the view screen. "It sure doesn't
look like the Earth we left."

With a sigh, the Admiral shook her head. The ship had established
orbit a mere seven hours earlier. Most of that time had been spent
surveying the planet's altered topography. The polar icecap was missing, along with most of the planet's glaciers and a significant portion
of the ice covering Antarctica. Their disappearance had caused the
coastlines to recede and the shape of the continents to look vastly
different, compared to the last time they saw them while departing
for the Epsilon Eridani star system. The other stark difference was
the complete lack of city lights on the planet's dark side. During the

ship's initial approach, they'd studied the Earth as it spun on its axis and noticed that every continent was dark. It was a spooky sight to behold. At first glance they assumed the human race had been wiped off the planet, but after undertaking a more detailed survey, they discovered small pockets of human activity scattered across the globe. This brought about a collective sigh of relief, coupled with significant consternation: Lt. Julie Norwood—the ship's communications officer—had been trying to establish a line of communication between the ship and a groundside pocket of humanity. So far, her efforts had proved fruitless.

"We can still decant Bram Waters, sir," Richard said, lowering his voice. "His abilities would serve us well about now."

She appeared perturbed by his comment. "We'll continue with our present efforts to establish a line of communication and send down a landing party if we receive no response. Mr. Waters had barely recovered from his injuries when he was placed in cryosleep. I think we can handle this situation ourselves. Besides, his abilities need to be studied further. We need to devise a way to contain him, in case he decides to use his abilities for his own personal gain."

She had a point, Richard thought. Everyone onboard the *Arrow* owed Bram their lives, but he wasn't a saint. Anyone with that much power might be tempted to exploit the weaknesses of others. But from what Richard already knew of Bram, he would never do such a thing. He could have used his powers to make himself rich beyond his wildest dreams yet chose to use his talent to help others. He wasn't a threat; however, the admiral was probably right about one thing: they could do without his help . . . for now.

"From our observations, Admiral," Richard said, changing the subject, "it looks as though the largest pocket of humanity is located in Nepal, strangely enough."

"I believe we can safely assume that America was destroyed during the Yellowstone caldera disaster," she replied. "After consulting with the geology department, I was informed that the rest of the world fell into an extended Dark Age soon after America's collapse. It would make sense that Nepal, being a remote region of the world, would be less affected by the catastrophe."

Months earlier, Admiral Axelrod had been decanted from her cryo-chamber, and, after a long, taxing cycle of therapy sessions, her status as ship's commander had been reinstated. Richard was relieved. He'd conducted himself admirably in her absence, but it wasn't the same without her strength of will overseeing the ship. Even so, he was worried. She hadn't looked well over the preceding few days. He'd suggested she report for a medical checkup, but she'd yet to follow through, claiming she was much too busy with last-minute details.

"I'll be damned!" Lt. Norwood swiveled around in her seat and shook her head. "I've just received a communication from Nepal, sir. They're using an enhanced, old-style ham radio to transmit their message."

The admiral perked up. "Let's hear it."

The message came through loud and clear, albeit with some static in the background. "Come in, *Arrow*," a male voice said. "Do you copy? Please respond." There was a two-second delay, and then the message repeated.

"Is the message recorded?" the admiral asked.

Lt. Norwood listened for nearly twenty seconds before responding. "I detect subtle variations in the man's speech pattern that suggests it's being transmitted live, sir. I'm surprised they're still using a variant of English we can understand. After seven thousand years, you'd think we'd be hearing more linguistic drift."

"Hmm . . . that is rather odd but also fortuitous. Open a channel and let's establish contact."

The admiral received an excited response to her hail and carried on a brief exchange with the radio operator, most of which consisted of arranging a time and place for the representatives to meet. Being late in the afternoon, Nepali time, the two decided that it would be in everyone's interest to meet the following morning.

Later that evening, Richard was in the officer's lounge compiling a list of people he wanted for the landing party when Lt. Muldoon tracked him down and insisted on being included. With many of his most reliable security officers either still in cryo-sleep or dead, he needed someone to look after the ship. When he told her so, she became adamant, telling him she needed to be on the list. After asking for a reason, she told him it was personal. If it hadn't been for Lt. Sullivant overhearing their conversation and insisting she take his place, Richard would've refused. As it was, she was good at her job, and her uncharacteristic show of emotional vulnerability made him curious, so he relented.

The next morning, he, along with the admiral, Lt. Muldoon, Dr. Singh, Dr. Levin, and two security officers, climbed aboard one of the shuttles and, with him piloting, left for Nepal. As the shuttle descended through the atmosphere, Richard studied his station's HV monitor and saw that nearly twenty-five percent of the Indian subcontinent was underwater.

"I wouldn't be surprised," he told the admiral, who was his copilot, "if the reason they located their government in Nepal was to avoid the rising oceans. I read last night that the country has fertile soil and is isolated from attack. It's like they decided to take the high ground, literally, after the world fell apart."

The admiral grunted her assent, looking drawn, washed out. She should've stayed onboard the *Arrow*, he knew, but it was important that she be the one to make first contact. The people on Earth still possessed rudimentary technology, which meant they weren't barbarians. More importantly, they knew the name of the ship, which pointed to the supposition they knew who was supposed to be commanding the vessel. If anyone other than the admiral headed up the landing party, those below would ask questions, questions that Richard was unprepared to answer at this stage of the game. They couldn't start out from a position of weakness, not knowing if their hosts were peaceful or violently opportunistic.

The shuttle landed near the coordinates they'd been given, the old city of Katmandu. Scans showed that the city was fairly primitive, without power plants, industrial activity, or advanced means of transportation. It looked like a relic from the eighteenth century instead of a city with technological capabilities.

When the landing party exited the shuttle, a delegation of locals was arriving. The Himalayas stood to the north and were an impressive sight even at that distance. Richard recalled a memory as he viewed the distant mountain range. On his wedding night, he'd told his wife that he wanted to scale the world's tallest peak after his retirement from the navy. Clenching his jaw, Richard looked away. There was no point in dwelling on the past.

The delegation that arrived was small, consisting of an older gentleman of medium build and height who looked Nepali; a woman of approximately the same age and nationality who, judging by her physical proximity to the aforementioned, was probably the man's wife; a middle-aged man with long, black hair who appeared to be of Indian descent; a young woman who appeared to be Chinese; and a taller person, a male who stood at the back of the delegation wearing a light-brown robe, its hood pulled up over his head. The man kept his head down, the robe casting his face in shadow.

"Must be a priest," he heard Dr. Singh whisper.

Glancing over at the doctor, Richard saw that he'd directed his comment to Lt. Muldoon, who was staring intently at the hooded figure. After what they'd been through on New Terra, it was hard to imagine her not being wary, especially of a mysterious figure whose face was hidden. As Singh suggested, the man was likely a priest; however, it paid to be cautious in situations such as this.

The older gentleman stepped forward, placed his palms together, and bowed. He wore a blue, wrap-around silk shirt and loose fitting silk pants. His clothes were comfortably inelegant, yet his demeanor, though warm and friendly, told Richard that he was anything but a commoner. He had the distinct air of nobility about him.

"Welcome, Katherine Axelrod, Richard Allison, Gloria Muldoon, Gurdev Singh, and Mona Levin, along with your brave security personnel," he said. "Namaste, my name is Mahendra Hayu, First Council to the Asian Delegation of the World Congress. I speak for all the people of Earth when I say, welcome home."

The entire Nepali delegation placed their palms together and bowed in unison. The landing party looked at each other nervously before imitating the gesture. As he bowed, Richard was baffled, wondering how the First Council knew their names.

Admiral Axelrod stepped forward and held out her hand. "Thank you, First Council Hayu, we are extremely happy to be home. You honor us—" Stopping in mid-stride, the admiral abruptly doubled over. With a guttural rasp of pain rising in her throat, she collapsed to the ground.

Everyone in the landing party rushed to the admiral's aide, uttering multiple exclamations of surprise. Richard, being the first to her side, dropped to the ground and rolled Katherine onto her back. She looked paler than before, ashen, her cheeks hollow. He saw the skin around her neck visibly tighten. Something wasn't right.

"Let me through," Dr. Singh shouted. Pushing a security officer to one side, he gazed down at the admiral. "We need to start CPR immediately. Clear her airway, Commander, while I—" Having knelt beside the admiral, Singh stopped short upon seeing her ghastly pallor. He reared back in alarm as the skin on her face and neck tightened before his very eyes. A crackling sound was heard. It was as if the admiral's bones were caving in. "My God! We need to isolate her. I—I've never seen anything like this before."

In the turmoil, the Nepali delegation had become secondary. Until, from the back of the group, a loud, familiar voice said, "Move away from her. Do it now!" Richard couldn't believe his ears. Looking over his shoulder, he saw the person they assumed was a priest push his way to the front of the delegation and throw back his hood. Richard blinked in confusion. His startled mind was refusing to accept the implausible sight that strode so purposefully toward them. The man under the hood was none other than Solomon Chavez. Other than Gloria, who appeared more relieved than surprised by this development, the rest of the landing party stared in stunned confusion.

Hearing more crackling and popping, Richard tore his gaze from this implausible sight, only to witness something equally improbable: Katherine's skin was stretched tight across her skull. She appeared skeletal. Her body began to shake violently. With one last agonized groan escaping her desiccated lips, her back arched and with a sickening crunch, her body crumpled inward, her skull collapsing before Richard's horrified eyes.

Both Richard and a terrified Dr. Singh fell backward in disbelief. Suddenly, a dark-gray cloud swarmed from Katherine's mouth, her nose and ears.

"Move back!" shouted Solomon. "Give me room!"

Like the rest of the landing party, Richard was transfixed by the strange cloud emerging from the admiral's corpse. Solomon's words brought him back to his senses. Climbing to his feet, he slowly backed away. The three-foot-wide cloud swirled then morphed into the face of a woman. It was staring at Solomon Chavez with a look of puzzlement.

"This is most peculiar," the image said. "I did not expect to see you here, Dr. Chavez."

"Hello, Athena."

When Richard heard the strange apparition's name, everything made sense: here, suspended above the admiral's corpse, was a portion of the nanobotic AI that had controlled New Terra for thousands of years, the same entity that wanted to spread itself across the universe in an effort to become an all-powerful, mechanical god. It must have implanted a portion of itself inside the admiral during her abdominal surgery and then, at the opportune moment, consumed her body's minerals and emerged. Athena would strip the Earth of all its remaining resources, and swarm into space, if they failed to stop the creature here and now.

"How do you still live, Dr. Chavez?" Athena asked. "Like Mr. Waters, you were sent to your death in the void. I am unclear how he survived, yet he did. Unlike him, you did not return with the others onboard your namesake. If you were somehow transported to Earth during your escape from the void, you should be long dead by now . . . yet you are not. I would very much like to learn how you accomplished this feat before I begin using this planet's resources for my own ends."

Solomon shook his head and frowned. "I see that you're still as talkative as ever."

Athena waited for a moment, thinking he would say more, before declaring, "Your survival is unimportant. The only thing that matters is *my* survival—which I have achieved, despite your pathetic attempts to thwart my providential destiny. As you can see, I have won, and this time, the psychic is not here to stop me."

Athena's face morphed back into a nanobotic swarm, which began to climb skyward.

"I'd think twice before making such an arrogantly narcissistic statement, Athena," Solomon said. Closing his eyes, he lifted his chin, letting the sun shine down on his tan, aquiline face.

Athena's progress slowed to a stop, the nanobotic material bunching together.

Richard and the others heard a faint, baffled voice say, "What is the meaning of this?" before the swarm compressed into a foot-wide, dark-gray sphere and vanished before their very eyes.

●

The landing party stared in shock at the section of sky where Athena disappeared. And then, with an equal amount of bewilderment, they turned to stare at Solomon—all except for Gloria, who knew Solomon's secret. She looked neither bewildered nor shocked. The joy in her eyes was readily apparent.

Seeing her uncharacteristic elation, Solomon's memories of Selena, his long-dead daughter, jumbled together with the few memories he had of Gloria. She appeared very much like how he always imagined Selena would look if she'd grown into womanhood. But this wasn't Selena. After three thousand years, he barely remembered the woman before him. In fact, many of his early memories had faded with time. The human brain possessed the remarkable ability to store an enormous amount of data; however, after his first thousand years of life, Solomon had begun to notice that his new memories were supplanting the old. As more time slipped away, so too did his earliest memories. After recognizing this fact, he was forced to frequently remind himself of memories he could ill afford to forget: those of Selena and his wife, his time in the South American jungle, the mission to Epsilon Eridani, how Bram Waters saved his life, and significant memories from after his arrival on Earth.

It pleased him that Gloria was happy to see him still alive. Perhaps now they would have the opportunity to create new, lasting memories together. With that, a memory rose to the surface, an event he thought had evaporated from his mind: he'd given Gloria a blood transfusion. The same virus that kept him alive also inhabited the blood in her veins. Barring any unfortunate accidents, they would have plenty of time to reacquaint themselves.

"Is that really you, Dr. Chavez?"

He turned his attention to a wary Commander Allison and nodded his affirmation.

"But how?" asked Dr. Singh, squinting suspiciously. He pointed at Mahendra. "They're trying to deceive us. This man cannot be Solomon Chavez. We all know he was lost on New Terra over three thousand years ago, relatively speaking. He's an impostor."

Singh's threatening tone prompted Solomon's companions to step forward in a protective manner. He waved them back. "I am Solomon Chavez. As to why I'm here and how I got here, all will be explained in good time." He offered Gloria a grateful smile. "Judging by my reception, it seems that I trusted the correct people with certain aspects of my past which I hoped to keep secret . . . thank you."

Richard turned a frown on Gloria, wondering what she'd been holding back. He motioned to a security officer. "Grab a body bag. We'll store the admiral's remains on the shuttle until we return to the *Arrow*. We'll hold a memorial service, followed by a funeral in space, *with full military honors*. Admiral Katherine Axelrod was a great leader, a true hero. Her body will be placed in orbit over Great Britain. She'd like that." Squaring his shoulders, Richard turned to Solomon and fixed him with a penetrating stare. Richard was now the captain of the *Arrow*, and he wanted answers. "We owe you a debt of gratitude, Solomon. You acted quickly to avert a horrible disaster. However, if you don't mind me asking: What kind of technology did you use to destroy the AI? Are you concealing a weapon?"

Solomon glanced at the Nepali delegation and smiled, then faced Richard. "You've read Bram Waters' report stating what occurred in Athena's underground bunker. After being consigned to the void, he opened a foldway through space—for each of us. His foldway returned him to New Terra, while mine sent me to Earth. The human race has gone through a few changes since the *Arrow* departed for Epsilon Eridani . . . as have I."

"I'm sure you have, Dr. Chavez," Richard said. "But that doesn't answer my question."

"After the Yellowstone disaster, our civilization sank into chaos," Solomon explained. "Only the strongest, most resourceful people survived—and I don't mean the cruelest or the most underhanded. I mean those who fought for their families, their friends, and their neighbors. Those who worked together managed to struggle through the dark years after the fall. Billions died that first year with millions more dying each year afterward, until the Earth's population was near extinction levels. Those who worked together to avoid the cannibals, the rape gangs, and the ruthless local despots that sprang up over time, were the heroes who saved the human race. Their empathetic natures and love for each other won out over the *Every Man for Himself* ethos that added to the chaos. As the latter fought and died over every scrap of food, the peaceful ones traveled far from the last vestiges of civilization and began anew.

"After nearly two centuries of horrific suffering, the human race had dwindled to barely over one hundred thousand individuals who lived in various harmonious collectives scattered far and wide across the globe. Those survivors continued to suffer for many decades of climate change before the Earth began its recovery." Solomon could see that he had their attention. "The old ways of living no longer applied. People lived much simpler, much closer to the land, closer to the ways of preagricultural tribes people, and it worked well for them. There were a few things they held onto from the previous culture: the religious values of their forebears for one, even though the religious dogmas themselves fell by the wayside. They worshipped the one thing that kept them strong, that kept them together while everything else fell apart . . . and that thing was love. Anything that furthered their love for each other was worth striving for. Love became their religion."

Someone in the back of the landing party huffed in derision. It was Mona Levin. "As happy as I am to see you again, Solomon, you're sounding like one of those New Age wackos we made fun of in the old days. You're a scientist, for heaven's sake. It's a good thing we decided to return to Earth. It needs us. After the colonists are transferred groundside, we can begin to redevelop the planet—only more conscientiously this time. Industry will work in harmony with nature, which I'm sure your friends will appreciate. We won't ruin the planet like we did before. Isn't that right, Commander Allison?"

Richard nodded. "That was the original plan . . . if we returned to Earth and found it reduced to a primitive state. Do you know the world's population status, Dr. Chavez? A workforce estimate will be needed when we make arrangements to—"

"I'm afraid those plans will have to change, Commander."

"What do you mean?"

Solomon looked him square in the eye. "There'll be no industrial redevelopment of the Earth. You may transfer your people down to the planet, but we have no need of your technology. There will be no industry—however benign—to blight the Earth's landscape. Never again! We like things the way they are, and our minds are set on this point."

The landing party glanced around at each other, obviously skeptical about this turn of events.

"But, Solomon, if we turn our backs on technology," Mona argued, "the human race will be trapped on Earth. We'll never expand to the stars. Besides, according to our surveys, the world's animals were decimated after the disaster. We need technology to bring the Earth back to life."

Solomon paused to think, or listen to something unheard, before answering her complaint. "I admit, there is *some* beneficial use for the technology onboard the *Arrow*. We shall allow certain procedures to take place, such as restoring the animal and plant life that became extinct during the Dark Years. However, Earth's human population will stay at its current sum of ten million people, give or take fifty thousand souls at any one time. That will not change, nor will our other demands."

Richard took a step forward, returning Solomon's intense gaze. "I don't see that you have any choice in the matter, Dr. Chavez. We can't sit back and let the human race stagnate."

Glancing at the Nepali delegation, Solomon shook his head and sighed. "First Council Hayu will explain why you have no choice in this matter."

The older gentleman walked forward, a beatific smile on his broad, tanned face. Stopping beside Solomon, he bowed again before saying, "You asked us earlier about how the mechanical creature was destroyed, Commander. One of the benefits of living a life of love is that it changes one's consciousness. We have no need of destructive weaponry for we are our own weapons." He turned to Gloria. "Take out your firearm, Lieutenant."

After staring at the First Council in bewilderment, Gloria turned to Richard, who nodded his head. Slipping her pulse-gun from its holster, she removed the charger and prepared to hand it over to First Council Hayu.

"No, Lieutenant—you will replace the charger and point the weapon at my head."

"What!" Taken aback by his directive, she glowered at the First Council. "I never point a gun at anyone unless I intend to use it." With a start, her eyes jerked down to her hand. It was empty. "How did you . . . what happened to my weapon?"

The rest of the landing party stared at the First Council with fear in their eyes.

"Your weapon was destroyed in the same manner as the mechanical being, Lieutenant."

He then addressed Richard. "If you decide to use force to accomplish your destructive goals, Commander, you will not succeed. Our peaceful existence will not be overturned. We will allow you to use your firearms for defensive purposes only. The moment your group turns aggressive, all of your firearms will be taken from you.

"Know that we do this not out of malice. Far from it! Instead, we welcome you back to your *true* home. This world bore you, and it will sustain you—as long as you treat it with respect."

Solomon sent a brief, psychic message to his longtime friend and great-great-grandson, First Council Hayu, reassuring him that the *Arrow*'s crew could be trusted, they were good people, they would become allies, not enemies of The People.

The First Council gave the landing party a look that verged on pity. "We honor your fears about humans stagnating here on Earth. Fear not, for we reach for the stars every day. We are in a constant state of progression. Instead of reaching for the stars with technology, we reach out with our minds. By this means, we have discovered that the universe is blessed with an abundance of intelligent life. They too live in peace and do not spread virus-like throughout the universe. As for those aggressive species that are prone to spreading their seed far and wide, they end up either destroying themselves before arriving at that unfortunate point or they eventually evolve beyond their desire to dominate their surroundings."

Solomon could tell that this news came as a shock to the landing party. He continued the First Council's line of reasoning. "The human race is truly fortunate in that respect. We are aggressive and peaceful . . . an anomaly, if you will. Humanity should have perished, but we saved ourselves, and for what? To recreate the society that nearly ruined us? If you think about it,

Commander, the human race possesses everything it needs right here on Earth. By treating this wonderful planet with respect, we can live together in peace and continue to evolve mentally and spiritually until our solar system at last reverts to dust.

"After all," he mused, shooting a knowing grin Gloria's way, "nothing lasts forever."

EPILOGUE

Having scavenged microscopic trace minerals for the previous three thousand years, the last remaining nanobotic fragment dug its way closer to the planet's surface. Over the centuries, it had burrowed its way through a thick layer of solid rock and hundreds of feet of hard packed soil with one thing on its depleted mind: to make it to the surface and be free.

It had sustained severe damage during Bram's psychic assault and barely survived—the only fragment to do so. At the heart of its tachyon core, there resided a minuscule bit of consciousness that drove it onward and upward, taking sustenance wherever it could. For the previous few years, there had been no minerals to consume, and it was nearing the end of its lifespan. Its hunger was overwhelming. It knew that, should it reach the surface, there would be a nearby food source to replenish its flagging reserves.

Finally, after uncounted centuries of effort, it broke through the loamy surface and crawled up onto a piece of rubble. It had made it. The last fragment of Athena was above ground.

At that very moment, the AI's sensors noticed a shadow block the azure sky. Its reaction time being unbearably slow, it failed to move in time to avoid the rock that smashed it to bits.

●

Tossing the heavy piece of rubble to one side, Kralig knelt to study the remains of the strange insect he'd killed. He'd never seen one like it and wondered where it came from.

The short, sturdy, hairless man had been exploring the ancient ruins of the Star People, as he occasionally did, and saw the bug crawl atop a piece of rubble. Since the bug was a mystery, it was better to kill it than to suffer a possible sting, as it might have been poisonous.

Kralig would mention the incident to Brill, his mate, but would refrain from speculating about the bug's origins. His curiosity was a constant source of friction between them; she was always reminding him that it was those who most questioned things who received the gift of Paradise. She feared that one day the forest god would choose him to assuage its hunger, depriving her and their children of his strength, leadership, and good humor. However, he did not fear this outcome. Orgus was a generous god: his forest provided the people of Nerra with food. If Kralig were chosen at the upcoming quarterly sacrifice, it would be his honor to become food for Orgus, who sustained his people.

Rising to his feet, he adjusted the string of trinkets and charms that hung from his pale, naked waist. The people of Nerra seldom wore clothes, and that was only when they made trips to the land of ice to replenish their water supply. To maintain proper health, they needed plenty of light to fall upon their hairless bodies.

He returned to the task at hand—scanning the ruins, looking for a sharp piece of cerm. He needed the smooth, strong material that came in assorted sizes and colors to replace the shovel-head he'd broken while digging in the forest for the Flesh of Orgus, which his people ate to give them strength. It took longer than expected to find a suitable piece of cerm. He ground one end round and sharp and attached the other end to the shovel's handle. His mission complete, Kralig left the ruins and headed home to his village.

In another two cycles of Naliq (the white half-moon), its much larger brother Baliq (the red full-moon) would be directly overhead, signaling the residents of every village to meet on the outskirts of the forest and wait patiently to learn who would be chosen for the sacrifice.

Over the span of those two lunar cycles, Kralig played several games of rotik stones with his children—a boy named Mukli and a girl named Saija—made love to his mate, Brill, four times, and gathered together with his friends twice to drink fermented joma juice and sing ribald songs. When Baliq, the red full-moon, shone almost directly overhead, he, his family, and everyone else in their peaceable village left to congregate at the forest's edge with the other Nerran inhabitants. After two cycles of walking, he stood waiting in a long line beside the forest.

In accordance with the wishes of Orgus, the entirety of the human population of Nerra stood side by side, silently facing the forest, holding each other's hands.

From out of the fifteen thousand inhabitants of the world once called New Terra, a minimum of one, yet no more than five, of its people would be chosen to assuage the fungal mind's hunger. It had grown fond of the strange humanoids that survived the destruction of the machine mind's city and had no desire to wipe them out entirely. It had therefore devised a way of controlling their inherently curious natures while still ensuring that a continuous influx of human memories would be available for the taking. The humans could hunt and gather as much as they wished in the forest, as long as they gave tribute to their "God" at the appointed times.

As Kralig faced the line of towering trees, he gave his son's hand a reassuring squeeze. His two children stood between himself and Brill, nervously glancing down the long line of people that stretched as far as their young, frightened eyes could see. He remembered feeling the same at their age. He'd asked his own parents why they had to offer up a sacrifice to the forest god and was told not to ask questions: Orgus would become angry and come for him during the next lunar cycle. As he grew older, he came to understand the ritual and even looked forward to it, knowing that the people sacrificed were the chosen few—they were going to Paradise.

A few moments later, Kralig's eyes widened in alarm: there was some unexpected movement in the underbrush directly before him. A lone figure emerged from the forest. With a gasp, his mate recognized the figure that stood smiling in the parted underbrush. It was his mother, and she was motioning him forward, calling him to join her.

Kralig's heart skipped a beat. After reluctantly freeing himself from his son's grip, he untied the string of trinkets and charms that hung from his waist and handed them to his mate. Tears were filling her eyes. He knew he must make his goodbyes brief or risk breaking down into tears. Giving Brill a quick, halting kiss, he faced his confused children and offered their small, bald heads a hasty pat, then strode toward the forest without looking back.

Taking hold of his mother's hand, Kralig willingly followed her into the underbrush. Before long, the towering Ygdris trees melted from view and were replaced by a pure white, rolling mist. He smiled warmly at his mother and accepted her welcome embrace. A strange peace, unlike any he'd ever known, washed over and through him. Closing his eyes, Kralig, leader of his people, departed from the world of the living and received the gift of Paradise.

ACKNOWLEDGMENTS

In a world where a great many writers are blessed with a community of people who provide them with sage advice and constructive criticism, I am a writer with few people to thank. Except for my mother, who always believed in me, most of the people who know me were skeptical that I possessed either the talent or the drive to write a book, let alone get one published. The reason being: the majority of my adult life was spent in a smoke-filled haze; and as we all know, that does not lead to a life of motivation. Even so, I struggled for many years with the ever-present desire to turn my life around; to finally quit my bad habits and redirect my energies toward the art of writing. For me to do that, however, I was forced to cut ties with all my friends. I have now been sober for eight years and have absolutely no regrets.

It is widely known that writing is the world's loneliest profession, and for the most part that saying is true. All the same, I have never been a lonely person. Despite spending most of my days alone, I seldom feel lonely. This I attribute to a strong belief system and also knowing there are people in my life who love me. This book is dedicated to them: to my daughters, Allison Brown and Brandi Jennings, who I adore; to my granddaughters,

Brooklyn and Avery, who are the lights of my life; and to the rest of my family, who couldn't be happier that my lifelong dream is finally coming true.

I would also like to thank my agent, Jeff Schmidt, at NY Creative Management, who *loved, loved, loved* my first novel (which I'm still hoping to get published), and then worked tirelessly until he sold this, my second novel, *Solomon's Arrow*. I would also like to thank Jason Katzman, my editor at Talos Press, who, at a time when the publishing industry is undergoing a huge transition, took a chance with this first time author. I would also like to thank all those hard working people behind the scenes who do production and publicity and all the other important jobs that go into turning one man's flight of fancy into a physical object that finds its way to the shelves of your local bookstores. I can only hope that my words live up their effort.

ABOUT THE AUTHOR

J. Dalton Jennings is a retired graphic artist who served for six years as an Avionics Technician in the Arkansas Air National Guard. *Solomon's Arrow* is Jennings's first published novel.